About the Author

Joni Daniels studied for her degree in Humanities specialising in Creative Writing and Classical Studies with the Open University and proudly graduated from The Barbican in September 2014. Her passion for music, particularly Duran Duran, and classical history figure heavily in her daily life. Joni lives with her family in the seaside town of Sutton-on-Sea on the east coast of Lincolnshire 'not far from Skegness', which incidentally, is not in Scotland!

To Les + Emma
Lovely to meet you!
Best wishes
Joni Daniels

The Hub

Joni Daniels

The Hub

Olympia Publishers
London

www.olympiapublishers.com
OLYMPIA PAPERBACK EDITION

A CIP catalogue record for this title is
available from the British Library.

ISBN: 978-1-78830-282-1

This is a work of fiction.
Names, characters, places and incidents originate from the writer's
imagination. Any resemblance to actual persons, living or dead, is purely
coincidental.

First Published in 2018

Olympia Publishers
60 Cannon Street
London
EC4N 6NP

Printed in Great Britain

Dedication

To all my guides in this world and the next, thank you for your constant support. You lead with love, I follow with love and that's all you need.

Acknowledgements

The Hub came about as a result of tragedy. My husband Nigel and I had spent three years looking after my beautiful mum who sadly lost her life to a brain tumour in June 2015. She passed away on a warm summer evening at home the moment that Nigel finished mowing her beloved lawn, happy, I believe, in the knowledge that he had done a good job. We had only been married the previous year, so we began our life as a couple rather than an odd little trio. We spent the weeks and months afterwards grieving for her and yet moving on as I know she would've wanted. That Christmas, we had planned a New Year's Eve party and it was on the 27th December that Nigel went off to play with his friends, racing their motorbikes at an organised event on the beach. It was a crisp sunny winter day, the sky was bright blue, a day to enjoy breathing in the clean sea air. I had decided to stay at home and do a thorough clean, getting everything ready for the celebrations. I had just sat down for a sandwich and was singing along to '*A spoonful of sugar*' with Mary Poppins, when my phone rang. I picked it up seeing Nigel's picture, smiling to myself that he would be home soon. Only it wasn't his voice that answered me but that of his best friend. I knew in that instant that something terrible had happened. Time stood still as he relayed the awful news that my beloved husband had had an accident. The events in The Hub are based on this true story but at the time I wasn't ready to tell it exactly as it happened so I altered the accident to happen to the main character Kate, based on myself having ridden competitively in endurance horse-riding for many years. Sat in the waiting room outside the intensive care ward, our lives in tatters, relying on the fabulous staff at Hull Royal Infirmary to bring him back to us, was horrific; something I would not wish on my worst enemy. The doctors all called him Miracle Man, and now, although partially sighted, suffering from anxiety, and with a brain injury, he is and we are going from strength to strength individually and as a couple. We still have the odd day where it is so hard but I am proud of him and how far we have come since those dark days, getting stronger with every day that passes. Kate's experiences are based on my own experiences dealing with mental illness, in which I spiralled upwards not knowing how to deal with all the information I was being given and being ripped away from my family. My life now in the hands of others, some caring and wonderful, some sadly preying on the weak and vulnerable. I have seen both sides of the mental health system and now count myself as a survivor rather than a victim.

Thanks go to the wonderful friends and paramedics at the beach who were first on the scene of the accident, then to the guys of the Lincs & Notts Air Ambulance, and of course, the fabulous staff at Hull Royal Infirmary Intensive Care Unit who undoubtedly, along with Nigel's own determination and the support of thousands of well-wishers, all combined to bring him back to us.

Thanks to those at Rape Crisis for their counselling service and to my psychiatrist who, after knowing me for nearly two years now, appears to take my experiences on board.

Thanks to our dear friends and close family who all rallied round, you know who you are, especially our wonderful children who saw things they shouldn't have seen and coped with situations which must have been very frightening for them.

Thanks to Geoff, my original editor who asked if I had an aversion to commas, and was I mad? Your harsh critique made me work even harder on my manuscript and your words inspired me when you emailed after the edits to say it was 'prize-winning material'. I live in hope!

And massive thanks to Olympia Publishers for loving The Hub and supporting me in my quest to reach a larger audience.

I had to write this book; I could not keep it inside my head. I have a voice and am speaking on behalf of myself and countless others who may feel that nobody cares. The stigma of mental illness is still with us, but, I hope that with books like this, and the support of many others who work tirelessly to raise awareness, the sheer agony of battling with this illness will enable our voices to be heard. The essay I include at the end of The Hub is one which I wrote as part of my degree back in 2011. I had no idea at the time that Aphrodite would play such a massive role in the events which led me to being hospitalised.

FOREWARD

The Hub is a novel which deals with the difficult subject of mental illness and the thin line we, as humans, tread as we go through our lives. Nobody knows how they will cope under extreme pressure and what their breaking point may be until it actually happens. The future is not ours to predict, thank goodness. This story, my debut novel, is based on true events of people known to me. Although based on the truth, I have used artistic licence to weave a fictional story; names, places and events have been changed to suit the narrative.

I have included an academic essay for interest at the back of the book which traces the goddess Aphrodite throughout antiquity to present day.

PROLOGUE

The radio provides its usual accompaniment to my daily routine. The familiar voice of a local DJ washes over me as I sit staring blankly at the page glowing bright white on my laptop. I have written 'Dear Sir...' over an hour ago and that's the result, two words. I cannot go any further.

It's just a letter, yet it's more than that. It's an attempt to bring some semblance of justice back to the living hell I escaped from. What might be called by some 'closure'. I don't know if it will do any good, but I have to try... I have to try, for my sake, for the sake of my family and for the sake of the ones I left behind.

I am safe. I have to keep reminding myself that the worst is over. I am home. As long as I keep my end of the bargain and take the tablets I have been prescribed, they won't send me away again.

My hot chocolate has gone cold, and I know that my husband will be back soon. He and the rest of the family are so protective towards me; they never leave me alone for very long, and for the first time since I came home I am enjoying my own company. I know he won't be long, maybe an hour or so, and that gives me comfort too. I'm not scared, I know he won't let me down.

He's gone to do the food shopping. He does mostly everything now. He has become self-sufficient whilst I have been away. That's how we refer to it now in the family. 'Whilst you were away.' It's our code and it's much easier to say 'whilst you were away' than 'whilst you were sectioned' or 'whilst you went crazy'. And it's definitely easier to say 'whilst you were away' than to contemplate the truth, 'whilst you were locked up, drugged and abused'. Nobody wants to say those words because that makes it real.

I need a drink. Kettle on again and more hot chocolate. I have developed a sweet tooth since I have been home. I think it is a comfort thing. The rich milky drink is like nectar, the chill that has settled in my bones is starting to ebb. Four weeks ago, they ripped me away from everything I loved. I was supposed to be going 'away' to get better; to focus on getting better and not trying to solve everyone's problems. I had thought I would never see my beautiful home and family again.

The laptop screen has gone black, but the little blue light on the keyboard flashes, beckoning me. For a moment I am transported back to that place; the place where colours were sent as signs to guide me, to keep me safe. Blue. Blue could go either way and meant be careful. I look around in awe; I am safe, I am in my kitchen. Nothing is going to harm me. I used to take this for granted. How many of the friends I left behind will ever see their homes again? The thought spurs me on. I have to do this. I owe it them, I owe it to myself, and I owe it to future patients who may find themselves in my situation.

Deep breath. I tap a button on the keyboard and the screen lights up, cursor flashing where I left it, ready, waiting for my words to spill the truth about The Hub.

'Dear Sir…'

BOOK ONE
POSSESSION

Kate - The Origins

I was born in 1967, during the Summer of Love, where hippies fuelled by hallucinogenic drugs preached of free love and peace from the warmth of California. In the UK, their contemporaries followed suit adorned in paper flowers, flowing multi-coloured garments and Afghan coats, California dreamers of Woodstock doing their thing in a slightly cooler climate across the pond.

The Beatles were at number one with '*All You Need Is Love*' and my family were happy with their new arrival. A new reality had been delivered to them that day, a Leo child; a little girl with a strong will who shared her birthday with many other strong personalities, people well known in their chosen profession. Mick Jagger, Helen Mirren and Stanley Kubrick had all made their first appearances on Planet Earth on this day in history.

As well as new souls being ushered into this world on this day throughout history, to keep the balance, there were others who left behind their mortal coils to move on to the next level; a number of significant figures throughout the history of the world: Offa, King of Mercia; Atahualpa, the Inca ruler overthrown by Pizarro; Eva Peron in 1952. All leaving their mark and helping to shape the future as do we all in our own ways. Each and every soul has a purpose and a destiny to fulfil.

My parents were of a different generation. They already had their children who were now in their teens, and the appearance of another baby had been of great surprise to the rest of the family. By the age of two, I had beautiful blonde Shirley Temple curls and a volatile temperament; when I was good, I was indeed a model child, but when I was bad I would throw tantrums of epic proportions. A penchant for banging my head on the concrete floor repeatedly was a worrying trait, but I did not seem to suffer any ill effects from this behaviour. Although some might say this may have had some bearing on events in later life, or at least indicated a sign of things to come.

For such a young child, I developed an unusual love of history, on holidays, dragging my parents into every museum I could find, to the point where distraction tactics of bribery sweets were deployed. Nobody knew or bothered to ask why I was so fascinated with antiquity at such a tender age. It was just another symptom of my boundary-pushing behaviour.

Always a pain in the arse, I would be found standing between crenellations on the top of a high castle, looking down to see what was on the other side; on one occasion falling into a waterfall when curiosity, and a yearning to join my grandad on the slippery stones near the edge, was too much temptation to resist. A postcard home followed, recounting the tale, with much raising of eyebrows and tutting ensuing; nobody expected anything but trouble from the feisty little girl.

Back home, I liked balancing my way along the foot-wide ledge outside my bedroom window, practising dance moves and wobbling fearlessly with eyes tight shut, and pushing limits I didn't even know existed. A goddess in training, and a source of constant aggravation for aging earthly parents who really should've - by this time - been out and about enjoying child-free weekends away and holidays relaxing or rambling; normal pursuits for a couple in their late forties.

In school, I was bright, lively and popular. Always into one scrape or another, with many friends, some of whom became friends for life and remain in contact until the present time. As a teenager, the local Grammar School had no clue how to handle high spirits and antics. I followed my heart not my head, and broke every rule the stuffy school tried to impose. Too much make-up, too many earrings, hair bleached then in turn dyed purple or red, skirt too short, smoking. The list was endless, as were the letters home, some of which made it to home to my parents, most finding themselves confined to the bottom of my school bag. They labelled me a rebel and left me to it, a sad reflection of the poor teaching methods common in the 1980s. Many of the school's staff were near to retirement age. My friends and I could not get out of there fast enough, and as soon as exam leave began, that was the end of my Grammar School education as far as I was concerned. They had failed me, and I left with nothing but a handful of 'O' levels and a scathing report.

My parents were pleasantly surprised when I excelled in college, and went on to complete a degree in Classical Studies. The keen interest in ancient history and mythology has stayed with me throughout my life, and may go some way to explaining as to why when the chips were really down, my brain turned to familiar subjects of which I was passionate about to utilise as a coping strategy when the shit really hit the fan.

The Prophecy

Summer 2015

So it began. I had fair warning of what was to come in the future but I chose to ignore it. It was a beautiful summer's day, and I had visited the stables, as I did every day. Nothing strange about that. My beloved horse Ebony and I had been out on the beach once again. It was our favourite place, perfect for blowing away cobwebs. My beautiful Ebony, coat brushed so she shone jet black, gleaming muscles rippling under the sun, tossed her mane and whinnied with pleasure as we galloped along the shore without a care in the world. The smell of the sea air rushing by was making my nostrils flare and eyes water. We raced sea birds, as they flew alongside us, cawing, their cries carried by the wind until we left them far behind. Sand flew up, sticking to her powerful limbs, only hoofprints left behind to show our journey; only to be washed away again by the inevitable ebb and flow of the tides. Ebony and I enjoyed each other's company, we were best friends and she knew all my secrets. She was a friend and confident, I was her protector, her comforter, the human who cared for her every need. We had a solid bond and made a good team. We competed in long distance riding events and travelled all over the country in pursuit of ribbons and trophies, meeting others engaged in the same pastime. We cantered through forest trails, over moors, on bridleways and paths less taken, enjoying every second and never knowing what was around the corner. But it was here on the sand that we felt most at home and free. The morning had been the same as any other. All stable duties done, my lovely Ebony's black glossy coat brushed, white stockings cleaned of the sand which stuck grittily to the feathers around her hooves. Ebony, with her long black lashes and white blaze, whinnied at me and, turning abruptly, kicked up her heels, tossed her mane and let fly. Happy in her freedom, she cantered and bucked with joy as she left me watching her from the field gate, looking for a suitable place to roll and stretch after our morning exercise. I loved this horse as unconditionally as any parent loves a child, and watched with pride as she cantered out into the field, snorting and whinnying to her friends who had been left behind waiting for their respective owners.

'See you later, gorgeous,' I called after her as I closed the gate and headed to the tack room to put her saddle and bridle away.

It was still early morning, all yard chores done, and I felt a rush of pride at our progress. The training was going well and our competitive long distance rides had been successful so far.

'Is that you on your way then?'

It was Adam, the yard manager, who interrupted my daydreaming. He was striding towards me carrying a large bag of feed. 'Here you go, they dropped this off with my order yesterday. Said I'd make sure you got it.'

'Thanks, Adam, that's good of you. Yeah, I'm heading home now, no rest for the wicked,' I grinned back at him. 'What are you up to today?'

'Just off to the sales, I'm looking for another coloured cob, and I heard on the grapevine that there may be some Travellers turn up with some Irish stock,' he replied. 'Hey, why don't you come with me? I could do with some advice if I'm going to find something decent to enter into the sand race this year.'

'Love to, but I've got a date with an old school friend. I haven't seen her for years so I'd better not. Thanks though, maybe I'll join you next time. I'll see you later. Good luck with your hunt,' I called over my shoulder as I exchanged yard boots for my battered converse.

Adam was such a nice guy, we had always had a connection and hit it off from the moment we met. I could sense it when we spoke; I knew him from old, but how? We often exchanged glances and caught each other looking inquisitively when we thought the other was not paying attention. When our eyes met, there was a jolt of recognition that remained unexplained. I was sure there was something deeper there, and I knew that we both felt it. It puzzled me; it was as though I had known him forever even though we had only met a year ago when I had to move Ebony to new stables. It was better left unspoken. We had settled for mutual appreciation and friendship; it was far too complicated to let things go any further. No, things were better left unsaid. Still, it didn't hurt to appreciate a nice looking member of the opposite sex, did it? What harm was there in looking? He was a handsome man with hair as black as my Ebony's coat, long dark lashes framed eyes the colour of rich dark chocolate. He was slightly built, sinewy, and used to the heavy lifting that goes hand in hand with anything to do with horses. He had told me how when he was younger, he had been quite successful as a jockey and a well-known part of the racing fraternity back at home. Those days were long behind him and he had come over from Ireland to help out relations with their busy yard and ended up staying, gradually taking on more and more responsibilities until they handed the reins over to him completely last year. He was full of ideas and had started as he meant to go on, the yard was now a bustling place, always running at full capacity and with a growing waiting list for an empty stable. Adam was a godsend for many reasons.

No matter how we felt, I was determined I was not going to fuck up another marriage. I was no longer free and single, so whatever feelings lurked under the surface they could stay exactly where they were, hidden and locked away where they could do no harm to anyone.

I already had one divorce behind me and I didn't intend to add another one to my little black book of failed relationships. There were countless failed relationships in that particular book, more than enough to fill its pages twice over. I don't believe in regret. I believe things happen for a reason. Sure, I feel bad that people had been hurt in the past as I bounced from one guy to another and back again, but that was back in the day. Pick yourself up, get up, show up, and get the fuck on with it. I told myself off if I felt my resolve starting to weaken. 'Suck it up, Buttercup' was a mantra I used when there was nothing to be done but get on with it.

I fall in love easily, and my heart has been broken and mended more times than I care to admit. I was forty-five before I finally met my match. The relationship had come out of the blue; passionate, unexpected, a rollercoaster ride, the yin to my yang. Boom, with a libido that not only matched mine but sometimes overtook it; I'd never been happier. In less than a year I found myself saying 'I do' for the second time in my life, and since then had never looked back. Four years later and I had remained faithful, as had he, a fact which surprised the pair of us given our respective track records.

As I turned the ignition, bringing the engine to life, I sat for a moment breathing in the sweet warm air. A mixture of fresh hay, sugar beet and manure filtered through from the yard, familiar and comforting. Life didn't get much better. With a broad grin on my face,

I put the roof down and the music up, full blast; I drew away from the yard and set off.

'You be careful now,' Adam shouted after me as I left.

'Always,' I answered, and winked mischievously. Well, a little flirting didn't hurt, and it put a smile on both our faces. I caught him reflected in my rear view mirror, shaking his head as he turned and went back to his daily chores in the yard. Duran Duran, my constant musical companions, provided the tunes for my short journey back home. The yard was just ten minutes away, another reason in my choice of livery for my equine friend.

'*Reach Up For The Sunrise*', I yelled to the world at the top of my voice as I sped through the countryside towards home accompanied by my 'boys'.

As a product of the sixties, I had grown up with the sound of music playing every day on our old radio in the kitchen as my mother baked cakes or made pastry. *A Whiter Shade of Pale, Puppet on a String*, then Ed Stewpot Stewart on Radio 1, request shows, The Carpenters, The Osmonds, quirky comedy songs by Benny Hill or Terry Scott. The sounds of my childhood, the sound of happiness, music and the smells of freshly baked bread filling the kitchen, the bread waiting to be topped with homemade luscious jam crammed with whole succulent strawberries.

I had had a wonderful childhood even though I had not been an easy child. My parents gave me a solid upbringing and never gave up on me despite my antics, which had them pulling their hair out. I suppose they always hoped that I would turn out alright, as my brother and sister had done before me. I was just a different generation. One on my own, an in-between. My cousins were all of the same age as my elder siblings and consequently I was raised more as an only child, with the others having fled the nest when I was still a small child.

Being in-between I had the luxury of having siblings without having to live with them, and by the time they had children and their children had grown, I was the in-between generation cool auntie who was invited to parties of the generations either side of my own. I was, in fact, someone who could mix with all ages of the family and feel comfortable in either situation. A born socialiser.

My formative years were lived in the eighties; punk, new wave, new romantics and the age of synthesisers joined the more traditional sounds of drums and guitars. The Sex Pistols, Adam and the Ants, my Duran boys, I loved them all. I loved music, always had, always will and I point blank refused to be categorised into one genre. Music is life. I know that I cannot live without it, or at the very least I am sure that I would shrivel up and die without a song or a lyric to lift me up to higher levels and make my soul sing.

I drove home that day in a haze of happiness, my right foot hit the pedal to the metal and I sped along in my comfort zone cocooned in utter bliss, roof down with the sun blaring down and singing in harmony with Simon Le Bon to *'Planet Earth'*. I rounded a sharp right hand bend, tyres only leaving a small amount of rubber behind on the tarmac. As I did, a voice shouted in my ear and rudely interrupted my journey home.

'Dead by Christmas' it screamed into my ear. For a moment I thought my car stereo was playing games with me. I looked at the display and it had not moved, the red lights still reading CD ONE. What the hell had just happened? Where had that come from? Shaken, I slowed down and pulled over to the side of the road, breathing shakily. 'Dead by Christmas.' What?

I looked around me. The sun was still shining, cars were passing me on the familiar road, and I was halfway home. Nothing strange to see. So why did I feel so frightened? It was as if in that moment my reality had somehow shifted or changed. My brain could not make sense of where those words had come from.

After what seemed like hours, but on checking my watch was only a few minutes, I pulled myself together enough to resume my journey. Nothing else untoward happened and by the time I had made it back home I had almost put it out of my mind. I decided to keep the experience to myself because maybe I had just imagined it, and if I hadn't imagined it, who would believe me in any case? I put it down to the heat of the sun and a trick of the mind.

My husband had already left for work. An open newspaper on the table with an empty coffee cup next to it, the chair pushed out and abandoned; a familiar sight which both irritated and comforted me at the same time. He was so untidy, I couldn't help but smile, and a rush of love swept through me as I thought about him. I had never met such a kind and decent man in my life. In fact, I probably had met many, but nice guys did not normally hold any attraction for me. I had a penchant for those of the opposite sex that exuded danger, treated me like shit and screwed me over without a second thought for anyone but themselves. Selfish beautiful men were my choice of lover. I could win them over in a second and initially be in control. This never lasted long, and I fell hard and fast. They all had similar traits; I wanted romance, flowers, poetry, what I generally got was great sex, broken dates and a wounded heart.

So when I decided I wanted my current husband, he really stood no chance. None of them did; I won hearts easily. He did put up a bit of a fight at first, being a local guy and having heard of my fearsome reputation. Yes, I had a bad rep in my hometown, which was why I generally sourced my lovers from other areas. The thing is, when you grow up in a small town everyone knows everyone and what they don't know they make up. I had, as I think I have said, been a pain in the arse most of my life. I had moved away as soon as I could but found myself back in later years to look after my elderly mother.

Nearly thirty years had passed since I lived in the area, but the people who I had left behind here still saw me as the hell raiser who had fucked the whole village. I hadn't, but it didn't stop the tongues wagging. Funnily enough, it was the male population of the area that were the worst for rumour spreading, and I soon realised the instigators were my contemporaries, school friends who I had declined to spend any time between the sheets with. Jealousy? Who knows, but it was a fact that if I ventured into my local pub, the same old faces were there propping up the same old bar, telling the same old stories. Barely concealed stares and stage whispers carried above the hum of conversation and the clink of glasses. I felt a bit sorry for them that they had to hold on to gossip from our school days. They had never stepped out of their comfort zones or taken a leap of faith. That's not a problem. Who am I to tell anyone how to live their lives? And sometimes I envied them with their safe little lives, familiar faces, same old routine, day in day out week in week out. Sometimes. But mostly I shuddered at the concept and felt an immense sense of pride of all that I had managed to achieve thus far. Funny how such narrow-mindedness can cause so much trouble, and stories of my adventures in love seemed to have taken on legendary status.

The local gossips had excelled themselves over the years. The Whore of Babylon had nothing on my reputation. Initially I found it amusing, but it soon became tiresome. Luckily I had one or two friends from school who had also returned to the homeland and we gravitated towards each other, safe in the knowledge that we had all actually experienced life out of the county and broadened our horizons. We met once every few weeks to chew the cud, share a nice meal and a few drinks. We were educated women who enjoyed a chance to speak candidly about anything and everything and, knowing that we would not be judged, we spoke frankly and listened without prejudice. We had all turned out just fine despite our youthful antics.

It was on one of these nights out that I became reacquainted with the man who was to become my significant other. He had been at the bar with his brother when we walked in. I later learned that those gossips from my formative years had warned him off when he showed an interest. Luckily for me he had integrity, and his intellect took him above the lower levels of those pathetic human beings.

We were on our second bottle of wine by the time I spotted him.

'Girls, look over there. Who is that? I feel sure I know him from somewhere.'

The other three ladies who made up our cosy foursome all followed my gaze.

'Him? The taller one? Yeah, he looks familiar. Not your type though, Kate,' my oldest friend Anna replied.

'I think he was in the year above us at school, can't remember his name. Anyone?' said Mags, my second oldest friend.

'I'm going to go and say hello,' I stated taking a large swig of wine.

'Kate, no. Slow down please, you don't want to give them lot any more to gossip about.'

'I agree with Steph,' said Mags

'Me too,' Anna agreed.

'When did you lot become so boring?' I shot them a look of disgust and stood up, wobbling slightly.

'Sit down, you nutter,' said Anna, and grabbed hold of my arm.

'Get off me, no need to be so rough,' I shot back at her.

Looking at the concern on their faces, I decided for once that maybe they were right. Annoyingly. I sat down with a thud, managing to spill my drink as I collapsed back onto my chair.

'Bloody hell, Kate, don't be making a show of yourself in front of those knobheads,' said Mags.

'Whatever,' I replied sulkily. 'I was just going to go and say hello and ask his name that's all.'

The others glanced at each other, and at my pouty face before bursting out with laughter, causing the rest of the pub to stop mid conversation and look our way.

'Shhhh. I thought we were supposed to be acting in a proper grown up manner,' I retorted.

'Aww, Kate, he's looking over now anyway. You managed to get his attention,' said Mags.

I looked over and saw she was right. The rest of the cronies had resumed their conversations more than ever, and now I knew that I had once again proved them right that I was a complete slapper. The focus of my attention caught my gaze and winked. I felt myself blush. I don't blush, and I put it down to the alcohol coursing through my veins. Keep it cool, Katie, keep it cool, I told myself, and then blew it all by winking back at him and raising my now empty glass.

Despite my fearsome reputation and my friends' opinions that he was not my type, after some very careful negotiations we went on a date and the rest as they say is history. Maybe he wasn't 'my type' and maybe that's just why this time it worked. I had found my match; a kind, hardworking generous guy coupled with a ferocious libido was exactly what I had been looking for all my life. He was perfection. Our wedding was intimate, with just the closest family and friends in attendance. We had a rockabilly theme, my dress being full on fifties-style rock and roll, black with red cherries, red and black sequinned shoes with a killer five inch heel, coupled with his red and black bowling shirt and the reception at an American-themed diner, it summed us up divinely. We were blissfully happy.

Why then just a year later did fate cruelly step in and systematically strip us of everything we had come to know and love? Our lives thrown into turmoil.

The Sand Race

Sunday 27th December, 2015

The preparation that had gone into today's occasion has been second to none. Many weeks have passed since the summer, which is way behind us. We stepped up the training in the autumn. Now winter has come around, and with it the biggest competition of the year for local equestrians and their trusty steeds. A chance to shine and revel in local glory in The Psamathe, a sprint race along the beach which had been run since the 1960s. The race was inspired by the success of a similar event, which was held yearly just north of Dublin. A young bookie had seen an opportunity of making a few quid out of the crowds it pulled in, and The Psamathe race had turned into one of those 'see and be seen at' type of events patronised by high society, celebrities and the rich and powerful. The first year had attracted a few local competitors, but after the inaugural race, word had spread and the second year had pulled in more than double. He ran it along the same lines as its Irish forefather, with no more than ten horses in each race. By the time it had reached its fifth year, there were more than fifty entrants and word had rapidly spread that this was a worthy race to attend. It became as much a part of the racing calendar as any point to point race. The exotic name, 'The Psamathe', came from his mother, who was of Greek descent and was an expert on Greek mythology.

Psamathe was a Greek goddess of sand beaches who had, according to legend, been seduced then ambushed on the beach by a mortal king. To escape his unwanted advances she transformed herself into a seal. This stretch of beach where the race was run, transformed in November and December each year to become the birthing grounds of hundreds of common grey seals. Further along the beach the protected area became a bombing range for the Ministry of Defence, but in-between these areas were desolate hard flat sands that stretched away to the north for ten kilometres, perfect for hosting The Psamathe, which ran over six furlongs. The event was otherwise more commonly and affectionately known as The Sand Race.

Although friendly, it was extremely competitive, and to triumph here gave the winner kudos amongst their fellow horsemen. Since hunting with hounds had become illegal, the local hunt had decided to hold the race on Boxing Day. The landed gentry and other red coats enjoyed showing off their hunters and thoroughbreds as well as giving them the chance to brag off to their mates about their six-figure salaries, newest car, and last exotic holiday. Spectators came from near and far and the event had become more and more popular as the years went on. It was a real spectacle and riders were coded by colour to denote their level of handicap.

The ex-huntsmen and their cronies, who competed in their own class, were labelled The Reds. The Greens were made up of novice entries, plus the youngest horses allowed to compete. Yellows were riders who came from other countries and Blues were veteran riders over the age of forty. The colour coding worked well, not only for categorising competitors and aiding a fair race, but for the assembled crowd to be able to follow the somewhat chaotic proceedings.

As each year went by, the race grew in its popularity. This year had seen its biggest number of entries yet. The whole of the beach had been transformed into an open air arena. The track was clearly set out, the dunes providing a natural grandstand for spectators. Even though the wind whistled harshly off the North Sea, it hadn't stopped a record turnout. Stalls were set up all along the edge of the dunes; coffee, soup, hot dogs, chips, burgers, all vied for trade alongside the more unusual and expensive pop-up stalls selling anything from tofu to lobster. A large beer tent was full of punters enjoying a Boxing Day tipple, helping to keep the cold at bay.

Bookmakers were doing a roaring trade and the atmosphere was one of jovial good nature, everyday punters rubbing alongside celebrities enjoying their VIP passes and hospitality, lanyards proclaiming their importance but not affording them any better view than the rest of the race goers.

Ebony and I had yet to win, and we certainly didn't move in the same social circles as the Reds and had no desire to join them. They always looked down their upper class noses at the likes of us, but they couldn't escape the fact that despite our low breeding we were the ones to watch, and in the last couple of years had risen through the ranks of also-rans to coming an impressive third in our category last year.

Today I am buzzing and so is Ebony. Today is the biggest event of our year and we have trained hard for this. The three words that had been shouted in my ear on my way home last summer were locked away safely in the back of my mind. Not entirely forgotten, just stored away in my head, in a place where I put things that were too painful or just plain weird to waste brain power on.

Our intense training has paid off and Ebony is a shining testimony to the work we have both put in. I pat her neck and talk calmly into her ear. We understand each other. Her head is held proudly in the air, ears pricked listening to my every word, muscles rippling under her glowing black coat. We are not fazed by the competition, we relish it.

I have upped my physical training too since this race is more of a sprint than the usual endurance races we are used to. As such, we have had to develop and change our training to suit. I have changed the way I train and forced myself to go running on the beach. I figure if I am asking Ebony to do it then the least I can do is join her. I alternate our routines, and a couple of times a week instead of saddling up, I exchange the bridle for a head collar and run alongside her to try and improve my fitness too. Headphones ever present so I can sing along to my favourite tunes wherever we are; my whole life has been accompanied by music. It invigorates me when I need some encouragement, calms me, makes me cry, makes me sing with the pure joy of being alive. Today's well-chosen playlist was made up of The Eagles, AC/DC, Duran Duran, obviously, and many other bands, an eclectic mix that was for sure. '*My Own Way*' by the Duran boys, their lyrics appeared to fit the day's activities rather well and I hummed the familiar song whilst undertaking my final preparations before the allotted time for the vet checks.

We are well prepared. My family have come along to support me, my husband and children are well used to the interruption of seasonal festivities and they wave excitedly at me from their vantage point on dunes.

'Hey there, Kate. Ready for the off?'

Ebony snorts a greeting at Adam before I can answer. He has pulled alongside us riding Pilgrim, the cob he had purchased that day back in the summer. Pilgrim was a typical black and white coloured horse, rough around the edges, but what was known as a good sort. With Adam's training regime, he had come on in leaps and bounds over the last few months. He had raced in The Psamathe last year with his previous owner, finishing mid-field, earning him a place in my category.

'Hey, Adam, looks like we are in the same heat then,' I gestured at the blue tabards we had been issued with.

'I think we stand a good chance; the competition doesn't look half as fit as we do.'

'Hmmm, well we've had a good year training,' I replied.

He grinned at me with mischief in his eyes. 'Think you can beat us then do you?'

'Have to wait and see won't we, but we are as ready as we will ever be that's for sure. We had better go to the assembly area. It's the first novice heat and then we're up.'

'I'll follow you if you don't mind. You've got more experience than I have.'

There were definite undertones in Adam's reply, but I chose to ignore them. I needed to keep my wits about me; Ebony was winding herself up for a fight and it was like being sat on top of a coiled spring. I could feel her muscles tightening up underneath me and she pranced from one leg to another in anticipation. 'Behave yourself, follow me if you must, then I suggest you try and keep up.'

There the gauntlet had been thrown down, and this was the closest we would get to having intimate relations with each other. We could show our passion and share our joy of racing without having to take our clothes off or using any protection other than the obligatory riding hats and boots.

'I'll let you take the lead then, but don't get too comfortable up there, Kate, I won't be far behind you. Shall we have a little bet then? Are you up for that?'

'Depends what the stakes are.'

'Well, I think a little game of truth or dare when we get back to the yard. How about it?'

'Are you sure you want to go there?'

'Entrants for the blue race, that's the blue race, please make your way to the start line.' The tinny sound of the Tannoy announcing our race drowned out my reply and we both tightened our reins and prepared for the tense walk down from the holding area to the start. I glanced behind me and saw my family jumping up and down, waving and cheering. I raised my hand in return and turned my thoughts to the task in hand.

There were ten of us in this heat, ten horses, the maximum allowed in each race to comply with health and safety. Despite the competitiveness, the event had a good reputation of being run safely, and its track record was one of the best in its field. Any type of racing has its element of danger, and those who partake in it understand the risks but do it anyway for the love of speed. Horsepower is exciting in all its forms. But here on the sand it was back to basics and had an air of inevitability and understanding of the thrill of the ride that dated back many hundreds of years. It was a feeling that was felt in the very soul; fear, suspense, danger and speed that got the adrenalin racing through the bloodstream of horse and rider alike, the sound of hooves pounding the hard flat sand and the sweet smell of success on everyone's minds.

'Good luck,' I mouthed at Adam as we lined up with the other entrants.

A thin tape ran across the starting line, similar to the Grand National but more basic.

'Competitors ready?'

The sound of the crowd rose as the starter held up his gun.

'Three, two, one,' he fired the gun in the air with a flourish and the race was on.

At six furlongs, the race was less than a mile and usually took just about ninety seconds. What it lacked in length it made up for in brutality. Each and every competitor was in it to win, and getting a good result here ensured horse and rider had a well-deserved place on the winner trophy, their name recognised in the racing fraternity the world over.

Ebony and Pilgrim were neck and neck at half distance, chasing the front runners, pounding along the sand. We were running our own private race, spurring each other on, and loving the thrill of competition.

'Come on, let's show them how it's done,' Kate urged Ebony on, and feeling her respond to her encouragement they started to pull away, and friendly rivalry gave way to the urge to be triumphant in their quest for a win. She glanced behind to be sure they were leaving the rest of the field behind. Just two horses in front of her now and the winning post fast approaching.

'Kate, watch out!'

Kate was in her element, oblivious to Adam's warning shouts which were lost in the wind. Too late, she spotted the dark figure that had come out of nowhere and stood in the middle of the track.

The horses in front had not been so blinkered and their riders were struggling to keep them under control. The grey horse that had taken the lead swerved dangerously to avoid the figure, the one in second suddenly put its anchors on leaving Ebony nowhere to go.

Too late, the warning. Kate tried to slow Ebony down but the collision was inevitable, whilst most of the rest of the racers had seen the carnage ahead unfolding and managed to pull up.

Kate was thrown head first over Ebony's neck, and she landed with a thud on the hard sand. Ebony tensed her hind quarters and took flight over her, determined not to put a foot on her beloved owner. Not so the horse behind. The equivalent of a motorway pile up followed.

As horse after horse went down, their riders scattered across the beach like a bad game of Buckaroo.

'Kate… Noooooooo.' Adam had managed to steer his horse around the mayhem ahead. He leapt off Pilgrim and ran towards the tiny form of his friend who lay motionless on the ground. Ebony stood next to Kate, nostrils snorting and prancing from leg to leg, eyes on stalks and ready to take flight at any minute.

'Somebody help me please,' Adam cried as he knelt over Kate's body.

Paramedics were on their way, running from their posts carrying a stretcher. The crowd had fallen silent. Adam held onto both horses, helplessly looking down at his friend.

Kate's body suddenly started twitching involuntarily, arms and legs no longer under her control.

'Oh no, Kate, Kate. Come quickly, I think she's fitting. Come on, come on.'

'We'll take it from here, sir,' the medic said, kneeling down and pushing Adam to one side.

Adam stood with their horses and tried to placate them as he watched. The other competitors had managed to calm their horses down and had made their way back to the start. The spectators looked on in horror, and realising that there had been a horrible accident, stood in reverent silence

Adam looked away as the paramedics worked, and staring into the distance he noticed a lone figure stood on the edge of the dunes silhouetted against the winter sun. A sudden chill washed over him and the wind swirled around them, bringing a sulphuric aroma which engulfed them within its rising vortex. Sand whipped up, stinging his eyes. Ebony and Pilgrim strained and pulled to get away from him.

'Sir, please go and join the others. Let us get on with treating your friend. The helicopter is about to land, we need to get her to hospital as quickly as we can.'

'I'll take the horses back, but what about her family? They're over there watching. Her husband will want to come with you.'

'No room I'm afraid. The best thing you can do to help is take the horses away and let her family know what is happening. We have stabilised her and are taking her to the nearest spinal unit. Can you do that?'

'Yeah, of course. What shall I tell them? Will she be ok?'

'Sir, please just tell them we are doing all we can and she is in good hands. Now really we have got to have some space.'

'Ok, ok, I'll do that. Kate, you hold on, do you hear me? Hold on. Oh Jesus, this can't be happening.'

Adam struggled to calm the two horses down and it took him all his skill to lead them back to the assembly area. TV cameras and reporters who were there to capture the races and broadcast them globally, suddenly descended on him. Adam stoically ignored them and made his way through the crowds, leading his highly-strung cargo to the relative safety of the competitors' enclosure. Kate's family awaited. Adam felt his heart sink as he approached them, not knowing what to say, but knowing that they needed to hear the facts.

'Adam,' Kate's husband John arrived, out of breath and visibly shaking flanked by her two daughters.

'John, let me find some help to get the horses sorted and back to the yard and I'll drive you all to the hospital they're taking her to. '

'I need to see her. Is she badly hurt? Is she conscious? What the fuck happened?'

'She's in good hands, give me five minutes. I know it's only words but try not to worry, I'm sure she'll be fine.'

Adam turned and led their horses away, wondering what would await them when they arrived at the hospital, his heart breaking for them all. He wasn't sure that she would make it and he had no clue how they would all manage to go on living without her

The Primary Level

Adam, John and the girls stood and watched as various hospital staff came and went in and out of the cubicle where Kate had been laid to rest. Hardly a word spoken between them, in stunned silence they watched and waited. Hoping, praying for good news to come every time the blue curtain twitched or opened, a hive of activity revealed. But no answers forthcoming as the medics prodded, poked, scanned and tested Kate's lifeless form. Half an hour passed, an hour, two hours, every second lasting an eternity in the waiting room opposite.

'I can't stand much more, Adam. Why won't they tell us what's happening?'

'Just let them do what they've got to do, John. We can't disturb them, they are doing everything they can to save her.'

Silence once more as the four of them contemplated the unthinkable, each wondering if things would ever be the same again. Suddenly a large man in hospital scrubs appeared from behind the screen.

'Which one of you is her husband?'

'That's me. Can I come in? What's happening?' John got up and started toward him.

'We've managed to stabilise her, but she has taken an almighty blow to the head. The good news is that all the scans we've done have been positive, no broken bones, nothing untoward, but we won't know for sure until we bring her round just what damage has been done. All we know is that there are no fractures visible. We will probably keep her sedated for the next twelve hours just to give the painkillers time to do their job and get her through the worst.'

They all breathed a collective sigh; she was going to be ok. John hugged the girls tightly and they wept with relief. 'Oh thank you, thank you so much,' he breathed in-between sobs.

'Can we go in and see her?' Adam asked the doctor.

'Yes, but only quickly. We are just organising a transfer for her upstairs to go to a bed in the Intensive Care Unit.'

'Intensive Care? Oh my God,' John answered, barely able to speak.

'Try not to worry too much. We're fairly confident she has just sustained surface injuries, but we will have to wait until the swelling to her head goes down a little before we can properly assess. Until then, she will be monitored every second and kept under to allow the drugs to do their job.'

'You can come in now,' said a young nurse as she drew the curtain back and beckoned them over. 'She probably looks worse than you were expecting, but as the doctor says, it appears to be mostly superficial. What on earth was she doing? She is covered in sand.'

'Racing her horse on the beach,' Adam replied, tears choking his reply.

'Oh Katie.' John held her hand as best he could in-between the tubes which protruded from all over her body. 'She looks so tiny laid there plugged into all that machinery.'

'It's all necessary, I'm afraid. I'll have to ask you to be quick, they're waiting for her upstairs.'

One by one, they bent over and negotiated the tubes to try and lay a kiss on a free patch of skin. It was too much for the girls and they held each other, sobbing as they watched the motionless form of their mother being wheeled away.

'She's in good hands,' Adam tried his best to reassure the family but it was hard to say it with conviction he didn't feel.

'Kate, can you hear me?' The voice in my head was unfamiliar. Who was it? I tried to answer but there was something blocking my mouth. My hands reached up to remove the obstacle only to be caught and placed gently down by my right hand side. Whoever was there with me in the dark had now taken a firm hold of my hand. I tried to respond, but once again was thwarted by tubes, pipes, wires, I didn't know what else. Who are you? I tried to will my thoughts into the head of my companion. No answer. Nothing worked. I couldn't make sense of what was going on around me. I tried to open my eyes but was unable to do more than a slight flutter. I had the feeling that I had been asleep for a very long time. My fingers grabbed onto what felt like wet bed sheets covered in some sort of grit. No, not grit, sand. Sand. I struggled to try and remember what had led me here to this blind chaos. Many voices, the sound of machinery, blips, a brightness trying to seep through my eyelids, and I had a brief notion that maybe the someone I had heard was just in my head and not a real person. Was I going mad? I didn't know. I didn't know anything. Confusion took over. I had to get up. I had to find Adam. Nothing. The thought had gone again, as much as I tried to chase it I couldn't hold onto it, gone again in a split second and the dark engulfed me once more.

'John, come on, you've been sat there all night. Please go and get some rest,' Caitlin, the elder of the two girls spoke softly their step-dad.

'I can't leave her. What if she wakes up and there's nobody here?'

'They said she's heavily sedated. Come on, shall we just go and get some fresh air? You can't sit here all night.' Charlotte took hold of John's hand with a comforting squeeze. 'Let's let the nurses do their job, she's in safe hands isn't she.'

'Your daughters are right. It won't do any of you any good sat here just looking at the numbers on the machines all night. She won't be able to respond as we've increased the sedation to help stabilise her overnight. Go and get some rest and if there is any change we will come and find you.'

Adam had spoken to the hospital staff and managed to secure one of the relatives' rooms for the night. It was tiny, with a bed settee and a chair, but it was private and meant that they could at least get a little bit of rest and enabled them to be at hand for Kate.

John sighed and stood up wearily. 'If you promise you will fetch us if there is any change.'

'Of course. Now if you'll excuse me I have some checks I need to do on your wife. Just routine, but we monitor very closely on this unit. She's doing ok and holding her own.'

'Thank you for everything you're doing. What time can I come back in the morning? We are staying in one of the relatives' rooms.'

'The doctors do their rounds at nine o'clock, so if you come at half past eight you'll be able to have some time with her before they arrive.'

'Come on, John. The girls are right, you look exhausted. You're no good to her in this state. I noticed a coffee shop downstairs. I don't know about you but I'm ready for a drink.' Adam put his arm round his friend's husband.

The four of them left the unit and made their way down to the ground floor.

'If you want to go home, Adam, please do.' John took his hand. 'You've been very kind, but we'll be ok, won't we girls.'

'I'll stay and have a drink with you, then I had better go back; the horses won't see to themselves in the morning. I'll come back tomorrow. Ring me if you need anything bringing.'

'Adam, I'll cadge a lift with you. I'll go then I can come back in my car tomorrow, and if you need anything I'll bring it. You've been more than kind, Adam, but we'll be ok,' Caitlin said firmly. 'I need to get home and organise the kids, poor Dave will be tearing his hair out. I'd like to go straightaway please, Adam, if you don't mind.'

As the elder daughter she had always taken the lead. Her and Kate had a tempestuous relationship and had often clashed in the past, but they would do anything for each other if need be. Caitlin had grown into a strong woman who had her own business as well as three-year-old twin boys to keep her busy.

John and Charlotte knew better than to disagree with Caitlin; she was like a force of nature once she had made her mind up. Adam looked from one to the other and decided it was best not to interfere with the family dynamics at play.

'Ah, right then. I'll be sure to ring you tomorrow, John. Try and get some sleep later.'

'I'll try, thanks for everything. Speak to you tomorrow then. Thank you, thanks so much.'

John shook his hand and gave Caitlin a swift hug. And they were gone.

'Shall we get a drink then?'

'I don't really want anything. I don't know what to do, Charl.'

Charlotte's heart went out to her step-dad. He was such a kind man and the best thing to have happened to her mum in a very long time. They were so blissfully happy. John had been a breath of fresh air and a welcome break from the normal kind of guy her mother brought home. He was a little older than Kate and had had his fair share of accidents in the past, which had left him with a slight limp, hardly noticeable unless he was tired. Tonight he looked ten years older, and every accident he had suffered in the past now showed on his weary face. He rubbed his left leg, vaguely aware of a dull ache as they stood in the hospital foyer watching Caitlin and Adam head off towards the car park.

'Shall we get that drink then?'

'I can't face anyone, Charl. I think I'd like to go outside. I need to get out of this building and try and clear my head a bit.'

A blast of icy cold air hit them as they stepped through the automatic doors of the main entrance of the hospital. One or two hardened smokers, including a guy in a wheelchair, were getting their nicotine fix just outside the doors. Their cigarette smoke following John and Charlotte as they wandered along the slabbed pathway. Neither of them smoked and usually John would have stressed about selfish people polluting the atmosphere. Passive smoking was the last of his worries tonight and he didn't bat an eyelid.

'I can't believe this, Charl. That bloody race. I knew something was going to happen; I had a bad feeling in my gut. Why didn't I stop her going?'

'You weren't to know. Anyway, even if you had asked her not to go, what do you think she would have done? You know what she's like. Nothing would've stopped her going. She'd have only ended up having a strop with you and gone anyway. That race meant too much to her to forfeit her place.'

'I know you're right, but I still can't help blaming myself. I need to find out what happened. What caused those horses to spook so badly?'

'Don't even think about it, we must try and focus on Mum. Shall we go in now? I'm bloody freezing and it's getting late. It's been a long day, you look like I feel.' Charlotte put her arm around John and gave him a hug.

'Thanks, Charl, you're so brave. It should be me comforting you, not the other way round, especially in your condition.'

'Don't be silly, everyone needs support at times like this and we are there for each other, that's the way it is. And I'm pregnant not poorly. Love you.'

'Love you too. You're right, I can hardly feel my hands with the cold. It's bitter.'

The wind whipped through their coats, making them shudder as they headed back to the entrance, their breath as heavy on the air, as visible as that of the oxygen polluters.

'Excuse me, can you help me?'

Charlotte looked over to the source of the plea. It was the guy in the wheelchair calling to them. He was on his own now having been abandoned by the other smokers. Both his hands were bandaged and his legs stopped short at the knee. He was wrapped in a blanket and wore a battered trapper hat.

'I'm stuck,' he gestured at his wheels, demonstrating his predicament. 'They're stuck in-between one of the slabs. There's a big crack and I can't move them. Could you give me a push please?'

'Of course, we can,' said Charlotte. 'Here, let me try,' she added, taking hold of the wheelchair handles and setting him free. 'Would you like us to help you back inside?'

'Er, yeah, if you don't mind. I feel a bit of a stupid twat to be honest. But I'm really struggling with these fucking bandages. I can just about manage to smoke if someone else lights it for me. Filthy habit I know, but look at the state of me; I figure I've survived a war zone so a little nicotine ain't going to be a problem.'

John could only follow blindly, tears streaming down his face. Tears of sorrow for his beautiful wife and for the man in the wheelchair, tears of pride for his step-daughter, and tears of regret that he was unable to protect Kate as he should've done that day. Events had taken over and were out of his control, but it didn't stop the guilt.

'Which floor are you going to? We might as well take you all the way back.' John wiped his eyes and caught up with Charlotte and her charge.

'Seventh floor, Surgical Ward, if that's ok. Cheers, appreciate it. I'm Gary by the way.'

'Nice to meet you, Gary,' said Charlotte.

'Yeah, you too. How come you're here so late? It's past visiting.'

'Mum is in intensive care. We're staying over,' Charlotte replied.

'Sorry to hear that. That's crap, especially at Christmas, eh.'

The odd trio travelled the rest of the journey up in silence, each lost in their own world. John studied the injured man, and he wondered where he had sustained his injuries, assuming it was fighting for his country, but not knowing or wanting to ask any further information. The faded 'Help for Heroes' t-shirt, the scraggy beard and eyes full of pain prevented John from embarking on a difficult conversation. John was shocked at how he had misjudged the man, assuming that he was in his forties, and once he had seen beyond the injuries he realised that he was probably in his early twenties, the same age as his girls. John wondered how much more misery he could take; he had enough sorrow to deal with without taking on the rest of the world's problems.

The lift 'binged' their arrival at floor seven, interrupting his painful daydreams.

'I'll be ok from here. Thanks very much.' Gary wheeled himself out of the lift.

'If you're sure, ok then. Well, nice to have met you. Er, Merry Christmas,' John replied. The irony of his salutations cut through him as bitterly as the ice cold wind.

Charlotte bent over and gave Gary a kiss on the cheek. 'Next time you go for a smoke stay away from broken slabs. You could've frozen to death if we hadn't been there.'

'Bossy aren't you,' he replied with a wink. 'I'll try and keep out of trouble.'

'Make sure you do,' Charlotte replied with a grin.

As the lift doors closed they watched as Gary wheeled himself to the security door leading into the ward and pressed the intercom.

'Are you ready to go back to the relatives' room?'

'I think so, I'm exhausted,' John replied. 'I don't know if I can sleep though.'

'It's going to be a long day tomorrow, and if we are going to get through it we need to try and rest.'

'When did you get to be so grown up?'

'Today,' Charlotte answered, her voice cracking with trying to hold back the tears.

The two of them held each other up for support and walked slowly back to the little room that would become home for the next week, both lost in their own thoughts, but both knowing that things would never be the same again.

Level One

New Year's Eve, 2015 - daytime

I open my eyes. The light hurts so I shut them again quickly. I am scared. I don't know where I am. I don't know where my family are. I don't know anything. All I can remember is a buzzing, a loud whirring. What was that noise? I am trying to pluck up the courage to open my eyes again but it hurts so much. This isn't normal is it? I am scared. The whirring, buzzing, rushing of air. I can hear it faintly in the background. Am I flying? Am I dead? The confusion flies around in my head like butterflies flapping, trapped in a bell jar trying to escape to the world beyond the glass prison. I try and pin one down but it escapes me.

'Hello Kate.'

Who is that? I don't recognise the female voice. Nobody I know could speak in such a mocking tone and convey the menace in such a short sentence. Yet somehow it sounds familiar.

'Who's that? I can't see you.'

'We've known each other a long time. You've just forgotten.'

'Where are you? Can you help me please? I'm scared, I don't know where I am.'

'You're coming home, Katie, just go with it. Let go and follow my voice.'

I try with all my might to remember who the disembodied voice belongs to. I don't know if I can trust it. The name is there but just beyond my grasp. I suddenly feel very scared and alone.

'I can't even move so how can I follow you? I'm not going anywhere until you tell me who you are.'

'Oh, you know me. We've known each other for many, many years. I'm disappointed in you. I did try and speak to you a few months ago but you ignored my warning.'

'I don't understand. What warning?' I managed to open my eyes at last but my vision was blurred and I could only make out that I was in a small room, no windows, just a door opposite the end of my bed and a lot of machinery.

'Am I in hospital?'

Silence. Whoever had been speaking to me was certainly not present in the room as I looked around trying to locate the source of the voice. I was alone and the sense of something bad enveloped me. I tried to remember what had happened to me. Where was John? My girls? Adam? Ebony! The race.

Memories came flooding back but oh so jumbled. My tired mind tried to make sense of the images that flashed in and out of my head. That whirring sound, I still couldn't identify it. What the hell was it?

'I had an accident, didn't I?'

Silence.

'Hello, hello. Answer me, please. Where have you gone? I don't want to be here on my own, please come back.'

I was aware of my heartbeat, which seemed unnaturally loud. My breathing accompanying with a whoosh in and out with controlled regularity.

I felt so tired, I couldn't hold onto consciousness and my body gave way to a purplish black fog which engulfed me. I went under once more, but this time aware that my life was in danger.

The day dragged, minutes passed so slowly that time appeared to stand still. Kate's family tried to keep themselves occupied. Flicking through dog-eared magazines on the coffee table, staring at the TV screen on the waiting room wall, the sound off, sub-titles displaying dialogue that none of them read, all absorbed in their own thoughts. John was alternating between pacing up and down, answering text messages, and keeping up with social media messages. Kate's daughters trying to maintain brave faces and nearly succeeding.

'Surely they should be finished by now?'

'I'm sure they will come and fetch us as soon as they can, John,' Adam replied.

Another hour came and went. The morning gave way to afternoon. None of them had risked going to get any lunch, and they daren't leave their positions in case they missed being called to the ward.

The clock showed that they had been waiting four hours when eventually Kate's nurse came.

'How did it go? Can we see her? Have you got the results?' John's questions came thick and fast.

'If you would like to follow me, the consultant will have a word with you,' she replied calmly. 'The scan went well and he will update you on the results.'

John, Adam and the girls followed the nurse as she walked briskly down the corridor and directed them into a room near to Kate's ward.

'He will be with you shortly if you would all like to take a seat. I will let him know that you are here.'

'I don't like this,' John said quietly.

'Let's not jump to conclusions, she's a tough cookie your wife,' Adam replied with more conviction than he felt.

The nurse returned as promised with Kate's consultant, who greeted them all warmly with a firm handshake.

'Hi, my name is Daniel and I'm part of the neurology team who have been taking care of Kate,' he addressed them all with a smile. 'Nice to meet you all and I'm sorry you've had such a long wait, but we have done a thorough scan and as you're aware, it involved a trip to another part of the hospital. It all takes much organising to ensure the welfare of the patient is utmost. It is quite stressful for the nursing staff, but I want to assure you that Kate is receiving first class care.'

'What did your tests find, doctor?' Caitlin asked briskly.

'Well, we can tell you that there are no fractures as we already knew, but we have found that the pressure in her head is very high and there is some swelling in the brain. This does explain a little why she has not responded as we first hoped, but I can tell you that we have taken steps to bring the pressure down and it does appear to be working.'

'What does that mean? Will she recover and be ok?' John asked.

'Your wife is a very lucky lady and seems to have managed to avoid serious injury, which having heard the details of the accident, is surprising. We are reducing the sedation and will try and take her off the life support. She is breathing more and more on her own now and holding her own, so all in all it's a positive result. But the next twenty-four hours are crucial.'

'So she is going to be alright?' asked Adam.

'As far as we can tell, but until we try and bring her round again it really is a case of having to wait. The brain is such a complex organ and there may be things going on at microscopic level that don't show up on the scan. A patient with the same injury could be sitting up and talking, but on the other hand they could be the same as Kate and on life support. There is no way of telling. All I can say is that we will be monitoring her very closely and I am happy that things appear to be moving in a positive direction at the moment. Now, if you'll excuse me, do you have any questions before I go?'

'No, thank you.' John stood up and shook the doctor's hand. 'I can't thank you enough for everything you've been doing. Can we go and see her?'

'It depends if it's convenient with the nursing staff, I'm afraid. Is she settled back in the ward?' Daniel asked the nurse.

'I'll just check, if you'd all care to wait here, but it's two at a time, so you will have to take it in turn if that's ok?'

'More than ok. Thank you so very much,' replied John.

'You and Caitlin go first,' said Charlotte, giving him a hug. 'We can go after, can't we, Adam?'

'Sure, that sounds like a good idea. Good news, eh. Good news.'

'As Daniel says, the next twenty-four hours are crucial. We need to take her off life support, but yes she appears to be responding more now. Just try and bear in mind that it may not be successful. If it doesn't work tomorrow then we will try again the next day. I just need to make sure you all understand that.'

'Yes, we do. Thank you, nurse,' Caitlin spoke for all of them. 'We fully understand.'

'I'll just check and see if you are able to go in.'

'Thanks very much,' John replied.

'We'll go back to the waiting room,' said Charlotte giving John a hug.

'Ok, we won't stay too long with her. Grab a coffee or something. Can you ring your grandparents please, Charl, but stress that she's stable. This is taking its toll on them as well and we need to take care of them.'

'Of course. Don't worry. I'll ring them soon as we get back to the room.'

I am aware that someone is in the room with me again. This time I'm not so scared; I feel that whoever it is will not hurt me. There is a totally different atmosphere, one of love and caring. I sense movement, the scraping of a chair along the floor by my bedside. I try and speak but no words will pass my lips, my tongue is squashed flat in my mouth, my lips are so dry they are almost numb. I try to move the obstacle that is blocking my mouth but it is wedged in tightly. I can hear my voice inside my head but I cannot make the words audible. Someone squeezes my left hand, a strong firm grip. I know that touch. It is John, and he holds my hand tightly and raises it to his lips. I feel the soft scratch of stubble. John. I feel safe. I feel love.

Another is present, my right hand being stroked gently with a feminine touch. I cannot tell if it is Caitlin or Charlotte, but I feel sure that it is one of my daughters. My eyelids are glued together. I so desperately need them to know that I am aware of their presence but my efforts are in vain. It is no good, I am paralysed. Fear comes again and makes my heart race. I hear blips and beeps, the whooshing sound drowns out my voice. Something is happening to me and I have no control over it. Whoosh, beep, beep. John's voice. Caitlin. Ah, that's who it was. They sound frightened. Another person arrives. The fear is now a tangible thing. Please help me. Please don't let me go. I scream in my head to no avail. The purple is coming again, enveloping me in its velvety touch. It rises slowly, I can see it creeping up from my toes, which seem a hundred miles away. Past my knees, my tummy hurts, a sharp pain. What is that sticking into me, a sharp scratchy pain.

A needle. Oh no, what are they doing? Someone is trying to hurt me. My arms lay by my side, useless, heavy and leaden. Bip bip bip. The purple comes higher, now at chest level, rising unchallenged until my neck is engulfed. Purple lava, warm, soft. My chin has disappeared. I try and fight it because I am so scared I will suffocate. It reaches my nose, colours my cheeks, darkens my eyes and fills my ears, gradually removing all my senses. I cannot move. I cannot see. I cannot speak. I cannot hear. I am left with a vague aroma of something sweet and sickly, something familiar I try to decipher where I know it from. I cannot, it is too hard. My whole world has succumbed to the purple blanket I find myself trapped under. Lost. In an underworld. I think I may be dead again. Something is with me. I want my family. I am vaguely aware of a wetness on my cheek. Purple turns to black. And I am gone.

'Kate, Kate, can you hear me? You saw that right? You all saw that?' John looked at Caitlin and the nurse who was topping up drugs and doing the hourly routine checks that were now becoming familiar to Kate's family.

'It's just the body getting rid of secretions,' the nurse answered him calmly.

'No, no, it was a tear, I'm sure it was. She cried a tear. It had blood in it. Is that normal? Has she got damage to her eyes?'

'Your wife has suffered a severe blow to her head. There is some trauma around her eyes, but the swelling is going down. It's part of the healing process.'

'But I was talking to her and she cried a tear. I'm sure it was because she heard me. She's in there fighting, I know she is.'

The nurse carried on with her checks, adjusting drug levels, noting readings from the machines. She knew better than to disagree with a relative; sometimes it was only hope that kept them going and to correct him again would be cruel. Who was she to take hope away with her professional opinion so she kept it to herself and wondered how she would cope if it was her loved one laying there on the bed, so helpless, with their life in someone else's hands.

It did not matter how many years' experience one had, the pain and suffering of relatives never got any easier to deal with. It was almost harder for them than it was for the patient who slept in a drug-induced coma, oblivious to the heartache.

Omnia Somnia (Everything is a Dream)?

'How nice to finally meet you again, it's been a long time my friend. I'll bring you up to speed. There is much intelligence that you need to be familiar with.'

'Sorry, but do I know you? I think I do but I'm really sorry, I cannot remember your name?'

'Names are not important here. The important thing is you are back. We all have our jobs to do and it is time now to act.'

The being who stood in front of Kate was strangely human, but something was not quite right. Kate looked around her and could not make out her surroundings. The ground was rocky and she could see a building shrouded in mist in the middle distance. She had the feeling she was high up, the air was thin and her head felt muddled. A beautiful rainbow rose above them, and the colours of the spectrum shone so brightly they made her eyes hurt. And that smell; violets, lavender, lily of the valley. A sudden thought entered her state of confusion. Mum? Grandma? The thought slipped away and she looked at the figure who stood before her.

'Can't you tell me your name?'

'Follow me, come and meet the rest of the family. We've all missed you very much.'

'I'm not going anywhere until you tell me who you are and where the fuck I am,' Kate replied angrily. 'I don't like playing games, so quit it and tell me what is going on? Where are my family? What have you done with them?'

'Ah Katie J, that's the woman we know and love.'

'You say you know me and you know my name. Please tell me who you are.'

'I'm hurt and offended you don't remember me. It will all come back, you just have to trust me. Can you do that?'

Kate stood and looked at the figure, a powerful rush of love filled her and as she looked a golden light shone down and bathed them both in its hue. The man's face transformed into a face she knew well.

'John!' she wobbled in danger of losing her footing on the uneven surface.

The man rushed to her and caught her before she fell. Strong arms held her and set her on her feet again.

'Hello beautiful,' John smiled down at his wife.

'I don't understand.' She held on tight to her husband and a sense of relief flowed through her. 'Am I safe now?'

'You've always been safe, my dear. We have always been here watching you. But it's time now for you to join us.'

'Where are we?'

'Home, my darling, we are home.'

More figures appeared, striding towards us. The confusion present in my brain started to fade away as they came closer. My beautiful mother, my grandparents, my daughters all approached me as I stood, held captive in the loving arms of my husband. More questions came; how could this be; the living and the dead joined together and all here present waiting to welcome me? How was it possible?

John looked down into my eyes and I knew the answer. In a split second I understood. I nodded to let him know I had heard him. As my mind cleared I knew that spoken words and physical gestures were unnecessary in this world. I had returned to a home that I had long forgotten. I had transcended the trappings of my physical body. Love overtook all my senses and my family welcomed me back with open arms.

I sank back into silk cushions and tried to take it all in; I didn't want to miss one single thing. My eyes devoured the scene in front of me; a table adorned with the most succulent buffet I had ever seen. Bowls of bronze were filled to overflowing with luscious fruits, slabs of cheese, cold meats, flagons of drink jostled for room amongst goblets and tankards. Beyond the table, a fireplace which housed a whole suckling pig rotating on a spit. The sounds of laughter and the hum of warm friendly voices filled the air. I was so completely happy. My appetite satisfied, I gazed up at my wonderful husband in awe. He had rescued me; he was my saviour once again. At the head of the table sat a formidable-looking man, I immediately recognised him as the father. He stood up and caught my eye. Smiling, he raised his tankard.

'Listen,' he commanded.

Immediately the gathering fell silent. This man was the leader of the assembly, and when he spoke they stopped and did as he commanded. Nothing but the utmost respect was worthy of the head of the family. Zeus was the father of many of the assembled. He was also the lover, the brother, the grandfather of many; some dual relationships in a world where incest was common place and single parentage not unknown. Anything was possible in this world of the gods.

'Today is a momentous day for our kind. We welcome my daughter Aphrodite back into the fold. Now is the time that we draw our plans against the evil that is threatening to overtake the Earth.'

The rest of the deities present murmured in agreement.

'I propose a toast to our lady. Raise your goblets and drink, we will rain hell down on the wicked and we will avenge the worthy. The ones who possess and embrace the evil will turn and flee, but we will follow them to all the four corners of the Earth and beyond. They will not defeat us and they will know of our existence. Too long have we watched and waited in vain for the mortals to take action and defeat the malicious. How dare they try and destroy our earthly home? It is time to fight. Time to return.

'I say again, raise your glasses and drink, to the family, to Aphrodite, welcome. To our enemies, eternal pain and sorrow.'

The gods toasted the safe return of one of their own, Dionysus (Bacchus), hosting the banquet, Zeus heading the table. Kate looked on in wonder as the memories flooded back and filled her skin as fast as the wine flowed and the food consumed.

John turned his attention from the father and down to his wife. 'Happy, my love?'

'Oh yes, blissfully. So you are Hephaestus and I am Aphrodite,' Kate replied, stating a fact rather than asking a question. She knew that this was the case but had to voice her opinion so as to make it real.

'Yes. I had to come for you. The time was right.'

'What would you like me to call you? Hephaestus? Vulcan?'

'Just John will be fine. How about you? Aphrodite? Venus? Kate?'

'Whatever you choose. All I know is I want you very badly. Show me to our quarters.'

'You know the way. Do what you've always done in your current human form. Follow your heart, it has served you well.'

'So many questions, but they can wait. Take my hand and come.'

'Who am I to refuse such an offer my lady? It has been far too long since we shared a bed.'

The two of them slipped away from the festivities, leaving the rest of the family to drink and celebrate the return. Things were moving forward and their human forms were starting to take action. Fate was taking over and the gods were returning. It was time.

Hours passed and daytime gave way to evening, then night. Kate and John enjoying getting to know each other once again, but this time on a level which she had forgotten. Time in human years passed much the same as on Mount Olympus and in this respect the gods were able to keep an eye on their human counterparts.

'There is much I don't understand, my husband,' I said, my body tired after our lovemaking, and I studied his face and tried to take in everything he had told me.

'You will, my darling, but it may take a little time to fully appreciate the situation. For now, try and rest a little. We may be subject to a different way of life than our human counterparts, but we still need to stop once in a while and take stock. We have been asleep for a very long time, just waiting until the time our earthly homes started to need us once again. Many hundreds of years have passed since they built our temples and asked for our help in all manner of matters. As time passed they became arrogant and fought amongst themselves without asking for our intervention to thwart their enemies; without asking for a miracle cure or seeking an oracle for guidance. They thought their scientists held all the answers, science battling with their faith and ridiculing our priests.'

'That may be so, but why then didn't we intervene sooner? Surely we could have shown them some proof of our existence and won their faith once again.'

'How many signs do you think we and other gods gave them? You must realise that other races and religions were suffering the same fate as ourselves. Over different periods of time, the higher beings came and showed them how to build their pyramids. The Inca's, the Aztecs, the Mayans, the Egyptians to name but a few eventually gave up on their gods, the same as our followers left us behind in their quest for knowledge.'

'But there are still many faiths and religions on Earth. The Catholics, Muslims, Buddhists and many others still hold their gods in high esteem so why did they forsake us?'

'I do not know all the answers, none of us do, but I do know that their beautiful planet is in turmoil.'

'I keep thinking about their city of Paris. I don't know the reason, but as my mind is becoming clearer, the sense of evil I feel about that place is steadily growing. What is it about Paris that makes me feel that way, John?'

'Don't you remember our earthly wedding anniversary? Think back just a few weeks ago. Try and remember what happened. I can tell you, but I want you to try your hardest to bring it all back. I know you can do it, my love. Please try for me.'

Kate lay her head against John's chest and closed her eyes. As her mind searched for the answers her exhausted body took over and she fell once more into a deep sleep.

Friday 13th November, 2015

The venue was filling up nicely. Kate and John had arrived at the perfect time; not too far ahead that they froze to death queuing up, but just early enough to ensure their usual place in front and centre of the stage. They had it down to a fine art, coats tied around their waists to avoid the lengthy wait to collect them from the coat check after the gig. A bottle of water each to quench their thirst, walk calmly to the front of the venue and wait patiently for an hour until the support band came on. They were hardened music lovers. Beer and spirits could wait until after the music; they did not need artificial highs to enhance the event.

Tonight was another special event. Their first wedding anniversary, and coincidentally their local venue had provided the stage for what they knew would be a brilliant night of music. The Queen Extravaganza were playing tonight; they were the official tribute band for Queen, each and every member hand-picked by Queen's drummer Roger Taylor and put together for their level of expertise. It was turning into a memorable night for many reasons.

Kate had booked them the Executive Suite at their usual hotel, 'The White Lion', which provided comfortable rooms and decent meals. It was their favourite place to stay and the location was perfect, being just a couple of miles away from the venue. The university was in the heart of the city and boasted of new premises suitable for all kinds of entertainment. Comedians, bands, exercise classes, foam parties, all kinds of events were held in this massive room which used to house railway paraphernalia. The coming of the new university had given the place a new lease of life and brought hundreds of students to breathe new life into the city.

Yes, it was filling up nicely. Friendly banter and a sea of expectant faces jostled for position as the time came for the lights to go down and the band to take their places on the stage. A curtain, emblazoned with the logo of a large eagle with its wings spread, billowed across the stage front. The curtain obscured the stage but the occasional hint of a silhouette came through as different coloured spotlights shone from in front and behind. The level of excitement was building nicely as the audience waited expectantly.

John stood behind me, his arms wrapped around my waist. Being a good foot taller than me, this was the position we generally assumed at gigs. We made it to the front and he protected me and defended our position; not always an easy job, especially at some of the more aggressive gigs we had attended in the past. Madness being one on the black list where out and out fighting took over the mosh pit with the lead singer, Suggs, trying to calm things down with humour whilst at the same time keeping his street cred intact. Guys our age who had never grown out of their skinhead roots. Thankfully they were in the minority, and for the most part the violence had been left behind many years before.

This gig was not in the same category and the audience was a mix of younger student types and an older generation made up of forty and fifty somethings coming to listen to the anniversary tour of 'A Night at the Opera', which was celebrating its fortieth birthday.

The tension was building nicely as the lights in the venue went down. The curtain fell to the floor with a flourish, revealing the musicians behind lit up by red, green and blue. Bright white lights blazing out over the audience lit up our faces and highlighted the silhouetted members of the band. The drum kit raised above the guitarists and the singer stood on a platform in a typical Freddie Mercury pose, one hand held high in the air and his face upturned as if in praise of the gods of music and expectance of hero worship from the fans here assembled. Boom. The music began, and there began our evening of singing, dancing and revelling in the excitement that came from soaking up the atmosphere of a live band. So much talent, it was easy to see why these musicians had been chosen to represent the original members of Queen. The replacement front man strutted and posed and performed to perfection. It was as though he was channelling the real Freddie. We couldn't imagine any other doing such a brilliant performance.

The evening was over too soon. Smart phones had done their job, updating statuses on social media, checking in to the venue, taking photographs, and 'selfies' already uploaded before the end of the gig. We were guilty of that as much as anyone. We both love our social media, Facebook and Instagram being our choice of sharing our lives with the waiting world. John and I had both grown tired of Twitter; it seemed to have of late been a place where keyboard warriors excelled at being clever and trolls lurked around every tweet waiting to intimidate or abuse innocent victims. It certainly seemed to be less fun that it was a few years previously so our tweets were now few and far between for us.

We headed out into the brisk November air, smugly walking past the novices queuing to redeem their jackets and coats. Not us, we happily drove away towards our waiting executive suite, looking forward to having a nice bath and a bottle of wine before our next session of lovemaking.

As John drove, I uploaded a few pictures of the evening. Something brought me back down to earth with a massive thud. Something had happened. Something was badly wrong with the world tonight.

'John, put the radio on will you please?'

'Yeah sure, what's up?'

'I don't know, but there are some very disturbing statuses on Facebook. Something about a shooting.'

'The news won't be on for a little while. Don't worry, it's probably something and nothing. You can't believe everything you read on there.'

'I know, but there are a few people saying there has been a shooting in Paris.'

Five minutes later and we were back at the hotel. I found the remote and put the news channel on. Instead of relaxing in a bath of bubbles and sipping Prosecco we found ourselves sat on the end of the bed, speechless as we heard of the events that had taken place at the Bataclan that evening. As we were enjoying our gig and singing and dancing to the music, our contemporaries just a few hundred miles away were being shot down and killed. Fellow lovers of music, lovers of life, people out socialising and enjoying a meal or a drink with their friends had been cruelly killed. No reason, no explanation forthcoming. The whole world watched in horror as reporters told of the horrific events that had taken place on the Friday, 13th November. Our first wedding anniversary, the date that would now hold significance for many others for entirely different reasons. We sat on the edge of the king-size bed in silence, both lost in our thoughts and grieving for the loss of so many innocents across the channel. Reports that there were still people held hostage added to our grief. The band that had been playing were The Eagles of Death Metal, a band who had ironically covered the song *'Save a Prayer'* by Duran Duran and had, only two weeks previously, appeared with them on a TV show. Many bands, including my Duran boys, had already done their sets and left Paris just a few short hours earlier. I shuddered and wept silent tears at the total waste of human life. And for what? Who knew how these terrorists justified their actions, but that night I prayed for a long time, safe in my husband's arms before we fell into a troubled sleep.

Level Two

New Year's Eve, 2015 – Night time

John had stayed at the hospital once again, this time with Adam for company. Initially refusing the offer of a companion, he didn't have the strength to argue against the rest of the family who were not taking no for an answer. John insisted that the girls go home and get some rest. Caitlin and Charlotte had both offered to stay, but it made more sense for Adam to be there as Caitlin had her own family to look after and Charlotte was due at work; she managed a busy hotel. It was full to capacity, in full swing with the season's festivities. Her boss had offered to get cover for her, but Charlotte declined, preferring to keep busy to keep her mind occupied, especially with only a few weeks left until the baby was due. As long as her mum was recovering, she felt she could leave John with another male for company, one who knew her mother well but was one step removed. She trusted and liked Adam and he had proven to be a rock solid pillar of support for all of them since the accident had happened almost a week ago.

New Year's Eve, and John and Adam found themselves sat in the relative room waiting for the time when John was allowed back onto the ward to say goodnight to Kate. Adam hooked up to social media, updating their friends and acquaintances to take the pressure off John, who was receiving hundreds of messages, which he was both physically and mentally unable to cope with.

'Bloody phone never stops.'

'It's only because people care, John. You're lucky to have so many good friends and family.'

'I know, but I can't keep up. It's so exhausting.'

'That's why I'm trying to update everyone for you. Switch your phone off. It's not doing you any good.'

'I feel so helpless, Adam. I still can't understand what exactly happened out there. Tell me again please.'

'Look, I don't entirely know either. Just something spooked the horses. It all happened so quickly. Everyone I've spoken to says the same; something spooked the front runners, we all agree on that, but a couple of the guys say they thought there was a figure on the track, but they can't be sure because there was no evidence of anyone running across the track and the sands were empty. It is just one of those mysteries that I doubt we will ever get to the bottom of.'

'There will be an inquiry, that's for sure. I hope they shut it down after this. That race is far too dangerous. I've never been happy with Kate entering into it, but you know what she's like. She won't take no for an answer, and who am I to stop her doing what she loves. I blame myself, Adam, I really do, I had a bad feeling about it and I didn't voice it.'

'Do you really think she would have taken any notice? You know very well how headstrong she is. At least she was doing something she loved.'

'Thanks. I know, but it doesn't make it any easier.' John put his head in his hands. 'Oh God, what a bloody mess. What a way to spend New Year.'

Adam's phone buzzed again. 'There are literally hundreds of people all sending their best wishes and praying for you and Kate. The power of social media, eh.'

'I don't really bother with it. Kate does. She loves it, but it's not for me.'

'Well, whether you like it or not, the amount of prayers people are saying is a miracle in itself. She will be ok, you know. She's tough.'

John checked on his watch and picked up his phone. 'I'm going to go and say goodnight to her.'

'Leave your phone with me, John.'

'No, I'll take it. I've been playing her a song every night at bedtime, and the nurses say she may be able to hear the music.'

'Ok, mate. I'll sort the bed out so you can get some kip when you come back.'

John forced his aching body up and left Adam engrossed in texting, or whatever it was he was doing on his phone, his legs made of lead; it was as though he was wading through treacle as he made his way down the corridor and back to the ward. Leaning against the wall for support, he pressed the buzzer on the ward door. A minute passed before the answer came, or maybe an hour, he wasn't sure.

'Hello, who is it?'

'Kate's husband. Can I come in please?'

'Can you take seat in the waiting room for five minutes please? We are just turning her. We'll come and fetch you.'

The waiting room opposite the ward had just a few chairs, a broken drinks machine, a coffee table, and a large flat screen TV with its volume off, subtitles on. John was familiar with this room and the protocol regarding going onto the ward. He leant his head back and dared to close his eyes, concentrating on fighting off sleep. His whole body ached; injuries he had received in earlier life became tiresome when he was lacking in sleep. He rubbed the aching muscles in his left leg and allowed himself to relax, a little vaguely aware of activity around him. He kept his eyes shut, not wanting to engage into contact with anyone else. He just couldn't face the questions, the sympathy, the explanations, or having to be sympathetic to other poor souls who instead of partying and raising a glass to the coming year, were instead stuck in this miserable reality. Not that he didn't have sympathy, but the stories from others whose relatives were fighting for their lives alongside Kate were just as harrowing and heart rending as his own. They were all trying to come to terms with this reality, bearing the brunt of the pain, no sedation for the ones left outside. Waiting, caught like frightened rabbits in car headlights, staring into space trying to make sense of what was happening.

John's heart broke for all of them, but he couldn't save the world as much as he would like to. Keeping his eyes tight shut and avoiding any human contact from fellow sufferers was how he managed to just about hold on to his sanity. Deprived of sleep since the day of the accident, John was barely functioning. Voices floated across to him from the corridor and he squinted to see if it was somebody coming to fetch him. Three hospital staff were stood outside the entrance chatting and laughing. John put his head down and tried to blot out their cheerful conversation. He didn't want to know how they were going to celebrate or hear of if they'd had a good Christmas. People going about their normal daily business; how could that be when they were living in a nightmare?

The ward door opened and John stood up hopefully. The nurse who came out walked past him without a second glance. Another false alarm. He sat back down heavily, numb with exhaustion yet on edge with worry. He couldn't eat. He couldn't sleep. The most he'd managed was a couple of cups of coffee that he had been given. He had gone off the taste of it, and now could only stomach water. He figured that if he drank water he would survive. No amount of nagging by his family and friends changed the nauseous feeling he had when he thought of food or stopped the churning of his stomach from worry. He was surviving on water and his nerves. He had even contemplated taking up smoking again only to decide that he wouldn't want to face the wrath of his wife if he did start again. That's if she survived and the Kate they knew and loved came back to them all. Nobody could tell them the how the injury would affect her or how she would recover. It was in the lap of the gods. John wasn't a religious man, but he had started praying to anything that may or may not be out there. He didn't care if by doing so he was being a hypocrite, but he defied anyone in this situation not to look to a higher being in hope of salvation.

As he waited, the staff in the corridor went on their way, one going home, the other two pulling a night shift. Pleasantries exchanged washed over him as he tried to make sense of what had happened. A familiar face appeared, interrupting his reverie.

'Hey there, are you waiting to go in to your wife?' the woman addressed him as she took a seat opposite.

John looked up and realised it was the mother of the young lad in the bed opposite Kate, another family ripped apart by tragedy. They had spoken a few times during the course of the week. Andy had been minding his own business on a lad's night out when a fight broke out and he had stepped in to try and help a friend and ended up taking the brunt of the beating. John's heart went out to this woman; at least Kate had been doing something she loved when she'd had her accident. Jemma's son had been playing the Good Samaritan and ended up in here for his trouble.

'Yes, seems like I've been here hours. I don't know what they are doing in there,' he replied with a sad acknowledgement to her question.

'Oh John, we shouldn't be stuck in this place. There is so much pain and misery everywhere you look; families like ours torn apart by awful accidents and stuff. We should've been at a party tonight and look where we are. Sat...' her voice broke and she started to weep, unable to finish her sentence.

'It's not fair, Jemma. I know, I know. Here,' John got up and reached across to give her a handkerchief. 'Here, take this. You're not on your own, none of us are. We must try and support each other though these terrible times. I know it's not easy, but we must try and stay strong and keep fighting for them. They're going to need us more than ever when they come out of there.' John gestured towards the door and paced up and down.

He spoke with more conviction than he felt. Although he had Adam to chat with, he felt that this woman could empathise with his situation. He wasn't entirely comfortable with Adam as he always had a feeling that Adam felt more than he let on for Kate. It was a fear that he had never spoken out loud to Kate. He knew she would never betray him, but just as strongly, he felt that she and Adam had an understanding and there was more to their relationship than they would ever let on to each other let alone to the outside world. He supposed what he felt was jealousy; irrational, but there it was. Something inside pricked at his mind when he thought of how much time Adam and Kate spent together. Again, he would never ask her to move her horse away from the yard or interfere in her life away from him.

When they had first gotten together there had been many frank conversations where they each promised that if the spark ever went or they fell out of love then they would be honest with each other and part amicably. Neither of them were prepared to put up with an affair or betrayal. That had been the way they lived with former partners until fate had brought them together; in their late forties. They had made a pact that they would be totally honest with each other. And so far that had been how they lived their lives, enjoying each other's company and supporting each other in their various hobbies and pastimes.

No, John was confident that Kate had kept to her word as had he. But still, Adam was a kind, caring guy and he clearly loved Kate. It was good of him to be there for them all, but John could not fully open up to him. Having met Jemma a few times already over the week, they had hit it off and were able to blow off steam without being afraid of being judged or having words used against them at a later date.

The ward door opened and this time the nurse beckoned John over.

'Can I come in as well please?' Jemma got up and followed John's lead.

'Just a moment, I'll check. Please come in and wait inside the ward entrance. Make sure the door is shut behind you. I'm sure it is fine, but I just need to check with your son's nurse. I won't be long.'

'I'll see you later, Jemma. Hope he is improving,' John said as he left her hovering behind him.

He went over and washed his hands, the routine now familiar, reading the hand washing guidelines as he did every time, mundane instructions; wet your hands, add the soap, how to wash in detailed diagrams, rinse and dry properly. All done blindly without thinking, it now came as second nature. Hands done, he walked quietly down the ward. Kate's bed was near the end; past the lad with his head caved in, past the old lady whose family had found her at the bottom of the stairs on Christmas Day, past the farmer in his nineties who had lost a leg in a farmyard accident on a farm that he refused to give up, past the Asian lady whose family attended in groups of ten or more, occupying the whole waiting room for hours and arguing with the nursing staff, a number of family members being doctors themselves, demanding treatment, tests, answers that nobody could give no matter how rude they were or how much they pestered. A very selfish attitude which had rubbed other patients' relatives, including Kate's family, the wrong way to the point that Caitlin had had to get up and leave on more than one occasion before she blew her top. A fact which John was thankful that she had left rather than caused a scene; it wouldn't have been helpful to any of them.

And there she was. She looked so tiny under all the tubes. Marie, the nurse who was looking after her tonight, was bustling about recording numbers off the various machines, checking drug levels, blood gases and every other million and one checks that the specialist ICU nurses did constantly. John had gotten to know them all this week and had nothing but praise for the professional and caring way in which they looked after the unfortunate people who found themselves in intensive care.

'She's doing ok, John. Very stable, and we are gradually decreasing the sedation as you know. She is responding well.'

'That's good then. Am I ok to play her some music again?'

'Yes, just as long as it's not too loud. I'll leave you to it for a few minutes then I'm afraid you'll have to leave the ward for tonight. Are you still staying over here?'

'Yes, myself and a friend. Are you sure we're ok to have the room?'

'Of course you are. There are only two rooms, but you are more than welcome to stay, and my advice is - don't give it up, because once you vacate someone else will take it. You stay where you are. And if you don't mind me saying, try and get some rest. You need to be strong for her.'

'Thanks, Marie. I'll do my best. I hate leaving her.'

'I know, but believe me, if anything changes we will come and get you. You will just be sat looking at numbers that you don't understand. I'll leave you alone for as long as I can, but if I say quarter of an hour max would that be ok? I will still be hovering doing my checks, but I will try and give you as much privacy as I can.'

'Thank you, I appreciate it.'

Marie turned away and left them to it, wondering how she herself would cope if it was one of her loved ones in the same situation. She doubted she would be any use at all. It was heartbreaking to see, and she had initially found it hard to remain detached from her patients, but she had been working on ICU for seven years now and it was still as painful now as it was when she had first started. The only thing that kept her going was the hope that she could make a difference to her patients and their families. Sometimes they made it, and that was wonderful, but for all those she had lost, she had never given up hope and had maintained her standard of caring until the very end.

'Hey darling, I'm here again.' John leant over and spoke to Kate. 'I know you can hear me. Marie, your nurse, says you are doing ok. Looks like the swelling on your right cheek is going down. You've still got a massive shiner though. Looks like you've been in a boxing ring.'

The only answer was the beep of the monitors, and the whoosh of the ventilator steadily controlling her breathing. The rest of the ward was bustling with activity, nurses purposefully going about the business of saving lives, plastic aprons rustling, wheels squeaking, curtains swishing back and forth.

'They put the radio on this time of night. It was 80s night last night and I told the nurse how much you love your music. I thought I'd play you some music tonight too. Marie says she thinks you might be able to hear it. Can you hear it, sweetheart? I know you can't answer me, or maybe you can blink your eyes at me? Can you do that? I'm talking too much aren't I, sorry. I found it hard to speak to you at first, but now it doesn't seem so weird. I know you can hear me, you're just not able to reply yet, but you will. I know you will.'

John took the smart phone out of his pocket and placed it on the pillow next to Kate's ear.

'I'm wearing the t-shirt from the Def Leppard gig we went to. Hard to believe it was only a couple of weeks ago. I didn't know which music to play you and I've only got a short time with you so I've chosen a few and done a playlist. Something to do whilst I've been waiting. I'm talking too much aren't I? Shall I just play the songs? Yes, I will. I hear you, get on with it, John.'

John found the track and pressed play. As the music flowed around them, John stroked Kate's hair and got his face as close to hers as possible. 'I love you, Kate. Don't you dare leave me when we've only just found each other. I won't let you go. You come back to us, do you hear me? We've got so much left to do together, so many good times ahead. We can beat this, I know we can. Keep fighting, Katie.'

Def Leppard played their song *'Love Bites'*, and John sang along sadly as much as he could until the tears choked his throat and singing was no longer possible. The next one up, by Whitesnake, was *'Is This Love?'*

'Oh Kate, these songs aren't really helping me to cope to be honest, but I thought they might reach you and you could sleep easily with nice memories to think about. I've got one more to play before I have to go. It's our favourite from the new Duran album.'

John clicked the play button on until he found '*What Are The Chances?*'

'This song, I don't know why we fell in love with it so much, but it's strange that the video that goes with it, it could be us, Kate. I can't wait to show it to you when you wake up. Even the nurse at the end of the video, she looks like Marie your nurse. It's bizarre.'

As the song played and the guitar solo spiralled beautifully, it happened again; a single tear from the corner of her eye. He reached out and captured it on his hand.

'Oh, my beautiful Kate. I know you can hear me. Just come back to us, please.'

So much for coincidence. This was the second time that she had responded to him. He decided not to mention it to Marie as he couldn't bear for her to contradict him and say it was just secretions again. John knew his wife and he knew better than that. He knew his Kate and he was sure she was on her way back to them.

'I'd better go now, my love, I'm only just down the corridor. Sleep well and I'll see you in the morning. I love you with all my heart. Night night, darling.' John held Kate's hand to his face and kissed it. 'Love you.'

The Revival

Adam was dozing in the armchair next to the bed settee by the time John got back to the room. John put the light off and laid down in the dark.

'You ok, mate? How is she?'

'Doing ok, thanks. I'm sure she can hear me when I speak to her. She cried a tear again when I was talking to her and we were listening to our music.'

'See, I knew she was still in there. Proves it, John. She's coming back, I'm sure.'

'We can only hope and pray, but yes, I think so too.' John got up again. 'There's no way I can sleep at the moment. I think I'm going to go for a wander around.'

'Shall I come with you or would you rather be on your own?'

'Up to you, although to tell you the truth I could do with some company. Thanks, Adam, you've been such a good friend to us all since this happened.'

Adam joined John and put an arm round his shoulders. 'That's what friends are for, John. I couldn't let either of you go through this on your own.'

The two of them headed down in the lift for a walk outside again just as John had done with Charlotte the first night. They walked silently, each lost in their own thoughts, out into the cold night of New Year's Eve, a night where the whole world celebrated the passing of the old year and welcomed in the new one, filled with hope for the future.

'Shall we go back now, John? It's getting on towards midnight.'

'I think I want to go to the prayer room, if that's ok? You go up if you want to.'

'No, I'll come too. It can't hurt us both saying a prayer.'

They followed the path back to the main entrance and from there the signs led them to the prayer room on the ground floor. Adam let John go ahead and decided that silence was the best option. He switched his phone onto silent since it was buzzing all the time now with questions and good wishes from their many friends. Adam was glad he had been able to take some of the pressure away from John. He couldn't let on how much he cared for Kate, although he supposed it was obvious to anyone who stopped to look. He loved her, he had loved her for thousands of years. He didn't know how it worked, just that when they met there had been an instant recognition for both of them. He was in love with her, he knew she had once loved him and probably still did, but now she was so happily in love with John. The pair of them were so in love that Adam would never come between Kate and her happiness so he contented himself in being the best friend he could be. They enjoyed each other's company and flirted relentlessly, but that was where it stopped.

Adam put his phone away and looked around the prayer room. John sat staring into space at the front of the room. Adam looked around him. A statue of Buddha drew his attention and he went over to it, and on the table next to the statue was a book, '*The Teachings of Dharma.*'

Adam flicked through it, reading passages but not really taking it in. The room was light and airy, and it catered for many different faiths. A screen sectioned off a private area for prayer at the back of the room; an area for prayer mats was set out on the opposite side. A glass case held a book with names of people who had donated organs, their loss of life enabling another to live. Adam's breath caught in his throat as he read the names, all beautifully inscribed in copperplate writing. He had never seen such a book before and it tore at his heart. The sacrifice of one family to another; it was the most touching thing he had ever seen and he fought hard to hold back the tears that he had managed to keep at bay so far. He turned his back to it and rubbed his eyes. The last thing John needed was to see him falling to pieces; he had to keep strong for all of their sakes.

'Shall we go back up? It's getting late.'

'Ok, yes. I've prayed to whoever may be listening. Don't know if it will do any good. I feel a bit hypocritical, I never pray. I don't expect God or whoever to take any notice.'

'Well, it can't hurt. I do have faith. I was brought up Catholic, but I don't practise it these days. I still think that there is something there, something good to pray to that will listen,' Adam replied.

'Look at this.' John pointed to a watercolour painting on the wall in the entrance. 'I didn't notice that on the way in.'

The picture was of a Ferris wheel, each car painted in a bright colour. Underneath the painting on a plaque two words were inscribed, 'Scarborough Fair.'

'I can't believe this, Adam. Scarborough Fair. You know how much Kate and I love Scarborough. We had our first weekend away in Scarborough; we went to watch the motorbike racing at Oliver's Mount. Four years ago now. How can it be that long ago? It seems like yesterday. Good times there, Adam, such good times.'

'And you will again, John, I'm sure. If that's not a sign, I don't know what is.'

'Yes, maybe you're right, we've got to keep hoping. I'll hold on to that. Whatever it takes, we can't ever give up on her.'

Midnight came and went. John had fallen into a troubled sleep eventually at around three in the morning. Adam had sent out a generic message wishing Happy New Year to all their friends at John's request. It urged people to have a drink for them and party on their behalf as they were unable to do it themselves this year. Adam thought it was one of the bravest things he had ever seen. He watched John sleep, grateful that he had managed to go off eventually after the fireworks at midnight had kept them both wide awake. How ironic that it appeared that everyone else in the world was out there partying and celebrating the coming of 2016, whilst those here in the hospital were stuck in limbo, waiting for a miracle.

A figure leaning against the door frame went unnoticed as John and Adam each succumbed to a restless sleep.

Friday 1st January, 2016

John entered the ward again, a little more rested than previous, his sleep interrupted by troubled dreams. He had tossed and turned for most of the night, but had maybe managed a couple of hours, which had made a difference. The doctors had done their daily morning rounds, and one by one family members were allowed back on the ward to take up their bedside vigils.

'Morning, John.' It was Paul who was in attendance to Kate this morning. 'Good news, we are going for the extubation this morning. She's had a really good night. I'm afraid you will have to leave whilst we do it, but hopefully it shouldn't take long. Go on in, we'll tell you when it's time for you to go.'

'Thanks, Paul.'

John pulled a chair up and took hold of Kate's hand and squeezed it. She squeezed it back.

'Oh my God. Kate, Kate, you're there aren't you? I knew it. Do that again,' John babbled excitedly.

Nothing. 'Please Kate, try and do that again.'

Nothing. John stood up and put his hand on her shoulder, giving her a gentle push. 'Kate. Please.'

As John stared at his wife, imploring her to try harder, he looked down at her hand enclosed tightly in his and brought it up to his lips once again. At the same time, Kate opened her eyes, staring at him, the confusion and questioning in her stare causing him to squeeze her hand even tighter at the shock.

'Paul, come quickly. She's opened her eyes.' John shouted across the ward where Paul was stood with another nurse.

Hearing the urgency in John's voice, Paul broke off his conversation and came straight over.

'Really? Well, that's good news.' Paul addressed Kate who had shut her eyes again. 'Hello there, young lady. I hear you've decided to wake up.'

Kate blinked and nodded her head cautiously, the movement to the tube in her throat causing her to cough slightly. She moved her hand up gesturing to the tube.

'It's ok darling, don't panic. You're wired up to lots of things that have been helping you breathe and keep you safe,' John spoke to his wife, hardly daring to move in case it was a fluke and she went under again.

'John, I hate asking, but we need to get things moving now so your wife has minimal distress. I don't want you here watching this, there are things we need to do and you really don't need to see everything. Take a seat outside and I'll come and fetch you when we are done.'

'You promise. She is going to be ok, isn't she?'

'Let us do our jobs and I'll fetch you as soon as I'm able. I promise.'

John gave Kate a kiss, her eyes growing wide as he turned to go. 'I'll be back soon, my darling. Don't be scared. Let them help you. I'm only just outside. Love you.'

John ran back to fetch Adam and update him on the good news.

'Oh, that's brilliant news. Can I come back and wait with you?'

'Yeah, of course. Let's keep this to ourselves for now because I don't want to tempt fate and have anything go wrong.'

'Ok, if you're sure, but people will want to know.'

'I hear you, I really do, but please respect my wishes. I cannot get people's hopes up only to dash them down again. We will tell the whole world as soon as they have done what they need to in there.'

An hour later they were called back on to the ward, neither of them prepared for the transformation that had taken place in such a short time. Kate was sat up in bed, her face free of wires and tubes. Bruises now turning shades of purple and yellow covered her face. Her right side had taken the brunt of the accident, and she was propped up with pillows. But, she was awake and smiled weakly at them as they approached her bed.

'Hi guys,' Kate's voice whispered croakily.

'Kate. I can't believe it. You're awake. Oh my God, we've been so worried.' John wept as he leant over her, carefully kissing her injured skin.

'John…' she managed, smiling and then wincing as a sharp pain caught her off guard. 'Adam…'

'You gave us such a scare. I knew you'd be ok though. Didn't I say that, Adam? We never gave up on you, not once.'

'Ah, we knew you were made of strong stuff.'

'How... how... long have I been here?' Kate struggled to speak.

'It's New Year's Day now. Do you remember the accident? It happened on Boxing Day. Nearly a week has gone past.'

'A week?'

'The longest of our lives. Oh, you are going to be ok. Thank God. We prayed, we've all been praying for you to come back to us.'

'Have you been here all the time?'

'Mostly. Don't try and talk too much.' John held on to her tightly not wanting to let go in case she slipped away from his grip again.

'I'll leave you to it for a while,' said Adam.

'Will you let the rest of the family know? Caitlin and Charlotte. Oh, and Kate's parents please.'

'Course, no problem,' Adam replied, keeping a calmness in his voice that he did not feel. He wanted to take Kate in his arms and kiss her as John was doing. He would not betray his feeling in front of John, and with difficulty he turned his back and left them to it. Somehow he knew it was just the beginning of something new and different. He could not put his finger on what had changed, but there was an aura around her. He felt it, he was sure Kate had felt it too; he had seen something behind the pain in her eyes that gave it away. John too. But John was in denial of the subtle shift of reality. Time would tell, Adam thought, as it always did. That was one thing that you couldn't escape.

The waiting room had filled up once again. Adam had done his duty and called the family as John had requested. First to arrive were the girls, who had both now gone in to see their mum. Next were Kate's elderly parents. They had been next to go and sit with their daughter, and they now returned to the waiting room, ashen faces

87

replaced with beaming smiles. They looked twenty years younger. The accident had taken its toll on all of them in one way or another. They all loved Kate so very much that the thought of losing her had been unbearable.

Adam had also updated social media, once again his phone bleeping constantly with all the responses and well wishes.

Satisfied that he had done all he could, Adam felt the need to run away from the happy family reunion. He made his excuses and left them to it. They didn't need him now. Kate didn't need him hanging around whilst she was so weak. She knew he had been there and that was all that mattered. The urge to run came over him in waves and by the time he reached the car park he realised he was sobbing uncontrollably. The cold had numbed his face and hands, his cheeks wet with tears and his eyes unable to see clearly. He fumbled for his car keys and got in, slamming the door, the car providing him with the sanctuary he desperately needed. He turned the engine over and put the heater on full blast. The radio came on automatically. Nickelback sang out at him 'Are we having fun yet?'

Dreams can come true

Thursday 7th January, 2016 – daytime

'Are you sure you can manage?'

'John, stop fussing please. I'm absolutely fine. There's nothing wrong with my legs. I can walk perfectly well on my own.'

'Let me look after you, Kate. You have no idea how poorly you've been.'

'Get off me, will you,' Kate snapped at him. 'Who was it that was laid up in hospital for over a week? Do you think I have no idea? How dare you. Get off me.'

John let go of her arm, taken aback. In all the years they had been together, Kate had never ever spoken to him in that way. He stared at her, dumbfounded. She brushed past him and left him standing outside the back door of their home. A sudden chill smothered him and he shuddered before following her inside, wondering what the hell just happened.

'It's cold in here; why is it so cold?' Kate looked at John enquiringly.

'I'll put the heating on. Here come and sit by the fire. I'll put the kettle on; what would you like?'

'Hot chocolate please,' Kate answered smiling, all trace of animosity gone.

'Coming right up. Are you hungry?'

'Biscuits please, if we've got any. Oh, I must go shopping. I'll go tomorrow. What day is it?'

'Thursday, my darling. We can do an online shop if you're not up to going out,' John ventured warily.

'Ok, I'll have my drink and do it. Are the girls coming over? We must have our party. I'm so sorry to have caused all this upset. We must invite Adam over too; he has kept me informed about Ebony. Seems that none of the horses were injured in the accident, thank goodness.'

John sighed. He really didn't want to think about that although, knowing Kate, she would be wanting to go to the stables as soon as possible. This was the longest time she had been kept apart from her beloved horse. It wasn't a conversation that he relished having, especially having just received the sharp end of her tongue. Her words had cut into him like a knife through butter. John tried to put it out of his mind and put it down to the stress of the situation they all now found themselves in. He looked across at where Kate sat huddled in front of the fire. His heart went out to her. Kate turned and looked back at him with emptiness behind her eyes. It was as though her body had returned but her mind was struggling to keep up. Before they left the hospital, Kate's consultant had been frank with them and advised she stay in for a few more days. The pressure in her head had returned to normal, the bruises were healing and she appeared to have made a miraculous recovery. The worry was that she had taken such a severe knock to her head that she may have a relapse. Although the MRI had not shown any severe damage, there was still bruising present. Kate had been so insistent that she returned home, it was decided that they would concede and let her go on the proviso that if she felt any pain or any change she come straight back. John now wondered if the damage was deeper than they had initially thought or if it was a form of post-traumatic stress that she was displaying. Whatever the cause, he hoped it was just a blip and that she would soon return to the Kate they all knew and loved.

'Everyone else is fine, you don't have to worry about anyone. Why don't you go up and try and have a nap; you need to take it easy and let us look after you.'

'John, please. I know you're worried but can you stop fussing, I am absolutely fine.' Kate reached out to her husband who looked so dejected at her reply. 'I know it's because you care, but I feel suffocated. You need to let me adjust. Please?'

'I'm sorry. It's so wonderful to have you home again. I only want to take care of you. We are all so relieved to have you back, my darling. Don't be cross if we seem overprotective.'

'I'm going to ring Adam, then I promise I will go and rest.'

John knew better than to argue again, the last thing he wanted was to upset her.

'Hey, Adam. Yes, I'm home. How's Ebony?'

John left them to it with a heavy heart; he had never felt so isolated from her. She may have come home, but she was different now, and he realised sadly that the road ahead was not going to be as straightforward as they had all hoped. At least she was here though and he thanked God for that. The amount of well wishes and prayers sent their way had been nothing short of miraculous in itself. The power of love, ironically also the name of 'their song' by Frankie Goes to Hollywood, seemed to have aided her recovery.

John had set up a charity page for fund raising for the air ambulance that had, in his opinion, saved her life. The donations had come in thick and fast, and it was testament to Kate's popularity. It was only when you suffered an event as bad as this that you saw who your real friends were and theirs had been outstanding; John would be forever grateful for the amount of support they had received.

Kate was feeling much happier now that she had spoken to Adam and he had reassured her that her beloved horse had not suffered any physical injuries. He had promised Kate that he was keeping a special eye on her and that Ebony would be cared for just as well as if Kate herself were doing it. She trusted him with her precious friend, and with no doubt in her mind that he would keep his word, she hung up.

'John, I will go up to bed for a while now, if you don't mind.'

'The girls are going to come and see you tomorrow. They send their love, but they are going to give you some space to settle back in.'

'Perfect, thank you.'

John took her in his arms and held her for a moment before he felt her becoming anxious again. He quickly let go and took a step back. 'Sorry. I don't mean to make you uncomfortable. It's hard to keep away from you; I missed you so, so much, my darling.'

'I know. Sorry. Look, I'll be ok. I just need to be on my own for a bit. I'll probably watch TV if I can't sleep. Just leave me to settle back in please. I don't want any fuss.'

She turned, picking up her bags, and left John stood watching as she went upstairs, struggling with her bags, bristling with stubborn independence. She had made it quite clear that she didn't want his help and he knew better than to contradict her.

The bedroom felt empty and bare. Kate took it all in; the curtains were closed, bed made, everything tidy and clean. John had obviously given it a once over before she came back. It was perfect. She was so happy to be home. So happy. Kate dropped her bags where she stood and burst into tears. So happy, so why did she feel so disturbed? What the hell had changed since she was last here? The bedroom had been decorated only last year, the wallpaper carefully chosen to fit in with the French theme they had chosen. The soft furnishings in deep red and gold silk with paisley sequins, expensive soft pile cream carpet and new furniture all blended in perfectly. They had good taste, and it showed in the ongoing refurb they were undertaking of the Victorian farmhouse that had been her childhood home; her parents were settled now in an easy to manage bungalow which suited their aging bodies, no longer willing to look after a large rambling house.

The 'Fleuriste de Paris' clock ticked quietly as she sat down exhausted on their bed. Kate undressed quickly and slid under the quilt, shivering despite the warmth of the electric blanket and the 'Paris in Love' throw that provided another layer of protection from the cold that houses of that age were prone to despite the central heating; the house faced north and it was cold all year through, even in the height of summer.

She found the remote and switched the TV on through force of habit. Kate pulled the blanket up and wrapped it around her shoulders; try as she might, she could not get warm. The bitter January air had seeped through her skin and settled icily in her bones. Flicking through the channels back and forth, Kate couldn't find anything interesting to watch. Click click click, the channels flickered and offered the usual daytime quizzes, home improvement and gardening programmes. She flicked it off again for a moment but the silence became too much so on it went again. Settling for a radio channel, she buried herself under the covers and tried to free her mind of the unnerve she felt.

'Welcome home. We've been waiting for you.'

'Oh, it's you again. How did you find me? I'm so glad you're here. I felt so alone, please don't leave me alone again. I've been scared.'

'You are never alone, Aphrodite. I told you last time we met. Your family have always been there for you in the shadows, you just

93

did not have the capacity to cope with it in your human brain. That is why we kept it hidden until the time came for you to be reincarnated and known to your present carrier.'

'I don't know what to do, you have to help me. I am here in this house with my husband. Is he Hephaestus, my lord of the forge?'

'Yes. Well done. You see my beautiful lady, you do know. It will become clearer every day. You must beware though. As we return, so does the evil. It has followed you and there are steps we need to take to prevent it taking over. Tomorrow is a very special day.'

'Is it the Eighth Day? I feel there is great unrest in the airwaves.'

'You are recovering so much faster than we dared to hope. The humans have helped with their prayers. It was a very clever idea of Hephaestus to enlist the power of their communication network.'

'He is known as John in this human form, isn't he?'

'Yes, my love. You also have another lover nearby.'

'Adam. Yes. I have loved him for many years.'

'By another name. Do you remember now my love?'

'I think so.' I remember. Oh how I feel pain. Oh the pain...so great, my tears, his blood. The boar has killed my love. My Adonis. His blood drips on the ground and turns into red flowers, anemones, RED, RED, RED danger, oh my love. My tears fall and are transformed into red roses, RED RED RED...'

I can feel myself crying and moaning. I know I am asleep, but I have never felt so alive.

'Adam...' I cry out as I weep uncontrollably.

'Kate, Kate, wake up, wake up.'

'Where is he? Where has he gone?' I can feel the panic rising and I struggle to sit up.

'Kate, you're here at home. It's ok, I'm here.' John cradled her.

'I, I was dreaming I think. Was I? Was it a dream? It seemed so real, who was I talking to?'

'I think you were having a flashback to your accident. The doctors said it may happen. You were shouting Adam. He is safe, and you were the only one to get injured in the race.'

'Adam is ok?'

'Yes, perfectly. Calm down, you're ok now my love, you're ok, I promise.'

Kate leant against the solid mass of her husband's chest and felt the love pouring from his presence, soothing her and reassuring her that everything would be ok. She relaxed and let him comfort her. The dreams she had been having in hospital were now becoming more intense. Now she was home and had dreamt of the voice again. She closed her eyes, and faces and names flashed in her mind; John, Adam, were they really reincarnations? Was she really Aphrodite? Or was it the effects of the accident and her brain injury jumbling up her love of history, mistaking mythological beings and transforming them into the guise of John and Adam? She did not have the answers, but she felt calmer now as she processed the latest images that had come whilst she slept.

'What time is it?'

'Just gone four. Shall I bring you something to eat?'

'No, I'll come down soon. I'm not really that hungry.'

'Maybe some toast?'

'I'll just have a wash first and then I'll come.'

Kate gave John a kiss.

'I'm worried about you. Shall I ring the doctors and see if there is anyone who can do a home visit?' asked John.

'I don't want a fuss. I'll be fine. I've already told you I'll come downstairs soon. John, you have to stop all this fussing. You're stressing me out and I really don't need this pressure from you.'

'You can't blame me for being concerned, especially when you shout another man's name so loudly. And you're obviously distressed.'

'John, I am not doing this now. I refuse to get into an argument over something I was dreaming. Leave me alone, please. I'll come down when I'm ready. I don't want to talk about it any longer.'

The truth was, Kate wanted to sit and think about the new information she had been given, and she needed time to process it. She felt bad that she'd snapped at John, but it was too much being questioned when she had to try and remember everything that had been said to her.

'I Want To Break Free,' by Queen was playing on the radio as Kate sat lost in her thoughts. Freddie. Mercury. Queen. Was he speaking to her? Yes, that's exactly what she wanted. To break free. Kate giggled at the coincidence and sang along whilst she got ready to go downstairs and face her earthly husband, John, so she could try and see if she could see signs of her heavenly husband, Hephaestus, within him. Things were starting to snap into place at a quite alarming rate. Her ancestors, her family tree, was coming to life in front of her eyes and she wasn't sure if it was reality or as a result of her accident, but she decided to go with it and see where it took her. After all, nothing ventured, nothing gained. She had followed her heart all her life, so maybe this was her destiny, and who was she to argue with fate?

Power Up

Thurs 7th January, 2016 – night time

During the remainder of the afternoon after I had my first vivid dream at home, I had followed John downstairs and eaten toast, drank tea, taken some painkillers and then told him of the revelations I had seen and heard whilst I slept.

And now I could not believe what was happening. I had been home for less than twelve hours and they had come into my house uninvited. Well, I didn't invite them. It seemed that my family had become concerned with my behaviour. I didn't understand why. All I had done was ask the doctor they had sent to check me over to leave. There was no point him being there. He asked me questions and then didn't listen to me. He wouldn't accept the answers I gave him when he asked about my health. I was fuming: with John; with the girls, with the medics they had now sent to assess my mental health. Why would nobody listen to me?

'Can you come downstairs, please? We would like to speak with you,' said one of the assembly who were gathered at the foot of the stairs.

'No. Leave me the fuck alone,' I screamed down to them. 'Get out of my house… Now.'

I stood at the top of the stairs, something heavy held tightly in my grasp ready to launch down at them if they dared try to come upstairs again. I checked what the object was; it was a book this time, *'Metamorphoses'* by the Roman poet Ovid. I had gathered books and evidence together to aid in my explanation of events so far. My words had fallen on deaf ears. Ironic that I had resorted to using them as physical weapons. I raised the book above my head ready for it to follow the other objects I had already sent sailing down on my intruders.

My heart was pounding so loudly I could hear it echoing in my head. I stood ready to attack, shaking with rage.

I thought I could trust John; he had listened, smiled and nodded at me. We sat curled up together in front of the fire after I had awoken from my nap earlier. He listened to my account, took the revelations in his stride. Then he did the unforgiveable and betrayed me.

At first, I had been amenable and accepting when the 'men in white coats' arrived, even though I was mad as hell inside. John had explained he had phoned the hospital and they had sent a couple of members of their outreach team to come and talk to me as apparently I had been hallucinating. I was sure that was not the case, but I was determined to be co-operative, and I welcomed them in with a smile painted on.

I had made them a cup of tea and offered biscuits. They were polite to begin with. I showed them around our home and began to explain about who we really were. They nodded and smiled at me, as he had done. They nodded and made notes as we went from room to room, and I gathered books and photographs and explained our ancestry and that all was becoming clear. How things from my past explained the situation I now found myself in.

I invited them to come and look at our bedroom; how the French theme was linked to the horrific recent events in Paris. Again they nodded, made noises of acknowledgement and smiled without answering.

I led them back downstairs and thanked them for coming, but assured them that I was absolutely fine. They ignored my reassurances and whispered to each other, then dropped the bombshell. Their words hit me like a thunderbolt from Mars himself.

'Kate, we think that your injury has produced these, er, symptoms,' said one of the three. 'We are going recommend that you go back to hospital. We are sending a car to fetch you.'

'No, really. I am perfectly fine. You know all about me now and you can see I'm ok. I don't understand why you want me to go to hospital. I'm just happy to be home and I know I'll be fine. Thanks for coming though. Sorry to have wasted your time. John worries about me but really there's no need,' I replied, aware that I was babbling.

'Well, I'm afraid that we strongly advise you to take our advice, Kate. The car will be here in half an hour or so.'

'No. I thought you'd been listening to me. Haven't you heard a word I've said?' I shouted at them. 'I'm not going anywhere. Go away. Please. John, how could you?'

'Listen to them, my love. You're not well,' John replied anxiously. He had never seen me in this mood before, but he knew how strong I was if I made my mind up about something, there was no shifting me. I was as stubborn as they come, this trait inherited from my father.

I shot him a look of pure hate and, turning my back, slammed the hall door behind me, leaving him stood with the medics.

They hadn't taken no for an answer and had tried to come after me. I couldn't leave now. Why weren't they listening? That's all anyone needs isn't it, to be heard?

They had been into our bedroom and violated it, they had been in our private sanctuary. I had trusted these people, offered them my hospitality, and they had thrown it all back at me, laughed at me and decided to take me away. There was no way I was going with them. It was past eight o clock at night now and I was tired, I just wanted to go to bed and there they were trying to drag me out of my home. No fucking way.

'Kate, we are coming upstairs now,' one had called after me.

He put his foot on the first stair. I threw a book, not at him exactly, but it sailed past his right shoulder and caught him off guard. He hastily retreated. And this is how the land lay now. They were whispering to each other, still at the bottom, but now surrounded by all sorts of paraphernalia strewn around them. Books, DVDs - some with their cases open and the disc hanging out, broken picture frames, perfume bottles, ornaments, they all adorned the stairs and the floor around them. Broken glass shattered as it had hit the wall on the way down and left shards sticking up dangerously from the stair carpet.

'Fuck off. Leave me alone. You'd better not try and come up here. I mean it.'

My last outburst appeared to work and they retreated back to the safety of my kitchen. I sat on the top step straining to hear what they were saying, but they had taken refuge behind the closed door and all I could hear was the mumble of male voices.

I giggled as I recalled the look on their faces when the first missile sailed past them. They hadn't expected that. Serves them right for taking the piss out of my good nature. John had looked very scared, and although I was still mad with him, I realised that he had rung the hospital in good faith. I was sorry I had upset him, but not sorry enough to forgive him just yet.

Five minutes passed, then ten, then half an hour, an hour maybe and I realised I had dozed off. All was still downstairs. I went back into our bedroom. Michael Jackson filled the screen of my TV at full volume. I must have put his DVD on whilst having my meltdown. The perfect song accompanied my path through the wreckage, '*The Way You Make Me Feel*', and I stopped as I caught my reflection in the window. I looked like a crazy woman. I looked past the crazy lady who stared back at me and turned my attention to the scene beyond the window. No strange cars on the drive, no traffic going past either. I half expected blue flashing lights. But there were none. I hummed along to Mr Jackson, letting the music filter through the turmoil in my head, letting it flow into my being. It felt good, at one with the elements. I remembered '*Earth Song*' playing and the wind blowing stronger and stronger the madder I became. The tempo of the wind and the rain matched my mood as I became angrier and angrier. The wind battered the trees and bushes in the garden outside, it whipped around the house, ever increasing with its ferocity. Rain lashed down sideways.

The window was open. Cold air washed over me, and I suddenly realised I was naked. I shivered and bathed in the icy wind. It felt good. I felt more alive than I had done for a very long time. I looked around our bedroom and realised the mess I had made. I surveyed the scene with calculating eyes. The walls were bare where pictures had once hung, bookshelves had been cleared free of trinkets, the two chests of drawers were annihilated, the drawers pulled out and thrown out of the window - their contents had joined them soon after, vest tops, knickers, t-shirts were now covering the front garden, a bra hung jauntily off the bay window below. The ottoman that had housed papers and gig memorabilia was open and empty, the contents stuck in the privet hedge which surrounded the front garden and littered across the grass below. Red silk curtains hung off their rail and billowed out into the waiting night, the wind whipping them in and out of the open window. What had I done? Where was John? I hoped I had not hurt him. I had never struck anyone in anger in my whole life, but at that moment in time I had no idea what I had or hadn't done.

I calmly found a vest top and pyjama bottoms to put on, and luckily there were still a few items of clothing that had escaped my wrath. My pink fleece dressing gown had made it in one piece and I reached up and took it off the back of the door, thankful that whatever I had done, the madness had passed and I was aware of who and where I was again.

John, I needed John. 'John, are you there?' I shouted down from my vantage point on the landing.

The hall door opened. 'Is it safe for me to come up to you, Kate?'

'Are you ok?' I answered hesitantly.

'Just about. Stay there, I'll come up to you. There may still be some broken glass on the stairs. I'll bring some slippers for you.'

I slumped down onto the step, exhaustion passing through my body now the adrenalin had subsided.

'Here darling, put these on.'

'They've gone now haven't they? I don't like those men, John, why did you call them? I trusted you,' I whispered.

'Yes they've gone. What the hell, Kate? You scared me. I've never seen you act like that before.'

'You betrayed me. I trusted you. I thought you had understood.'

'Kate, do you remember everything that happened this evening?

'I'm not sure. I don't really remember doing that,' I pointed to the bedroom. 'The last thing I can remember is screaming at them to go away. I couldn't leave here. I thought you understood, John. Why would you ask them to take me away?'

'You've had a bad injury. I didn't know what to do. You've changed. I was scared, simple as that. The things... the things you were saying didn't make any sense, Kate. I thought you were having a breakdown.'

'I'm going to bed, I'm exhausted.'

'I'll come with you.'

'No, please, can you sleep in the spare room. I'm not ready to share a bed with you just yet.

I feel so claustrophobic.'

John looked at his wife and the determination in her eyes told him not to argue. 'If you're sure?'

'Positive. I'll see you in the morning. I think I'll take a couple of painkillers.'

'I'm not surprised after everything that has happened this evening. You must be exhausted.'

'Yes.'

As he made his way up to the guest room, he paused outside their bedroom door, which was ajar. The TV was on, flickering and lighting up the darkness. John stood for a moment wanting to go in and kiss his wife but not daring to disturb her. He shook his head sadly, wondering if things would ever be the same again.

The Eighth Day

Friday 8th January, 2016

The sunrise was beautiful. I had tiptoed downstairs before 7 am, and the last thing I wanted was to wake John. I'd had the most contented night after eventually managing to settle down. Rocked to sleep by the music coming through the TV, soothing and familiar, it had washed over me and transported me to a place of safety. I couldn't remember having dreamt of anything, but I had a vague impression of beautiful light, golds and silvers and maybe feathers. I felt almost serene. The sun was bright, blue skies above, a crisp frost had tipped the lawn with white icing. I put the radio on - it was already tuned in to the local station, the DJ happily informing me it was going to be a cold but sunny day. I made myself a coffee and took it back upstairs again. No sign of John yet. I was glad. I wanted to be on my own with my thoughts and watch the world wake up. Today was a special day. I switched the radio on and moved the dial until I found the local channel. I needed to know what was going on in and around my home county. I wanted to know everything and, as I listened, the more bizarre things became. The DJ, the adverts, and most importantly the music, all seemed to be addressing me directly. Then a switch flicked in my head and suddenly it was me controlling the airwaves, I was communicating through the radio. It may have been the voices of the

DJ, of the adverts, of the newsreader, but they were channelled through me.

'And to take us up to the news, here's Duran Duran with '*Reach Up For The Sunrise*'.'

I grinned and opened the window, and grabbing my blanket, I wrapped it around me and sat on the ledge watching cars drive cautiously on the untreated winter tarmac. I snuggled into my vantage point, steaming hot mug keeping my hands warm. I watched over my subjects going on their way to work. I had their backs, these were my people. I would keep them safe. Some were going too fast; I implored them to slow down. They obeyed. I could feel the power of my newfound persona flowing through me, coursing through my veins, filling my mind. Today was a special day. I was becoming. Again. I had work to do. I needed food first and then a nice shower. My mind had never been so clear. Ever. My world seemed calm and bright. I felt cocooned in love. The rage that my family and I had dealt out to the unbelievers last night had now subsided and the only emotion I was left with was that of overwhelming love and peace.

The local news washed over me as I ate my breakfast. Local radio, with all its annoying adverts, had suddenly become my mouthpiece. The weather report became a reflection of my mood, a cold bright day. The news became my wisdom. The adverts, all promising of many bargains to be had in the January sales, they became my gift to my listening subjects. I was having a wonderful time; for the first time since the accident I felt happy and in control.

I heard movement upstairs; John. The electricity meter flashing faster as he put the shower on. I smiled. A surge of love for this man overtook me. I had to forgive him. I turned the radio up and sang along to Lionel Richie. My Destiny was upstairs and he was naked and wet. It was about time I joined him. If he'd let me. Time to put my newfound persona to the test. The Goddess of Love, a powerful entity, she filled my soul with sexual longing. It had been far too long. Time to put things right and show him just how much I loved him.

I couldn't wait any longer. My feet barely touched the ground as I flew up the stairs to join my husband. I knew he would welcome me with open arms. Our lovemaking had always been off the scale. The sound of the shower and John's singing masked my arrival in the bathroom. I was mesmerised by the outline of his body behind the screen and stood for a few moments watching him, but the need to be naked and wet with him overpowered me. Hot steam filled the room as I slipped off my robe and slid back the glass door to join him under the hot jets.

'Hey there,' I put my arms around him and kissed his neck.

'Kate.' He turned and our mouths found each other hungrily.

The rest of the world was back at work as we sat in the kitchen eating a leisurely breakfast. No words had been needed; our bodies had spoken to each other and come to a mutual agreement. All that was left was love and contentment. We were at peace again after the turmoil of last night and the events leading up to it.

I had decided not to voice my newfound information about family. I needed to be much stronger before I broached that discussion again. The last thing I wanted was another argument. It could wait. After all, we had waited hundreds of years for the right time when we made our comeback; a few more days was nothing in the grand scheme of things.

'Are the girls coming round today?'

'Maybe later. They want to see you, but they want to give us some space as well, especially after last night. It's going to take me most of the day to clear up the mess outside, but I want to do it before they come round again. It would be quite upsetting for them to see that.'

'I'm sorry. I can't remember everything that happened. I just have flashes of me throwing things and shouting. I'm so thankful that I didn't hurt you.'

'Me too. Don't worry, it's in the past now. I'll go and make a start. Why don't you go put your feet up.'

'If you're sure you don't need me to help.'

'You can help by doing as you're told for once; go sit down.'

John gave her a kiss and went out to make a start on clearing the garden of the contents of their bedroom.

Kate watched him for a while, ashamed of the mess she'd made. Her mobile phone bleeped. It was Adam. A brief twitch of lust coursed through her, immediately replaced by a twang of guilt. Kate allowed herself to think about her friend. Much as she tried to put the feeling out of her mind she found she couldn't get rid of it. Her Adam. Her Adonis. A vision of ripped jeans and black converse etched itself into her mind. She tried to think of the first time she had been aware of this presence and was drawn back to a summertime many years before.

July 1983

It was the summer of 1983. A special year. The year Kate and her friends had left school in the May for what was laughingly known as study leave. Kate had a job waitressing, which she loved, and only had a few exams to go back in for. The school was as glad to see the back of them as they were to leave it. It was a long hot summer as far as she could remember. Her beloved Duran Duran were playing a charity gig at Aston Villa. Kate had tickets to go to see them, but she had been forced to take her French exchange penfriend who, unfortunately, was visiting the week of the gig, a prospect that did not sit well with Kate as she had wanted to take her best friend. It wasn't to be, and Kate grudgingly agreed that the unwelcome guest would have to go with her. Her worst fears materialised when Kate, jumping up, screaming, singing dancing in the stands at Villa Park, was asked to sit down by her unwelcome guest.

From that moment, the exchange went from bad to worse, the journey back in silence as Kate silently fumed that the French girl had tried to ruin her day. It had only been a minor blip and spending hours on the coach in silence were worth the few hours of being in the presence of her musical gods.

Kate had arranged to meet her best friend the next day in the local wine bar, which they frequented every day to play pool. It was the only bar in their town that served them alcohol no questions asked, Kate and the French girl arrived early, Kate desperate to show off her gig memorabilia; a silk scarf emblazoned with the group's logo had taken pride of place around her neck. She ordered half a lager and black and stood surveying the rest of the bar. It was the end of July and holidaymakers mingled with locals. In the far corner were a group of lads, four of them. Kate studied them with interest; one with a Magnum-style moustache and skinny jeans caught her eye. The next one had a long flicked fringe and a small ponytail. Next to him sat a sporty looking lad, all three of them dressed in skinny jeans and t-shirts. But the one that stood out had jet black hair, his fringe long and covered one eye, long black eyelashes, faded ripped jeans cut off at the knee and a black t-shirt.

Kate stood in awe. She had never seen such a beautiful boy in her life. He looked up and caught her staring at him. She was mesmerised and didn't even feel the need to look away. At that moment there were only the two of them present in the bar. She grinned, and to her delight, he grinned back and raised his glass. The spell was broken with the arrival of her three friends; the four of them had become inseparable over the last few months. Her best friend followed Kate's gaze and back again.

'Oooh, where did they come from?' said Anna.

'I don't know, but I think I'm in love,' Kate replied with a grin.

'He's nice, that one with the black hair.' Anna raised her glass over to where the lads were sitting, devising their own plan of action.

'Hands off, he's mine. I saw him first so I get first try ok?'

'I like the Magnum one,' said Mags.

It was an unwritten rule and a taboo between them that if one of them fancied a guy, the others left well alone until either a first kiss was made or a rejection followed.

The lads in the corner were all still involved in their own conversations regarding the girls who stood at the bar. Warily they got up and approached the waiting girls. As they jostled for position at the bar, someone pushed Kate and she spilt her lager and black all over her new scarf.

'Bloody hell, watch out, you wanker,' Kate snarled before realising it was the object of her affection who had been the culprit.

'Er, sorry.'

'I only got this yesterday.' Kate was annoyed, but she couldn't help thinking it was fate that had got them talking to each other.

'Duran Duran. Yeah, they're ok,' he replied. 'Want another drink?'

'Er, yeah, seeing as you spilt most of mine on my scarf,' she shot back at him with a smile.

And the rest was history. It transpired, as the evening wore on, that they were all sixteen, the same age as the girls. They had all just left school and on their first holiday alone without parents. Alliances were forged and Kate and Rob became an item. Two by two they paired off, and that was how it stayed for the two weeks of their holiday, the French girl being waved goodbye that weekend, never to be seen again. She was far too square in Kate's opinion and she had very poor hygiene; the unusually hot summer did nothing to help matters in that respect. No amount of hinting made any difference and Kate was glad to see the back of her.

A school leavers' disco had been organised at a local club and the girls managed to blag tickets for their holiday romances. It was a magical time, making memories that would last a lifetime. He was a musician her Rob; he played guitar. Kate knew that she would never forget him. Even as their romance came to its natural end by the end of the summer, they remained friends for a few years and met up in both hometowns a few times. He played his guitar to another girl at a party they attended, whilst Kate watched, and that signalled the end of their relationship. Kate was more hurt than her attitude let on. After that they drifted apart. He lost interest and she found solace in another guy. The inevitable happened and time and life took over and she lost him.

Friday 8th January, 2016 – lunchtime

Kate had been sat watching TV and dozing on and off for a couple of hours. She had dreamt of her teenage summer love and realised with a jolt that he was her Adonis, all those years ago. It made sense now. The power of attraction and the depth of loss felt when they parted, she had put it down to a teenage crush, a first love, a holiday romance. But the more she thought about it, the clearer it became. No wonder she always remembered him with fondness. Kate had lived being ruled by her heart. The amount of loves she had endured so passionately and grieved so tragically each time the romance ended now made perfect sense.

I awoke with a start, my neck hurt from the awkward position I had been sleeping in on the sofa. The TV was on the horror channel for some reason. I was scared. I was wrapped in the blanket from our bed, and my pyjamas were in a heap on the floor by my feet. Where was John? I reached for the remote to switch off the zombies who were rampaging through deserted streets. Ugh, zombies. Why had I been watching that? There was an empty plate on the coffee table next to me, and a half drunk bottle of beer. I went into the kitchen, acutely aware that I was alone.

'John? Where are you?' My voice bounced back in my head.

The hall door, which was normally shut, was wide open. I walked through cautiously. There was something wrong. How long had I been asleep? The door to the snug was also wide open and I stepped back in horror as I surveyed the scene in front of me. John was sat on the leather chair by my desk, head in his hands. The room had suffered the same fate as our bedroom. Papers covered every surface. The heavy velvet curtains had been torn down, books littered the floor. The devastation was not quite as thorough as the previous evening, but it was clear that there had been another incident.

Was it me? I couldn't remember anything this time. I looked questioningly at my husband. He lifted his head up, his hand pressed against his right cheek where he held a hanky which was covered in blood. He had been crying. My heart went out to him and I went to give him a hug, but was stopped cold in my tracks as he sank back from me with fear in his eyes.

'Was it me?' I implored him to answer me. 'Oh no, it can't have been me. You're hurt. What happened?'

'Yes it was.'

'I can't remember anything. What's happening to me? Please forgive me John. I never meant to hurt you. You are my world, you know that don't you?'

'Leave me a while please Kate. Why don't you go and put the kettle on. I'll be through in a minute.'

John sat for a while wondering if Kate had come back to her senses. She appeared rational once more, and apart from the dark shadows under her eyes she almost looked like the Kate he knew and loved. He daren't tell her he had rung the hospital again and they were sending a car for her to take her to a secure unit. The events of last night and this morning had frightened the life out of him and the rise in temper and violence had escalated this morning. He knew she was in a blind rage, and there was nothing he could do to stop her.

She had worn herself out and as she calmed, had gone into a trance-like state with eyes glazed over and had taken herself into the lounge with a bottle of beer and settled in front of the TV with the curtains closed. Once he was convinced she had finished destroying things, he had made the call. They would be here within the hour. John was dreading them arriving, but knew he had to act quickly to protect his beloved wife from destroying their home and turning her temper on the rest of the family.

'Go and put some clothes on before you freeze to death.'

'I'm ok.'

'No, you're not. Please, Kate, do as I ask.'

'Let me see that cut on your temple.'

'It's stopped bleeding now. It'll be ok, don't worry.'

'I never meant to hurt you. Oh God, what have I done.'

John held out his hand. 'Come and give me a hug. I know you didn't mean it.'

I picked my way through the chaos and let John hold me. The tears came thick and fast, my body wracked with grief knowing I was responsible for his injury.

'I'm going to make a drink. I managed to tidy up most of the garden from last night, but then this happened so back to square one again.'

'What happened?'

'I think you were hallucinating again. Came out of nowhere.'

'Hello, is anyone in?'

John looked at me with a guilty look on his face.

'What? What have you done?'

A policeman stood in the doorway of the snug. I looked at my John questioningly. He averted his gaze and looked out of the window.

'Can you come outside with me please, miss?'

'Why are you in my house? What do you want?'

'We've had a report of a disturbance.'

'Everything is fine, isn't it, John. Nothing to worry about.'

'With all due respect, it doesn't look fine. Can you tell me what happened, sir?'

'Everything is in hand. We are just waiting for a hospital car to come.'

'A hospital car? What? No. You've done it again. Why do you keep betraying me? I thought you loved me?' I stared open mouthed at him, screaming accusations.

'If you will just step outside with me.' The policeman addressed Kate again, this time in a firmer tone.

'No. No I won't. I'm not leaving my home.'

Two more policeman, one short and stocky and one with bright ginger hair, had now joined the party and stood nervously watching as I backed myself into the corner of the room, picking up the nearest object to use as a missile. This was becoming a habit. I was in a blind rage again. I couldn't believe he had done it again after all we had spoken about; after our wonderful lovemaking this morning. I had stupidly believed everything would be ok.

John tried to appeal to me to calm down, but I was too far gone. Spiralling one might say. The police in my house? The next few minutes are all a bit of a blur, but in the ensuing moments somehow, I managed to throw all of them out of my house ripping off two doors in the process.

I am outside, on the floor, handcuffed, covered only by my 'Paris in Love' blanket. John is stood with the police, looking sadly on. Not long ago I was sat enjoying my lunch and a beer. How did that transform into me being naked on the ground? I try and wrack my brains. There are blanks in my memory that just won't come back. I look up from my position on the floor they all look very tall. They are eyeing me warily as if I am some kind of dangerous lunatic.

'Hey, any chance of taking these handcuffs off, please?'

'Not until you calm down. You can stay there for now,' the tallest policeman, that is near me, replies.

'I am calm. Never been calmer. I'm just bloody freezing and I need to get up.'

'Stay where you are please. Do not attempt to get up. You have no clothes on.'

'I'm well aware of that. For fuck sake, I'm catching my death here. Don't you know I've been really poorly. I'm sure this is not doing me any good.'

'Kate, please don't make things any worse.'

I look at my husband and laugh. 'Worse? What the fuck John. How can they get any worse?'

I know who I am. I know what I have to do. Worse, I'll show them worse. If they don't let me go the whole world will know what can be worse. It is the Eighth Day. The day that the good need to rise up and fight the evil. I have until midnight to get rid of the evil that has tried to penetrate my home, my family. We will not stand for it any longer.

'Let me up now, please,' I call out again, my pleas falling on deaf ears. 'I'll come quietly, I promise.'

John and the policeman are in deep conversation so I try another tactic.

'If you don't take these cuffs off, I am going to get up and go back in the house and I don't care if I am naked. You can all fuck off. Let me up now,' I scream as loud as I can.

'If you don't calm down, I'm going to taser you,' the ginger one threatens.

'Go on then, you wanker. See if I care. Taser, fucking taser?' I start laughing and I can't stop. 'I'm a forty-eight-year-old woman, naked and handcuffed. Are you really that scared of me?'

It is bizarre, but that remark transforms my mood from mightily pissed off to amusement. I look at the 'boys in blue' a bit closer and decide to have some fun.

'Oi, you,' I shout at my audience. 'Yeah you, the one with the hard on. Will you help me up please?' I don't know how I know he has a hard on, but I know I speak the truth.

'Oh Kate, don't please,' my husband responds. 'It's bad enough. Behave yourself please. The hospital car is coming, it'll be here any minute, and this time you have no choice but to go with them.'

'Ok, how about you then?' I address the one who came into the house first. I decide he is the bravest one of the trio. 'Will you help me up?'

He ignores me. No movement from any of them. Annoyingly. I try again, third time lucky maybe.

'Right then, 'Ginge', you'll help me won't you, prove to your mates that gingers aren't whingers. You can give me a hand can't you?'

John is stood in disbelief, holding his head in his hands as he realises I'm just getting into my piss-taking stride and I am having fun. I wink at him. Still no movement and it is another half an hour before they decide I am no longer a threat and they get me up.

'Go and get dressed please. The car will be here soon,' John asks me, his voice heavy with sadness.

'No problem. As if I want to stay here with you now. I can't wait to get away from you after what you've done. You have no idea of the trouble we are all in do you? I'm better off on my own. Where are they taking me anyway? I need to be in a place of safety so I can fight the evil.'

John shook his head. 'Just go and get dressed. I've put some things in a case for you.'

'Of course I will. No problem. Are the police coming with me?'

'They are going to stay outside until the car arrives. You're lucky they haven't arrested you for assaulting a police officer.'

'They're lucky I didn't hurt all three of them. Leave me alone now, I don't want to talk to you at the moment.'

I turned my back on him and went to find my clothes. I knew exactly what I was going to wear and what else I needed to take with me to the unit.

I find all the items with no problem, do my hair, put my make-up and high heels on, they match my wedding dress. I'm wearing the red petticoat underneath. I know exactly which items to take with me and which to leave. I am being guided by my family on high. Today will be the turning point when good starts to fight back. John is waiting in the kitchen. The car has arrived. I pick up my phone and hand my case to the driver.

'I will forgive you because I love you. I'm sorry that I hurt you, I didn't mean to do that, John. There are things that I need to do, and I'll be able to focus on them if I am away. I understand now that my path is marked out for me.'

'We just want what's best for you, my darling. You need help, and I'm sorry I had to call the hospital, but it really is for the best.'

'I know that now. I'd better go then, they're waiting.'

John looked beaten as I gave him a kiss and followed the waiting security staff that had been sent to escort me to the unit. I got in the back of the silver car and did my seatbelt up. The security staff got in, one either side of me and one in front; they weren't taking any chances. I was apparently classed as dangerous. They had no need to worry as they were the good guys and were there to ensure my safe journey to the unit. I waved at John as we drew away. My husband and my home disappeared from view as the car sped towards my date with destiny. I had a job to do. The car was protected by many deities and I knew we would be assured a safe journey. I also knew that as we neared our destination the evil would start fighting back. It didn't bother me because I was now aware. I knew we would make it. There was no alternative.

The Countdown

Friday 8th January – 7 pm – midnight

The journey down was an interesting one. Our silver shuttle sped along carrying its strange cargo. I was sandwiched in the back between my security guards disguised as paramedics, dressed in green. No guns, but I suspected they had a whole bag of tricks at their disposal if I lost the plot again. I looked at my feet, five-inch stilettos gleaming back at me, red and black sequins adorning them. I loved my shoes. It may seem a bit inappropriate attire for my final destination, but I knew exactly how I should be dressed and nothing else but my wedding outfit cut it. My companions were amicable; a woman on my left, a man on my right, a youngish guy opposite and a driver behind a Perspex screen, presumably for protection in case I had a relapse. They had been pleasant and chatty so far. I babbled away, hardly stopping to draw breath. The radio accompanied us at my request.

Outside, the skies were still blue and the sun shone down on us brightly as we sped our way south through the countryside. The quiet lanes of my county gave way to busier A-roads, and then we hit civilisation and its motorways rammed with vehicles, lorries, motorbikes all travelling at speed with purpose. I spent some time hiding under my blanket when the feelings of the evil hunting us down became overwhelming. My companions seemed to accept this as par for the course and neither encouraged or discouraged me. They appeared to be nonplussed at my previous behaviour. I decided that they were probably used to dealing with strange behaviour and they had probably seen it all. I was not violent; I was the epitome of agreeability. We had been travelling for a couple of hours when I emerged from under my blanket to ask how far we had to go before we reached the final destination. It seemed we were around half an hour away, and my alter ego came back and took over my persona. I knew what I had to do.

This time, I was aware of her doing it. I was no longer Kate; I was my higher being, and she had taken over my body again. This time it was seamless and we became one. She brought me back to a higher level of consciousness and it was time to defend the good once again. I had to be on guard and alert so that we reached the journey's end safely.

'Please would you turn the radio up?' I asked the driver.

My request was granted and I took a look outside. We were on a busy motorway still heading south.

'Half an hour away, yeah?' I asked.

'Yes,' the lady on my left replied. 'Nearly there, are you ok?'

'Fine. But I need to warn you all that the closer we get, the scarier things will become. Please be alert.'

Nobody answered me, they were professional and did not engage in much conversation.

'Please believe me. I know we will be ok because the sun is shining, and the music is on. I may have to ask you all to sing and think positive thoughts. We need all the help we can get if we are going to make it to the unit safely.'

'It's ok, love. We are nearly there, try and relax,' she replied at the same time as the car in the lane next to us pulled out sharply, causing our driver to brake suddenly and the car to swerve dangerously into the fast lane to avoid a collision.

'Fucking hell, that was close.' The driver caught my eye in the rear view mirror.

'Listen, I know you all think I'm crazy, but surely that proves I am just trying to protect us. Just humour me will you.'

My companions didn't answer, but I could see the looks that passed between them.

'How far away now?'

'Fifteen minutes,' the driver answered.

'We are all going to have to be vigilant now. I will do my best to protect us, but just imagine you are on the scariest rollercoaster ride ever and you won't be far off.'

I noticed the opposite carriageway start to get snarled up. Suddenly there were blue flashing lights and sirens everywhere, a multiple car pile-up, fire engines, ambulances, police cars, all trying to make their way through the traffic to get to the scene of the accident. Our side of the motorway started slowing down and it was all our driver could do to try and pick our way through the congestion.

'See what I mean.' I shook my head in sadness at the carnage.

'*Beat It*' came on the radio. My influence was starting to win the situation over.

I started singing. 'Please join in with me, and if you can't sing just tap your fingers or something. Please turn the music up, we need all the power of good we can sum up between us. Just humour me. I know I'm on my way to the looney bin so just pretend that I need this to stop me becoming angry.' I pleaded with them and started singing along with Michael Jackson.

'His music will help us, I promise. I'm going to focus on making the sun shine brighter too as I'm singing. I promise I will protect us. How long now, please?'

The driver mouthed five minutes back at me. I looked at my other companions and they looked a little shaken by the events unfolding. I decided to keep my mouth shut as they appeared to be quite spooked.

I looked out of the window and saw the sign to our destination; a mile away. The rest of the journey took far longer than it should have done and we dodged accidents time after time until we drew up into the car park and alongside the entrance to the secure hospital. I realised with a jolt that to come here I must have had to be sectioned under the Mental Health Act. I wasn't upset. This is where I was supposed to be. I had been transported here for a reason. It was no longer safe in my home and I needed to be here in my sanctuary so that I could fight the evil that had risen up. Today was a day of judgement; it was the day when forces of good and evil gathered in the battle to control our planet. The evil had gone unchallenged for far too long. This unlikely place was destined to be where goodness would step up the fight back. The Eighth Day. The Gods were all gathering together in various locations across the world. Unseen, silently, we were arriving at our temples armed and ready for the onslaught.

I wrapped my blanket around me for protection and surveyed the exterior of the building. There were two sets of steps to go up. Danger. I took off my wedding shoes and slipped on my battered trainers that I had picked up in the porch on the way out of my house. I knew I needed to take them with me for some reason, and here it was. The evil was just waiting for any opportunity to injure me. A fall down the stairs would have weakened me. Ah, so that's why I needed the trainers then. I had always followed my instinct. Now my gut instinct had been joined by a voice in my head. I didn't exactly hear a voice, it was more that I knew the course of action which I had to take. Something told me to pick up the trainers. And here in front of me was the reason.

My guardians signalled for me to get out of the car and follow them, one in front of me and two behind. They carried my bags and I followed the lead, thankful that we had made it in one piece. They all looked a little shaken and relieved that we had arrived. They handed me over to the staff who were waiting and I was shown to a small room and told to wait for staff to come and check me in.

'Thanks guys, I really appreciate it. Safe journey back.' I waved as they left the building.

I sat and waited in the little room. I must look mental, in my wedding dress and scruffy trainers, a hoodie hastily thrown on for extra protection and wrapped in my ever-present Paris comfort blanket. One other item adorned my head, a bright red fez topped off my outfit and confirmed my diagnosis. It read 'Complete Madness' on the front, another souvenir from a gig that John and I had attended before Christmas. If I am sectioned then I may as well embrace it. My thoughts turned to John and my family. I knew they were safe, that the evil that had lurked outside my home had attached itself to me; one less thing to worry about. Adam had texted me earlier to let me know that Ebony was safe and well. He was doing such a good job looking after my friend. Of course he was, and blissfully unaware of his true identity, as was John. It is difficult to explain to a human how our kind can possess different mortals. We can be one person or a hundred all at the same time. Our beings do not follow the laws of physics and boundaries that humans are tied into. We have our own planes, levels, dimensions, whatever you want to call them. We can occupy humans, animals, birds, fish, insects, in fact anything that has a life has a soul and we can slip into any form without the carrier even knowing it. We only bring ourselves to the attention of our hosts when it is unavoidably necessary, content with guiding from within and letting freewill take its natural course.

I only have to wait a few minutes before a lovely doctor comes to assess me. She checks my stats, blood pressure, temperature, weight, etc. before inviting me to follow her. Chatting casually as if I were a long lost friend, she showed me around the ward and then to my room, which was at the end of a corridor, last door on the left. It is all beautifully clean and brightly lit. My bags have been taken to my room. I looked around my new environment, and a feeling of deep contentment settled easily in my mind. Here was a home from home, where I would be safe. We come to the lounge, occupied now by a few patients and members of staff.

'Everyone, this is Kate. She's just arrived. Please make her welcome.'

A few blank faces stare at me. I stare back and give them all a beaming smile.

'Hi, pleased to meet you all.'

There are comfy sofas and chairs and a couple of purple beanbags on the floor. A large flat screen TV is playing on a music channel. In the corner is a kitchen unit and worktop with a kettle and tea, coffee, biscuits and fruit.

The doctor follows my gaze. 'You are most welcome to help yourself to drinks whenever you want one, Kate. We will be doing supper soon. There will be a variety of sandwiches; I'm sure you will find something that you like, and if you don't then we can try and sort you something different out. I'll leave you to it. Why don't you go and have a freshen-up in your room, then you can come back and get acquainted with the others, ok?' She smiled at me.

'Yeah, that's fine, thank you.'

I make my way back down the corridor to my room, immediately feeling at ease. My room has purple and cream décor, a comfy-looking bed, with a purple and cream throw across the bottom of the bed to greet me, along with a small en suite. I decide to have a quick wash before supper and grab my toiletry bag from my case. The basin has odd looking taps, round and flat like a tiny upside down saucer with a hole on the front where the water trickles down the side of the sink, and there is a blue and a red button adjacent to indicate hot and cold water. I have never seen taps like it before. The shower is operated by pressing a button on the wall which starts a feeble spray of water lasting a couple of minutes before needing to be pushed again. I assume they are special fittings for a hospital such as this, maybe to prevent people flooding the bathroom or drowning themselves. No plug in the sink, confirming my suspicions.

I feel very safe and at home. It's still quite early, too early to go to bed, and I'm quite hungry so I head back to the communal lounge to see if the sandwiches promised have materialised. They have. I join a small queue made up of a couple of guys and a young girl. Egg sandwiches and some crisps, a cup of coffee and I am more than happy.

A tall guy with a beard comes up to me as I walk across the lounge to find a place to sit. 'Hey, new lady, I like your dress.'

'Thanks, it's my wedding dress, and my name is Kate,' I reply and do a twirl, causing the full circle skirt to flare out showing the red petticoats beneath.

'I know you, Kate. I'm Gareth,' he replies with the biggest smile I have seen for a long time, yellowing teeth revealed through an overgrown beard and moustache.

I was still wearing my fez too, which caused some interest. The other patients wander over to introduce themselves. I really like it here; I feel as though I have come home. We chat for a while and most of them lose interest in the new lady and carry on what they were doing before I made my entrance. Not Gareth though, he stays. I've clearly made an impression and he stays to question me.

'Do another swirl, I like that.'

'Ok, but I'm not doing it all night. I'm hungry.'

'You're my nemesis aren't you? I've met my match,' he grins at me.

'Yes, I am,' I grin back. 'I know you, don't I? We've known each other a long while I think.'

'You're my nemesis,' he repeats, seemingly very happy with the prospect that he may have met his match.

I decide to test the water to see what reaction revealing my inner identity will provoke.

'My real name is Aphrodite, and I'm here to fight for all of us.' I wait for laughter and prepare to have the piss taken out of me for the length of my stay. It doesn't come.

'I knew you were here for a reason. My mother was a sibyl. Do you know what that is, Kate?'

'No, I've never heard of that before,' I answer him questioningly.

'A white witch. She was a good lady, like you are. Aphrodite? Really?'

'Yes, really. Your mother, was she locked up too like us?'

Gareth tells me the sad story of how he has grown up in various children's homes and passed from one place to another as his mother had been sectioned. Then he had lost his way until the same fate had befallen him. He had been locked up for thirty years of his life. My heart went out to him. He was the same age as me, but his life had been one of tragedy after tragedy through no fault of his own.

'We will be ok now, I promise. I'm fighting for all of us,' I reassure him.

Quite a crowd formed around us whilst we were chatting. A young girl of Romany origin sidled up and introduced herself, LJ, her wide dark eyes bright with curiosity and wariness as if she may take flight at any moment.

Five minutes later and there are half a dozen of us now sat round chatting. Everyone has a sad tale to tell, but as we talk I realise that these are my people. We are misunderstood, and the majority of the others that have joined our group all have one thing in common; they have all been given medication and have been taking prescription drugs for one thing or another for many years.

A large lady waddles over towards our little group. Her eyes are sunken into her face, dirty blonde hair stuck up off her head as if she has received an electric shock. She stands in front of me. I feel a great sadness descend on me like a cold heavy blanket as she holds my gaze, unblinking.

'Hi there, I'm Kate. What's your name?'

'Oh, she doesn't speak. Her name is Jenny. She never speaks to anyone. She barely comes out of her room,' says LJ.

Jenny points at me, stands for a few moments looking me up and down and then turns slowly and ambles slowly out of the lounge back down the corridor where the female bedrooms are located.

'Is she ok?' I ask.

'Been here longer than I have,' says Gareth, 'and I've never heard her speak a word.'

A couple of staff members are lurking on the outskirts. I feel a little jolt of unease. I have come into contact with a few staff members and the majority seem lovely, but there are one or two that I take an instant dislike to. Evil masquerading as good people. Since the takeover, I can read people like a book. They may pretend to be good, but I can see through the façade.

Nowhere for the badness to run. I see past a sickly sweet smile. Nowhere to hide. I am a force to be reckoned with, and as the evening wears on I can feel my power growing.

We are having a brilliant bonding session. I launch into a version of *'The Lunatics Have Taken Over The Asylum'* by Fun Boy Three, which goes down a treat and we are told to quieten down as our singing becomes louder and louder. Being told off just makes us laugh harder. It has been a brilliant evening and just what I needed, music being my salvation again and the song choice a perfect icebreaker.

We calm down before, as Gareth so rightly says, 'we get a needle up the arse'. This makes me giggle, but I also realise the repercussions of his words. I decided to warn him and the others of the trouble which is coming our way. I cannot leave them unaware and defenceless; we are all in this together. Not only is it the Eighth Day, but it is a full moon, and I need to make sure my newfound friends are as safe as possible.

'Listen up, guys. Can I have your attention for a minute please?'

LJ, Gareth and the others form a circle around me.

'I know I've only just arrived here, but I need you to all follow my instructions. I want to keep you safe.'

To say that they have only set eyes on me a couple of hours ago, they all listen attentively whilst I give them instructions on keeping safe for the night.

'I need you to all be in your rooms before midnight. Lock the door behind you and don't come out no matter what you may hear. Is that ok? Things are going to get batshit crazy around here. Please don't be scared. The nearer it gets to midnight, the worse it is going to get.'

'I'm scared of being locked in. I can't do it, Kate. I'm too scared. I've been locked up all my life.' Gareth looks petrified at the prospect.

'Ok. Well, could you stay outside your door and then go in a few seconds before midnight?'

That seems to work and he nods in agreement. The others all promise, but I'm not convinced they will follow instructions.

Banished

The next hour passes peacefully. Nine. Ten. Ten-thirty and the madness begins. The atmosphere shifts and I can feel the evil entering the room as two support workers that I haven't seen before enter the room. I don't like the way they are speaking to us. A very subtle shift from calm instructions to passive aggressive, the menace in their voices barely concealed. I have a very bad feeling which is becoming more and more intense with every minute that passes. I cannot wait much longer before I have to take action.

'Everyone, it's starting.'

Gareth catches my eye and leaves the room, beckoning the others to go with him. The staff are on edge, sensing unrest in the air.

'Guys, it'll be ok, I promise,' I call after them. 'Trust me, just lock your doors like I asked you. That'll keep you safe.'

My attention is drawn to a pair of double doors that lead into the dining room. Something was in there. As I got nearer, the evil increased until it was tangible. A sense of foreboding overtook me and I knew I had to act fast to stop it spreading. A voice in my head screamed at me, 'It's coming. Getting stronger. You must contain it. Now. Do it.'

I had no clue what I needed to do to be able to 'contain it' so I followed my gut and threw open the doors to confront whatever it was that had managed to infiltrate our sanctuary. The air was foul, heavy, oppressive and menacing. I entered the dining room. I couldn't see anything untoward at first. Then my higher consciousness took over and my body followed her instructions. Moving tables, chairs, art equipment. I sorted out the good from the bad and put a barrier between it. I piled all the badness up onto a table in the far left hand corner of the room. Jigsaws with pieces missing, a broken chair, felt tips that didn't work, anything that felt unclean added to the pile.

Then it started fighting back. A knife whizzed past my head. A chair slid across the room, its leg slamming into my shin. Ah, so that's the way they were going to play it. I went crazy and picked up the offending item and launched it back across the room. The whole place was in an uproar. Windows had slid themselves open and the winter night rushed in. I fought my way over to close them again, because the longer they were open, the more evil tainted our safe haven. I had been transported to the next level and could see a small black demon oozing black filth from every pore, laughing at me and standing on top of the evil items I had piled up on the table in the corner.

I saw red and picked up a table, launching it across the room. The place was in uproar, and my new friends had all returned to see what the commotion was. The two staff members that I knew were part of the evil approached me. I found myself being restrained and marched to my room.

'Don't worry, guys, I'm ok. Just go back to your rooms and lock the doors. Promise me, stay safe,' I screamed over my shoulder as they dragged me down the corridor. My feet scraped the floor behind me and the flesh on my arms pinched in a vice-like grip.

They sat me on my bed, one either side holding me firmly so I couldn't get up. I decided there was no point struggling and sat waiting for them to show their next move.

'Go on then, what next? I'm perfectly ok so you're wasting your time holding me down. I'm not going anywhere.'

The one on my left shot me a look of venom.

'Look at me again like that and I will spit in your face,' I challenged her.

She looked away quickly. The one to my right, being a bit braver, nodded at her companion and they both tightened their grip on my arms.

'Go on then, bitch, do your worst. You think that hurts? That's nothing. I could crush you, you pathetic piece of shit. I know you and your kind. We won't be walked over any more. Today is payback. I suggest you leave me alone whilst I'm calm or I will crush you like the insects you are.'

Another member of staff arrived.

'We are going to give you an injection to calm you down,' the new one spoke to me gently.

'Do your worst. I don't care. It won't make any difference. Just get on with it and leave me the fuck alone. Oh, and lock the door after you. I need some peace so I can think.'

They did as promised and injected me, not up the arse as Gareth had said, but in the arse cheek. I was relieved when they cleared off as I was suddenly exhausted and I needed to regroup. I had half an hour left to hold on. We were getting close to midnight. I opened the curtains and looked out the window. The wind had died down. There was a bus stop opposite, and a lone figure stood under the shelter. As I watched, it turned its attention on me, and although I could only see the silhouette, I knew it was smiling at me. An angel had come to help. An angel was there watching over me. No, not an angel, an archangel. I knew as sure as I knew who I really was that we were all coming together in a bid to turn the world around. Archangel Michael had my back. I waved and left him in charge of perimeter security.

'Cleanliness is next to godliness, Kate.'

On autopilot, I stripped naked and went into the bathroom. Suddenly my stomach cramped and I hunched over the toilet. Vomit and bile hit the bowl at force, and I retched until there was nothing left to come out. Shakily, I rinsed my mouth and cleaned my teeth. Cramp again. This time I had to rush to sit on the toilet as my bowels emptied themselves as violently as my gut had.

'The evil is leaving you. Don't be scared.'

I sat until I dared move again. I stood under the shower and tried to cleanse myself. Water trickled down and eased my mind as the dirt soaked away. I was aware of something watching me. The water suddenly stopped and I turned to see the door of the bathroom swing open. My Paris blanket, which I had laid on my bed, was curled up, and I could make out the form of a body underneath it, head at the foot end of the bed.

'Get out of my room, you fucking bitch,' I screamed across at the form.

I pushed the button to switch the shower on and let the water flow over me whilst I shouted obscenities at the evil in the room. I was alone with it, I had the advantage. I was in my sanctuary. I had been emptied of dirt and my body was now clean inside and out.

'Cleanliness is next to godliness, Kate.' The mantra repeated itself over and over in my head.

The blanket moved, the figure underneath appeared to be shrinking slowly.

'I need help, guys,' I beseeched my heavenly family. 'Send her to the moon until she learns some manners. It is full and ready to receive her.'

'Not far enough away,' came the answer.

'Oh, my family, help me. Which planet?'

The answer came thick and loud as had the 'Dead by Christmas' so many months ago.

'Mars will take the bitch away. To Mars. Mars. Mars.'

'Are you sure that's far enough?'

I pressed the button again and a fresh trickle ran over my body. The water had turned red and I realised with horror that I was bleeding, bright red blood from my womb was trickling down my legs and over my feet to join the clean water. It was bizarre. I had not had a period for over a year. The revelation brought me to my knees. I was suddenly exhausted.

'Go away. Leave us alone now.' I sat curled up as the water switched off after its allotted time once again.

I stayed where I was, eyes closed and repeating the Lord's Prayer over and over again. After what may have only been a few minutes but felt like an hour, I opened my eyes, not knowing what to expect. The blanket was flat. The entity had gone. My room was free from the evil that had been present. I was suddenly cold and shivering. A fluffy white towel had been provided and I wrapped it around me rubbing it over my skin to try and get some heat back into my flesh.

My beautiful blanket had been tainted and I removed it carefully from my bed, threw it into the wardrobe and shut the door. I went back into the bathroom and washed my hands.

The battle had been won. The evil had been banished for a while and left our planet. An immense sense of relief washed over me and I flopped down onto the bed.

My family and I had done all we could for the moment. Earth and its population were safe for the time being. The drugs started to take effect on my exhausted body and finally I allowed myself to fall into a deep dreamless sleep.

BOOK TWO

THE MUSIC

I Am – By John Clare

I am—yet what I am none cares or knows;
My friends forsake me like a memory lost:
I am the self-consumer of my woes—
They rise and vanish in oblivious host,
Like shadows in love's frenzied stifled throes
And yet I am, and live—like vapors tossed

Into the nothingness of scorn and noise,
Into the living sea of waking dreams,
Where there is neither sense of life or joys,
But the vast shipwreck of my life's esteems;
Even the dearest that I loved the best
Are strange—nay, rather, stranger than the rest.

I long for scenes where man hath never trod
A place where woman never smiled or wept
There to abide with my Creator, God,
And sleep as I in childhood sweetly slept,
Untroubling and untroubled where I lie
The grass below—above the vaulted sky.

John Clare, poet – certified insane in 1837 and admitted to an asylum in Northamptonshire where he spent many years. John wrote the above poem during his time in hospital. A melancholy account of a man who spent many years feeling persecuted; a man struggling with being incarcerated; a man longing for an escape from a world that didn't understand. John told them he was Shakespeare, he told them he was Lord Byron, he told them his daughter was Queen Victoria. Nobody believed him. I do.

A New Day

Saturday 9th January, 2016

I awoke with a clear mind for the first time since before the accident. It was still dark and I had no idea what time it was. The foreboding that had weighed me down had lifted. The curtains were wide open, as was the door to the en-suite. I lay on my back staring blindly at the ceiling, inspecting the darkest recesses of my mind, hunting for clues as to which demon had attached itself to my being and followed my journey. How had it penetrated the inner sanctum of my place of refuge? Had it really been with me since the day I had heard and ignored the deadly warning?

I was safe now. I knew it had gone, far away to another galaxy. Evidently, Mars had still not been far enough, that I knew. My Mars, my Ares, had given me his attention last night for the first time in many, many years. I did not know how it would work out with this former lover, but I did know that he would, and had, killed to protect me. His intervention last night had saved my soul from being dragged down the depths of Hades. I shuddered, and a bolt of fear swept through me at the thought of the underworld.

As a small child in this world, I had an unnatural fear of going underground. My parents found out to their cost whilst we were on a family holiday in the Peak District. No amount of cajoling or bribery would entice me down into the Blue John Mines. I vehemently refused point blank to go past the entrance, and so I ruined yet another family day out.

Who was it that had sought me out? I did not know. My guides assured me that it was not the time for me to be informed, there was much to do before the earthly identity of my enemies were fully revealed. I allowed my thoughts to wander and to inspect close friends and acquaintances, seeking out the suspects, placing them on trial in my head. I had a notion of three. Three graces opposing three witches, earthly friends and foes, I needed to speak to Gareth and glean some information about his background. Answers lay unspoken on my lips as I drifted back to sleep.

Meal times were busy on the ward. The food was plentiful and delicious, so the majority of patients attended every meal. The dining room furniture had been put back into their normal places after my outburst, with the exception of the table in the farthest corner. I remembered putting all the 'bad' objects into a pile and cursing the evil. I had forgotten that I had covered the whiteboard on the far wall with writing. I had rubbed off the menu and information on various activities and replaced it with my own text. A flow chart starting at the top with the year 2016 in large black numbers led by arrows to the word Exodus at the bottom. 2016 – 6102 – Dios – Year of the Gods – Exodus.

It all made perfect sense to me, and the more I studied it the more I believed that this was meant to be. I had to come here, it was written.

The rest of the ward seemed largely oblivious to the alterations. Except for Gareth. He came into the room and immediately stopped in his tracks.

'Was that you?' he shouted across the din of the breakfast sitting.

I nodded in answer to him and put my finger to my lips, mouthing at him that I needed to speak with him later.

He studied the board and queued for breakfast without a word.

'Kate, can I sit with you?'

I turned around as LJ, the girl with dark hair who I had spoken to last night, stood waiting for my reply.

'Yes of course. Sit down, you don't have to ask.'

LJ looked to be in her early twenties, extremely thin, with the palest white skin and bright blue eyes.

'How long have you been here?' I asked as I sat enjoying the beautifully cooked breakfast of thick toast, crispy bacon, fried eggs, mushrooms and hash browns.

'Three months now,' LJ replied, pushing the food around her plate. 'I had a breakdown, but I think I'm getting better.'

'I'm sure you will, it's a nice place in here. You're safe here, LJ. I know you will be ok.'

'They took my baby,' she said so quietly I barely heard her.

I had no answer for her. I couldn't imagine how painful it must be to have a child forcibly taken from you. I left the subject alone and changed tack quickly to try and lighten the mood a little. She was so painfully thin, it was obvious that food was an issue. She had only eaten a couple of mouthfuls when she pushed the plate away and left me sat there on my own without a word.

The thought came into my head of a large group of people, maybe her family, horses, caravans. Ah. Travellers. They wanted to look after LJ, but she had run away only to be picked up by the authorities and her baby taken. I knew this to be the case. My powers were stronger today. I had washed, I had slept, I had washed again, I had eaten and the demon had been severed from my aura. I felt clean and calm. Ready to face whatever the immediate future had to offer.

I finished my meal in peace and took the empty plate over to the staff, who were clearing up. 'Thanks very much, that was really lovely.'

'The food is good here. Yes, we are lucky we have good cooks in our kitchens.'

I walked over to the round table in the far corner. The nearer I got, the more unease I felt. I carefully examined the objects I had labelled as evil. They all had one thing in common in that they were either broken or had pieces missing, and some pieces of artwork had been crafted in such a way that they made me feel ill. Images crudely drawn in wax crayon, a face with a snarl and covered over in scribbling. My attention was drawn to a wooden box. I examined it carefully, wondering what it had done to end up on the pile. I picked it up and turned it over in my hands. On the underside someone had written in blue felt one word. 'Aspen'. The word ripped through my being like a butcher's knife. Aspen, Aspen, Aspen, Colorado. Pure evil. Why? I had a vague notion of seeing this word printed somewhere, but I could not for the life of me remember why I felt such unease. It would come to me.

I put the box back down and left the room, desperate to wash my hands. The day passed without anything untoward happening and I felt happier than I had in a long time. Gareth came and sought me out after lunch and we found a corner in the lounge where we could chat.

'Last night, Kate. You did it, didn't you? I felt a shift in power. I did it too. I managed to lock my door, just for a minute, but I did it. You've come here for a reason haven't you? Do you know why? Tell me. Help me understand, please?'

'I don't have all the answers, Gareth. I'm being guided, and I cannot see very far ahead in the future. I just know I have things which I have to do. We were meant to meet, I do know that.'

'I know we were, Kate. I was told someone would help me. I knew when you walked in wearing that dress that we knew each other from a long time ago. Did they stick a needle up your arse?' he asked, grinning all over his face when I nodded in reply. 'I told you they would. The bastards. That's what they do when you get too close to the truth.'

'It didn't have much effect on me. In fact, I was glad when they did because they left me alone after that and I was locked in, safe and able to do my job.'

I explained the events of the previous night and he sat listening, taking it all in, not laughing, not interrupting me, just believing.

'We spoke briefly about your mum,' I spoke cautiously, not knowing how he would react to being questioned, but I knew he had answers that I could only get from him and that I had information he needed to know.

'Yes. They locked her up too. She died in a place like this. Not as nice. A shit hole. She died twenty years ago. They killed her like they're trying to kill me,' he whispered, looking around furtively for any eavesdroppers.

'You said last night she was a 'sibyl', a white witch?'

'Yes. She only ever used her powers for good, but they locked her up anyway. Said she had lost the plot. I wasn't very old when she first went away.' He tailed off, lost in his own tale of sadness. 'I was put into a children's home, nobody cared. I was locked up and by the time I came out she was put away for good.'

'She is ok now, she is on another level. I'm here and fighting for everything that is good. You know the world is upside down don't you.'

'Yes. I've been waiting for you to come. My mum has been coming through and she told me a lady in black and red would be our saviour. And then you turned up last night. I couldn't believe it, Kate.'

'I had no idea that this was my destiny. It's only since my accident that things have really started happening.'

Gareth and I spent the afternoon chatting and discovering things we had in common. We talked of witches, good and bad. I had been exploring script writing. I had developed one which I named 'The Fallen', dealing with the injustices of women and men who had been put to death unjustly in the 1600s; intelligent strong women accused of witchcraft on both sides of the Atlantic.

'In Pendle and in Salem, people were burned, hanged, drowned and tortured for no other reason than the power of the witch-finder generals, who earned themselves a lot of money in the process, Gareth. I think I am channelling these women and fighting their cause. Don't ask me how I know, I just do.'

'Talking to you has made me realise that I am not completely mental, like they say. The medics just don't have the insight that we have, do they?'

'No, and they try and solve everything with medication. I think they've put me on an antipsychotic drug. I'll take it, but it won't stop me following my gut.'

'You are doing what you have to do. And if that means you came here just to help me, then it was worth it. I know now that my life has not been a complete joke. I'm just going to get better and better.'

'You're one of the reasons. I'm happy here. I think if I can stay and get some rest for a few days I will be ready to go home and face my family again.'

I decided not to tell Gareth of my heavenly identity. It was enough that we had spoken of the witches. My heart told me that was enough. Any more could be of detriment to my mission.

As it transpired, I stayed in my sanctuary eighteen days. During that time, I cleansed my body and soul, regained my strength, and was discharged as perfectly sane. I kept my inner feelings to myself, played nicely, took my meds and behaved impeccably. I had met some beautiful people, and I left with a new honorary daughter in the form of LJ, who I swore I would always be there for. Gareth and I had an understanding and communicated without having to speak. His mother came through to me every day and I acted as her mouthpiece, giving him the solace he needed to enable him to lay his ghosts to rest and overcome his fears.

'Bye then, everyone,' I addressed the patients who had gathered to see me off.

One of my best friends had come to pick me up. She had driven for hundreds of miles, no questions asked, to come and take me home.

I stopped for a moment and looked up at the first floor window where some of my fellow patients had gathered to wave me goodbye. They were smiling.

The Light

Tuesday 26th January, 2016

We travelled home that afternoon in good spirits as it were. My friend had no idea of her true identity and I knew it was not the time to tell her of how we came to be such close friends, back in those heady days when we were first washed ashore.

Aglaia, was one of my three graces who were also related to each other, being sisters fathered by Zeus. My grace of brightness, beauty and splendour had come to transport me back to my rightful place on this earth. Aglaia's reincarnation had chosen to inhabit the body of my beautiful friend, Stephanie. Aglaia's influence on her personality was plain to see; she was beautiful, she liked beautiful things and often would fulfil her role as a messenger, making sure we were all informed of new beauty products, gig dates, dinner parties, anything that involved getting the four of us together for a catch up would generally be instigated by lovely Steph. So, it was no surprise when it had been she who offered to come and carry me back home to my husband. Steph had always got on extremely well with John. I knew that eventually she would become the wife of his higher being, Hephaestus, when our heavenly marriage ended, a fact which I kept to myself. It was hard enough trying to cope with the amount of epiphanies I was experiencing without having the task of explaining our very complicated mythological family tree to my earthly friends and family.

We both loved music, and the radio blared out familiar songs to accompany us on our journey home.

'Oh bugger, it's never done that before,' Steph swore under her breath.

'What's up?'

'I don't know. That light has come on, on the dashboard and it's telling me the car is overheating.'

'What are we going to do? Do you think we will make it home?' I asked, wondering if the evil had once again found us.

'I'll just take it easy. I'm sure we will get there. We are less than half an hour away now, aren't we? And if not, I'll ring the AA.'

The rest of the journey was a little tense as we both watched the light on the dash flicker red. Red, red, red. Danger. Colours were becoming increasingly important. Colours and the radio. Another mystery for me to try and unravel. I put it to the back of my mind to join the ever growing list of weird shit that was being thrown at me daily.

Luckily as yet, I did not have the power to predict future events. We made it home without any mishap, each individually saying a silent prayer of thanks to whichever god had taken notice of my pleading.

They pulled into the long driveway - home. The house had been home for as long as I could remember. It was more than just bricks and mortar; it was home, it was a living thing, I adored it. Yes, it was cold and draughty in the winter; it had some damp, it needed a new roof, but it was homely and welcoming. It was a real family home, always had been and always would be. I had fought tooth and nail to keep it and seen off discouraging remarks from various family members, but no harsh words or threats had ultimately made any difference. Between us, John and I looked after it and it looked after us. A lot of things had become clear whilst I'd been away; I'd identified the three witches, they hailed from different areas of their lives, but each one had turned their disenchantment with the world onto John and I, bitterness and jealousy eating them up as they watched in envy the love and respect we had found in each other. Love that they had themselves once courted but that their evil had destroyed bit by bit over the years when the world did not deliver what they deigned their right to have. All three of them had the love of money ingrained within their beings. Money. They hated anyone who had it, yet they chased it relentlessly. Money had been their downfall, greed trampling on any love which may have been present. I'd had misgivings about the three individuals months ago, but it was only since the accident that I'd come to realise, as with every other revelation, just how much they hated me and were vying for my downfall. I wasn't scared of them, not any more. They would show their true colours before much longer and I'd already exorcised one. One down, two to go. It wouldn't be long until the time was right to send the next one a million miles away from us and the people I loved so desperately. My closest friends were the three graces, how obvious now I was in possession of higher knowledge; everything was beginning to make sense.

John watched the car come down the drive and went out to meet them.

'Here, let me help you with those bags,' he said after wrapping his arms around Kate, squeezing her in a bear hug and helping her inside their home.

'Thanks, darling. Oh it is so good to be back.'

'Hey, Steph, pass me that case. I'll take it in.' He strode across to Steph, who was struggling trying to lift Kate's luggage whilst holding the boot open.

'So good of you to bring her home. How can I ever thank you?'

'We've been friends forever, no thanks needed. I'd do it again in a heartbeat.' Steph smiled back at John.

Steph had moved south, and although they only met up a few times a year now, Kate knew that she could rely on her for anything, time and again proving their friendship had been built to withstand many of the hard knocks that came between people throughout life.

'I've got the spare bedroom ready for you.'

Steph looked at her friend's husband, and her heart skipped a beat. She had a lot of time for this man. He was the best thing to ever have happened to her beloved friend. She realised with horror that actually she thought more of him than she ought to. Ashamed at the betrayal, Steph kept her distance from him, avoiding the usual bear hug he gave out so warmly. He gave her an odd look as she went into the house, without getting near enough for him to greet her as he normally did. John put her aloofness down to the stress of recent times and tiredness after the journey and thought no more about it.

Kate shot her friend a questioning look, a fleeting vision of John and Steph together came and went as quickly as it had appeared, leaving her flustered; she wasn't ready to see that vision just yet.

The three of them chatted easily over coffee and biscuits. Kate had been away from her family and friends longer than they had envisaged and they were all so relieved to have her home again and seemingly in better health. The only proviso that her doctors had given her was to take her medication. Kate had reassured them that of course she would and they had discharged her from their care without a second thought, certified as sane, and the section she had been detained under now lifted.

Kate had chosen to sleep alone again that night. She wasn't up to being close to John for that length of time. She had managed to cope with his embrace and his kisses, but the thought of spending a whole night in the same bed when she had been used to sleeping on her own for weeks was too much. John had sadly agreed and took himself into the bedroom opposite. With Steph occupying the guest room, the night took over and they succumbed to tiredness, each lost in their own thoughts.

Kate settled back into their bedroom, and it had been transformed back to a neat and tidy haven, her family working hard to clear up the chaos Kate had left behind her the day her mind had broken into a million pieces. Kate looked around and took it all in. It was comforting and disturbing at the same time. Her possessions had been returned to the room but, in the hands of others, now occupied different places. The Duran Duran framed poster from Shepherd's Bush now hung in a space on the right hand side of the windows. A large framed photo of Kate and John had been placed on the left, leaving a blank place opposite from whence it came. Knick knacks had been set on the shelves opposite her bed. The ornaments nudged at her senses as they sat awkwardly in different positions. Kate couldn't really feel at ease with these changes, but she was thankful to whoever had tidied up the carnage she had wrought on her beloved home.

Her mobile phone buzzed and lit up with a text message.

'Adam.' His name felt good on her lips and she spoke it gently as she picked her phone up from the bedside table.

She felt a pang of guilt at the way he made her feel. Since the accident, her feelings for him had refused to fade into the background where they belonged. In hospital, she had the luxury of being able to think of him as more than a friend, trying to remember the time when they had been lovers in their previous lives.

'Kate. I'm so happy you're home. I need to see you soon as possible. A.'

She answered back straight away then switched her phone off before he had chance to reply. Kate only had one thing on her mind as she allowed herself to fall into a deep sleep, and she slept soundly in her own bed, unaware that her husband was dreaming of another woman. Steph dreamt in the guest room, uncomfortable realisations tugged at the edge of her senses as she tossed and turned trying to fight them off. Four individual souls drowning in affairs, love, lust, entangled the four and joined them in betrayal. Their earthly hosts could do nothing to stop events that had been set in motion. It had been written thousands of years before, as inevitable as the rising of the sun in the morning.

'I'm going to the stables,' Kate announced after breakfast.

Steph had left early that morning, making the excuse that she had a ton of work to catch up on after taking the day off to collect Kate. In reality, she could have stayed much longer, but after the vivid images her brain had served up overnight she could hardly look her friends in the eye. They hadn't questioned her, for which she was grateful, as telling lies did not sit easily on her conscience. She needed to get away and back to her life as quickly as possible. Steph didn't know what was going on. Blaming stress and tiredness after the journey helped to ease her mind a little. She had never felt such a strong attraction to a man for a long time, and the fact that he was her best friend's husband was very disturbing. She made a pact with herself that she would keep her distance. Steph had no idea that as she left, John was watching her leave, feeling exactly the same way about her.

'Did you hear me?' Kate nudged John, who sat opposite her reading the paper.

'Sorry?'

'I said, I'm going to the stables. I'll be back before lunch.'

'I don't suppose there's any point me arguing with you is there?' John looked up at his wife, who had already left the table to go and put her coat on. 'Don't forget, you're not as strong as you were, take it easy.'

'I will, of course I will. I'm getting straight off. I can't stop thinking about Ebony. I've not seen her since...' Kate's voice trailed off as painful memories flooded back. 'I mean, I'm going now. I'll be back by lunchtime, ok.'

John did nothing to dissuade her, having known Kate long enough to know that the more he objected the more she would put her foot down. He watched her go. Strange things were happening, but he could not put his finger on the change. One thing he was certain of was that Kate was not only missing her horse. He had a niggling thought that it was Adam that was the main reason she was so desperate to get back to the stables. He also realised with a frown that as he thought of Steph, he had become aware that he was more turned on than he had been for a long while.

Kate. John. Steph. Adam. Four individual minds, four human beings, four higher level spirits fighting against their earthly hosts. Kate and her lover, Mars, may have banished one demon to another galaxy, but the fight for the path of righteousness, the way into the light had only just begun. A battle won. A war begun.

The Radio

February 2016

February flew past in a blur. John and I settled into a new routine, and I assured him that I was fine as I took over my duties at the stables once more. Adam and I had talked in depth about the accident. We had both seen the figure on the track and neither of us could come up with an explanation as to who it could have been or how it was physically impossible that whoever it was had vanished into thin air. Adam had been at the inquiry which had taken place whilst I was in hospital. There had been a call to get the race banned, and eventually it had been decided that it was a one-off freak accident, but future races would be supervised more strictly, with spectators kept behind fences away from the actual course.

John had asked Adam to speak on behalf of the family as he felt that my accident would be held up as a bad example and a tool for the naysayers to get the race banned. He knew that I would be furious if they used me as a scapegoat.

Gradually my physical health improved. My mental health was still fragile but getting stronger with each day that passed. I had decided to keep quiet about the things that were happening all around me on a daily basis. I was certified as sane, but if I divulged information about who I really was and the reality that ordinary mortals did not understand and could not see, I felt sure if I tried to explain they would send me straight back to hospital and increase my medication.

Adam and I had talked, and things were getting back to normal. We had reached a mutual understanding that whatever had passed between us would remain unspoken, our friendship intact and my marriage safe once again. Adam had started dating for the first time since I had known him and I was glad. That episode was now behind us. My head and my heart knew who he was and that was enough. I had been ridiculed by the other gods because of my love for Adonis and I knew that it was in the past. Adonis, for his part, let Adam be in control of his own body once again and we had mentally waved goodbye over the last few weeks until he had disappeared altogether.

My Ebony was fit and well; she had been treated like royalty whilst I had been away. Another one of the stable hands had been exercising her on my behalf, and her muscles rippled and her coat shone once again. I had decided to keep to the indoor school arena for a while until I got my confidence back and overcame the fear I had when I first got back in the saddle. A few minutes later and we were trotting around the arena as if I'd never been away. After half an hour, I was exhausted.

'Oh, I'm so unfit,' I called across to Adam, who had come in to watch me, and I suspected to be on hand in case I had a wobble.

'You'll soon get it back again. Looked great.'

'I'm going to call it a day; got a headache coming on.'

'Yes, do that. Otherwise I'll have John to answer to.'

'He fusses. I know what I'm doing,' I shot back at him.

'He cares, Kate, that's all.'

I swung my leg over and hopped down to join him on the sand. 'Well done, my darling.' I patted Ebony on her neck and she turned to nuzzle me in acknowledgement.

'You two, it's so good to see you back together. She was not herself when you were away. I swear she knew something was wrong. Good to have you back, Kate.' Adam smiled and left us to it.

I threw the reins over her neck and turned to lead her out of the school. Ebony started to follow but suddenly stopped dead in her tracks and pulled me back.

'Whoa, what's the matter, girl? It's ok, come on,' I tried to placate her with no joy.

She pulled back and reared up, whinnying. Something had spooked, her but I couldn't see anything untoward.

A white flash blinded me and sent me down to the ground holding my head. The pain came sharp and fast, cutting into my head. I groped around on the floor, trying to find Ebony's reins. There was nothing there. The sand felt cold and scratchy on my hands. I could hear Ebony snorting as I groped around the arena floor to try and take hold of her reins again.

'Adam,' I shouted. 'Help.'

Nothing. I crawled towards the edge of the arena, hardly able to see where I was going. Eventually I managed to stand up shakily. What the hell had just happened? Ebony was standing where I left her, nostrils wide, eyes on stalks. I was transported back to Boxing Day and the accident. I looked up and saw the outline of a figure in the entrance of the arena. I squinted, to try and see who it was. It disappeared and I was left alone once more. I had the uneasy feeling that the badness was coming back. The freedom I had felt since being home from my sanctuary was in danger of being taken away again.

I brushed the sand off and walked over to Ebony, soothing her with my words and stroking her neck until she was calm again. This time, I had been luckier and had not sustained an injury other than being momentarily blinded by the flash of light. The figure, the tension in the atmosphere - all in all I was as spooked as my equine friend, but I was stronger than I had been a few weeks ago.

'Come on, let's get you back to the stable, I'll give you a nice brush down and we can forget what just happened. It's ok, my friend, there's nothing to be scared of. Whatever it was has gone now. You're safe, I promise.'

I led her back through the yard and to her stable. Fresh water and hay net awaited and I brushed her down as she ate her feed. I still felt a bit spooked as I tried to figure out who it had been and what had caused the flash in my eyes. I was better prepared to cope with the weird shit these days. Once again, I decided to keep it to myself. I would write it in my diary, and maybe things would become clear later.

Adam was nowhere to be seen when I set off for home. I drove back in silence, rubbing my temples. A nagging pain had settled across my forehead, and it was causing me to squint as I drove. I was glad my home was only a short distance away. Home again with no other strange happenings. John was waiting for me, my lunch ready on the table as I walked in. This man was my saviour, he never gave up on me. I loved him dearly, and whatever we were now facing, I knew that we would face it stronger together. If and when the time came for us to part, we would always remain friends; whatever the future held for all of us, it had already been written.

As a result of my awakening, I was in possession of the year of my death. It didn't frighten me. I had stared death in the face on more than one occasion and believe me, there were much worse things than death. It had come calling last year and I had kicked its arse into touch. The grim reaper had backed off in reverence to a force greater than the scythe he wielded. Once he cut down my earthly body, I would be free to return to my heavenly home and family on Mount Olympus. I was, in a funny way, looking forward to it, but for the time being, for the next few years, I would enjoy what was left of my life with my earthly husband John. I would keep observing the human race and their planet. I would do what I could along with all the other deities. We would try and bring peace to the planet. We would try and overthrow the badness and lead by example. I would follow the signs given to me from a higher level. I was soon to meet more of my kind. It was lucky for me that I could not see very far into the future because I thought I was over the worst, when it turned out that being in a coma and surviving was nothing compared to the trouble that was heading my way.

So, I kept quiet and kept a secret diary, noting all the 'coincidences' and just plain weird shit that was happening more and more frequently. I was being instructed on how to live by a higher force; I followed the instructions as far as I could. I listened to the radio and heard my angels speaking directly to me, and I answered them using the same method, across the airwaves.

February was a month of recuperation. Both John and I had worked hard to recover from the shaky start that 2016 had brought us. We worked hard to bring some normality back into our lives once again. He had moved back into our bedroom and my claustrophobia had abated. We enjoyed being close again and our home had come back to life. We were looking forward to getting back into the garden in the springtime. We had a large lawn which gave way to orchard at the far end, and elderly apple trees which had survived for over a hundred years spread their branches over meadow grass full of cowslips and bluebells. Neither of us were big gardeners, but we did keep it neat and tidy and it flowed naturally as an extension of our house. The exterior was as welcoming as the interior, a lazy welcoming environment filled with love. That was the atmosphere we had created for ourselves and our families. Caitlin and Charlotte visited regularly and we had all relaxed and let down our guard these last few weeks. How wrong we were. The evil was just biding its time until it paid us another visit.

I had to switch certain songs off when they played over the airwaves into our home. John was used to my not being able to listen to certain bands and switching the radio off mid song. It was one of my quirks that had both annoyed and amused him when we first got together.

'Get out of our house, you bitch,' I swore at the radio as I flicked the switch off.

'Bit harsh, Kate,' John replied surprised at my tone of voice.

'Hmmm, I just can't be doing with her. She sets my teeth on edge every time I hear her,' I replied, unapologetic in my actions.

'She's won a lot of awards…'

'I know she's popular and, yes - I know she has a good voice, but I wish she would cheer the fuck up. Gets on my wick, moaning all the time.'

John came up behind me and gave me one of his bear hugs. 'You are a funny one.'

'You wouldn't have me any other way would you?' I grinned up at him.

'I guess not.' He smiled back at me. 'Love you, Kate.'

'Love you, too. Are you still off out with your mate later?'

'Yeah, he wants to look at a new car. We will probably get something to eat whilst we're out too. Is that ok?'

'Yes fine, it'll give me a chance to get some housework done without you under my feet.'

'You sure you're up to being on your own?'

'Stop fretting, I'm fine,' I promised.

I had the music on full blast, local radio providing the soundtrack to hoovering, polishing and sorting out some of the mess I had made all those weeks ago. I was impressed with my singing as I listened and sang along to one awesome song after another. The Eagles, Duran Duran, Queen, Madness, as I listened I realised with a jolt that every single song was directed at me. I was so happy that the airwaves were accompanying me in perfect harmony. By the time a couple of hours of this phenomenon had gone by I was almost predicting which song would come next. Eighties hour, next song, '*Venus*'. Oh, yes indeed. Yes, I bloody well am. I am Venus. Laughing loudly, I polished and tidied, '*I Want To Break Free*'. Freddie filled the kitchen with his fabulous voice. I channelled him as I vacuumed, a little hysterical at the weirdness that was happening.

Enough housework I decided. I made myself a coffee, locked the back door and went upstairs to have a rest. I put the TV on. A James bond film, Casino Royale. Perfect. Daniel Craig to admire as Bond. I was a happy lady. I was in control. Nothing could come between me and my family again. We were winning in our campaign. They may have sent another demon to spook us, but it had held no fear for me. My beautiful Ebony had soon calmed down. I was fine. She was fine. My family were all fine. I nodded off happily, secure in the knowledge that we were protected by all the gods in heaven and on earth.

The Descent

Friday 4th March, 2016

'*There Must Be An Angel*' blared out, and I sang along with Annie Lennox and giggled. There were people trying to get into my house. My logical mind told me that I knew them. Was it my husband? My cousins? My children? I didn't really know. I knew that the evil had passed me on the stairs, because James Bond had told me so. I couldn't let these people in because what if I didn't really know them? What if they were demons in disguise?

Bang bang bang on the windows and the doors. No. I am not answering. Go away. Leave me alone. You are not who you say you are. I am being summoned back upstairs. I am scared for the first time since I left hospital. The demons are trying to possess me as they have possessed my family. I have to get away from them so that I can save everyone else. It passed me on the stairs. It is up there waiting for me. How can I protect myself?

The bedroom is empty. I have made it upstairs; the evil there had been easy to get past. I recited The Lord's Prayer over and over and it shrank away, leaving nothing but a bad smell.

I put my Duran boys on the DVD, *Sing Blue Silver* played, the familiar songs and images filled the room. These were my demigods. I was safe with them watching over me. I don't know how long I laid there because when I woke up it was growing dark outside and there were three people stood by my bed.

'Who… who… who…?' I stammered.

'It's ok, Kate, we've come to help you.' I vaguely recognised the man.

'Who… who… whooo?'

'Kate, it's ok. I'm here.'

'John?'

'Yes, it's me. You're going to be ok. These people have come to help you. Come downstairs with us.'

'I don't want to. Who are they? Are they bad?' I struggle to reply, taking deep gulps of air. Scared again. I was so scared.

'They won't hurt you, I promise. I had to get help, Kate You had locked yourself in. You wouldn't let anyone in.'

'Because I didn't know if I could trust them. Can I come downstairs? Is it safe?' I looked up at John warily; could I trust him? I didn't know.

'I promise. They've come to help. You've been badly let down by the mental health team, Kate. We won't let that happen again. We need you to come downstairs so we can find a solution that will help you. We think you've had some flashbacks to your accident.' John took my hand and helped me up from the bed. 'Come on, sweetheart, let's go down, you gave us such a scare. I promise it will be ok.'

My hair stuck to my forehead, my cheeks were streaked wet with tears, and I had no idea why I was in bed and my house was full of strange people.

I let John guide me downstairs and into the kitchen. I sat at the table looking blankly from him to the other two men who stood uncomfortably in the background.

'Kate, we have to talk about you getting help. You had a psychotic episode this afternoon and scared us all to death.'

'I was singing. To the radio.' I rubbed my hands through my hair and tried to remember the events of the afternoon. 'You had gone out I think?'

'That's right. Do you remember what happened after that?'

'Not really. I think I've got bits of my memory missing,' I answered slowly. 'Things were looking in at me, something passed me on the stairs. What was it, John? What has happened to me?'

'We think it's stress. You've held everything in and been so strong and, I think you've stopped taking your tablets. I found a full bottle in the bin. Kate, you shouldn't have stopped taking them; they were helping to keep you stable.'

'No. No, they weren't. They were keeping me from remembering who I am. I don't need them. I'm not taking them. You can't make me. I won't do it.'

'I had to break in; you'd locked all the doors. I couldn't get in. Jesus, Kate, you had us all so worried. The girls were here but I sent them home; I didn't want them to see you like this. Charlotte's baby is due soon. The stress of this isn't good for her. We need to get you sorted. You were screaming all sorts at me when I came upstairs. I couldn't make any sense of it.'

'I'm not mad, John, I'm not. I know what I saw and heard. The radio. It told me. The things come through the radio. You don't know who we really are. I do, I know everything.'

'Kate, you need to calm down. We won't let you down again. We want you to go back to rehab. Will you do that?'

'Where to? I will if I can go back to the one I was in before. Can I do that please?'

'Not this time. There are no beds there at the moment. There aren't any in our county either. I'm afraid it's further away than last time. It's north, about three hours away.'

'I don't want to go north. If I have to go away I want to go back to where I was. They were nice there. I think I just need a rest again. That's it, isn't it? I just need sleep. There's nothing else wrong with me. I'm just tired.'

'I'm sure it will be just as nice at the new one. Please, Kate. Just for a few days. We're all so worried. You must take the medication. It will help you. Do you promise to do that?'

The other two men were taking notes. I vaguely recognised them. I looked from one to the other and back to John again.

'You promise it will be the same as the other one?'

They all nodded. One of the doctors pushed a form in front of me. 'Sign there, please.'

I hesitated before signing. I had a bad feeling about this and I was sure that I was in the presence of evil. I could not put my finger on it. I was aware that I was babbling. John and the doctors faded in and out of my vision. The doorbell rang. Three people dressed in green came in. Someone had packed a case for me. I felt sick. I was speaking Spanish. I was giggling. I was throwing up bile into a cardboard receptacle. I was in a car. Red. Red. Red. Green. Green. Green. It was dark. The lights outside. John. Not there. Dark. Bad. Dark. Traffic lights. Sat nav. Are we there? No. My mind was spiralling up, then down again, way down. Where had reality gone to? Every time I looked at the sat nav it had moved back half an hour, we had been on this road before. I struggled to keep level. Ugh. Sick again. Scratching at the card, flecks of paper stuck under my fingernails.

Laughing with the people in green, Janet? Who was Janet? Moves? What? They were laughing at me, we were singing '*Moves like Jagger'*. Moobs like Jagger, I was giggling but tears streamed down my cheeks relentlessly, and I was so scared. I didn't understand. The night flashed by outside. Two hours gone. No. One hour gone. Red. Red. Red. Danger. Are we there yet?

Yes. It's ok. Here. The car has stopped. I don't know where we are but we have stopped.

A high fence. A bright light. Wire. Can we go in yet? I'm so tired, I'm struggling to stay awake. Sleep deprivation. Nasty. Why are we sat here in the dark? What is happening?

I look at the floor, and it is covered with bits of cardboard, all ripped up into tiny pieces. I look from one green man to the other. What happened? Don't worry about it, they assure me. Have I made this mess? I can't remember. I'm struggling to stay centred. If I let go, I will die. I know I will. I just want to find reality again. I can't sleep until I find it. Who will help me? I'm terrified.

Half an hour until they let us in and we follow an unspeaking member of staff up the stairs. Every step takes all my effort; how can it be so hard to climb a few stairs? I don't like it. I have a bad feeling. I want to go home. They have ripped me out of my home to bring me to this place. I'm scared. My heart has been torn from my body; I have left it at home. I am starting to panic.

'I don't know what's happening,' one green says to the other.

'Don't leave me here,' I beg them. 'I don't like it. Please take me home again.'

They don't speak. We are hustled into a small waiting room. Bang. A door slams. Bang another door slams, making me jump. I don't feel safe.

'I'm so tired, I hope these doors don't slam all night,' I speak out loud but my words fall on deaf ears. I see a look of concern flash across their faces and then it is gone.

The door opens and a tall thin woman comes in; she has curly hair and an Irish accent.

'You can leave her here now. I'll show you out.' She addresses my travelling companions and ignores me.

I get the feeling that they don't want to leave me here either, but there is nothing they can do about it.

'Please take me home?' I plead with them. They ignore me and disappear behind the door, which bangs with such a force that it hurts my ears.

I sit alone with my suitcase. The room is tiny, like an examination room. It has a red leather chair and settee, red curtains and red carpet. The walls are dingy white and need decorating. The carpet is threadbare and has unidentifiable stains on it. The bad feeling I had has been replaced by blind panic. I am in trouble here. I am lost. I cannot stay here. I will stay the night and go home tomorrow. That settled in my head, I concentrate on staying awake because I know if I let go and sleep I am lost forever. If I go to sleep now, I will die.

The door opened and the curly-haired woman came back in. She had very pale skin and dark eyes which studied me closely as I picked up my case.

I held out my hand, 'I'm Kate.'

'Yes. I know. Follow me.' She ignored my greeting and held the door open impatiently. 'I will take you to your room, you can wait there until the doctor is ready to see you.'

'Will it be long? I just need to sleep. I'm so tired. I've come here for rest, that's all I need. Rest.'

My voice sounds tinny and detached. I shake my head to try and focus on reality again. The level, I need to be on the right level. The woman turns left along the corridor where I came in and then right to a long corridor with numbered doors on either side. There is a blue armchair at the far end. It is positioned in front of a window. A sign reads 'Obs Room' and I can see a computer lit up within it. She strides ahead of me so I have to almost run to keep up, then stops abruptly and points at an open door on the left. Room 11.

'This is your room. Wait in there.'

'Ok, thank you. Do you know how long it will be please?'

She has already turned her back on me and is gone, leaving my words hanging in the air.

I take in my new surroundings. There is a single bed which lies along the left hand side of the room. At its foot, a small sink with the same type of taps that I had become familiar with in my happy rehab place. Behind the door is a built-in closet with the door wide open. I put my case inside and try to close it, but it swings open again; no catch to keep it shut. Opposite the door and half way up the wall is a window probably measuring three foot square. It has frosted glass at the bottom and a clear rectangle of glass at the top on a catch which has been propped open, making the room feel cold and hostile. The ledge is about a foot wide. Below the window, a radiator that has been boxed in, and when I go to touch it, it is cold as ice. To my right, and running alongside the wall to the right hand corner of the room, is a unit which has drawers both sides and acts as a type of desk. On top of the desk are a couple of towels. A large notice board above the desk is blank except for a few random animal stickers and scratch marks gouged out as if the previous occupant has been climbing the walls. The only other furniture is a bedside table. The carpet is mottled purple, the walls the same off-white of the waiting room. I sit myself down on the bed to wait. The bed squeaks and is unforgiving; a thin hard plastic-covered mattress lies under a threadbare fitted sheet and the thinnest quilt I have ever seen. The cover is pale pink and stained. One pillow, its case the same state as the rest of the bedding. A large picture of a beautiful waterfall with a rainbow cutting through it is the only thing in the place that I can look at without feeling a sense of dread. My fears are materialising before me. I don't possess a watch and I have left my phone at home. I estimate it must be around midnight although time seems to be playing games with my mind. My memory is like a DVD that has been paused then clicked on forward, then back again. I feel horrible, sand in my eyes, sweaty, my breath is stale and I can smell vomit. Another half an hour goes past. I can hardly keep my eyes open but daren't go to sleep. I decide to have a wash and find my toiletries. Someone has kindly packed my expensive skin care products and shower gel and a scrunchie, but no toothbrush or toothpaste. I try and remember to ask for one as soon as someone comes. My skin feels lovely after using the creamy cleanser. The hot cloth soothes my face and for a moment I am transported back to our beautiful home, and breathing in the familiar eucalyptus comforts me and momentarily clears my head. The illusion ends when I pick up a towel to dry myself with. It is threadbare like the rest of the linen, hard, scratchy, and worst of all has a huge dirty mark across it. That's when the awful reality sinks in. Nobody here so far has spoken to me like a human being. The environment is filthy. I am absolutely petrified. My legs are shaking and I peer around the door to look up and down the corridor. It is deserted, and I vaguely hear the sound of someone coughing.

'Hello.'

Silence.

I decide that I need to ring my on-call team. I vaguely remember a name from earlier. I will ask for him; he will help me. They will have the number here; they can find it on my notes. I take some deep breaths and grab my pillow, a plan now forming in my head and calming me down. I would sit in the blue armchair at the end of the corridor so that the staff would see me and I would be able to make my phone call. I would stay awake. There was a clock behind the glass of the 'Obs Room' showing that it was nearly two-thirty in the morning. Ridiculous. I had no choice now but to wait. But tomorrow, I would go home and get some sleep there. I'd been dragged all this way because I was suffering from sleep deprivation and here it was, the middle of the night and I was still straining to stay awake.

The woman reappeared. She beckoned me to follow her again. The doctor had eventually sent for me and subjected me to an interrogation before they allowed me to go back to my room. It was three in the morning when I climbed, exhausted, into bed. I still hardly dared go to sleep and lay staring at the ceiling. A red flashing caught my eye. On the ceiling was a round disc which I assumed was a smoke alarm. It was flashing red intermittently. I blinked a couple of times and it blinked back. Red three times. I blinked again. Green three times. The lights were coming from various parts of the disc. I knew that whatever forces had followed me were watching. The disc was communicating with my higher being. I was in danger. Three red. Danger. My brain registered the signs. This place was where matters were decided. I knew I had to be on my guard. Eventually I allowed myself to let down my guard, checking with the lights on the ceiling that it was safe. They blinked, three green, safe.

The bed was unforgiving, the hard plastic creaked as I turned over. Doors continued to slam for what seemed like most of the night and my nerves were in pieces. I wanted to go home. I had never felt so desperate and frightened in my whole life. Eventually blackness crept over my body and smothered me until I fell defeated by its strength, swallowed up into an abyss. Then the nightmare began in earnest.

Medication

Saturday 5th March, 2016

I woke with a start. My neck hurt. My head was sore. I ached all over. I lay quietly, allowing my brain to catch up. My eyes felt gritty, like I had slept for a week. The awful reality of where I was dawned on me and I caught my breath as it flooded through my senses. Foreboding, the air in the room was heavy, weighing me down as I struggled to rouse myself. I could hear people in the corridor, footsteps drawing near, hesitated by my door and then carried on past. Why did I feel so scared? I would speak to my family today, or the team who had sent me here. I would be able to go home by tomorrow at the latest. That thought in my mind, I decided to get up and freshen up. More activity outside my door as I washed and found fresh clothes. I checked out the contents of my suitcase. I estimated I had enough clothes for a week, more than enough. There were trackie bottoms, vest tops, a couple of soft jumpers, two pairs of pyjamas, my short pink fleecy robe and for some reason, my fringed black knitted shawl that I tended to wear for funerals. What? Why had they packed that? I stared at the contents and my brain registered that things had been packed for a reason I was as of yet unaware.

I felt much calmer now, fresh, clean clothes, ready to set the wheels in motion so I could go home. I decided that as it was Saturday, they probably wouldn't be able to organise anything today but I would leave on Monday. That in mind, I took some deep breaths and headed out into the corridor. A short stocky woman with glasses and short mousy hair stopped me. She wore two white lanyards; one which bore her name and a photograph and another which bore a number three. She turned the number over when she saw me looking at it.

'You arrived last night didn't you? Room 11? You need to go to the clinic for medication.'

'Oh. Well, no, I don't think I need to do that because I don't take any meds in the morning.'

'It's down the corridor that way and to the right.' She pointed in the direction I had come in last night.

'I think there has been a misunderstanding. I don't have medication in the morning.'

'I haven't got time to stand here and argue with you. Go to the clinic.'

The sense of foreboding returned and I brushed it aside. Obviously there had been a mix up. I could sort it out easily enough. They would have my prescription, I was sure that I had handed it over last night when I explained to the doctor about the tablets that they had prescribed me when I had been in my happy place. Yes. This would be sorted out easily and I told myself off. It was just the stress of yesterday that was making me feel this way.

'Ok, well that's fine. Sorry, I'll go straight away and sort it out.' I smiled at the woman.

She scowled and left me to it. I watched her go and wondered if I had just been unlucky meeting three staff who were lacking in bedside manner. Surely they weren't all like this. I had tried to remember their names; I knew that there had been a tall Irish doctor, but I had only glimpsed her badge. The woman who had just left me was called Jane.

I would remember her. I shook my head and followed her directions to the end of the long corridor.

Each door had a number. I was number eleven, in between twelve on the left and ten on the right. I wandered up the corridor, taking in my surroundings. The door opposite was number five, then six, the numbers going up on the left, seven, eight, and down on the right, twelve, eleven, ten, nine. Some doors were ajar, some tight shut. On the right, opposite number eight, were two doors that stated they were bathrooms. A laundry room on the left. I could hear people talking. I reached the end of the corridor and turned right as Jane had told me to. There was a queue of around six or seven people in front of me, presumably waiting for the clinic.

'Next.' A thickset man with glasses stood behind a hatch. The woman at the front of the queue held out her hand and he passed her a small pot and a plastic cup of water. She put the pot to her lips and threw her head back, emptying the contents into her mouth all at once. A swig from the cup, a gulp, and she was done. She ambled off leaving behind nothing but the smell of an unwashed body, the stale odour making me retch as she passed. Her clothes were tight, a grubby t-shirt riding up over her lower back leaving mottled rolls of skin on show. Her jogging bottoms were stained, her dark curly hair matted against her scalp. I smiled at her as she passed. Her face was blank, expressionless and she disappeared from view as she went back down the corridor from where I had come.

The rest of the patients in front of me followed suit, each one going up to the hatch in turn, responding to their name being called. None of them spoke. The man behind the hatch barely made eye contact as he dished out the medication. Finally it was my turn. I would explain that I didn't need any. There had obviously been a mistake.

'Morning…'

'Room number?'

'Eleven. But if you check my notes, you'll see that I don't take anything in the morning. I have my tablets before I go to bed. I don't need anything else, thank you.'

'Take this,' he replied, ignoring my response.

'I don't need to, thank you. Can you just update my notes, please? If it's written on your paper, it's clearly a mistake. Thank you.' I turned to go but found my path blocked by Jane, the woman who had been outside my door earlier.

'Take your medication, then you can go to the dining room for breakfast. Hurry up, they serve until nine, but if you're late you won't get any.'

'Sorry, I was just explaining to your colleague... Nick is it?' I peered at his name badge. 'Nick, sorry about this. I've only just arrived last night you see. There has been a mistake and I think I will be going home very shortly.'

'Take the medication please,' he answered.

'I can't, it doesn't have my name on it. It's not mine.'

Nick produced a box and thrust it through the hatch under my nose. The printed label had the name of a drug on it that I'd never heard of; the dosage two tablets three times daily. My name was printed at the bottom.

'I don't know what they are for? I've never taken that before. What is it?'

Nick and Jane gave me a look which said they were less than happy with my response.

'Are you refusing to take the medication?' Jane grabbed hold of my left elbow in a vice-like grip. 'We don't take no for an answer here. Now, do the sensible thing and shut up and take it. If you don't, I will have to call the team.'

I tried to pull my arm away but she had a firm hold on me. 'You're hurting me. Please let go.'

'Are you going to take the tablets?'

'Well, no but...'

She signalled something to Nick and he took out a radio from his pocket. 'Assistance required on the first floor. Patient uncooperative.'

I looked at them both in disbelief. I wasn't being awkward, I just knew my rights. I knew that I had the right to refuse. I had learnt an awful lot about the rights of people sectioned under the Mental Health Act during my last stay down south and they were breaking the law.

'I need to speak to my local team. Please let go of me. There's been a mistake.'

'Are you going to take the fucking tablets or not?' Jane spat at me.

'No. I'm not. I know my rights,' I spat back at her. I hadn't wanted to have an argument but there was no way I was putting a drug into my body when it wasn't prescribed and when I had no idea what it was for.

'Urgent assistance required. First floor clinic,' Nick said again into his radio.

Jane held both my hands behind my back. The door at the top of the stairs opened. The team had arrived. I counted eight of them. Really? I needed all these people to restrain me?

One of the team addressed me by name, the first time anyone had done that since I arrived. 'Kate, we're going to take you to the isolation room unless you comply and take the medication. Do you understand?'

'Yes, I understand. I don't want any trouble, but I know that legally I don't have to take the meds.'

'Last chance. Take the pills.'

'No.'

Jane and a member of the team took an arm each and frogmarched me back down the corridor past my room, past the 'Obs station' and into a room on the left at the far end of the corridor. As they dragged me inside, another team member approached, and he had a syringe on a cardboard tray.

'No. Please. I don't want to be injected. I'm not being awkward. I just don't want to take drugs that aren't on my notes. Please? Why won't you listen?'

The fear and panic rose within me and I knew that no matter what I said, nothing would now make a difference. The evil had got to these people. They all wore white shirts and dark trousers. I tried to look at each of their name badges so I could report them to my family and my team from home.

'This isn't right. You're all breaking the law,' I screamed.

'Lie down on the floor,' Jane said and gave me a shove.

I had no choice but to do as they were telling me. They pushed me on the floor face down, one member either side of me kneeling on my legs, another pair at my head, each holding an arm. I lay on my front, my body in the shape of a cross. Jane took the syringe off the tray.

'We are injecting you because you are spiralling. Your condition has worsened and you refused to comply. The injection is to prevent you from injuring yourself and to protect the staff and other patients from your violent behaviour.'

I was powerless to stop them. The needle only stung for a moment. I wasn't scared of injections but I was beyond petrified at the situation I found myself in now. I was in trouble. I needed my phone call. But for now, the sedation had started to take effect and I felt myself slipping away into unconsciousness, vaguely aware of the staff leaving and the sound of the door being banged shut behind them. My first day in this place hadn't gone exactly as planned. I struggled in vain to resist the drug that was flowing through my body. I lay on my back trying to focus. Red. Red. Red. The disc on the ceiling blinked at me. I blinked back three times before the sedation robbed me of my senses.

I was cold and hungry when I eventually came round. My stomach cramped painfully and my neck was once again twinging. I took stock of my situation. Not good. I got up off the floor, my body complaining at the treatment it had received. Everything creaked and ached, I wasn't getting any younger. I was alone once again. There was a single solitary red padded chair in the corner, the only other item in the room apart from myself. A TV monitor looked down on me showing images from a camera attached to the ceiling in the far left hand corner. According to the clock on the wall, I had been asleep for six hours. Unbelievable. There was a window which had frosted glass, similar to the one in my room except it had bars across it. I noticed from the images on the TV screen that the room was L-shaped, a feature I had not taken in when the team had forced me in here. Around the corner of the 'L' on the back wall there was a white iron studded door with a circular window like a porthole. I shuddered. It looked like something from a horror film. Despite my misgivings, my curiosity got the better of me and I went to investigate. I grabbed the handle and it swung open. It was a cell, about half the size of the rest of the room. The walls were green with a marbled effect. On closer inspection, there were scratches in the surface; the white door was covered in them too. On the floor in the corner was a cardboard receptacle which presumably was to urinate in and a long mat which I took to be instead of a bed. I quickly retreated, not wanting the door to shut. The sense of evil in the cell was overwhelming. I couldn't breathe and I had a vision of the door clanging shut as I tried to escape. I did not want to be trapped in there forever. I backed out and gave the door a push to close it behind me. It was heavy, I was weak, but I used my body weight to lean on it and it closed with a thud. There was another screen above the door of the cell. I had not noticed it when I went in. The TV lit up the interior. The cardboard vessel looked small and almost like a small animal. A rat. No, not a rat, a guinea pig. What? Where had that come from? My mind was so confused. My stomach growled and I remembered that I hadn't eaten anything for a long time. I couldn't remember the last meal I'd had. Maybe breakfast yesterday? Everything was so jumbled up in my head.

I walked to the door. I was desperate for the toilet but didn't want to use the pot in the cell. There was nobody to be seen. I shouted for someone to come. Silence greeted me once more. Opposite the isolation room were two doors which stated they were toilets. I banged on the door in a bid to alert someone to my predicament and to my surprise it swung open. So, I had been out of control and spiralling I think they called it and a danger to myself and others, yet they had left the door unlocked. The new information did nothing to help my confusion. The only thing I knew for sure was that I needed the toilet. I stood in a quandary, what should I do? If I wet myself they would think I had done it on purpose, but if I left the room and went to the toilet, they would think I had tried to escape. My body made the decision for me and I made a dash for the toilet opposite.

The toilet was in keeping with the rest of the place, filthy, but I was in no position to be fussy and sat down with great relief. I flushed, washed my hands and dried them on a paper towel which I deposited in an overflowing bin.

Leaving the toilet, still alone, I took the opportunity to have a look around this end of the corridor. A locked door was on the left, a small rectangle of frosted glass let in some light. A sign saying 'Lock it. Secure it' in bold red letters was stuck directly underneath the glass. As I tiptoed past the toilets and level with the 'Obs Room' a strange sign in yellow that said 'Oxygen' was stuck on the wall. Next to that, a red box which said 'Fire' above it. To my left, another corridor with a bathroom on either side and yet more bedrooms. I followed the corridor, past the two bathrooms, past the bedrooms to a door at the end. The room it opened into was large and airy. It had settees all around the edge, a window and a door at each end. On the wall adjacent to the entrance was a large television boxed in behind a thick glass panel with a wooden frame. The furnishings were plush, purple velvet and a cream carpet. I found it strange in contrast to the rest of the ward. This room was the polar opposite to the squalor I had so far witnessed. I wondered who was allowed to use it and why it was so utterly different.

Aware that I was not supposed to be out of isolation, I ran back to the room before anyone came and caught me. I had already had one injection for 'non-compliance' and I didn't relish another one. I needn't have worried. It seemed that I had been forgotten. Another hour went by and still no sign of any staff. I decided that I would risk it and go back to my room. The ward seemed deserted as I tentatively made my way back. I sat on my bed wondering what to do for the best.

I could hear voices coming from outside. They were male voices, laughing and talking loudly. I had to see who was making the noise. The desk provided a step up to the windowsill, so I balanced precariously on the ledge and peered out to see a group of three guys kicking a football around. One of them looked up and noticed me staring down at them.

'Hey there. What you looking at, lady?'

'Hi. I just wondered who was making all the noise,' I replied with a smile.

'I'm Carl. Nice to meet you.'

'Kate. Likewise.'

He was the tallest of the three, with long limbs, gorgeous rich black skin and an infectious grin.

He reminded me of someone. I couldn't quite put my finger on who it was.

'You allowed out unescorted?' he shouted up at me.

'I don't know. I've only just arrived here. I won't be here long.'

'That's what they all say,' he replied.

'But it's true. There's been a mistake, I shouldn't be here. I'm going to speak to them and they will let me out on Monday so I can go home.'

'Really? Well good luck with that.'

His response hit me hard and I was suddenly angry. 'I am anyway. I'm going to talk to them right now,' I shot back at him. 'Nice to have met you.'

'You too, Kate. Take it easy.' He saluted me and went back to his friends.

The smell of smoke wafted through the window and made me cough. I jumped down from my vantage point and went in search of someone who would get the ball rolling and get me home again.

Orientation

March 2016 – Sat 5th– Mon 7th March, 2016

The weekend passed. I had resigned myself that I just had to get through the next few days, do as I was told and then I could speak to my family on Monday. I had decided to pretend to take the med, co-operate and avoid any more sessions in the isolation room. So far it had worked. I queued up for my medication when they told me to. When it was my turn, I accepted the little pot and tipped my head back as if to take them all at once but instead flicked them under my tongue and then spat them out into a tissue once I was out of sight and flushed them down the toilet. I knew if they caught me I would get another injection, but so far I had managed to dupe them into thinking I had taken them. The only pills I swallowed were the ones I had been prescribed before being sent here to this purgatory.

I had spent the weekend wandering around the ward, finding my way with no help from the staff, who were pretty much all made of the same stuff as the ones I had encountered when I first arrived. They must have very strange job descriptions with sullen, moody, sarcastic, and just plain nasty listed as desirable qualities. The staff were, as far as I could see, mainly made up of bad people. There were one or two who I thought that maybe I could trust, but for the main part I had experienced nothing but hostility and bad attitude. I had tried to remember all their names and secretly wrote them on some paper I had pilfered from the art cupboard. I started to write down names, times, incidents, everything that I witnessed I made a note of. My gut feeling told me to keep quiet about what I was doing, not to even mention it to the other patients. I had no clue who I would be able to trust, so I trusted no one.

I had introduced myself to the rest of the patients on the ward. It was a female only ward. Some had been here many months, some just a short time, and all together we numbered thirteen. We came from all walks of life, a diverse cross section of women who had mental health issues. At least half self –harmed, and their poor limbs were covered in scratches and scars made by razors, plastic daggers made from biro pen lids or any other object that had a sharp edge. It was amazing what damage a harmless looking everyday object could inflict if one was so inclined. These ladies were not allowed anything that may be used as a weapon against themselves, even their shoelaces confiscated to prevent the making of ligatures. Other ladies had less visible problems. I counted myself among this group. But we all had one thing in common, we wanted to leave. I had come to realise that once admitted here, it was very hard to be set free again. This place was the complete opposite of the refuge I had been in at the beginning of the year. This place was hell on earth as far as I was concerned. At least that is what I christened it in my head. We were patients on 'Chrysalis' Ward. Here to be transformed back into valuable members of society. Our families had entrusted our lives to this place not realising that our very souls were in danger.

I had come to realise that I had been sent here for a reason. The hospital had two floors. Chrysalis was a ward on the upper floor. This was where souls were sent to be transformed. To be delivered. Souls were inspected carefully by higher beings. If they were worthy, they were allocated bodies, born again to occupy a new carrier and sent out into the world from the upper floor to go and spread goodness; to help redress the balance. They were delivered back to Planet Earth once they had proved themselves. If, however, the soul was found to be lacking, if there was evil present, then they were then sent to the ground floor, the floor that was easily entered down the stairs. The ground floor was where the stench of stale smoke filtered up to us on Chrysalis; they were sent down to hell. I had been delivered into a living and breathing purgatory. A waiting room, a place of judgement. It was up to me to fight to prove myself. Once again, I had luckily been spared the gift of predicting the future.

I was becoming familiar with the layout of Chrysalis. The bedrooms were all pretty much the same from what I could see. The bathrooms were for the most part, dirty. I had only seen one cleaner up to now and she had her work cut out with four toilets and four bathrooms to keep clean as well as the rest of the ward and the laundry. I felt sorry for her. She did her best. She always smiled at me when she bustled past carrying a mop bucket, or a net of washing. I had the feeling that she saw everything that went on but kept quiet about it. She was on my list of good souls.

The whole of the ward was laid out as a large circular building with a courtyard downstairs in the middle, a bit like a tyre or a wheel without spokes. Along the left or west quadrant lay the corridor containing most of the bedrooms, the laundry, the 'Obs Room', two bathrooms and two toilets. At the north were two toilets, the clinic hatch then the door to the stairs. Moving forward, the small waiting room that I had been left in when I arrived. Opposite that, still in the north, a library to the inner side, the office further along and to the outer side then a door at the end leading into a square landing. On the left of the landing, a computer room, on the right a 'Quiet Room', the kitchen, directly in front the dining room, and to the left of the dining room door another door with a small square window. This door was always locked, and when I looked through the window I could see another door directly behind and to the east quadrant. The sign read the same as the door near the isolation room at the other end of the building. 'Lock it, secure it.'

Through the door window, I could see a corridor beyond another door opposite with the same window and the same sign. The corridor had a red carpet. People came and went, jingling and clinking with the many keys that they carried. This corridor led to the guards. I don't know why that thought came to me when I peered through the small window. Immediately, I knew that was where the good angels came and went, through this corridor of locked and secured doors. They had to be vigilant so that the evil could not escape via that exit.

On the opposite side of the ward from the bedrooms, the eastern quadrant of the circle was finally joined by a walkway which led away from the 'guards' door' and corridor; the walkway led to a large cage which covered another exterior door which I realised led to the outer side of the plush lounge which lay in the southern most point of the circle, the south pole. I counted four satellite dishes and two antennas fixed on the side of the building near the computer room.

Along with names and incidents, I drew myself a map. I hid the map with my other secret items, and I had decided that if I wrapped them in my black shawl and put the shawl in the bottom of my case, they would be safe. I didn't realise at that point how powerful the items in my possession were. It was still my first week in Chrysalis. I had a lot to learn.

I had settled into a routine over the first week, firmly believing as each day dawned that that would be the day I went home. My requests for a phone call were largely ignored. Each time I asked a staff member they would reply that they were too busy, or that they would sort it out later. I started to familiarise myself with the daily routine. A general call for medication would come at eight-thirty; we would queue up at the clinic. I noticed there was an 'Oxygen' sign above the hatch the same as near the 'Obs station' at the end of my corridor, and I struggled to reason why such a sign would be needed. Just another mystery that I had to unravel.

After meds, we made our way to the dining room for breakfast. It was always busy and the food was served from a hatch similar to the one at the clinic. The kitchen staff were on the whole much friendlier than the support workers and nurses. I generally went for a safe option of toast and coffee, at least for the first week, until things started becoming strange. The food was not a patch on my safe place, but my stomach did not require much to keep me going. I was too upset to eat much. After breakfast, I had got into the habit of going for a shower and washing my hair. I generally used the purple bathroom in the south because this was the one that tended to be the cleanest. It had a shiny purple wall opposite the door and was large and spacious. I could easily wash away the dirt and hair on the floor that tended to be ever present when I went in. The rest of the bathrooms were normally squalid, and this was the only one that I felt comfortable in using. I luxuriated in hot water and my expensive shower gel. I spent a long time cleansing; my skincare regime was the only thing that had stayed the same after leaving my beautiful home. I had decided to ration my toiletries so they lasted, and luckily they were so good that I only needed a tiny amount of each product each time. Anyway, I would be leaving next week, I was sure of it.

Week one dragged, and there are big chunks of it missing from my memory. The whole week merged into one long day and night. I have memories of playing hide and seek and covering my face in purple and pink felt tip, drawing on a moustache and beard like the 'V for Victory' mask and hiding from terrorists. I have recollections of a support worker hiding behind the settee in the 'Quiet Room' with me and giggling like maniacs when the others couldn't find us.

I had an obsession with the fruit bowl in the dining room, apples in particular and satsumas all found their way into my pockets or down my cleavage to be hidden from sight. I thought they represented the galaxy; a satsuma was the Sun, a red apple was Venus, a green one Mars. The fruit bowl had to be central in the middle of one of the round tables in the dining room, the fruit had to be symmetrical. If any of the fruit was going bad then I had to dispose of it straight away or the galaxy would be in danger. The other patients tended to stay out of my way during this time. I kept to myself. I did not trust anyone. I wanted to go home but knew I was trapped. This room became the centre of my universe for that first week.

The Dining Room

Week One – Mon 7th- Sun 13th March, 2016

The dining room was situated at the north-west quadrant on the outer side of the circle, and it had two large windows on the outer side which overlooked the car park. There were four round tables with four dining chairs at each. On the immediate right of the door lay the serving hatch. On the same wall was a worktop with a small fridge, a water cooler and bin underneath. On top was a coffee machine and a tray of different coloured plastic mugs.

The table at the far side of the room had two high-backed chairs upholstered in purple, and to the left of this table was a door to the art cupboard, housing crayons, paper, and craft items. This was the table that became my command centre. It had a few jigsaws piled up on it along with a couple of board games, some magazines, some 'colouring for mindfulness' books but most importantly, the radio.

On the wall above this table were two large pictures depicting scenes of nature which had mixed messages. The one on the left was predominantly orange, portraying dark silhouettes of hanging leaves and branches; it made me shudder as all I could see were witches dripping in black grease hanging outlined against the backdrop of a fire. The picture on the right hand side also depicted silhouetted leaves on an orange background, but these were large sycamore type leaves, some of which were singed and burnt as though they had sailed too close to the sun. It was these images that dominated the room and from my table; I could sit with my back against the 'witch' one and keep it behind me out of sight.

There were only two stations available on the radio and I chose the one which played current hits and had an eighties hour every day. Nobody seemed to challenge me and I assumed this position from which to run my campaign for freedom.

After breakfast and a shower, I returned to the dining room each day to keep myself busy and simulate some sort of routine. Each day I would ask for my phone call, each day it would be denied. It didn't matter how many times I asked, what time of day, which member of staff, the answer was always the same, 'later'. Later never came, and after the first week I despaired of ever having success.

The radio became increasingly important once again. Now it instructed me on what to do and when to do it. I listened for my signs coming through those airwaves. I followed my instructions every day. By the end of the first week I had gotten my bearings, sorted out which were good staff and which were bad, made alliances with other patients - some of which became vital in the role I had been given. I spent more and more time at my table. Solving clues, obeying instructions, I was bound to do certain things. The fruit was of grave importance. I had a good view of the car park at the front of the building. It had thirteen spaces on the left and thirteen on the right. In the middle was a gap for disabled parking and the entrance to a smoking area in the form of a round picnic bench. Behind this area, the perimeter of the grounds was edged by tall trees. In the top of these trees, right in the centre, were two bird nests way up high. The nests had been made by crows. The crows became my friends and allies, as did the other birds outside. I watched with interest how the vehicles came in and out, each vehicle colour representing a different warning or mood. Each number plate a different meaning. I soon learned to recognise allies and enemies. Night and day. Day and night. Time was upside down in this place, I knew now why I could not make a phone call; it was the middle of the night in the ordinary world and the exact opposite here in the north. My birds, my six crows, aided my assessment of individuals as they came and left the car park. They were my friends. I trusted them, and they spoke to me every day.

The other patients kept their distance for the first few days; I suppose they were wary of this new inmate who had taken over the dining room and sang at the top of her voice all the time. I had moved on from just singing after the first day and taken to dancing as well. I danced to anything and everything, I couldn't sit still, I was possessed by an all-compelling urge to dance and nothing could stop me. When I wasn't dancing, I had taken up yoga, which I did in my room. I did not know that I could do yoga. I had never done it before, but somehow the moves flowed as naturally as the singing and dancing. I spent a lot of time balancing on my window ledge and practising more and more dangerous moves. Nobody ever stopped me. Nobody had any interest in me. The staff were not monitoring me. After the first day of my refusal of medication and my stint in the isolation room, they seemed to have washed their hands of me and it was as if I no longer existed. I moved through the ward like a phantom, slipping in and out of rooms with nobody raising an eyebrow or giving me eye contact.

Week one had passed in a daze. I had a vague impression of someone coming into my room in the middle of the night but I could not be sure; it may have been a dream. Anything was possible in this place. I realised that I had been transported to somewhere which lay between the dimensions of my normal reality and those of higher levels. I was awake during the daylight and asleep during the night, not so strange except for the day as I knew it in this place was actually night in the real world and vice versa. During the day I fought for justice in my reality; during the night I fought for justice in the real world. It didn't make sense at first. It took the first week for me to get my head round what exactly was happening, but when things did click into place, everything then made sense and I knew what my role in this awful place was and why I had been sent here to The Hub.

The Stakes

Week Two – Mon 14th – Sun 20th March, 2016

Higher beings now guided my every move. I was made aware that there was a game in progress. The game was being played in a different dimension to the one I was living in. It was on a much higher level than I was privy to. The gamers came from different worlds, the stakes were high; they were playing for control of the planet. I had my role to play. It was up to me to watch out for new players coming in, warn the others who were on our side and to raise the stakes when instructed to do so.

I stalked the corridors day and night now. The game was afoot. The dining room still played a major part in my role. The position of the fruit bowl was a distraction and no matter how many times I carefully put it in the middle, as soon as my back turned, something moved it off centre. It became a running joke between myself and the other beings who I could not see. Even in these troubled times we enjoyed being mischievous, our humour served us well and enabled me to carry on when times looked hopeless. It was all a game to my godly family. They had every confidence in me. I hoped and prayed every day that I would prove them right, and one thing was for certain; I would never give up.

The coffee machine in the corner of the dining room played a major role in the game. The display on the front showed only two options for drinks: black coffee and white coffee. None of the other functions worked. One of my tasks that I had been allocated was to check the display constantly. If hostile beings were landing ready to take control of the game, the display would flash and symbols would appear. A digital picture of a coffee cup on the machines display panel pulsed whilst what looked to me like a tiny hammer beat down on the cup as though to smash it. It would flash faster and faster as the threat came nearer. The beings entering our world came from many different dimensions. Some were the colours, the reds, the greens, the blues, coming in from other planets; some were time travellers, the Mayans, the Incas, the Egyptians, higher beings coming to take their nations back again. Not all visits were hostile and alliances changed depending on the game. My duty was to stop the machine flashing and ensure the display went back to black and white. Yin and yang, perfect harmony. In order for me to do this I had to make sure it was clean, the milk powder would block and a creamy fluid would appear under the tray. I had to flush it out. I used a cup and the hot water button, and it was essential that I did it three times and wiped away the tainted liquid. I flushed it through and emptied the dirty water into the large bowl next to the machine, after three rinses it became holy water, the symbols would stop flashing and balance had been restored, the safety net back up, and the threat diminished. This was my role. I kept an eye on developments. The fruit, the coffee machine, the car park showing players leaving and arriving, the birds, the radio and the games on the table were all signals. I was the only one who could interpret them and keep the badness at bay. It was if I floated through the levels, carrying out my duties as directed. I had little interaction with any of the humans during this week. I made my notes. I kept my secrets close to my chest and watched over the developments as things progressed.

I was not invited in to play the game. I was the sentinel, the watcher. I warned our players of incoming threats. The comings and goings of players centred on the dining room. They would come and take their place around the table nearest the door. I would flit in and out, watching the coffee machine, checking the fruit. My office for this role was situated in the 'Quiet Room', which lay a little further to the east on the same quadrant as the dining room. From here, I could keep my eye on the car park and check who was entering the game and who was leaving. It was strangely fun. Doors slammed as the other side lost and exited the building, shepherded by the good angels who entered and left via the red corridor with the door which never opened. This week was centred on Planet Earth and the stakes for who would take control. I did not know the exact rules, but the scene reminded me of a casino with the players sat around a table with piles of coloured chips at their disposal. The chips represented different areas on earth and other planets. Black were areas where the evil had taken control, blue were neutral, red were in danger of being taken over, green were safe, golden owned by deities and only played when absolutely no other course of action would ward off the evil. The croupier was on a higher level and never visible in the game. The presence was felt as an overwhelming power which all players were in awe of. Much arguing and debate between beings ensued. Some I recognised as famous people from our plane who had passed over to the next level. Some had become saints, and they took their seats if I called to raise the stakes. The saints would appear and join the game, sending lower life forms running back to the darkness they had come from. I liked it when the saints came, they were beautiful creatures. When they entered the dining room, the whole room lit up, a golden aura settled over the gamers, beautiful music would play from the airwaves. I would sing to welcome them and my voice would be that of an angel. I treasure the memories of these wondrous beings, and being in their company eased my fears and soothed my mind. I would sit in the doorway cross-legged and watch as they presided over the game.

The game was well underway and I was aware that things were going our way for the time being. I was busy all the time, so busy during this week that I had no time to become acquainted with the other patients and they, for their part, kept their distance. The chairs in the dining room had to be symmetrical, it had to be a pattern; I kept hearing songs and lyrics and following the instructions. To save Planet Earth I had to do as I was told, I had no choice. Week two in the asylum was all about making my presence felt. I had the tools at my disposal, all I had to do was listen to my guides as to how to use them. The fruit, the coffee machine, the furniture all needed to be perfect. I listened and acted accordingly.

As the days passed, I became more and more in tune to higher frequencies that and I spent more and more time on their level, listening and learning. It made us laugh that human beings were forever banging on about needing a 'sign'. We left signs all the time, many times daily when they were needed and what did the humans do? Ignored them, that's what. I began to think that we were wasting our time trying to save their planet, but inside me I knew I would never give up.

My grandparents (Eva aka Gaia - Earth, and Frank aka Ouranus – Heaven) had come to find me. I had missed their activities over the Christmas period. It had been they who had caused consecutive hurricanes around the world in their anger that my earthly body had been so badly injured in the sand race. For my part, I was glad to see them again and know that they were watching over our family. Luckily for the planet, I had recovered. They were taking a back seat once again, but I knew that if I needed them they would be there to step in. I didn't want our planet to be destroyed by the elements, but they had assured me that they would take their wrath to the next level if anything else were to happen to me. I knew that I was stronger than I had ever been and growing stronger each day. All I had to do was follow instructions and everything would be fine. I had always been a favourite of my grandparents and I managed to persuade them that I was perfectly capable of handling events from here on in.

The dining room was my headquarters; beings from many dimensions were channelled into my office. I examined them; I could see if evil lurked under the skin. I kept notes on which bodies they possessed, how long they stayed, and where they were destined for. It was exhausting, but it gave me a purpose. I was vigilant. I had to be. This place was the centre of everything. Funny how my children had always said to me that I couldn't save the world on my own... My response had always been 'maybe not, but I'll die trying'. It really had come to this. Never a truer word spoken.

I had figured out which staff were possessed by which beings. The ones from the blue planet tended to do nights. They were smaller in stature, the majority were coloured women with long straight shiny hair. The reds and greens worked the day shift. A constant battle between them. The good and bad entered their bodies frequently, many times a day, many times a minute, sometimes it was hard to keep up with the ever-changing entities and the shape shifters, the souls moving swiftly, the battle between good and evil fleeting and powerful. Their lanyards read earthly names but their security numbers constantly changed according to which soul occupied the body. I deciphered the system during week two. I had decided that I could no longer sleep at night. I had woken up twice to the feeling that someone had been in my room. Since the second time, I had decided to turn my world upside down to match that of the outside world. I slept for a while in the north daytime and stayed awake in the north night. The staff didn't approve but they didn't stop me from doing it. I was on guard duty. I had taken it upon myself to protect us all. I was sure that they were abusing all of us. If I stayed awake, then they couldn't go into people's rooms without me seeing. I stationed myself on the floor of my room with a pillow and laid on my front with my head in the doorway, surveying the corridor. For the main part the night staff ignored me. They were on the whole lazy and involved in their own games. Too much trouble to bother with a loony with insomnia. I stayed in this position until the day staff came on at seven-thirty every morning. I was winning the night time battle so far. As the week went on, the game intensified. I was on duty twenty-four hours a day. Signs came thick and fast. Every single action I completed had been given to me by a guide. I got up at a pre-ordained time. I ate exactly what they told me to for breakfast. I showered in a certain way, each product carefully selected. My need for cleanliness had reached new heights. I went into the shower but first had to clean the floor, finding hair and other detritus and disposing of them before I could clean myself. My eyes were constantly on the lookout for the 'shiny'. I had to pick up any bits of glitter, silver paper, foil, sequins and wrap them carefully in clean tissue which I then tucked safely into my cleavage.

My cleavage had become a haven for anything which I needed to hide. I knew that nobody would touch me in the daytime, and at night I folded everything up tightly and stashed it in the folds of my black shawl. I had been told that this shawl made things invisible. Anything in my shawl was safe. I hid the shawl in my suitcase and strapped it in using the fittings in the case to secure it in a cross shape.

It is round about this time that I found myself spending some time in the library. I had organised the books so they were in alphabetical order. Some of the books were evil and their pictures stared down at me. I had to turn them around so they couldn't watch my every move.

It was at the back of one of the shelves in the library that I found a bible. It was a bit worn for wear, but I knew that I had to have it and keep it with me in my bedroom. It would protect me. The day I found the bible was the day events started to escalate.

The Eighth Day had also been a turning point. I had managed to defeat the demon and with help, send it beyond Mars. The shape that had been on the race track was the same one that had followed me to my sanctuary. It was the same one that had somehow managed to come back from Mars and find me again at the stables. It had entered my home and I had passed it on the stairs. I knew that it had been instrumental in sending me to this place. It was powerful, and had been responsible for occupying the bodies of many a serial killer. It had taunted me with clues; Aspen, in my sanctuary, a haven for an American serial killer. Clues were left for me. Just as we left signs for mortals, the dark had been leaving signs for me. What it hadn't realised was that it was being observed by much more powerful forces and they had sent it here with me for me to defeat it once and for all. I was regaining strength. It was possessing various members of staff and also some of the patients. I was armed and ready for it. I knew it, it knew me, but what it didn't know was that I was plotting its downfall and this time it would never come back. It was small fry compared to the forces that protected me. I knew its name. It had spread its evil throughout the world, gradually converting goodness to bad. Events in Paris last year had brought it to my attention. It got closer and closer, bringing pain and misery to my contemporaries. Not content with that, it had decided the only way to beat us was to attack us personally. It thought it had won. Big mistake. My family and I were far more powerful than it had realised. We knew it, and now was the time to rid us of it forever. The devil himself. Small fry. We knew how to beat him at his own game.

The game was intensifying. I now lived in the shadows, defending souls who came in and out, occupying the bodies of human patients. We were on level three, myself in battle with the devil. The next level up, the game was on between members of different alien races. In the shadows of history, my family, the Greeks, conspired with other deities from around the world. The highest level of all only housed one being. God. He was overseeing the fight. He was the being we all ultimately answered to. He held all the cards. The role I played in the games was essential. I had had to come here and survive my own journey down into the inferno to be born once again. Cleansed. Knowledge coursing through my veins that had been de-scaled with the acid of bitter truth. I was the key to salvation.

The Shower Scene

Week Three Mon 21st – Thurs 24th March, 2016

As week two gave way to week three, I had no clean clothes left and the laundry was out of order. I had nothing but the clothes I stood up in. I had no money, no phone. My suitcase was empty other than the black shawl which contained my writing and other items from the library and the dining room that I had been instructed to hide.

My family had phoned a few times, but I could not speak to them. I had been told that it wasn't really them on the phone. A demon was impersonating them and anything they said was not true. The demon was trying to trick me into giving away personal information about my family. I would not be tricked this way; it was my mission to protect the people I loved. My youngest daughter was expecting a baby and the demons were waiting for her to give birth so they could steal its new-born soul. I would die before I let that happen, so in order to protect them I refused to speak to anybody from home.

I turned to the Bible more and more. First thing in the morning I would open its pages at random and read the passage I was directed to. It never failed to help and support me through the whole of my time in the place I had come to know as The Hub. Each passage spoke to me personally. During the third week, I was directed to the book of Job. Time and again, Job had been stripped of everything as a test, as had I; this was the only explanation I could accept. It was God's will. This bible was old, with some of the pages worn thin and tattered. Throughout the book, verses had been underlined in different colour felt tip pen, passages circled, prayers highlighted. I took great comfort in knowing that I was not the only one who had received help and guidance from above.

The amount of instructions I was having to follow now took all of my time, from the moment I awoke until the moment I went to sleep. After having spent a week being awake all night, I was exhausted and had succumbed to sleep. When I awoke in the morning, I had somehow moved from the floor to my bed. I was aware that I had been moved and had a vague recollection of being lifted up and carried to the bed. I knew something bad had happened. My legs were sore and I felt sick. As I woke up, I realised I ached all over, my head felt heavy and I could hardly open my eyes. I sat on the edge of the bed trying to wake up properly. I stood up and stumbled, falling back onto the bed again. As I sat trying to come round, I had an impression that someone else had dressed me, my vest top was inside out, my pyjama bottoms looked ok, but there was something not right.

Someone had left my toiletries on the sink at the end of the bed and there was a bath towel on the floor. I sat for a few minutes trying to piece together what I could remember from the previous night. Nothing for sure, but I had the awful feeling that I had been abused. I grabbed my toiletries hurriedly, I could not bear the thought of anyone but my husband touching me, so I had to get in the shower. I took my black shawl out of my case, hiding its contents in a zipped pocket in the case. I wrapped my shawl around me, knowing I would be hidden from sight if I did this. Next, I grabbed my bible, clutching it to my chest. I needed the reassurance and protection it afforded me. I opened my bedroom door cautiously, and the support worker who I had met on my first day was walking down the corridor away from me towards the clinic. She was with a man I had never seen before, and they were laughing together as I crept out and went in the opposite direction. I did not want her to see me. I had a gut feeling that if something had happened to me it had been largely down to her. I made it to the purple shower room without anyone spotting me. I went through my normal routine of checking the floor for hair and removing any that soiled the floor. It was only when I took my clothes off that I realised I had been subjected to some form of abuse. I had fingerprints on my thighs and my left breast. They were only faint, but there nevertheless. I felt sore between my legs, itchy. A blackness descended and a scream found its way out of my body. My clothes lay in a heap at my feet as I switched the shower on. I screamed and wailed as the water cascaded over my bruised body. I clutched my bible in one hand and scrubbed away the filth with a scrunchie filled with the familiar aroma of my shower gel. No matter how hard I scrubbed, I couldn't erase the stench of someone else, the thought that their hands had been all over my body. Sinking down onto my knees until I was crouched on the floor in the foetal position, my clothes lay wet through around me; my bible soaked, its pages sticking together, I could not stop and my screaming echoed around the room and filtered down the corridors.

I vaguely heard people approaching. My body tensed, I was vulnerable. I had an episode which I can only describe as undergoing a metamorphosis. I turned, and threw myself forward. I could feel my body elongating and stretching out, I was laid on my front with my arms reaching out. Someone tried to enter the room and I went to scream at them but it wasn't my voice which came out, it was a very loud and frightening hiss. I had the notion that I was now a snake, a cobra, fighting for my life against these people who were trying to steal my soul. I had shape-shifted to protect myself. My bible lay to my right, and as they backed away from me I reared up hissing. They would not hurt me again. I knew this was the case and I sank back down on my knees, knowing I was safe for now. As I sat under the shower, cold and shivering now, I was aware of a conversation taking place outside the door. There were two people present, a male and a female. I recognised the male voice as one of my idols; a famous actor. Surely I was hearing things? The female spoke to him saying that the actress in the shower had now finished her scene and they would edit his part in. He was required for a scene in the dining room with another actress who shall remain nameless.

I sat for a while not knowing what to do. I was alone once more. I checked outside the door, picked up my wet clothes and wrapped the towel around me. I managed to make it back to my room again. Nobody bothered about the crazies. We were in a mental health hospital, sectioned as lunatics. Nobody listened to our point of view, none of them cared. I sat on the edge of my bed, drying myself and feeling sick at having to put wet clothes back on. I had nothing else. I still felt nauseous. They must have drugged me. There was no way that I would have stayed asleep whilst someone was touching me. I felt sure that they had injected me. How could I ever go to sleep here again? I knew nobody would believe me; they would protect their own. But I had to try. Surely I could catch a support worker who was being a good angel to help me at least get some dry clothes.

I began to form a plan of action. I would report the abuse and insist on reporting it to the police. If they prevented me, then I would somehow break into the computer room and dial 999 from the phone that was kept locked away in there. They wouldn't get away with it.

I decided that I would sleep in the isolation room until I had spoken to the police. This room had a video camera recording day and night. I would go in there and speak to the camera and record everything that way, stating my name, the date and the time, and the identities of staff who I thought had been responsible. I decided that not only would I disclose abuse that I had suffered but that I would report on everything that I witnessed. As God was my witness, that is what I would do. One day, they would get what they deserved. Karma would come. The phrase 'I will rip off their heads and shit down their necks' became my catchphrase. I began to make friends with the other patients. They had been watching me and keeping their distance, but now as I confided in them about the abuse they had started to see me as a confidant. They now confided in and believed in me. I told them that I would make the bastards pay for what they were doing to us. They began to trust me, a few questioning exactly what had happened and scarily divulging abuse that they themselves had suffered at the hands of these evil, fallen angels.

Easter

Good Friday – Easter Monday, 2016

The day after the abuse had been a turning point. I had managed to speak to a support worker who I trusted, and there were only one or two that I actually believed in. She had been horrified and had gone against the ward manager in backing me and ringing the police. I was summoned to the 'Quiet Room' to talk with the manager. I took my duvet cover with me. I was sure that there were stains on it that would incriminate my abuser or abusers since I had my suspicions that there were more than one. She nodded and listened and said she would ring the police. The linen was put into a red plastic bag, tied up and taken away. My good angel brought the phone in and made the call whilst she was present. I couldn't believe that it had come to this, and I decided not to tell them what I had been doing in the isolation room with the camera. I felt sure that somehow the tape would be erased.

The ward manager did not seem shocked or bothered by my allegations, and I wondered if it was because she had gotten so used to hearing these tales that she was not easily surprised. Maybe she didn't believe the patients or maybe, as I suspected, she was part of it.

The first week I had spent in The Hub, I had brought my rights to their attention day after day; my right to be heard, the standards set by government to safeguard vulnerable adults. I had ripped posters off the wall stating the CPA standards, the Mental Health Act, all staff without exception had done one of two things; either ignored me completely or worse, laughed in my face. Jane had actually called me a loony and told me nobody would listen to me, I was sectioned as a lunatic. What did I expect? I expected to be treated like a human being. I soon found that my expectations fell on deaf ears. We were locked away. Out of sight. We may as well have been living in Victorian times. The only difference I could see in treatment being that we were not subjected to electrotherapy. No, they had replaced that with injections. If the injections didn't work then the next step was to be locked in the cell within the isolation room. I had so far avoided that. I could not risk being locked in there, and I knew that if I was ever shut in that room I would not leave it. I had fought for my life on more than one occasion. I would not risk being put in there.

I had one more session in isolation and again this was because of medication. They had caught me throwing away the tablets that had not been prescribed for me and once again, they called the team and I was marched down to the room, forced to the floor on my front with four team members holding me down even though I had not put up a fight or struggled. They held me so tightly that I developed bruises on my arms. They injected me again. This time it had no effect whatsoever and I was thankful of the opportunity to spend three hours practising yoga in the peace and quiet. Once again, they had forgotten to lock the door so I just stayed as long as I thought acceptable and then went back to room eleven once I had done enough exercise. The whole place was a complete farce.

We sat in the Quiet Room, and I was lost in my own thoughts. The ward manager was on hold to the police and reluctantly passed the phone to me so that I could speak to them. I recounted everything that I could remember and requested that they come and take a statement. The ward manager, I'll call her 'L', was none too pleased with the outcome and took the bag and the phone away, leaving me sat there alone once again.

I didn't hold out much hope for anything coming from the phone call to the police. I had done my best to give them as much information as I dared, but I decided to keep my diary and notes hidden. I didn't trust them not to take it away and it never be seen again. I had written down names, dates of incidents that I had witnessed either by myself personally or to other patients.

At this point I feel that I need to introduce the major players who inhabited The Hub during my time there. As patients, we were all in the same situation; all suffering from abuse in one form or another. The staff were the good angels and fallen angels depending on the roles they were given by the higher beings. We were all a part of the game.

The hospital hierarchy began with the doctors who visited twice a week, and on rare occasions they came by at other times. The ward managers, of whom there were two, managed the upstairs ward of Chrysalis and its polar opposite, the downstairs ward... which was in essence, Hades. The bad souls were banished downstairs until their personal hell was delivered to them. The upstairs was where souls were tested and the battle for salvation took place every day. The staff up here were mainly made up of the support workers, and there would always be a nurse on duty to issue out medication, and just one cleaner. The kitchen staff occupied another building and came and went at mealtimes, pushing trolleys laden with provisions in and out of our kitchen.

Our female ward housed at the maximum thirteen. During my time, I saw many come and go. I was trapped in limbo, harnessed and in chains which bound me to my surroundings until my work there was done. I had to slip from one dimension to the next and back again; hide in the shadows from the evil and fight where necessary. I was at the centre of every single level. I was the pivot around which events were linked and resolved.

In the foyer outside the dining room, there were two whiteboards and two more large pictures. To the right was the whiteboard giving the menu for the day. Each day, it was my job to wipe away the date from this board and also from the other one which detailed the names of the staff who were on duty. The boards had to be free of dates so that the ward was free to go back and forth in time. Time travel was an essential part of the game which we were all playing. If the date had gone, that left the time portals open to do their job. The higher beings were only then allowed access into the building. I rubbed away the names of all the staff so as to aid the golden angels to filter into the bodies of the support workers as much as possible. The picture on the left opposite the menu board was of a bright red flower, exquisite in its beauty but deadly with its power. This was a red anemone, the flower of death, synonymous with my Adonis but representative of Red, my Mars, and it served as a reminder to beware of the danger all around. The picture on the wall opposite was of a bright red tulip which had luscious green leaves either side. This tulip represented the spring time that was coming and hope for the future. It also represented my husband, Hephaestus, loyalty and a bright future. Above the entrance of the corridor opposite was a large rainbow above which read the words 'Welcome to Chrysalis Ward'. The rainbow represented all the colours of the spectrum. Combined with the tulip, these images were the hope I needed to be able to carry on and do my job. I would not let the evil win. Whilst ever I lived and breathed, I had sworn that I would do my best to protect the rest of the patients on the ward and to protect everyone I cared about in the outside world.

There was a baby due, a baby boy. My sources advised me that it was imperative to save this baby from the claws of evil spirits who were poised ready and waiting to carry him off to the underworld as soon as he was born. I had to be vigilant with concealing his identity as well as the rest of my loved ones, especially the beautiful untainted souls of my grandchildren. Each day was a new challenge to get to the information and remove the evidence before the evil came and found it. After rubbing out the date and the names, my next task was to hide the dates of the daily newspapers that came in to the ward.

The board games and jigsaw puzzles, the magazines, the colouring for mindfulness books, all became an intricate part of the game with no rules. I had to be as vigilant as possible during the day and on guard all night against the evil.

No date was as important as the Easter weekend. I had read my bible and had been privy to information that no mortal could possibly understand or wish to believe. The uneducated were ignorant of events that were unfolding. It was up to me to protect the new king and save his soul from the evil that was on its way to snatch him away from his earthly family.

They tried every trick in the book that weekend to try and find out where the baby was and who he was to be born unto. Good Friday was the start of a vicious onslaught. While the rest of the country enjoyed their hot cross buns and Easter eggs, I had the job of protecting mankind in order for the new saviour to be delivered safely.

I refused to take any phone calls from home as I could not risk the bad things sending their shadows to lurk in the airwaves and the phone lines gathering intelligence. I had to be vigilant. My bible was my guide. As the weekend intensified, I spent every single second obeying the commands which came from on high. The culmination came on Easter Sunday. I had commandeered the dining room as my headquarters. The staff had seemed to become resigned to the fact that they could not control me without injections and even they were wary of giving me too much of that. I expect the death of a woman who was fit other than suffering sleep deprivation would have taken a lot of explaining to the authorities. I was for the moment safer than I had been for a long time. This enabled me to be on guard and to do the job I had been given.

It was nearly midnight and I was alone listening to the radio. I had taken up my position, sat with my back against the art cupboard door leaning the chair against it and swinging my feet in time with the music. I was tired but on duty, so the radio was my saviour once again. I had my trusty bible with me as I sang along. Suddenly I had the feeling I was not alone. A hollow deafening banging came from within the cupboard behind me; I knew without a doubt it was the evil trying to come through and filter into my soul. A light from the corridor caught my eye and I saw a large figure floating in the corridor coming up to the entrance of the foyer. The sense of badness was tangible. I closed my eyes and prayed as hard as I could. The devil had sent a fallen angel to come and glean the information from my tired brain. My eyes were tight shut as it entered the room. The door behind me rattled loudly as the devil came up from the bowels of hell. I would not let it in. I pushed my chair back as hard as I could to prevent the door from flying open. Coldness touched my skin, a clammy vice like grip took hold of my arms. I would not give in. The Lord's Prayer would help me fend off these demons that had come for the new blood. I was scared. My worst fears were materialising in front and behind me; I was surrounded by the sense of impending doom. I could feel my soul being sucked out of me. A succubus had come. I dare not open my eyes to see what had caught me in its grasp. I knew that if I did as it was telling me that I would start to lose all hope. That was what it wanted, this demon, this succubus, this thing of evil. I was aware that the music had turned from the uplifting songs which kept the airwaves safe to a dour lyric, the words filtering through into my subconscious, urging me to give up. I would not win. But. I. Could. Not. Give. Up.

The wind rushed around my head and my eardrums were ready to burst with the violence of the beat that had built up and up; a heavy drum beat accompanied by a shrill whistle and manic laughter replacing any lyrics that may have been present in this song of the damned.

Suddenly, it was gone. I recognised a light within me. I had switched off the malevolence with the flick of an internal switch. The understanding had settled in my brain. I knew what to do. My light had been there all the time. I had unlocked an inner power that had, up to now, lain dormant. The wicked had come to take away things I held dear to me and when they had been in danger of being taken and lost forever, only then had my inner strength stepped up to fend them off and keep everyone safe.

'Hi Kate.'

I still had my eyes tight shut. I tried to decipher the voice but could not. It was deep and rich like beautiful dark chocolate slipping through the air and covering me with a layer of warmth the like of which I had never experienced.

'It's ok, you've done it. They've gone now. You are safe.'

'Who are you?' I whispered to the voice that washed over me.

'Open your eyes. You know me.'

'I can't. I won't be tricked.'

'You are right to be cautious, but I promise you that you are safe again.' The disembodied words floated around and settled in my brain, soothing and caressing with their softness.

I hoped and prayed that I could trust this being. My senses were still on edge after fighting so hard for what felt like hours but was probably only a few minutes.

'Who are you?'

'You know who I am. I do not need to tell you.'

I did know. I would open my eyes. I luxuriated in the richness of his words before I unscrewed my eyes and dared to open them again. I was still leant back, guarding the cupboard door, the front two legs of the chair hanging in mid-air. I wobbled back and forth before landing them down again with a thud.

I turned towards the direction where the voice was located.

'Hi Kate. Lovely, good, kind Kate.'

'I feel like we have met before. How do I know you?' I asked the man who sat leant on the table in front of me.

'You know we have. I've been with you a long time,' he replied with the kindest of smiles, revealing slightly yellowing but even teeth.

His black hair was greying at the temples with a mass of dreadlocks tied back in a scruffy ponytail. His eyes were dark and crinkled around the edges as he smiled at me. I estimated he was probably in his fifties. He wore a black baseball jacket, faded black jeans and converse.

'Have a good look.' He laughed harder. 'Oh Kate, your memory will be the death of me.'

'I know we have met before, but I have no idea where. You're one of the good guys though, I do know that. Thank you for helping me.'

'Ah, you did most of it yourself. You were winning already when I came by to check.'

'Those things… have they really gone for good?' I asked, pushing her hair back away from her forehead, tucking errant strands behind her ears.

'They've gone for now, yes. You'll be pleased to know it's now past midnight and we are into Easter Monday. You've done it, Kate. They won't come back now. You can relax for a while. I won't leave you just yet. I'd like to have a chat with you before I go.'

'I'm going to check the coffee machine and grab a glass of water. Can I get you anything?'

'Black coffee would be nice. Thanks. Always thinking of others aren't you?' he said as I cleaned the machine.

'I just do what I think is right.'

'Indeed you do. I've been sending you a lot of signs and you have been so vigilant. That's why I came to make sure you were handling things. I knew you could do it. I never doubted you.'

I studied his face as I brought our drinks over.

'I know you.' The greatness of the situation was not lost on me as I passed him his coffee.

And there we sat, and for the next couple of hours he questioned me. I answered him as honestly as I could. It was the best two hours I had experienced since being in The Hub. Being in His presence comforted me and gave me the strength to carry on fighting for everything I believed in. I knew that there was much work to be done but that He would be with me guiding my way. He would work with my heavenly family and friends and continue sending me signs to give me reassurance and light the path I was destined to follow. I now knew what I had suspected. I was here for a reason. I had saved my first soul. I had saved the baby boy who had been delivered safely into the arms of his earthly parents. Hell had sent its soldiers to come and defeat me in order to carry the new born away. I, with the power of my faith and the vigilance of my deeds, had saved him. This was why I had been sent to this place. It was what I was born to do. I had been reincarnated from my Greek ancestor, I was a goddess. I was a human. I was strong and had a job to do. All the tests that He had put before me I had passed. There were no stone tablets for me, things had moved on since those days.

I would fight for the good of the world. I would endeavour to save each soul and help navigate the way through to the earthly world if it was found worthy to be reborn; and send it to the depths of hell if it was found to be a carrier for the darkness that lurked ready to carry it on a downward spiral. I was doing work on behalf of much higher levels than I was able to ascend to at this moment in time. Now I knew my job. Now I was well ahead of the game.

The Transformation

Week Four – Monday 28th March – Sunday 3rd April, 2016

The breakfast sitting was busy the morning after. I had spent the rest of the night in paradise with beautiful creatures. After He had gone, the whole world looked different, the future became clearer and the confusion I had felt for such a very long time had finally left me. I had experienced the ultimate epiphany in the presence of the ultimate being. The darkness had threatened to consume me piece by piece until nothing was left of my soul; I had fought with every fibre and been found deserving of salvation. My spirit was flying through the solar system at breakneck pace. My soul was free at last, free to carry out the work which I had been brought back to Planet Earth to carry out.

I had been to cleanse my body before the rest of the ward started waking up. The shimmering purple wall that had shown my image as a wraith-like being of no substance appeared to become opaque, my reflection only just visible if I stared very intently. The world I was inhabiting was turning around. I estimated that we were no longer twelve hours adrift with our planet. I took my time in the shower and cleansed as thoroughly as I could. Each product from my bag was there for a reason. The eucalyptus cleared through the physical and mental blockages that had made my head feel so full of cotton wool and I breathed in the clean aroma letting it fill my senses. My toiletries were running low, and with no way to replace them I had to ration them out to ensure that would last me for what I knew would be another week. I cast my mind back to the day when I had transformed my physical self into the snake. I mulled over the conversation that I had overheard that day. I knew without a doubt that day had been shown to me. It had not happened in the real world yet; it was a vision of the future. The knowing strengthened my resolve. There was still a great deal of work to do, but every second that passed showed me the truth and the path forward.

Even the hooks on the back of the shower door were signals as to when threats were coming nearer, and they crudely were representative of an erect penis in their stance, sticking straight up to act as a hook. When I showered, I clicked them down so they were pointing at the floor, and the sexual connotation was plain to see. I had to take away the power and blind them so they could not use my body for sexual gratification. The day after I had been abused for the first time, the hooks were pointing skyward in every bathroom or toilet I entered. As I showered, I remembered the itchy soreness that had refused to be rinsed away no matter how much I scrubbed.

I was a different person now. The last three weeks had taught me well. I had learnt how to reduce the risk and recognise signs of the enemies creeping towards us all. Now, rather than being a prisoner trapped with no hope, I had been transformed into a soldier. I was employed as a guardian angel, a goddess, a golden child. I was not afraid. I had stared death in the face many times since I had arrived at this place. It would not and could not defeat me. This I knew for sure. From being sectioned, to this point, had been a test of my character. It had been necessary. Every event had been carefully planned by the higher levels. They had been using me. I had started as a pawn in the game. Small fry, cannon fodder. Only when the dark had come calling closer and closer had my true identity been revealed. It had started in Paris. The city of love. I was the goddess of love. Paris had seen many tragedies, our city of love had been turned upside down. The tower inverted, pointing its way down to the catacombs. Evil lurked in the nooks and crannies, it hid in plain view. It was omnipresent and it had been responsible for the killing of many beautiful angels. It had taken hostages and killed them. It had defiled everything my earthly incarnation and partner stood for. The music. The joy. The sheer love of living, loving and laughing. All had been taken away from us. The night of our anniversary, the evil had taken the city by storm, leaving it and us reeling in the aftermath. My musicians had only just gone by a matter of a few hours before the attack began. The shit had got real when it decided to attack us directly. I knew what had caused my accident. The shadow that had stood in the middle of the track had been stalking me for many years, biding its time, waiting for the moment when I would be most vulnerable. It had almost succeeded in taking me away from everything I held dear, but it had not counted on something far stronger than it would ever comprehend. The power of love. Ironically our song. *The Power of Love* and Frankie Goes to Hollywood. The powerful lyrics that John and I had tattooed on our flesh, served as a permanent and visible sign of our devotion to each other. The song that defined us as a couple and stood for our motto. Live. Love. Laugh.

My shower that morning cleansed my body and soul. Having saved the new born, I needed to clean and prepare my armour once more, ready for the next campaign against the badness. Every single item that I had taken in with me was a weapon against those who plotted my downfall. By the time I emerged, I felt as though I was walking on air. The evil had been washed away. The aroma of essential oils filled the corridor. I was cautious in checking for signs with every step that I took. I gathered up the shiny things that caught my eye as I walked back to my room. I inhaled the oxygen from the gap in the 'Obs room' door. My senses were now rejuvenated. Nothing escaped my glare, my eyes sharp, and I picked up the shiny things from off the floor as I was directed. I was reminded that all that glitters is not gold. The evil would be upping its game now to try and match my newfound determination. I would not let it win.

I made my way back to my room without seeing another soul. All was quiet as the rest of the patients slept soundly, none realising that their physical bodies were being inhabited by many souls, all trying to find their way out and escape to their next destination.

My body was clean and I had persuaded the cleaner to let me into the laundry so I could wash and dry my clothes. The washers were themselves filthy, but my clothes were a least a little fresher and once I had spent time picking off hair, they were at least the best I could do.

After I dressed, I sat on my bed and read the passages that I had been directed to that morning. The book of Job spoke to me and gave me comfort. Job had thought he had been abandoned by all his friends, but unbeknownst to him, he was being tested. He had been stripped of everything as had I. The words flowed through my brain and settled there happily. I put the Bible back on my windowsill and arranged the other objects in order as directed. I had an orange, a green apple and a red apple. These were good and evil. They were also Mars and Venus.

The green and the red were interchangeable depending on mood. Green could be interpreted as good and a sign to go ahead. It was also a sign that my heavenly lover, Mars, was jealous; it was also representative of the planet Mars and the Martians coming too close. Red was lust and danger; it could be the red planet Mars, it could be Red, one of his earthly incarnations. It could also be red for love and red for Venus, the planet, and Venus, my Roman love goddess incarnation. I could interpret these signs in conjunction with other events that unfolded at the same time. I had now had the gift to be able to read all the signs and act accordingly.

My windowsill was a portal that looked out over the courtyard and the smoking area. I arranged the fruit as instructed. The planets were aligned with the sun, all was well. I could see the dawn beginning to break. There was a green tinge to the mist. I knew this to be my Mars guiding our building back to the plane it was inhabiting. The Hub was basically a ship. I hesitate to say spaceship, but in reality that would be the most accurate description. The Hub was taken to many, many worlds depending on who had won control during the game that had been played that day. The green tinge that flooded the atmosphere this morning was synonymous with my lover Mars. I knew that we were way ahead of the game now and things were starting to turn the right way up. I hopped up onto the windowsill so I could breathe in the freshness of the morning air.

I stayed there for a long while, collecting my thoughts, planning my strategy. Bob Marley came through to me as I sat there. I realised that my powers in communication had increased tenfold at least. Bob sang inside my head as I watched the sunrise. *'The Sun is Shining'*, Kate, he whispered inside my head. I sang along with him and let his lyrics flow through me. I could feel myself smiling as the daylight rose and the mist thinned and finally oozed way. It was going to be a beautiful day. My powers were coming back in waves. I could not help but smile as I jumped back down off the windowsill, vaguely aware that I had already completed all my yoga exercises for the morning. I had stretched and danced on that windowsill without so much as a wobble. I had put my faith in the higher beings and they were holding me up, boosting my comeback as every second went by. I laughed out loud and immediately told myself off. I would not give the game away.

It was being played in earnest. Today I would save each and every one of the souls that was sent my way and woe betide anything that got in my way.

Flying High

Easter Monday – 28th March, 2016

I took my medication without problem these days. I had fought to ensure that they knew I would only take it if it had my name on the box and had been prescribed for me. I had seen one of the doctors and stated my case calmly and firmly. It appeared that I had been accused of spiralling when I had previously refused to co-operate. I had played them at their own game and employed the use of an advocate. One of the good angels had turned a blind eye and let me into the computer room to use the phone to ring an internal number. I had seen the advocate service on a leaflet that I had found sticking out from behind a poster on one of the notice boards. The number did not need an outside line so I could ring without having to ask a member of staff to dial out for me. Once my advocate had been in, it was amazing how quickly that I had been given an appointment to speak to a doctor who was on ward round that week when previous requests had been either laughed at or just plain ignored. The doctor had listened without interrupting and explained which drug he thought I should be taking. I was more than happy and as a result took my pills like a good girl. My only refusal, when being handed the wrong ones, I would politely decline and point out the error. I had been kept in this place for three weeks, and I witnessed mistakes with meds every single time we were called. I had tried to speak to the other patients to ask them to double check their meds, and one or two had started to follow my lead and since then I had become the person to confide in.

There were a group of six of us who had become close in the last few days. We had each other's backs. We were the ones who looked out for the rest of the ward too. I had unwittingly become the leader. We started standing up for our rights. The staff for their part seemed to now be a little intimidated by our newfound confidence. Yes. The tide was turning. We sat and spoke about incidents that had either happened to us or that we had witnessed happening to others. Until now nobody had stood up to the abuse. As the days went by, we became stronger and stronger. We gave ourselves code names. I had become Miss DJ. I was at the centre of The Hub. The six of us held court in the library, always with one on lookout. We were all from different walks of life and had different qualities. I could not wait to see them and fill them in on the events of the previous night. I looked around my room. It was essentially the same, but it felt fresh. The purple carpet was spotless. My quilt and pillow were now folded neatly at the end of the bed and I had wiped the plastic mattress, picking off any bits of fluff and the inevitable hair that found its way into every nook and cranny. I cleaned the sink, making sure that it was spotless and that my products were lined up in order. The mantra 'cleanliness is next to godliness' repeated over and over in my head. I took stock of my reflection; I had lost weight, my skin was pale and my eyes, although sunken, now looked more lifelike as I stared into the glass. The world beyond the mirror was calm. No demon dared show its face to me this morning. The picture above my bed drew me into it until I could almost feel the clear water that cascaded down into a lagoon. The sun shining through and creating a rainbow in the torrent of water that gushed down from a great height, no longer frightened me. I had made a point of ignoring it since I came to this place, but this morning it brought me something that had been threatened to never show its face again in my life. It brought me hope. Without hope, all is lost. I had nearly lost my fight, I had very nearly given up. Last night had been the turning point. Whatever happened from this day forth, I would never ever lose hope. I promised myself that I would keep the faith forever. He would be there to help me with whatever battle I was faced with. And it was with that thought in my mind that I eventually managed to tear myself away from the vision and leave the room to face the new day.

The rest of the ward was starting to wake up and I waited until it was time for meds before I ventured out into the corridor. All looked much the same to the untrained eye, but I spotted subtle differences along the way to the clinic. The pictures on the walls had altered, the same as the one I had just left behind in my room. The picture on the left of the corridor had solid rocks and bright green foliage surrounding a cool river mist.

Most of my fellow patients were up. The little lady in room eight was dressed and sat on the edge of her bed with a support worker stood in the doorway. I smiled at her, and for the first time there was a hint of recognition from her. I had been so very concerned about this lady. She rarely ventured out of her room, and every time I had seen her, her eyes would dart this way and that as though expecting harm to befall her. I knew without a doubt that she was scared half to death. She was taller than me but so tiny in stature. I could see every bone in her body, a thin veil of white skin mottled with blue tinges, bruises and scratches visible on her arms. Her collar bone stuck out as did her vertebrae. Her hair was dark and wispy, her eyes dark and wary. I always made a point of saying hello to her and a glimmer of recognition flickered across her face as I spoke to her this morning. I could feel her gaze on me as I left her behind and went to join the queue for morning medication.

'Morning,' I greeted Nick, the nurse on duty.

'Kate. I see you've been complying this week. That's better. You know your mediation is there for a reason.'

'I have no problem taking it if it is prescribed for me.' I smiled at him, taking the pills and swallowing them down. 'But, I'll be fucked if I'm putting any old shit into my body. You can't be too careful eh.' I didn't wait for an answer.

'You go girl,' said one of our six who had been stood behind me.

'You bet. You coming to breakfast? I'll wait for you.'

I wasn't entirely expecting her to come. Shakira, as I had named her, had her own issues and I had learned not to pressure her into doing anything.

'Yeah, I'll be there in five. Save me a seat will you?'

'No problem, lovely.'

I made my way down the corridor to the dining room. I took in the sights and smells as I passed each room. The corridor had been swept clean already. The pictures on these walls had been transformed in the same way as the ones I had already noted. The doors to the other rooms which led off the corridor were shut. The curtains in the library, the small lounge and Quiet Room were all shut. I was the first one to arrive in the dining room, and this was a rare occurrence. I was first to arrive at the hatch and ordered a bowl of muesli with toast to follow.

It was the Egyptian-looking guy who was working in the kitchen this morning, and he was one of the good people. Always a smile, and the food was always more than edible when he was in charge. He grinned back at me as I thanked him and took my bowl. There were a couple of clean green plastic cups next to the coffee machine along with a few blue ones. There were never clean cups normally. The coffee machine was showing black coffee, white coffee; no flashing, no milk powder to clean up. The fruit bowl had been placed on the windowsill, filled to the brim with fresh fruit. There was a full roll of kitchen paper stood on the opposite end of the windowsill. The room was clean and the green curtains were open, letting in the morning sun. It was a happy day.

My seat next to the radio was vacant and I sat down, taking in my surroundings with fresh eyes. The witch picture next to me was graphic in its detail, showing the witches that had been hung for their sins. The witches had been set free, their corpses still hung from branches, but their souls had flown away leaving only the empty husks behind. The picture nearest the window still showed the silhouettes of sycamore leaves laced with holes, and they now symbolised the rescue of souls which had been in danger of being dragged down into the eternal furnace below. My talk with Him last night combined with the growing beliefs of my contemporaries, had helped turn the egg timer back so the sands of time were flowing as they should.

I basked in the sunshine. The radio boasted of our small victories. *'Reach Up For The Sunrise'* played out and filled the dining room. The others came following Shakira with her beautiful smile.

'Shakira, Shakira,' I sang to greet her as she came to join me at my table.

Agent H, otherwise known as The Oracle, pulled up a chair. Next came my Romany ancestor, Eliza, with her infectious banter. She was related to LJ from my happy place. I did not need to tell her of our heritage; she was as well informed as I was. We called her Pocahontas as she had taken to wearing her jet black hair in two plaits, reminding us of another ancestor.

The other two who made up our group of six generally didn't join us for breakfast. CC was a lady who I had realised carried the souls of both my daughters, and she did not socialise a great deal. She looked as though she were pregnant, but the only thing she carried with her was a large fluffy teddy. I knew how special she was, but I could not tell her of the situation as it was hard enough for me to understand let alone try to explain it to her.

The other member of our six was a complex character who I had seen at the hatch for the clinic on day one. She was my next door neighbour and occupied room twelve. She had many issues and I didn't think it would be beneficial to her to know that her perception of day and night were completely wrong. She slept most of the day here in The Hub, her snoring echoing throughout the corridor. Her room was always in darkness, but she kept the door slightly ajar. The stench which wafted out was enough to make me gag; the aroma of unwashed body odour mixed with stale cigarettes. This unsavoury character was the most special amongst the six. She was my earthly husband, John; she was my heavenly husband, Hephaestus. It was too fantastical to even begin to broach the subject. Somewhere deep within her, hidden by the ungainly body, was my John. I listened to her breathing each night. I checked on her before I retired and went about my other duties. It was imperative that I kept this lady safe. For her part she did not interact much. Her conversation was limited, and bullet pointed with the need to smoke. She had anger issues when it came to smoking, and the need for nicotine outweighed any social pleasantries. We had clashed like mad when I first entered this place of judgement, and she had sworn at me and told me she didn't like me almost constantly. But, despite her unnatural dislike of me, the more I saw her, the more I knew who she really was. I never told her the whole truth, but by week three she had started to mellow, and although she hadn't voiced her change of feeling towards me there was a definite change in attitude. I simply called her Angel. She didn't question it. We came to have a mutual understanding and if she did dream of us when she slept in this place, she never revealed it. The crunch had come one evening when the six of us had occupied the library. It was getting late and the staff were getting nasty. They wanted their charges to all be in bed so they could put their feet up and sleep the shift away. We knew their game. They were the blues on duty that night; normally impartial, the blues were the colour of caution, the colour that denoted things could go either way. This particular night they had shown their true colours and had been influenced by the bad. No matter how much they tried to remove us, we stood firm. It had been my idea to start singing gospel songs. I did not know many but attempted to lighten the mood and bring God into our circle. Angel had suddenly stood up and burst into song with the most beautiful singing voice I had ever heard. The rest of us looked at each other in disbelief and gradually, one by one, stopped singing as her voice drowned us out in its clarity and tone. We let her fly solo and for the next half an hour were lifted to the next level where we laid back and let her transport us to the highs we had only dreamt of. As suddenly as she had begun, she stopped. The tide had turned and the blues left us alone, the power of good in the room too much for them to handle. We had won that battle. We all looked at each other in amazement and, one by one, began to clap. She was from that day known as Angel, purely on the strength of that performance. The singing over, Angel resumed her sullen character, but underneath we all knew how her heart and soul had been lifted that night. A fact that she hid from our guards but could never hide again from us her loyal friends.

Easter Monday carried on as it had started, filling my soul with hope and showing me the way in which I could help. The car park was less busy today. The beings who were playing the game were almost at a stalemate. It had been agreed to leave me be to run things on my level. A holiday, and somewhat of a truce, had been called from level three and above.

Although the car park was free from many of the comings and goings of vehicles, the balance was just right. The silver AV(Ares/Venus) number plates belonging to the minibuses were aligned properly; our families were in residence. Black cars were equal to the number of white ones and there was one red on each side. The scene was of perfect harmony. I was so happy with the equilibrium. My homies had left me to it after breakfast. I had become consumed with my duties. They understood. They all had their roles to fulfil. I did not ask them what tasks they had been given and in return they did not question me. We had parted for the time being, each left to their own plan until we would meet up again at the next meal.

I sat on the windowsill in the Quiet Room, watching my birds in the small copse behind the car park. I had pulled the curtains to behind me so I was no longer visible from within the building. I was able to sit, undisturbed, for the rest of the morning. My six crows had been lucky that their nests had stayed intact high up in the tall trees. We had experienced a storm the day before. The trees had swayed dangerously at alarming angles, threatening to dislodge the two nests that belonged to my boys. I tapped out the signal to them so they knew that I had done my best to save their homes. Planet Earth. I tapped out *'Planet Earth'* until I had their attention. They swarmed in their group and gave me a display of flight, intricate patterns performed in front of my eyes. I sang softly and clapped along, accompanying their song of salvation. A magpie appeared and we chased it away. One for sorrow was not on the agenda. My boys were in full flight. They controlled the forest. We, as higher beings, controlled the airwaves, inside and out of the building. Jack was in the car park along with his wife. I had christened the ducks, Jack and Vera. He nodded in approval as he waddled his way across the quiet tarmac, safe in the knowledge that I was watching him as he followed his wife. I nodded my head in return. They had been helpful in the game when I had to raise the stakes, I often called on my two jacks. Raise it. Two jacks, two jacks. And deal. I was proud of how far we had all come. I surveyed the outside world with new eyes.

There he was. I heard him before I saw him. My Mars, navigating his craft across the blue sky high above me. The bi-plane swooped and rolled in acknowledgement.

I waved manically. Please come and rescue me, my love. Please. I need you. My words were drowned out by the sound of the powerful engine as he joined my demigods; my birds, my boys in the clear airway above my head. My pleas had been noted, but it was not time for me to leave yet. My lover dipped his wings and left me waving as he disappeared. I called his name into the empty space. The void before me threatened to jump up and swallow me whole. I opened the window, wondering what I could find to smash it to pieces so I could make my escape. Surely he would come back for me. A loud bang brought me back to my senses. The door behind me had blown shut. I stopped dead. I was alone again, but back in control. The demon that had jumped onto my shoulder as I doubted my mission quickly disappeared again, knowing that he had been defeated in his whisperings.

These bastards were so sneaky. They crept up on you with no warning and before you knew, you were being carried away along the wrong path. Well, fuck you, darkness. I strengthened my resolve and recited a prayer. The Quiet Room had become a jealous place. The light in the ceiling had turned green. I had to get out of there or my soul would be in danger once again.

I jumped down from my vantage point and blew a kiss at my boys. They had settled down once again. Jack had disappeared into the undergrowth with his wife. All was well.

I opened the curtains, letting the light shine in and overpower the green above me. The game was still afoot. It was gone ten as I left the room and made my way to the library.

Saving Souls

Easter night – Monday 28th March, 2016

Angel surprised us and, after joining us for lunch, stayed up for the rest of the day. Although I had been careful to protect their true identities, the rest of my inner circle had started to work things out for themselves. They now accepted, without a doubt, that I controlled the airwaves. I was Miss DJ for a reason. They looked up to me. They loved me. I, in return, loved them too. They were a part of me. Shakira, Oracle, CC, Angel, Pocahontas, along with myself, we were the inner circle. The ones who were fighting for the good of the world.

Where it had once been down to myself as a solitary soldier to protect the gateway and oversee transformations, now they had all become a vital and integral part of the operation. Each one of us had been brought to this place for a reason. Each one of us had overcome a battle with evil. Some had had their children taken away from them; others, their husbands and other loved ones. We all had many things in common. We had all been stripped of our dignity. We had been ripped away from people who loved us and we had been brought screaming and kicking to this place. We had all stared death in the face and each of us had overcome it.

As we got to know each other, we listened with open minds at the events leading up to each of our incarcerations. All of us, with no exception, had witnessed a strange phenomenon. We had all been threatened by something inexplicable followed by a sign of some kind. Pocahontas told us of a stunning double rainbow, the like of which she had never witnessed before. The Oracle had witnessed a sudden violent electrical storm, forked lightning landing at her feet as she tried to run for shelter. I did not question CC and Angel as I knew that their tale would echo mine. I knew they had seen figures and heard voices without them telling me. We were in touch via other methods of communication. I did not need them to verbalise their fears, I already knew. I loved them all with all my heart. I would die for any of them and they knew the depth of my feeling without me having to tell them. Shakira was another special being, she was Mars to my Venus, Ares to my Aphrodite. I could not tell her this, but I knew she felt it too. We had connected on many levels and our spirits were entwined forever. We spoke of everything except of our true identities. If we had verbalised it, it would have spoilt the connection. I had to be very careful not to tip the balance. My head told me to let things happen organically. Let things unfold in a natural way as they were supposed to.

The day did unfold organically. What a difference the day made. Those twelve hours since midnight had enabled the world to shift. By mid-afternoon, we were very nearly the right way up again. I had been promised that by midnight the axis would match the earthly world. I had the rest of the day to conduct my duties as I saw fit before midnight came upon us. Midnight would mark the end of the nightmare ruling the planet and a new beginning. It would be a new moon tonight. I had a lot to get through in the following hours. I had been given a mission and I was determined to see it through. I would rest at the dawning of the new day tomorrow.

The bookshelves in the library had been turned upside down. My first task was to put all the books back in order and take off the ones that would cause problems. There were certain books that I needed to hide in my cloak; their covers featured children and young women who I knew represented my daughters and grandchildren. Once I was alone in the library, I began my work in earnest. I removed the family books and put the rest in alphabetical order. Some books had covers or titles which made me feel uneasy so I took them down and hid them at the back of the bottom shelf where they could not cause any mischief. Once I had taken my family books back to my room, I hid them in my black shawl and said a prayer for them as I zipped them up in my suitcase, the straps forming the sign of a cross affording them protection from above.

Next on the list were the DVDs, and some had a girl's name on. I knew that I had to hide these as this was the next soul in danger. She was a cousin. I had seen her family today. They had communicated on the next level, thanking me for my help. I handed over my cousin to their care. One soul saved. I watched as they made their way to the purple lounge and closed the door behind them. I felt the building twitch as their ship took off. After half an hour, I dared to venture over to the lounge, knowing it was empty. The plush purple curtains had been shut. I went in and pulled the drapes back. I straightened the sofa cushions, sweeping away imprints left by the previous occupants. Cousin A was safe. I knew her on two levels, one as a distant member of my family and another as a troubled musician. Both souls were now free to carry on their journey. I had not actually seen the physical body of my relation, but as I looked out the dining room window later in the day, I saw the figures of two girls walking down the driveway. I watched until they disappeared from view. Two saved so far today.

Seeing to the purple lounge was imperative. It had to be clean and ready for the next inhabitants, which I hoped and prayed would occupy its lush interior on their way to salvation. Bob Marley came through again. He was pleased at how things were progressing. I laughed with him and smelt the aroma of some strange smoke filling my lungs as we chatted. He called me his lion in Zion. He stayed with me for a while as I did my routine checks. The bathrooms, which were always so dirty, were all in need of my touch. I wiped surfaces, cleaning away what looked like charcoal splodges on the windowsills, and the carbon footprint we were leaving on this planet was never very far from my mind. I had, until today, walked around with nothing on my feet in order to demonstrate the filth in which we were expected to exist. I carried on my cleaning duties after Bob had left me. My mind had become wide open and I was receiving many spirits and souls loud and clear. The word had obviously got round and I was becoming more and more in tune with the hundreds of voices now clamouring to be heard.

'*All That Glitters.*' I hummed the Prince tune in my head as I examined the carpet in my room. After filing away the books, I had turned my attention to the floor. I walked with my head down, examining each piece of carpet and laminate as I passed over it. I collected the glitter. Strange pieces of gold thread had begun appearing as had tiny pieces of clear plastic, shaped as a diamond. Bits of silver foil, metallic bronze fibres, blue plastic, green plastic, sequins; all caught my eye and I snatched them up before they could be lost. I had to take them back to my room to investigate. I was in the process of separating them into their piles. Some I saved in a small plastic pot which I kept on my windowsill, and I had placed the pot in pride of place next to the bible. It joined a picture that I had drawn; on one side were two lions coloured in purple and red, on the other were crude drawings of the peace sign and the Eiffel tower. There were splodges of what could only be described as purple rain, covering love hearts with the initials JK within them. I turned this picture round according to whether it was night and day. As I set about my task I was aware that there were people outside in the communal area. I climbed back up onto my vantage point but the owners of the voices were nowhere in sight. I was about to jump down when I heard someone shout.

'And action,' a male voice called out.

I strained my neck to see if I could spot anyone. I could vaguely hear some dialogue, but it was not loud enough for me to decipher exactly what they were saying so I jumped down from my perch. I spent the rest of the afternoon going from one room to another, collecting the signs as they had been left for me. The more I collected, the more I noticed that I was becoming tired and irritable so I kept my distance from staff and patients alike. It was three in the afternoon when I heard the call for 'fresh air' come from the end of the corridor. I could not remember the last time I had been outside so I decided to join the smokers. Not to smoke but to socialise with the rest of the ward and try and find an area away from the pollution where I could breathe in some proper outside air.

'You don't smoke.' One of the guards sneered at me. 'I'm not sure I should let you come.'

'I've just started,' I sneered back.

The rest of our gang sniggered and the guard backed off, disconcerted at my arrogance and at the reaction from the others. I knew this one. He was a coward. He was normally a bully when he found us on our own, but in numbers we were more than he dared take on. So, I found myself clumping down the two flights of stairs towards the outside. At the bottom of the stairs was another door with a security pad on. It flashed red until the guard passed a lanyard across and the red changed to green, unlocking the mechanism which held us prisoner. Once in the foyer, there was another door which opened the same way. I noticed the picture on the wall opposite near some lockers. It showed a wooded area and underneath the trees the space was filled with the most vibrant bluebells I had ever seen. A path through the middle was lit up by shafts of sunlight and it wended its way through the flowers until it disappeared. This was an escape route. I knew it. I stored the image in my head before following the others out beyond the locked door; out into the yard, out to the nearest thing to freedom that we would experience whilst being kept locked away from our world.

It was cold but sunny. The blue sky had just a few fluffy white clouds floating lazily across it. I could hear the song of a robin, its shrill voice sounding like a rusty saw. I allowed myself to take in each element slowly. The noise of nature, birds, a slight breeze making the leaves whisper just beyond the fence. The cawing of my crows as they swooped around giving me the benefit of a flying display once again. My fellow smokers had all lit up and were huddled together in the smoking shelter.

'I thought you were smoking?' the guard quizzed me as I sat on my own away from the pollution.

'I decided I'd try it later instead. I feel a bit sick,' I replied before turning my back on him.

He walked away, leaving me to my thoughts. I could hear activity from the other side of the fence. I tried to work out my bearings and decided that it was the area directly below my bedroom window.

I hopped onto a bench so I could see over into the yard next door. There were a few men milling about smoking, and one kicking a football against the wall. I watched in silence until a face I recognised caught my eye.

'Hi, is that you? Carl?'

'Well, fancy seeing you here,' he replied and made his way past the others to come and speak to me.

'You have the biggest smile I've ever seen.'

'Thanks. Are you allowed out now, then? Are you escorted?'

'I have no idea. I pretended I wanted to smoke so I could get outside. I'm not sure if I need an escort or not?'

'Well, are you on levels? I'm guessing you must be sectioned if you've come from in there.' He gestured at my bedroom window.

I ignored his question, not wanting to explain what had happened to me. I had gone past that scenario now and had moved on. I couldn't bear a conversation bringing it all back again.

'Can I ask you something weird?'

He looked at me quizzically. 'Depends how weird.'

'You know I love your smile. You look like Dizzee Rascal with that grin.'

'Well thanks, lady. Nobody has ever said that before. What do you want to know?'

'Was there a film crew here earlier? I could've sworn I heard the words camera and action?'

'Ah, so you're the one they've been whispering about. I shouldn't really tell you, but seeing as I think I know who you are, I will just say that anything you may or may not have heard may well be based on the truth.'

'What do you mean?'

'Yes, you did hear a film crew. But you didn't hear it this morning. You heard it in the future. I can't explain properly now, but I know you understand about time here don't you?'

'Yes. I don't fully understand everything yet, but it is becoming clearer every minute that passes. Thank you, Carl.'

'Don't know what you mean. I haven't told you anything.' He winked at me and sauntered away as if we had never had a conversation.

I sat back down on the bench and stared at the sky, high above me a jet trail. Another plane appeared, and I wondered where it was heading. Some warmer climate I thought, full of passengers all looking forward to their week, or two weeks if they were lucky, in the sunshine. I wasn't really jealous of them. I just wanted my transport to come and take me home. A thrumming sound drew near and as I looked, my plane appeared again. It swooped and soared.

'Hey. It's me. Come back and save me. Hello, hello,' I shouted at the sky.

The rest of my companions laughed out loud. 'Oh Kate, you're so funny. Our Miss DJ, do you think you can control the skies as well?' They laughed good-naturedly.

'Worth a try, girls. That's my fella up there. He promised he would come and save me. Obviously the time isn't right just yet, but he will come. I know it.'

'Smoke break over, ladies. Put them out. Let's go.'

I took a deep breath and savoured every bit of air as it rushed into my lungs. I needed to fill my soul with the goodness of the outside before I headed back inside and up to the first floor again.

I hadn't anticipated how hard it was climbing back up to the first floor. There were thirteen steps in all on two flights of stairs. The first seven came to a landing and I had to stop and rest for a moment before tackling the next seven. A picture of sepia clocks was fixed above the first landing, and they all showed different times and portrayed confusion. No wonder I found it so difficult to keep a grip on what time it was. The portent was here at the entry, a picture I had missed on my way in late that first night that I had been brought here. I had learned so very much in the last three weeks. I was a different person now. I was regaining my strength.

My notepad was still intact. I had managed to keep it hidden from the staff. I flicked through it and made notes. I had managed to identify which souls were inhabiting which bodies. The very thin lady had a musician who had very recently passed over inhabiting her body for the most part, but she also had a musician who had refused to move on for many years. No wonder she was all skin and bone. I identified at least three different souls who were all present within the bones of this poor lady. No wonder her eyes had beseeched me each time I passed. I knew that this was my next mission. I also knew that the elderly musician would have been a prize catch for the dark side. I had my work cut out with this one.

The staff called for meal time. It was five o' clock. I decided that I would bring the lady from room eight with me.

'Hey there. Will you please come and join me in the dining room,' I asked her as I passed her room.

My question went unanswered, but her eyes followed me as I passed.

'Come on then, you can come and sit with me if you like.'

It took me the best part of half an hour before she made a move. As we walked together I gently placed my hand on her elbow, understanding flooded through me. My mission for the day was to shepherd the elderly music man through the correct door, where his parents were waiting to carry him home.

I had a song in my head and as we walked, I sang it to him.

The little lady turned and looked me in the eye. Her eyes had been replaced with the dark trusting eyes of a beautiful man who in his time had captivated the world with this soulful voice. Her face disappeared to be replaced with one of a familiar male. I knew him straight away.

'Hello sir,' I greeted him as he stared at me. 'Will you come and eat with me before you go?'

The music man nodded and followed me into the dining room. I took my place and gestured at the empty seat opposite. He hesitated and then sat down unsteadily.

'It's ok. I promise. I will fetch your dinner for you. You look ravenous.'

He smiled and nodded. I felt honoured to go and order his last supper for him. I chose wisely, taking heed of his requests as they floated into my head.

I said grace and we began the last earthly meal that he would taste before moving on to his Nirvana. We chatted about music and how things had changed since his day. My meal with this wonderful man will stay with me forever. He ate and drank, savouring every mouthful.

'It is time to go,' I said gently as he finished the last of his water.

'I know. Thank you so much, mam,' he replied.

'No need for thanks. This is my calling,' I answered him softly.

I gestured for him to follow me into the foyer. The sign 'Chrysalis Ward' glowed gold and the corridor ahead of us was flooded in a bright white light.

'After you.' I gave him a gentle nudge on the back.

'I'm scared.'

'That's only natural, and it is up to you whether you want to go or not. I cannot force you, but I can tell you that everything is ready and waiting for you on the other side.'

'I think I can believe you, but it's been so long. Would you do me the honour of singing with me.'

'Wow, it would be my honour, sir. Would you like to choose the song?'

'No, you do it... Miss DJ isn't it?' he stared into my eyes with a smile.

'If you're sure, then of course I will.'

I started singing the first tune that came into my head. As he joined in, the way in front changed from bright white light to gold, then the colours of the spectrum appeared, dancing in front of our eyes. He took a step forward, still holding my hand.

'*Swing low, Sweet chariot.*' We chorused together, our voices harmonising beautifully.

I gently removed my hand and took a step backward, leaving him to face his destiny.

He looked at me and we sang the lyrics together as he left me behind. The colours surrounded his form with every step he took until they had swallowed him up completely. I was left on my own, staring at a kaleidoscope of colours and patterns dancing in front of my eyes until nothing remained but a speck of gold at the end of the corridor.

The building shook and then became quiet again as I entered the dining room. She was sat there where I had left her. Staring into space. He had gone. She now housed only two other souls apart from her own. He had taken up a massive part of her being and now she had a space to build herself up again. The two who remained would soon be gone. He was the one that had fed from her soul.

I sat back down and carried on with my food, aware that I was being watched.

'You ok?' I asked her.

'Yes, thank you,' she replied.

I almost choked on my food at hearing her voice. Now we had a special bond and I knew that I would be able to exorcise the other souls and send them to their destinations. The one I had been tested with had gone and he had gone safely. I was tired myself. The exorcism had taken it out of me. I took my time eating the rest of my meal and made the most of the nice food that had been provided today. It seemed that with the turning, everything, including the food, was being transformed for the good.

BOOK THREE
EXODUS

I am – by Miss DJ

I am lost
I wonder who will hear me
I hear some hope this day
I see opportunities
I want my home; my love
I am waiting

I pretend you are here
I feel abandoned
I touch your image
I cry out in my sleep
I am sinking

I understand the plan
I say hurry please
I dream of your loving arms
I try to remain calm
I hope it will be today
I am saved

Live Music

Easter Monday 28th March, 2016

The evening came quickly on this Easter Monday. I was happier than I had been for a long time. The atmosphere had taken on an air of positivity for the first time since I had arrived. My notebook was filling up rapidly as I jotted down new developments. I used a code in case the staff found my hiding place and took it upon themselves to ship us all downstairs en masse. I now kept it on my person, hidden in my cleavage. My cleavage had served me well as a hiding place and I had secreted all manner of items down there like a human squirrel, filling my bra with my finds and notes. It was the safest place I could think of. Even the fallen ones would not dare to strip search me in front of the others and I was not a self-harmer so they had no reason to think I was concealing anything under my clothes.

I kept my vigil by the radio for the rest of the day. The songs being played became more and more relevant as the day went on. Spirits who had passed over years before came through via the airwaves. Apart from allowing myself a short break at mealtimes, I sang and danced with each and every one. It was important for them to know that their voices had been heard. Some had been made saints since they had left our world. I welcomed them all. Some came in person, occupying the bodies of the good angels. The fallen angels were keeping their distance today which made my job so much easier. We sang together, we danced together, we got to know each other. They thanked me for my help and I was filled with such a deep sense of joy and satisfaction. A job being well done. They warned me that I had to be on guard as the bad side would still try and sneak in wherever it could. It would be getting desperate and be even sneakier than usual. I was not worried just yet, I knew that until night fell I was more than safe. I had carried out all my duties as directed and not a stone had been left unturned. Prayers had been said. The environment was cleaner than it had ever been. The radio was tuned and in control. The occasional bad song came on and tried to sway me, tricking me into letting its voice be heard, but it only took me a few seconds to decipher the bad from the good and I switched them off before their influence took hold on any of us.

The bad singers were as influential on our souls as the sirens who had been the downfall of many sailors in times gone by. Their voices, beautifully crystal clear, soon became dangerous as they hypnotised their victims. They hissed at me as I switched them off, leaving empty space in the air where their treachery had materialised.

Today was a special day. It was a day of resurrection. So far, the resurrected had been good souls, but for every good soul there was a bad counterpart. Together we fought them off and our position was strong. I knew that as the night fell, I would need to be extra vigilant so I called a meeting in the library after our evening meal.

Five of our six were present. Angel had been unwell today and I was concerned that her health had taken a turn for the worst. My fears were based on the fact that she had not even wanted to go for a cigarette today. I tasked Oracle in policing the corridor; she did not have to be present to do this, her level of consciousness was way above the rest of us. She was a level five at least and as such could detect anything untoward way before anyone else. The Oracle's physical being was as stunning as her mental abilities; she had perfect clear dark brown skin, long dark lashes and a slight athletic physique which reminded me of a beautifully muscular toned racehorse. Her hair was swept up under a red turban and she wore a multi-coloured knitted blanket which she wrapped around herself like a cloak. The blanket had been given to her by a stranger who had passed her in the street; she had accepted it, not knowing why. Until now, I called it her dream coat; it had powers in itself and I had borrowed it one night when I felt particularly vulnerable. The cloak had protected me from whatever evil had stalked me that night, but in the process had become ripped down some of the seams. I knew that it was imperative that the seams were sewn up again since these were symbolic of the fabric of reality we found ourselves in. The Oracle and I set about mending them during this meeting. I could feel the fabric of time passing smoothly through my fingers.

Pocahontas sat quietly, lost in her own dream world. She was tapping into the psychic powers of our Romany friends. I had been able to help a little in locating some of the travelling fraternity as a few had turned up in my hometown the week before I had been taken from my home. I had felt them making enquiries as to who was in need of their help. My Romany spirit guide communicated on my behalf and had kept them updated ever since. I passed them over to my lovely raven-haired friend and let her update them on the situation as it stood.

My work with CC had already been successful. She had delivered our babies safely into our world without the dark side even realising they had been born. I thanked her for everything she had done and knew it was time for her to move on. She had been allocated a new home in a halfway house just that day and was all set to leave in the morning. CC always commented on how lovely I smelt, and she always looked a little envious when I told her of the products I used. She was beside herself with joy when I gave her a bottle into which I had decanted some of my special shower gel. I had brought one of the family books with me, and it had a picture of a small child on the front of it.

'CC, this book is symbolic of one of my grandchildren. I need you to take it with you to your new place. It is the only way I can keep it safe. Will you do that for me?' I asked when the others had left.

'Yes, of course. What do you need me to do with it?'

'Just keep her out of sight, that's all. If you take her with you, I know that you will both be safe.'

'I'd do anything for you, Miss DJ, you know that. Thank you so much for this.' She waggled the bottle at me.

'It is holy liquid. I blessed it before I filled it up. Your body and soul will be cleansed when you use it. It is my gift to you to thank you for helping to save my family.'

'I am going to miss you, Kate.'

'Likewise, but I am hoping I won't be here much longer. I have work to do, but things have changed. I am making some headway. Just pray for me. Pray that I will soon be following in your footsteps and leaving this place for good.'

'I know you will. Love you, mate.' CC gave me a massive hug, picked up her bottle and the book and left me to it.

The others had all gone on their way. I was satisfied that the library was in order before I, too, left to go and do my other hourly check. I had a system in place. I started from the purple lounge as that was the furthest point away from the dining room, it almost met and joined at the west side, with just the secure doors and cage in between the quadrant. Purple check done, all well. Then the bedrooms on that side which included our Oracle, opposite, a new patient, the bathroom and the purple shower room next door to her. Doors all shut. The two toilets, flushed and the carbon flecks cleaned up. Isolation room, empty. Cell empty. Obs room locked. All the time I was keeping an eye on the floor to pick up anything that needed collecting. I was on the lookout for good and bad, including staff. Moving into the corridor where the rest of the bedrooms were, I checked each room and looked in on each resident. Angel in residence, steady snoring told me she was still in bed. Room five opposite mine had a new patient and I was wary of her and as I checked on Shakira, I found that she had a new patient opposite her room as well. Three of the six of us had strangers nearby. The thought made me uneasy and I made a note of the room numbers which had new occupants. I needed to check them out. I had a bad feeling in the pit of my stomach. The rest of the bathrooms and toilets on this side of the circle were all dirty and I cleaned each one in turn, flushing dirt away, wiping sinks, wiping charcoal black marks off the windowsills, closing each door to keep the sulphur like smell trapped behind.

The rooms in the corridor leading up to the dining room and foyer were all clear. The office was occupied with four staff who were oblivious of me as I stared at them through the window. Two good ones, two bad. We were on level pegging at this moment in time. I went back into the dining room and switched the tunes back on again. 'Under Pressure' Queen and David Bowie sang out into the atmosphere.

The evening was drawing in, the light fading as Freddie and David harmonised. I joined in, my voice strong and clear; they had come to find me from whichever dimension they now occupied.

'Hey, David. You sound well, my friend. I hope they have made you welcome.' I felt his presence. Another music legend taken too soon from our world.

What was the reason? I knew things were escalating, but I had hoped that we had slowed it down a little. Too many of us were being taken from Planet Earth. Too many were being removed and sent on their journey, ahead of those of us who had been left behind. I wondered what the criteria was? We had lost Motorhead's Lemmy, but so far I had not come across him. Bowie was coming through, singing along with his friend Freddie, so I knew that he had gone to the right place. Who would come through to me next I wondered as I sang along and danced in complete unison with two legends of my earthly lifetime.

Night Moves

Easter Monday 28th March 2016 – The Night

Night time came at last. The night shift had come on. I had rubbed their names off the board and erased the date. These four were bad. They had come to try and take us down. They were working for the blues who had decided on taking the dark path tonight. I had no idea why they kept switching alliance, but I was glad that I was instantly able to decipher which side they were working for. I had met each one of them before and I was confident that I would be able to overcome anything that they may throw at me. I could not allow myself to let my guard down. It was ten o'clock at night, and for the most part the rest of my fellow patients had already retired, apart from Oracle and Pocahontas, who insisted they stay up with me to assist in the fight. I had argued for a while, but then gratefully accepted their help. With the three of us on duty, we had more than a good chance of getting through the dark hours with our souls still intact.

I was on first watch. I sent the other two to the library so they could at least sit in comfort and maybe doze off for half an hour if they felt tired. I knew that I could call on them if needed.

It must have been near midnight when the first demon came. The door to the art cupboard had started rattling again as it had done previously. Bang. I was wide awake, heart pounding. I wedged my chair against the door and turned the radio up.

'I can't hear you, I can't see you. Hear no evil, see no evil. You should know this, demon. I will never give up my fight. Do you think I am frightened of you? I have faced much bigger danger and survived. I suggest you back off before I open this door and rip your head off and shit down your scrawny neck.'

The door rattled harder making the chair slip.

'I know you,' it screamed.

A foul stench flooded the dining room, overpowering me for a moment.

'Oh yes, we know each other of old. Witch-finder General... I know how close you managed to get to my family. You possessed the weak ones and had them carry out your evil. Did you think I wouldn't fight back? You are not welcome here. Go back to your rocky home in Colorado. I know all about you.'

My head was spinning as the demon summoned up all its strength in its quest to defeat me. The chair flew across the room and landed with a crash against the far wall.

'Is that all you've got?' I screamed back at it. 'You fail every time you try. Give up, you pathetic piece of shit. Haven't you realised we've already won.'

'What's going on?'

I turned to see my friends stood in the doorway holding onto each other.

'Stay back, I've got it,' I called above the rising din that was filling the room.

'No, we are here to help. You can't do this on your own, Kate.'

'Ok, but don't come in, stay in the doorway. Pray as hard as you can.'

The room was spinning now and The Hub was throbbing with the energy created by the battle. Lights flickering, creating a strobe effect. I held onto my table to steady myself. I reached over with one hand to try and switch the radio back on.

'You think your music can save you? I'm in control now, Miss DJ.' It sneered at me.

The radio flew across the room, landing on the floor next to the chair.

'Kate,' the others shouted.

'The Lord's Prayer... do you know it?' I shouted back.

The three of us began reciting the familiar words, and as we chanted, I fought my way against the force gripping my limbs. The radio was within touching distance. Nearly there.

'Pray harder, girls. We are winning.'

The grip lessened and I grabbed the radio and clutched it to my chest. The Hub spun around on its axis like a fairground ride, it pinned me against the wall. Faster and faster, forces holding me rigid. Colours whizzing past my face, all joining until they merged to become a bright white light that dazzled me and I had to shut my eyes.

And as suddenly as it had started, it ground shudderingly to a halt. I fell to the ground with a thud.

'Kate, Kate, are you ok?'

The girls chorused as they ran in and grabbed an arm each, helping me up.

'It's gone.' I grinned at them. 'We sent it back to where it belongs. Aspen, if I'm not mistaken. That one has been trying to possess me for a long time. It managed to get Bundy, but I was stronger than it realised. I think it's gone back across the pond now, but I have a feeling it will try again in the future.'

The dining room was silent. Lights on. Curtains closed. I surveyed the scene and apart from a few magazines which had been blown off the table, everything appeared to be back to how it had been before.

'We couldn't get to you. Bloody hell, that was scary.' Pocahontas gave me a hug.

'That's him dealt with. I'm getting my strength back now.' I took the radio over to the table and plugged it back in, switched it on and let the music flood into the room once more.

'*Beat It*' blared out. We looked at each other in amusement at the choice of song. I had summoned MJ, and St Michael sang and we sang along with him. The power of happiness was amazing; the power of love, the power of good over evil. That is what the others who followed a dark path didn't understand. Good would always overcome; you just needed to have faith in your beliefs. I firmly believe that it doesn't matter what your choice of faith is, as long as you believe and you put your trust in it. It is nobody's business but your own whichever you choose. You can pray to a piece of cheese; if you believe it, then that's your religion.

We spent the next hour singing and dancing the negativity away. We were ecstatic in our glory. And that's when they sent the next test.

'Time you were all in your rooms. You're disturbing the other patients,' one of the night staff addressed us. 'And turn that radio off.'

'We are not hurting anyone. The bedrooms are nowhere near here, I don't see how we are disturbing anyone,' I replied.

We carried on dancing and ignored her.

'I will have to report this. You may all be put on levels in the morning.'

'What the bloody hell are levels?' I asked.' I've never understood what that is all about. You follow people around with folders making undecipherable marks totally at random. None of it makes sense.'

'I'm not prepared to have this discussion with you. It is not your business to know what we write.'

'I disagree. I think we're entitled to know everything that you say about us, but I really can't be arsed to have this conversation now. I'll bring it up with my advocate. Now kindly go away and leave us alone.'

The night staff turned her back and stalked off down the corridor.

'Now you've done it.' Oracle looked at me worriedly.

'They won't risk injecting three of us. They're cowards.' I smiled back at her. 'Go back to the library if you like or go to bed?'

'No, we're not leaving you alone now.'

I sat at my table and they came to join me.

'I'm going to sort some of these papers on this table. They've been annoying me. I know there is an internal fight going on between some of the images and I have to put them in order.'

The other two looked at me like I was in need of an injection up the arse.

'I know it sounds crazy, but look at everything else that is going on. Here, look at this.'

I separated two colouring sheets out. One showed an alien chasing a girl, the other showed a princess riding a horse.

'See, the princess is really being threatened. Look through the pile and sort it into good and bad. It's all about everything being in order.'

They looked at me like I was crazy, but did as I had suggested. After half an hour, they were not so sceptical.

'It's all about getting rid of the negative stuff. That is how the evil works, it puts negativity out there. Things get broken, mixed up, confusion takes over. It's not rocket science. Negativity breeds negativity and before you know it, things slide down until the whole world is upside down.'

'What she says is true.' The Oracle had been listening and remembering things as I spoke. 'You know I know things that none of you are privy to don't you?' she asked.

'Yes. We are nowhere near your level. You mustn't tell us because it will upset the balance and we are definitely making headway.'

'Everything is linked. That is all I can say to you.'

We carried on our tasks, separating the good from the bad. Picking pencil crayons, we coloured with love, masking the hate we found within the pages. As we coloured and sang our songs, the room started spinning again. We were the only solid thing in the room. Our feet dangled into thin air but we kept on. As we sorted and filed, coloured and sang, the evil spun us around. Another fairground ride. We were on a Waltzer, spinning this way and that. Colours whizzing by again. My head was spinning. None of us spoke to each other but we held hands, pressing our elbows into the table so that our work was protected.

We were dancing in the air. The airwaves sang out with my choice of songs. We spun and danced, sang and rocked, this way and that. Colours so vivid, beautiful voices joining in as we sang out. I knew that time was going back and forth. The Hub had taken over. We were powering it with our faith. All the saints, all the angels were with us. Our beloved musicians who had left our earthly plane carried us through the night on a crusade.

The demons could not keep up with us. They did not dare enter into a new battle. The three of us had joined forces, creating the perfect climate. We had been transported to the next level; we sailed through parallel dimensions, taking in the colours of the spectrum, dancing along wrapping themselves around us with the smells of incense and heavenly voices.

Apples

Tues 29th March – Early Hours

We landed safely back in the correct time and place once again.
The Hub was now under our control, and for the first time since I had
been ripped away from my family, I knew with certainty that we were
defeating the evil. It was a long process, an ongoing battle, but we
were on the up. The fight had been ongoing since the beginning of
time. Not since our days in Greece, not since the days of biblical times
had the fight been so visible.

There was a fly. I noticed it straight away. It buzzed around us,
settling on our work, polluting our atmosphere. Flies were bad news.
They were spies for the dark. Their hundreds of eyes, their dirty habits,
walking all over any excrement they could find then walking over
food, vomiting all over food, leaving their dirt on clean surfaces,
laying their eggs and leaving them to hatch into maggots. Nothing
good ever came about whilst there were those sneaky, nosy, evil little
bastards flying around watching our every move. Fly on the wall. Big
brother watching. Not this time.

I quietly folded a magazine and waited for the moment when I
could squash it dead before it could report back to the devils that sent
it. Thwack. Gone. It was a standing joke between our group that I

would always stop whatever I was doing and go on a fly hunt if one even dared to enter the room I was in.

'Kate, I'm going back to the library. Will you be ok?'

'Yes, you might as well both go. There's nothing else you can do here. I'll probably need your help later. I need to be vigilant here until the light starts coming again. When the night abates, I will come to you. I will need your help to bring the dawn in safely.'

They went without questioning me. They did not question my words. Whatever I said had now become accepted. They listened without ridiculing me. We had all been raised up in our levels of consciousness. What had started out as a nightmare was becoming a path that we all were sent on to follow. We were all here for a reason. As each day passed it became more and more obvious that we were meant to be together. We worked as a team. Since the beginning of time we had worked for the good of the world we inhabited. We were timeless. We were sentinels. We would never stop. Nothing was ever too much. Each time we were reincarnated it was for a reason, and we came back at times when we were needed.

Planet Earth was in crisis and we had been summoned to take control and turn the tables back to the path of righteousness. Once our jobs were done we could all go back up high or down low, wherever we were meant to be. We all had our tasks to do. For as much as the power of love was strong, it also needed something to fight against. As an individual, the doubters, the nasty bastards, had all served to make me who I was.

I scooped up the dead fly from the floor, wrapped it in a piece of paper and threw it in the bin.

I scanned the room, checking for any signs. The fruit bowl caught my eye. It had been placed on the worktop next to the coffee machine. A quick scan of the display showed that all was well, no threats of alien ships landing, black coffee, white coffee, no spilt powder or creamy liquids present. It had been brought to my attention that when the threat was near, the cream represented alien seed. Ugh. I decided to rinse everything with hot water anyway just in case. I cleansed the spill tray under the machine and emptied the water into the large bowl that was ever present. The fruit bowl had been placed on it. It made me feel queasy but I could not see anything untoward.

I poured some hot water into a clean cup and ripped off a large piece of kitchen roll. There were three red, three green, three golden apples and half a dozen satsumas in the large bowl. I carefully removed each one and wiped the bowl; something sticky had pooled at the base. Yuck, what was it? Sticky oily stuff that I could not identify. It took me a while to cleanse and wipe all the residue away. I started to wipe the fruit. The satsumas were all good but there was something not quite right with the apples. The green ones had a film of grime which I wiped away. When I examined the red ones, two of them had scars which looked very much like bite marks. The golden ones were puzzling. I held each one in turn, spinning them around in my hand and examining them closely. Three golden apples. My memory hit a wall. Three. Gold. A race. Something about a race. A transformation. Lions. Words came at me from all directions. I had the urge to throw one of the apples across the room. It glinted as at arced through the air towards the radio. It hit the floor and rolled under the table, coming to rest directly under the radio. Atalanta and Hippomenes' antics slowly came back to me. Racing. I gasped as the memories linked and I pieced together the images.

I, Aphrodite, had helped join together a man and a woman. Nothing special about that in itself seeing as I was the goddess of love, but this particular couple had needed me. They had needed my help. Atalanta was a hunter, a racer, and she was known throughout the land as a woman who could outrun any man. Her search for a husband was futile. In order to win her hand, a suitor would have to beat her in a race. None had been able to complete this task and she was in danger of never marrying. I had helped a young suitor named Hippomenes by giving him three golden apples. At stages during the race, I had instructed him to throw down an apple. Atalanta, on seeing the golden apple, stopped to pick it up. After doing this for three times, he had eventually won the race and won her hand in marriage.

The problem came when they failed to honour me for the help I had given and went into a shrine dedicated to another deity to make love. In my anger, I had turned them both into lions.

The events flooded back. I retrieved the apple I had cast away and set it on the table with the other two. Images of the race transported me back to my homeland. Head in my hands, I wept for the loss of my home. I wept for myself, I wept for Miss DJ, I wept for all of the poor souls trapped here in The Hub. It took me a while to gather my senses back together. I returned the apples to their bowl. The gold and green now glistened, the orange of the satsumas brightened the display. I threw the two bitten red apples in the bin. I was left with one red. It was large and had thick shiny deep red skin. Blood red. It was the colour of love. It was my apple. It was mine, representing love, lust, passion. I held it to my face, feeling the cool hard skin melding itself into the soft skin of my cheek. I pushed it hard into my flesh and rolled it across my face until it rested against my lips and under my nose. It had a sweet heady scent. I felt my lips part and my tongue shot out to caress the skin.

I was unaware of the presence as it crept up behind me. My body had thrown itself forward onto the table, my legs spread and my arms outstretched in the form of a cross. An inverted cross. I had sunk my teeth into the thick red skin, sucking the juice from the flesh. It dripped its nectar onto my tongue and I savoured each drop as it landed. I was vaguely aware that my body had become possessed by a spirit. I luxuriated in the feeling that had overtaken my senses. I was turned on. I was ready for the dark to take me. I wanted to make love to whatever it was that was sending chills through my body and soul. I writhed and swayed, opening my mind to the ecstasy that had taken over.

I crunched down and filled my mouth with the deadly fruit. I rolled it around in my mouth, sucking out the juice before crushing the flesh and skin ready to swallow it all.

My peripheral vision caught a movement. A jolt. I saw someone in the doorway. A figure leant against the frame watching me. It was him. He had come for me. My Mars was there waiting. I wanted him desperately. My lover had come to take me back to his planet.

'Come to me,' I begged the figure. 'Please, I need to see you.'

The figure took no notice of my pleas, shaking its head. It remained in the same position. I needed to be with this man. I turned my back. On the chair was a man's jacket. I knew it belonged to him. I picked it up and held it to my face. It smelled of him. I suddenly knew that I could not have him, the time was not right. He was watching and waiting for me. The closest I could get to him was to put his jacket on. My senses were returning and I almost choked as some of the apple skin stuck in my throat.

I spat it out. This wasn't right. The apple had been sent to poison me. I felt sick. It was the seed of the devil. I retched and retched until I had rid my body of any of the taste of evil.

When I looked up, my Mars had gone. He had saved me. He had brought me back from the edge of the abyss. My saviour. I pulled his jacket around me close.

I had let my guard down and the fallen ones had taken advantage. I would not allow this to happen again. Mars had left me his coat. It was a physical sign of his protection.

I turned the radio up. '*Photograph*' by Ed Sheeran blared out and I sat weeping for my loves. I would see them soon. Everything would be all right.

Bringing In The Dawn

Tuesday 29th March, 2016

I am mortified at what has happened. I nearly set us back a thousand years. If I had swallowed that poisonous flesh, I would have succumbed to the succubus that had come for me. My hero had come and saved me and I was forever in his debt. He would not let me close to him. It was not the right time, but he had renewed my resolve and given me hope for the future. I had faith in the plan. Everything was happening as it should.

The dawn was approaching. I went to join the others in the library. I had decided not to mention what had just happened. To verbalise it would give the evil some credence and I would not allow this to happen.

They were waiting for me to come. The atmosphere was full of positive energy. We were nearing daylight.

'Hey, girls. Anything to report?'

'All quiet. The staff tried to boot us out but we stood firm and they soon gave up,' Oracle answered me as I went to sit on the large brown leather chair in the corner.

'Thanks for your support, it means the world to me. You know I couldn't do this on my own. You are both an integral part of this fight. You know that don't you?'

They assured me that they would be with me until our duties had been carried out. The Oracle spoke of how she had come to be with us; the events which preceded her incarceration were similar to mine. Pocahontas spoke of our ancestors, and she had known that we were related as soon as she had set eyes on me. Her spirit guides had advised her. We chatted and discovered we had all been let down by our own mental health teams. Ultimately, nobody had cared where we ended up as long as we were off their caseload. The random events that had occurred before we had been sent to this hole had all happened to enable the universe to bring us together. We would be in contact now until the end of our days on this earth.

'I think we should relocate to the purple lounge. Are you with me?' I asked.

I needn't have asked, we all knew that we were being sent there by higher forces. As we followed the corridors around from the north quadrant to the south, I kept a lookout for our enemies. Some of them were sat on chairs in the east corridor. One had taken up position outside Angel's door, another sat in the Obs room watching TV. We passed them with no issue occurring. They only had a few hours left on their shift and now the daylight was approaching, they appeared to have resigned themselves to the fact that we would do as we pleased. We weren't causing them any grief, and to intervene would mean a shed load of paperwork which they didn't need. Essentially, they were lazy and liked as little fuss as possible. I checked in on my room on the way and suggested the others did the same. I needed to freshen up a little before my next duty. I had hidden everything including my toiletries in my case, wrapped up in the black shawl. They were safe and I retrieved the products I needed to wash away the last traces of the evil that had threatened to possess me. My cleanser washed away the dirt and I breathed in the familiar creamy eucalyptus; I splashed my skin with the cool holy water and finished with the soft moisturiser. These items had become a part of my armour. I was fast running out. I was careful not to let the staff see them as I knew they would disappear as had all my other possessions when I first came here three weeks ago.

Was it really only three weeks? It seemed like forever since I had been with my family. I had almost forgotten my life outside. I had so much to concentrate on in here that once I had been sure they were all safe I had had to put them at the back of my mind so that I did not give out any unnecessary information that may put them at risk. I wasn't with them physically to protect them so I had locked them away in the dark recesses of my brain. They were untouchable. I had prayed for them and put my trust in my heavenly family to keep them safe. My beautiful equine friend, Ebony, was back to full health and I knew that Adam was taking care of her as was she taking care of him. My Adam, my Adonis.

I put my case back in the cupboard. I cleaned the sink leaving no trace of DNA, not a hair. Nothing was left that could be used against me or cloned. I had had a very odd dream that they were collecting my DNA and trying to produce something to snatch my memories from me as I slept. I had so far managed to defeat them and now I was sure that they would not be successful.

The purple lounge felt welcoming as I entered. Now the three of us were back together and the light was starting to replace the shadows. I allowed myself to smile.

'Everyone ok?'

'Yes, we're fine,' they chorused.

'Right. I have to try and bring the dawn in now so that the new day begins afresh with us in control. I don't need you to do anything other than watch for anything that tries to come through to stop me. I don't think there will be any danger, but I need us to be vigilant. Nothing will stop me. We have broken its back now the light is coming.'

The others fell silent and sat one at either end of the large room, each on a large purple sofa. Purple, the colour of royalty. Always.

I checked the floor for any glitter and found three small diamonds which I put into my cleavage for safekeeping. They represented the three of us. Other shiny things were a distraction and I knew them to be a trick. All that glitters is not gold, the mantra repeating over and over in my head. I opened all the drapes and turned off the lights. They flickered and blinked before they were extinguished altogether. I closed the door and pushed a chair in front of it. I could not risk being disturbed.

This was where I had to explain to the others about my heavenly family. They sat, taking in my family history without interrupting. The Oracle already knew and my words confirmed her thoughts. My Romany had been given visions from her spirit guide. Neither of them questioned me. I felt calmer and confident that I bring forth the new day without any problem.

I walked up and down the room, pacing from one end to the other and back again. I felt my posture change. I was becoming the physical personification of my godly self. Aphrodite had entered the room and was in control of my body and soul. My stature lengthened until I was just a short distance from the ceiling. My shoulders back, chest out, I held my arms aloft and reached up far above my head, taking deep breaths in as I reached up and out as I brought my arms down. I was increasing my balance and control as I enacted a heavenly yoga-style routine. I spoke very little, but when I did have words, my voice had become louder and taken on an unearthly resonance.

'I call on Eos. You will help me bring in the dawn. You, whose actions made me attack you. You will help me this day.'

'Aphrodite, I will help you. This is not a day for quarrels. We need to work together.'

'You who fornicated with my Ares, I will put aside our differences. I thank you for your assistance.'

'My swans are arriving. They are bringing my golden chariot. I will accompany you across the skies. My golden basque, forged by my husband Hephaestus, will protect me from my enemies as we travel from the east.'

The room filled with light as I took up my position. My mythical swans had come for me. I mounted my chariot, the earthly laws of physics no longer holding me in their grasp. I followed Eos into the sky and we set off on our journey around the world.

My vantage point allowed me to view the world below me. I noted each country as we passed. I paused over Europe. I needed to give this continent a closer inspection. The light hovered over Paris as I sped around the streets before the city awakened. My swans knew which way to go without me having to ask. We worked in perfect harmony. We would leave our brightness over this troubled place. I wound my spell around the buildings, I poured my love down over the famous landmarks, leaving none out. The famous tower provided a nice vantage point and we halted above it.

'This city will once more become the city of love. It will overcome the sadness and the terror that has befallen it in recent times. We will triumph. We will not let the evil overtake everything that the good people of Earth have worked and strived for. And so it will be done. It will take some time, but we will make it so. I will not rest until it is done. My prophecy will come to fulfilment in this year of 2016. 6102. Dios. Exodus. The Year of The Gods. We will be triumphant.'

I took a last look at the scene. Paris lay before me. The city was coming to life. I spoke softly to my swans and we headed up and eastwards following the bringer of the dawn, making sure that we left behind nothing but love and goodness. The light would be brighter over the world today. A song came into my head as we left Paris behind. It would indeed be *'Hot in the City'* tonight. I grinned and hummed to the tune. If I had to go back again and again until my prediction came true, then so be it, then that is what I would do. I had never actually been to Paris in my current earthly form. I resolved that I would take my John there once I had settled back in at home again. It would be the first destination that we would travel to once we were reunited. Of that I was sure.

My girls had waited for my return. They had been reading the Bible and taken comfort in the words of the Lord as they counted down the last few minutes of the night. I arrived in a blaze of sunshine. My swans had delivered me back to our Royal lounge. I wished them farewell. My beautiful friends flew away back to Olympus, there to wait until I summoned them to earth once more.

I felt Aphrodite retreat into the back of my psyche once again. She was happier than I had felt her in a long time. For myself, a sense of peace had entered me. The lounge was tranquil. My girls were happy to see me and we hugged it out once they realised that I was back to being Miss DJ once again.

'I don't know about you, but I'm ready for a cuppa,' I said with relief.

'Too right. That was amazing to watch. We never doubted you for a minute as to who you were, but to actually witness it was truly awesome.'

'Thanks, darling,' I said to my Romany and gave her a hug. 'In fact, group hug, ladies. High five. We've had a major breakthrough today. Can you feel it?'

We hugged it out and set off to get a drink. A new day had come and with it fresh hope for a brighter future.

New Blood

Week Four - Tuesday 29th March, 2016

The call for meds had brought forth some new faces. The ones that had taken occupancy in the rooms opposite myself and Shakira. Another admission had come that I had missed, and she had taken residence in the room opposite my Oracle. They made me uneasy. I could not put my finger on the specific issues, but I knew that they had been brought in to put a spanner in the works.

My turn for medication came but I was turned away.

'We need you to wait until everyone else has had their meds.'

'Why?'

'Your med isn't ready yet. I am waiting for the pharmacy to send a new box of your antipsychotic up.'

I wasn't convinced that was the reason, but I went to the back of the queue. It gave me longer to study the new residents.

One was a white girl who looked to be in her twenties. She had long fair hair, bad skin and a Welsh accent. Next was a tiny black girl. She had the physique of a young teenager, barely developed, but her eyes gave away an older soul lurking underneath the skin. Last, a lady with shoulder length greying hair. She wore a nightie and stained pale green dressing gown. The three of them gave me the creeps and I kept my distance. I did not trust any of them. I felt sure they had come to cause trouble.

The meds were taking a long time to sort out with the extra workload that the new patients had caused. I was hungry. I wanted to go and have my shower. The rest of my crew had all been and gone. I was left alone with the new girls. I took a few steps back, not wanting to mix with them or breathe in their body odour. All three of them were unkempt and smelt bad. The combination of their odour made me feel sick.

It appeared that their personalities matched their hygiene. They reminded me of the three witches that had tried to interfere in my life outside the hospital. Had they been reunited in their quest to bring me down? It seemed so. There was a major difference this time though; I was prepared to take them on in the knowledge that I had beaten them before. They were all giving me the once over when they thought I wasn't looking. I could feel their eyes boring into me as they examined me from head to foot. I stood my ground. In my head, I recited prayers and armed myself with light. I invited the good angels to come and join me. It was amazing to see just how my powers had increased. No sooner had I asked for help than two staff members who I knew to be on the same side of the fence as myself appeared and put themselves in between me and the new ones.

The nurse in charge called them one by one. They took their pills without complaint and left me to it. My guards followed them down the corridor, and one of them gave a slight bow as they escorted my enemies away from me.

The clinic door opened. The nurse beckoned me in. I was hesitant to go because one of the support workers that I had suspected of abusing me loitered behind the door.

'What do you want?' I asked the nurse as I entered warily.

'Nothing to worry about, we just need to take some blood,' she assured me.

I didn't trust them and started to back out of the room but the door slammed in my face.

'Now don't be silly,' said my enemy. 'We just need some blood.'

'What for? How do I know you're not going to inject me?' I stood firm, not willing to give myself up to these people.

'Of course we aren't going to inject you. It's just a routine blood test that's all. You didn't have one when you came in. You were missed off, that's why we need to do one now. Nothing to worry about.'

'You want my blood do you? What are you using it for?'

My questions went ignored and I was ushered to the bed and pushed down to sit on the edge of it.

'Don't try and resist. We will take it one way or another so it's up to you. You can either make it easy on yourself or we can go down the isolation road again. Maybe put you in the cell this time. Up to you.' The nurse approached me with a needle.

I decided that I would let them win this time. I could not keep up my vigil if I was locked in the cell. That was my greatest fear. How did they know that I was scared of that room? My blood flowed quickly and they took four tubes full. Routine blood tests? My request to know what they were testing fell on deaf ears. The nurse handed me my medication and I took it without question. I knew that whatever they were doing with my blood, it was far from routine. I had been so careful to remove any traces of DNA from my room. I had carefully disposed of loose hair. I had rinsed out my washcloth carefully. I had done my best to clean anything that I had used. To what end? They now had my blood, they had taken everything they possibly could.

They did not know that they were too late. I had the upper hand and they would be powerless to do anything about it.

I left the clinic and headed to breakfast. The blood giving had left me feeling a bit shaky and I was in need of some sugar to give my body a lift. I was pleased to see the Egyptian guy on duty when I went to the hatch to order my food.

'How are you? You look a bit pale.'

'I'm ok. Just had a load of blood taken that's all. Once I've had my breakfast I'll be ok. Can I have muesli and a banana, ooh and some toast please?'

'Of course. Here, have this too.'

He passed me two small individual pots of honey. I couldn't believe it. I had been asking for honey every day since I had arrived and they had never had any.

'Where did you get those from?'

He didn't answer, just raised his finger to his lips and grinned as he handed them over.

'Nectar. Oh my goodness. Thank you so much.'

He nodded and winked as I walked away. Honey was something I had craved and been denied. It was a small sign, but a sign nevertheless, a sign that I was still in control. My seat was free and I sat in my usual position. The radio station had been running a competition every day, a mystery voice. Guess the member of our Pride today guys. The voice rang out loud and clear. I knew immediately who it was. The singer who had visited me whilst I had been here, he had come in the night under the guise of a security man. He was Adonis from my school leaving summer all those years ago, thirty-three to be precise. He had followed me in here when I thought I had been abandoned and now he was speaking to me from the radio. The mystery voice sang out a chorus of an Elton John classic, an acoustic version of '*Your Song*'. I didn't know the identity of the earthly body who sang out, but I knew Adonis was in possession of his soul at that moment in time. I felt calm, happy, and utterly loved with his presence coming through the airwaves to comfort me.

'Who is it? Phone in after the next record with your answers and if you're right you'll win a holiday for two in Barcelona.'

I couldn't ring. I had no phone. The phone they put calls through to was in the computer room which was always locked. They had assumed control of who we spoke to in the outside world. I knew who the voice belonged to but I had no chance of getting through let alone getting to the phone to actually make a call. I decided that I would try and call my family today. I could now risk ringing them without putting them in danger. Everything that I had done so far had been designed to keep them safe. It had worked so far.

The presenter took the answer form the caller who had been successful in getting through.

'Is it will.i.am?' he guessed.

'Sorry caller. Wrong answer. We'll be running the competition again, same time tomorrow. Would you like to request a song for us to play for you as a consolation?'

'Yes please. Could you play '*China Girl*' by David Bowie?'

'No problem, caller. I'll sort that out for you. Listen out for it before the next news. Thanks for playing 'Who's in the pride.'

I ate my breakfast deep in thought. I had been transported back in time once again to 1983. The tunes came through the radio thick and fast, each one synonymous with the year I had left school. The year I had first met Adonis in this world. There had never been a day go by where I didn't think of him, the memory bringing a smile and a pang of longing at the love I had lost. I hummed along with '*China Girl*', David's voice came from beyond the grave now. I knew he was ok.

He was singing loud and clear in The Hub. I was proud of him being so strong. Generally when a soul passed over, it took a while before they were able to communicate with their earthly family again. He was strong. A genius. His soul had found a happy place already even though he had not long left the earthly plane.

The rest of our inner circle had been and gone from breakfast. I had missed them this morning. It was not until much later that morning that we realised there was a thief moving amongst us.

'My tobacco has gone from my bedside cabinet.' Shakira was fuming.

'Are you sure that's where you left it?' I asked her, trying to calm her down.

'I think so. Yeah, I'm sure. I just had a new packet.'

Pocahontas joined the conversation. 'Mine has gone too. What the fuck?'

The Oracle was missing some chocolate. Angel had also had tobacco stolen. We checked our rooms, and apart from me, something had been taken from every room.'

'I'm allowed out to the hospital shop.' Shakira spoke after she had calmed down a bit. 'Anyone want me to buy some baccy or anything for them?'

She made a list and, good to her word, fetched everything that was on it. We all made our way down for fresh air after she had returned. The topic of conversation was obviously who had taken the items and how to catch whoever was responsible.

'She will show herself. I have my suspicions,' I said to the girls as they sat chewing over the events of the day.

'We all think we know too. Who do you think it is?'

'I'm not going to say, but believe me when I tell you that the truth will out.'

We returned to the ward, each one of us lost in our own thoughts as to who the culprit was. The rest of the day passed without incident. For the first time in a while I let my guard down and went to sleep in my room. My whole body had been elated since Aphrodite had filled me with her strength, but now I felt tiredness wash over me as I lay down. It only took a few minutes until I fell into a deep sleep.

Thief

Weds 30th March, 2016

I had the feeling I was no longer alone. Something had entered into my room as I slept. It stood at the foot of my bed, quietly observing. My eyes sprang open but I dare not focus to see what was watching me.

'Get out of my room.'

'I'm not in your room,' it answered back.

'Get out now.'

'Going to make me, are you?' it teased.

My valour returned. 'Yes, I am. You don't scare me whoever you are.' I swung my legs out of the bed and rushed at it, half expecting to fall through the shape.

To my surprise, my hands connected with solid flesh. I was used to being haunted by phantom shapes that disappeared into thin air when challenged. This shape was decidedly human. I grabbed it by its hair and frogmarched it to the door.

'Ouch, get off me, you fucking bitch,' it protested.

The light in the corridor showed the intruder to be the small coloured girl who had joined us in our prison the day before.

'What were you doing in my room? I have nothing to steal. I don't smoke and I have no money. You're wasting your time with me.'

'I wasn't going to steal anything, I must have got the wrong room.'

'Too right you got the wrong room. You've picked on the wrong person this time.'

'I'm not scared of you.'

'Likewise. If I ever catch you trying to come into my room, or for that matter any of the other bedrooms that aren't your own, shall I tell you what I'll do? It seems my current train of thought at the moment. I will rip off your head and shit down your neck. Mark my words, you don't want to mess with me.'

I let her go and she gave me a look that said she believed me. The cheeky cow. How long had she been standing there? What had she been looking for? I checked the contents of my suitcase; everything remained intact. As far as I could see there was nothing missing. It wasn't hard to check my belongings as I had nothing worth stealing. I had none of the usual contraband popular in institutions such as this. I sat on my bed musing over what had just happened. She had proved me right in my assumption that she had been the one who had thieved the tobacco from my friends. I had marked her cards. I would watch her like a hawk now, and if she was sensible she would not pursue her criminal behaviour. I decided to keep the incident to myself. Feelings were running high, and as much as I disliked the girl I did not want any harm to come to her. If the others found out, she would be subject to a beating. I didn't believe that would do her any good. I hoped that I had scared her enough to nip her thieving in the bud.

I risked a trip to the bathroom and made sure she had gone back to her own room. It was gone five in the morning when I checked the clock in the corridor. Too early to be up and about, I went back to bed and tried in vain to get back to sleep.

Wednesday. A new day in the asylum that had become my home for the best part of a month. I was in a much better position now than when I came in.

I wondered what they were doing with my blood, but the prospect of what was happening unbeknown to me was too daunting to think about for long. I did some of my yoga exercises and sat on the desk with my bible. The good book was definitely worse for wear, but it gave me so much comfort. When I had thought I was alone, it had directed me to the book of Job, showing me that it was just a test of my faith and I had to be stripped of all my possessions. The truth would set me free, I knew this. As I read, a plan of action started to take shape in my head. Today would be the day that the police came to interview me and I would give them all my notes. I would put my trust into the justice system. Once this thought had settled in my brain, I felt calm and ready for the day ahead.

I took my shower in the purple bathroom and luxuriated under the hot water. I stayed there, cleansing for a long time. The scent of what was left of my shower gel filled the air, and I scrubbed the negativity away down the drain and filled the bottle with water. I had to make it last. The thought came that I would be out by next week, but I didn't allow it to stay too long. I wouldn't tempt fate. I hugged the image of home, tightly wrapping my towel around me. My glass was changing from half empty to half full. I crept out of the bathroom and back to my room without attracting the attention of the night staff. This was a good time to be awake. The other patients were generally asleep and the staff were tired after their night shift, one of their duties being to write up the whiteboard listing the names of staff who were coming on duty and changing the date. I waited until they had finished before I snuck down the corridor to wipe them off again. I managed to do this without being caught every single day I stayed at The Hub. If they noticed, they never bothered to redo the board. The night shift was essentially made up of lazy people. They each brought in a thick blanket to wrap around themselves in the small hours; they each slept whilst on duty. I had seen them and observed their sneaky ways. They, in turn, knew I watched them, but they had been getting away with doing no work for a long time and hey, if I complained, I was crazy. A perfect job for anyone who shirked their duties - blame the patients.

I knew this to be the case when I had made complaints early on in my imprisonment. I had held up posters, I had quoted the Mental Health Act. All in vain. The staff either ignored me, laughed at me or called me a loony. I had long since given up trying to make new complaints against them. I had to make do with documenting my evidence as best I could to use at a later date when I had made my escape.

I decided that today I would follow up my original complaint. I would harangue the ward manager until she rang the police again and I could make another statement. I was adamant that I would not rest until I had done this. It was my mission for the day.

I bided my time. I played nicely and took my meds when they asked. I ate my breakfast and waited until everyone had left the dining room before I tackled the staff on duty. It was one of the male staff who I had come to know quite well. He was underhand and crafty, but he knew I was onto him and played it as a caring support worker. He knew and I knew that I had marked his cards so he played along.

'I need to make a phone call.'

'Who to?' he asked nonchalantly.

'The police again. I have a case number. I am going to follow it up.'

'You will have to wait until later. We will be doing handover next so there won't be anyone who can help you yet. Too busy.'

'It's ok, I'll wait. I'll stand outside the office door.'

'We could be quite a while. Why don't you come back later.'

'No, I'm fine, I'll just wait outside until someone is free.'

He walked off, knowing that I was on a mission and that nothing he said would sway me. I didn't mind standing in the corridor. I could watch the comings and goings of patients and staff from where I stood. It was a busy morning. It became apparent that my little friend had not only visited my room but had also crept into others and had found things worth stealing. My Shakira was on the warpath, Pocahontas had had items stolen, the Oracle had also woken to the feeling that someone had been in her room although she had not actually seen anyone.

The corridor was full and more and more people crammed into the small space. Everyone had a point to make and wanted to be heard. The result was that nobody was heard; their voices all joined together until the shouting brought forth extra staff to try and calm the situation down.

The Welsh one had added fuel to the fire by insulting Angel. Angel had flown at her and pinned her against the wall. The little waif threw in some comments and stirred up more trouble. My Oracle, who was usually so serene and above any violence, had taken a swing at her. By the time the staff had separated us out, it had become apparent who had been thieving. I did not have to say anything. She admitted it on the spot.

'I'm glad I took it,' she shouted at us.

'Lock her up and stick a needle up her arse,' Angel shouted at the staff. 'I swear to God, if you don't get her out of my sight I will kill her.'

I tried in vain to calm things down but it was too late, and before I could do anything to stop it, the team had been called and Angel had been marched down to isolation.

'Not her. She's done nothing wrong,' I called after them but to no avail.

Once the team had been called, it did not matter what the situation was, there was no stopping them in their quest to remove whoever they saw fit. They had made up their mind that Angel was responsible for the trouble and off they took her.

The thief stood watching as they dragged Angel away. She laughed in our faces. That's when all hell broke loose. Shakira lost it and took a swing at her and the rest of us joined in. She hid behind one of the staff still taunting us. The situation had escalated beyond our control and, one by one, they sectioned us off and locked us in our rooms. It was lunchtime before we were allowed out again. The ward manager made an entrance into the dining room and read us the riot act. Angel was nowhere to be seen.

'I told you she was a yardie,' the Oracle stated as we ate our lunch.

'I see she's been kept away from us anyway. One down, two to go.' I gestured at the other two new inmates. 'I don't trust either of them. We will have to be more vigilant. Keep your money, tobacco, etc. on you. I'm going to get the staff to lock my bedroom door whilst I'm not in there. I suggest you do the same.'

We all agreed to the new plan of action. We would look out for each other even more than we had previously. We had strangers in our midst and at least one thief.

I went back to my position outside the office door. Every time a member of staff went in or out I tackled them, asking for a phone call. Each time, they put me off, but I wouldn't be dissuaded. Eventually, after a couple of hours, the ward manager came out to talk to me.

'What exactly do you want?'

'I want to speak to the policeman about the complaint I made.'

'Ok. Well, I will ring them and see if he is available. Wait in the Quiet Room.'

'I'd like to speak to him myself, please. I'll wait here whilst you ring and then I'd like to speak to him, please. I can wait all day. If not, I will ask one of the girls if I can use their phone to ring 999.'

'You are not allowed to use another patient's phone,' she said coldly.

'And how will you know?' I replied.

She stared back with barely hidden hatred all over her face. 'I see. Well, if you are so determined to speak to them, of course I will organise it for you.'

'Thank you so much, I appreciate it,' I replied with as much sarcasm as I could muster.

Statements

Thursday 31st March, 2016

'The police are downstairs. Follow me.'

The ward manager herself had come to find me in the library to take me down to the incident room.

'Are they really?' I was shocked that someone had actually come to listen to what I had to say.'

'Hurry up. They won't be kept waiting,' she said briskly.

'Nice to know that you are so concerned about a patient in your care,' I shot back at her as I followed her down the stairs.

The further down the stairs I went, the more scared I became. I watched as the red flashed on the security lock. Red. Red. Red. She waved her card across and the red turned to green. The door opened and I could see a youngish man in a policeman's uniform standing in the downstairs foyer. Green. Green. Green. He stood in front of the picture of the bluebell wood.

'This is Kate,' the ward manager introduced me.

I slunk back to the wall. How did I know he was who he said he was? I couldn't trust anyone. He may be working for the badness.

'Hi, Kate. We spoke on the phone. Do you remember?'

I did recognise his voice and I pointed at his name badge for him to confirm he was the man that I had spoken to yesterday.

The ward manager led the way to a small interview room.

'You can speak in there. Shall I stay with you?' she asked in a sickly sweet voice.

'No, thank you,' I replied even more sweetly. 'I think I can manage.'

'I'll wait outside for you then. You know where I am if you need me.'

I felt so vulnerable. How did I know whether he was who he said he was? He could be working for them, in which case it would be a complete waste of time. I checked out his name badge. He caught me looking and confirmed his identity. He was wearing a radio. It flashed red red red. I shrank back into my chair and pointed at the flashing light.

'Red. Red. Red.'

'This?' he asked pointing at the light. 'It's just my radio.'

'I don't like red. Red is dangerous. Red. Stop. Like traffic lights, you know?'

'Oh. Ok. I understand I think. Look, it's gone green now. If red is stop, then green is go, right?' He smiled kindly at me. 'I'm on your side, Kate. You can tell me and I will write everything down. I can tape it, too, if you're in agreement.'

I studied his face and checked all the signs. Now would be a good time for a massive sign, please, I beseeched any deity who may be listening. Nothing came. I needed to trust my instincts. I took a deep breath and looked again at the policeman who sat patiently in front of me waiting for me to calm down. He tried again.

'Tell me when you're ready. In your own time.'

I took some deep breaths. The light was still flashing green. Go Kate. Go. Go. Go. It blinked at me. That was all the sign I needed. I started to talk and the words flooded out, tripping over themselves in their rush for the truth to be told.

I must have talked for an hour. He was very understanding. He let me speak without interrupting. I couldn't help feeling smug that the ward manager was sat outside wondering with every second that passed what exactly I was telling him.

I spoke frankly, answering any questions he had for me. I had taken my notebook which I had concealed under my clothes. I could not risk it being confiscated before I had divulged its contents to the authorities. I nearly handed it over but something stopped me. He didn't request to take it away as evidence so I decided not to offer. He seemed genuinely concerned at the statement I had made.

'You've made certain allegations about some members of staff. Would you be prepared to identify them?'

'Yes. I would. One of them is on duty. I can show you exactly who she is.'

'Is there anything else you want to tell me, Kate?'

'No. I think I have covered everything. Do you think they will let you have the video evidence I recorded when I was in isolation?'

'I'm sure if it comes to it, we will be able to access the files. I think I have everything I need for now.'

'What happened to the bed linen and underwear that was bagged up for DNA evidence?' I asked.

He didn't say that the evidence had never reached the authorities, but it was written all over his face. He ignored my question and fiddled with his radio, avoiding eye contact.

'Can't you get me out today?' I pleaded with him.

'You know that I don't have the power to do that. I understand the doctor comes twice a week. I suggest you see him. It has to be a medical professional that assesses you. I don't have the authority to have you released into the community I'm afraid.'

'It's ward round today. Would you do me a favour? Would you ask that I see the doctor; maybe tell them it's your idea? They will listen to you and they will have to let me see him won't they?'

'I can do that for you. I think we are finished here unless there is anything else you want to tell me?'

'Thank you so much. I just need to see the doctor. If you can make them let me then you've done more than enough.'

He opened the door and followed me out into the foyer, handing me back into the care of the ward manager.

'Thank you for coming. I'm sorry we had to call you,' she simpered.

'No trouble at all. Kate has the incident number and my name. I have told her to ring if she needs to add anything to her statement. We will be in touch. Kate tells me that the doctor will be coming today. I feel it would be beneficial for her to see him. I know she does have the right to see a medical professional'

I smiled at him in thanks.

'Yes. Of course she can. No problem at all. I will arrange it once we get back onto the ward.'

She moved to the security door and waved her pass over it so that he could leave. I spotted the woman I had accused as being one of my abusers and I flipped.

'Th-th-th-th-th-that's her,' I stammered and backed into the wall behind me. 'Get her away from me. Don't let her near me, pleeeeeeeeease.'

The policeman followed my gaze and looked from me to the ward manager whose face had turned to thunder, a red flush creeping across her cheeks.

'Kate, calm down.'

'No. That's her. That's one of them who touched me. Get her away from meeeee.'

The policeman took control of the situation and put himself between me and the bitch who had laid her hands on me. 'I suggest you take Kate inside. I'll wait here for you. I think we need to talk, don't you.'

She beckoned another support worker who had been supervising the fag break.

'Take her upstairs quickly. I'll be up as soon as possible.'

I backed away from them and did as I was told. I couldn't bear to be in the same place as her. The sight of her had brought back the trauma I felt from being abused. Although I had just spent the past hour talking calmly about what had happened, when faced with one of the abusers, fear overcame any confidence that had been built up over the past few days. I was a trembling mess once again. How did I know what they would do next? I needed to calm down so that I could see the doctor later.

I allowed them to lead me back to my room. I did not have the strength to fight any more. I needed to gather my senses together once again. The Bible flicked open and I read for a long time. My guides had come to rescue me once again. They stayed with me until I calmed down. The rest of the ward was quiet and I realised that it was time for ward round. I could not risk missing this one, I needed to calm myself down and convince them that I was as sane as I had ever been.

I followed my gut instinct, and suddenly I knew exactly what to do. It led me to the computer room. I tried the door. It was open. On the board next to the phone were a list of numbers. I rang the one I needed and, surprisingly, I got through straight away. I spoke concisely, aware that I could be stopped at any moment. Task done, I hung up and crept back out again with nobody any the wiser. Help was on its way.

'What makes you think that you are ready to be discharged?' the doctor looked up from his notes to address me.

I had been questioned for the last half an hour. My advocate sat next to me. She gave me an encouraging look which gave me the courage to carry on.

'I feel better now. I have caught up on my sleep and I'm taking my medication. I'm absolutely fine.' My voice held firm, despite my stomach being in knots.

'Do you understand that you have to take the medication we've prescribed? It is not long ago that you refused to take it. How do I know that you will carry on with it, if we release you?'

'I know my meds are correct now. I work in health services. I know that if the medication does not have my name on then I have the right to refuse it. I'm not taking anything that is not meant for me.'

'I understand from the staff notes that you were spiralling upwards with your psychosis and they had to sedate you for your own good.'

'I don't know about that. That's in the past though. I take the medication now I know it's the correct one. I haven't been taken to the isolation room in the last couple of weeks. I just need to go home now, please.'

'Is it ok if I speak, Kate?' My advocate was listening intently, making notes and taking in the information.

I nodded at her to go ahead.

'Kate has complied with treatment. I understand that the section expires tomorrow. It will be 28 days I think?' my advocate chipped in.

'Yes, you are correct.'

'Then there is no need to section her again. She has complied with everything as far as I can see.'

'The staff are concerned that she will spiral again. I am going to recommend that she have support in place at home before we let her leave. I'm going to put her under a CTO.'

'I don't understand. What is that?' I took some deep breaths before I spoke to quell the panic I felt rising within me.

'It is a Community Treatment Order. It means that if we let you go home, then you are legally obligated to comply with the course of treatment we prescribe for you, Kate. You have to take the medication.'

'No. I can't agree to that,' my advocate interrupted before I could speak. 'Kate, that means that you are on a higher section than now.'

'Is that all I have to do?' I asked him. I needed to make sure they told me the truth.

'Yes. It does obligate your local mental health team to look after you for the next six months. I think it would be prudent to have that in place.'

'Ok then. If all I need to do is take my med, I can promise that I will do that.'

'I don't think you should say yes to that.' My advocate was looking concerned.

'No. Really. It's fine. I just want to go home.' My eyes pleaded at her to agree with me.

'If you are sure you understand then it is, of course, your choice. I'm here to speak for you,' she assured me. 'When can Kate expect things to be in place?'

'I'll set things in motion as soon as I finish the ward round. I am pleased with your progress, Kate. Having taken everything into account and your agreement for the CTO, I am willing to sign to say that you can go home just as soon as the support at home is in place.'

'How long will that be?' I couldn't believe it.

'It depends on how quickly your local team can organise the support. I'm not willing to sign the release papers unless you agree to that condition, do you understand?'

'Yes. Yes, I do.' I struggled to keep my emotions calm. I didn't want him to think I was spiralling.

'In that case, there is nothing else to say.'

The doctor stood up and gestured at the door. 'Thank you so much.' I spoke as evenly as my voice would allow.

The advocate followed suit and we left the doctor filling out the discharge papers.

'How can I ever thank you?' I had to restrain myself from hugging my saviour.

'No need. That's what I'm here for. I speak for you. If you're sure you're happy with the CTO then that's all that matters. You do understand the implications don't you?'

'Yes. I know what it means. It's easy if all I have to do is take my meds. I just can't wait to get home. You'll never know how much you've helped me. I cannot thank you enough.'

'My pleasure. You know how to reach us if you need us again.'

'Yes. I'm hoping that's it now. I'm going home!'

'I'm happy for you. Nice to have met you, Kate. You take care.'

Then she was gone. I was ecstatic. We had done it. Between us, we had got the result I had been so desperate for. I was nearly free.

Jokers

Friday 1st April, 2016

The weekly community breakfast was in full swing. I had never managed to attend one before so it was all new to me. I had been too busy carrying out my given duties to have time to sit and enjoy the spread that was put on once a week. I sat happily with my friends and we watched as a member of staff who I didn't recognise rushed back and forth setting out a buffet breakfast the likes of which I had not seen since the last time I had stayed in a hotel.

Instead of having to form the usual queue at the hatch, we were allowed to help ourselves from the heavily laden table. Fresh fruit, hard boiled eggs, croissants, pastries, all jostled for room alongside the usual individual packets of cereal. A large silver toaster had been provided so we could help ourselves to fresh toast and waffles. I could almost see the aromas as they floated across the room, fresh coffee and warmed bread awoke my appetite and I poured myself a fresh cup of coffee to help wash it all down. The atmosphere in the room was genial, voices joining together in friendly banter. There was an air of optimism about the place. It suddenly occurred to me that I was happy. An emotion that I had long forgotten. I would soon be free and home again. I would ring my family later and tell them my good news. My attempts at trying to make a call yesterday had been thwarted each time I requested use of the telephone. The usual excuses of too busy, or being told to wait until later, flowed easily off the lips of the staff who were intent on denying me my rights. Why should they act any different now? I had nagged them on and off all day after I had been told I could go home. I nagged for a phone call to my family. I nagged them to make sure they were contacting my local authority. Nothing swayed them from their resolve to ignore every request I made.

Yesterday had been a turning point for me. My happy mood emanated from every pore of my body and washed over the others as we chatted and enjoyed our breakfast together. Even Angel had come to join the rest of us. I looked around the table with a sense of joy. Angel and Shakira were chatting, Pocahontas and Oracle had filled their plates from the buffet and were tucking in heartily.

'I don't understand how you managed to swing it, Kate?' Angel asked me in between bites of croissant.

'It was the advocate. She was just brilliant. I think she will be able to help all of us. Ring her. She will fight for you, I'm sure.'

'I don't hold out much hope.' Oracle looked at me sadly. 'I've been here a few weeks longer than you have and nobody has ever allowed me to see an advocate. I think I did ask once, but they told me there was nobody available.'

'You have to be sneakier than that. I managed to get into the computer room when it was unlocked.'

'I don't know, Kate. I've given up.'

'No. That's what they want you to do. I managed it and look how much shit I've taken from them. I mean it, I'll help you, but only if you want me to.'

'I'll think about it. When are you going home then?'

'Just as soon as they sort out some support for when I get home. It's Friday, so I'm hoping that I can go today. I'm going to bring up phone calls when the meeting starts. Anything you want to bring up or want me to ask on your behalf?'

'Fag breaks,' Angel chipped in. 'I was late this morning and they wouldn't let me out. It's not fair.'

The others all had their complaints and it seemed as though I had unintentionally been elected as spokesperson. I didn't mind, but I also was aware that if I made too many complaints there would be no chance that they would sort out my going home. I was a little scared that they would never let me out, but I was determined not to let negative thoughts bring me back down. I just had to be patient. I would be home soon.

We all pitched in to clear away the breakfast detritus and get the room ready for the meeting. I introduced myself to the lady who had set everything up. She was friendly and told me she was holding a poetry session later in the day if I fancied it. Things were spinning around and I had a flash vision in my head. The Hub had come full circle and we were now on the same time as the outside world. I checked for signs. The coffee machine, the car park, the glitter, all was as it should be. I took myself off to the Quiet Room before the meeting began. My crows circled above in a bright blue sky. I waved and signalled to them, tapping the rhythm on the windowsill. The signal they knew so well. I hoped the leader would remember it after I had gone. I sat, lost in my own thoughts, music and lyrics flowing through my mind. I projected the familiar song across the car park and high up into the trees so it carried through the airwaves to land safely with the boys, and they sang it back to me as they danced in the air before me.

'You have any more?' a male voice sang back.

I squinted to try and see which one of my crows had communicated. I knew the voice, but I could not decipher which one he was.

I did not need to speak out loud to reply. 'I have a lot more. I know every song that you ever created. Every lyric. Every tune. I've given you the signal. You know what to do with it. You don't need me to tell you more. I have every faith in you and the rest of my handsome boys. You will fill our world with the melodies that you craft. Only you can do this. It is already done, as well you know.'

The air filled with music as the notes rang out. My demigods were time travellers, shape shifters, musicians, muses. No wonder I had connected with them and their music. I had known they were special, but had not fully understood how important and how connected we were until I had been brought to this place.

'Are you having fun yet?' I sang out to them.

The flying display that they answered with assured me that they were having the time of their lives. They all knew their identities in the six. The original five and the new one. Five plus one. Perfect. I left them to it and went back into the dining room. The chairs had been set out in a semi-circle. The ward manager and the new lady had taken their places at the front.

'Is everyone here that is coming?' The ward manager shot me a look as I sat directly opposite her. 'Ok, then we will start with updates from the last meeting.'

She read out minutes for the previous week without looking up from her notes. Her voice wavering slightly. Something had changed. As she looked up I realised that her body was hosting a new being. Her features had taken on a new shape. It was subtle, and I looked around the room to check if anyone else had noticed the change. I knew this man. He was a saint, he had passed over many years before. A violent death of a peaceful man. His persona shone out from the ward manager. He looked me in the eye and winked.

The meeting progressed and matters which had been put aside were dealt with. The other patients hadn't realised who it was who was taking control, but they were starting to wonder what had happened. The change in proceedings did not go unnoticed. Suddenly, nothing was too much trouble. I brought up the matter of phone calls, half expecting to be shot down. The ward manager shifted uncomfortably in her seat and I had the impression that there was an internal battle taking place. I prayed with all my heart that the shining power of the saint outweighed any demon that had decided to fight back.

The meeting drew to a natural end. I had been promised that they would work on a new procedure for phone calls. Other items on the agenda had been discussed and, if not agreed to, then certainly promised to be looked into.

The staff left and the room emptied until only our inner circle was left to mull over how things had gone. We were all pleasantly surprised. Angel busied herself with making April fool jokes, and to be fair to her, she got each and every one of us with pointing to the floor and exclaiming at some invisible object. We were all in high spirits and fell about laughing as she made her jokes. It was the first time I had witnessed anything like this in the month that I had been incarcerated here. The whole place had taken on a new aura.

One by one the others left until I was alone with my thoughts and my radio. I had declined to go out for fag break. I just wanted to sing and dance for a while.

'Look at you, Miss DJ.' Angel laughed as she passed me on her way out for 'fresh air' as I danced around the tables tidying up as I went.

None of the others really understood how things were supposed to be. I had to ensure the chairs were in the right place. The colours had to match. Each had its own place and it was imperative that things were as symmetrical as possible. I hummed *'Planet Earth'* as I went about my business, making patterns rhyme. The airwaves were mine once more. Coldplay, who I normally could not abide, had a new song which had caught my attention and I actually liked it, the usual depressing tone of voice had been changed to one of hope. *'Adventure Of A Lifetime'* was a happier song full of hope and as I sang along with it, the lyrics filled me with optimism for the future.

The meeting had gone so much better than expected and I thanked the spirits that had enabled our voices to be heard. I smiled at the happening. The day I was born, *'All You Need Is Love'* had been number one in the charts. Today, John had come to reinforce his words and the mantra by which I had always lived my life on this earth. The lyrics now took on much deeper significance. Music was the key. Music had accompanied me throughout my life. My soul sang to familiar lyrics. I felt my soul flying as high as my birds as I carried out my duties. I was lost in the airwaves. I did not realise that anyone else was present in the room until the music stopped abruptly.

I turned to see what had happened to see one of the new patients, the older one with the straggly grey hair and shabby dressing gown sat cross legged in my chair.

'I didn't hear you come in. Can you switch it back on again, please?'

'Who do you think you are, Miss DJ?'

'Sorry, have I offended you? Don't you like music?'

'I don't like you,' she shot back at me.

'That's ok, you don't have to. I'll leave you to it.' I left before she had a chance to answer. I was determined that nothing would upset me today.

I knocked on the office door on my way past. Nothing. There were a couple of staff in there but they ignored me. I would try again later.

I remembered that the lady who had set up the community breakfast said she would be holding a poetry class in the purple lounge. I decided I would go and join in. I needed to write and get some of my feelings down on paper. Therapy came in many forms. Song, dance, yoga, colouring, and then my duties on top had all played their part in my recovery. I had tried to read too, but I could not concentrate on any story; my comfort had come from reading the Bible. The Bible never let me down. It drew me to it and selected passages especially for me to follow. It was my rock. I needed now to try and get some of the words down onto paper myself. Poetry would be perfect to enable me to express myself.

I walked into the room to find the new member of staff, who introduced herself again. Only one other was present. The one we had christened Thief.

The Lyrics

Thursday 31st March 2016 – Afternoon

I took stock of the situation, undecided as whether or not it would be a good idea to stay. The thief looked at me with a glint of a challenge in her eyes.

That made my mind up. I would stay.

'My name is Madeleine. Welcome. I'm sorry I don't know your name.'

'Kate, otherwise known as Miss DJ.'

'Ah yes. I've heard about you. You're the one who sings and dances all the time.'

'Well, mostly.' I grinned at her.

There were a pile of papers laid out on the floor.

'Have a look through the pictures I've laid out and pick one. Once you've chosen the image then I would like you to make up a poem about it. It can be anything you like. Have you ever written any poetry before?'

'Yes. I have, but not for a while.'

'How about you?' she addressed Thief.

'Not really, but I write songs. Can I do that instead?'

I looked across at the thief and suddenly my heart was filled with compassion. She was barely there. Her persona shrunk into the environment. She was tiny. She sat on the floor and had amassed a large selection of crayons and papers which she guarded. As I watched her, I let down my guard. She couldn't have been more than twenty. I wondered what had happened to her to make her so frightened. She was like a cornered animal, large wide eyes, ready to take off at any second. I had an image of her cowering in a corner, overpowered by a large man.

Madeleine was observing the dynamics of the situation and cleverly intervened by distraction, talking about different poems that she had written, discussing different techniques and offering to read out her poem first. She had skilfully stopped a situation from developing into a confrontation.

'Which image would you like to choose?' she asked me.

I studied each one in turn and decided on a water lily. The delicate pink petals which rose up towards the sky were reflected in the water. Green lily pads floated, forming a protective circle around the lone flower. I sat and thought about the significance that nature meant to me. Everything around me had a meaning. Flowers surrounded me. The sadness of red roses, tears cried for a dead lover, his red anemone dangerously enchanting, the bluebells leading the way from the darkness to the light and now this, this single solitary flower shining up at me from the page. The words came and flowed through my fingers, the pencil took on my life force as it scribbled across the blank page. I was lost in the beauty of language. I finished my piece with a flourish and passed it to Madeleine for her to read.

'Have you finished too?' she addressed the waif.

'Nearly. I'm writing a song. I can hear it in my head. It's not finished. Not yet,' she replied and was lost once more in her creation.

'There's a lot of sadness in this verse, Kate. Has it helped you to get things down on paper?'

'I think so. I find writing poetry helps to calm my mind. I used to write a lot, but that's the first one I've written in a while. I need to have another look at it, I think I can improve it if I take some more time.'

'Is it ok if I read it aloud?' she asked me.

I nodded and let her put a voice to my writing. I had heard a male voice in my head as I drafted the first stanza. John. John had come through.

'The Water Lily' she began.

'I examine the images before me, in their watery transparency. Where am I? Who is there?' a pause.

'Lily of the valley or floating in a pool of dark secrets, I wonder. I wander.'

'Lost. Like a phantom mist. Missing. Who will find me and come to my rescue and send me home? Away from the tomb of despair.'

'Is it you? Do you care, my love? Soon, joined as petals together once more laid bare.'

Madeleine pronounced each word carefully, pausing at each comma, taking a breath before reading the next line. I listened carefully to my words. Silent tears trickled down my cheek. I had been so very heartbroken, torn away from my loved ones. The last month had been worse than any form of torture known to man. I could not bear to hear any more; I snatched the paper away from her and ran from the room sobbing. I ran to the nearest refuge I could find, my purple shower room. Clutching my poem and my bible, I sank down into the corner of the room as I had done the day of the transformation. My body wracked with heaving sobs, and I tried to muffle the sound for fear of being accused of spiralling again. No matter how I tried, I could not stop. I wailed like a banshee until my voice gave way. The noise abated and I was greeted by silence, broken only by intermittent sobs catching my breath as I summoned every bit of strength I could muster to allow me to carry on the fight to get out of this hell on earth.

I had made progress in the fact that I had not turned on the shower to cleanse whilst fully clothed as I had last time. That was a good sign. Luckily for me, no member of staff had passed by when I had lost the plot and I was able to make it back to my room without being spotted. I did not know if Madeleine would tell anybody about the incident. I suspected she would keep it to herself. I couldn't be sure about the other one though. I hoped that even if she did happen to say I had been upset, that their lack of interest in me would mean it hadn't affected my chances of leaving. I vowed to be on best behaviour until I got out.

As Friday drew to a close, it became apparent that the staff had once again been unsuccessful in securing my external support. My heart sank as I resigned myself to the fact that nothing would be done over the weekend. I had to accept that I had another three nights at least in this place. I felt panicky. I wondered if I would ever see my family and friends again. Maybe they would inject me with something lethal next time and explain my death by saying I had overdosed myself; I was truly worried for my life. I resolved that if I had to stay in then I would be extra careful and keep myself to myself. I'd bide my time until Monday and if nothing had happened in that time, I would raise hell in order to get what I wanted. I was locked up against my will once again. My local crisis team had let me down once more. I knew that if I was to get out I had to play them at their own game. It was a game I was all too familiar with. I wasn't comfortable with telling lies, but if the means justified the end then I would join in and play it the same way they did. Covering up the truth and telling lies in order to get the result I wanted.

I read and re-read my Water Lily poem. I had signed it John Clare... who was he? I didn't know. I assumed he was just another soul who needed guiding away from this place. He came through to me loud and clear as I sat quietly on my bed. He told me some of his sad stories and I wept for him. He had died in a place like this many, many years ago, his story similar to mine. He told me he had come through as I was writing my poem; that was his profession, poet. No wonder the words had come so easily; I had been channelling his spirit. We spoke at length about the system and the utter despair that shrouded asylums in his day and how nothing much had changed in the present. It was a disgrace. I vowed that before I left, I would help every single soul who crossed my path. I would deliver as many souls as I possibly could. I would ward off the evil spirits and send them down to their level. I had been brought to this hell hole for a reason, of that I was sure. If I had to stay for the weekend then it would be productive. I vowed that by the time I left, I would have fulfilled my goal. My reward would be to be delivered safely back to my family. It was an epiphany. I understood exactly what I needed to do from that moment forward.

'Thank you, God. Thank you heavenly family for giving me the opportunity to redeem myself.' I spoke as Aphrodite came rushing back to take over once more.

I had become used to her coming and going when she pleased. I looked forward to the times when she possessed me; she made me feel powerful. I also knew that she could not stay too long in my earthly body as it was too much for my human brain to cope with. I had already been labelled as insane. There was nothing wrong with me; all I was guilty of was opening my mind. I knew that most humans had no clue of what was happening around them day in day out. It was better that they were kept in the dark. We could carry out our duties as directed by higher beings generally going unnoticed. It was when the darkness fought back that we had to up our game. This left us in danger of being discovered or, as in my case, thought to be mental and locked away. Clearly this had been going on for hundreds of years. It was only now coming to a head. Things had tipped to the negative far too much and we had only just stepped in before the world was lost forever. I dreaded to think what still might happen if I didn't complete what I had been sent here to do.

Power Up Ladies

Saturday 2nd April 2016

Today was the day when I knuckled down in earnest. This wasn't just about me anymore. The rest of the patients were equally as important. I was compelled to ensure that they were able to move on. I knew I had to do this before I would be allowed to leave this place for good. The day started same as any other with medication, except that when it came to my turn, the nurse on duty caught my eye and shook her head very slightly. The movement was not large enough for anyone else to have noticed and I gave her a puzzled look in reply. She did it again and emptied my meds into her hand before stuffing it in her pocket. She held the empty cup to me and gestured to pretend to swallow the tablets. I did exactly as she asked. The relief in her face said it all. What had they been giving me all this time? I dreaded to think.

'I feel a bit sick.'

'Come and see me after breakfast and I'll examine you. Don't eat any wet food today.'

I didn't know what she meant, but judging by her actions she had a good spirit inside her at this moment and I needed to take heed of any warnings. As much as things had turned around and I was no longer alone in my fight, I had to be very careful as the evil would do its best to stop me in my tracks.

I stayed away from the cereal and chose dry toast. I was hungry, but my stomach would not settle. I had a brief flash of something untoward happening in the night. I did not think I had been injected, but something had taken place, I was sure of that.

The little lady from number eight was sat at the next table. I waved in greeting and she put her thumb up. There was one more soul inhabiting her body. I knew who it was and how to handle him.

'Can I sit down here?' I asked her.

She nodded in reply and I sat down to eat my breakfast with her. I could see him just behind her eyes and I hummed a line from one of his most successful songs.

'Why am I here?' he asked me, suddenly coming into view and taking over her identity with his own.

'Don't worry. You were sent here to become a little stronger. It is time now that you moved on to the next level,' I reassured him.

'Where am I?'

'You know where you are, I really don't have to tell you. You have all the answers. Now let this little lady finish her breakfast. I'll sit with you and when you are ready I'll lead you to the exit. They are waiting to escort you.'

He looked at me and smiled. We ate in silence. He was lost in his own thoughts, questions popping into my head only to be answered by himself. It was as I said, he had all the answers and now it was his time to move on.

The familiar golden light flooded through the corridor as we approached, followed by individual colours signalling his time was now.

'How can I ever thank you?' he asked as we stood at the entrance to the next level.

'This is more than enough. That's all I need, to know that I have fulfilled my role and delivered you safely is all the thanks I need. Safe journey, music man. See you on another level.'

'You promise.'

'Yes. Now go, they are waiting for you.'

He hesitated. I held his hand and his soul parted from the earthly body. I smiled at him, the sense of tranquillity was overwhelming as he made his way out of The Hub and into the golden lights that waited.

The little lady looked at me and smiled. She was herself once again. I was sure that she would start to get better. She had already put a little weight back on by the look of it. I prayed that no other soul would take up residence in this carrier. She had done more than her fair share of feeding three men up and now, with only one other who would leave shortly, it was time for her to recuperate. My prayers were answered immediately as I had the reply affirming that this lady would soon be free. I gave her a quick hug.

'You'll be ok now.'

'I know,' she whispered. 'Thank you, Miss DJ...'

It was the most I had ever heard her say. I watched her totter away and felt an immense sense of pride. That many souls in one body just didn't work long term, I should know because my body was a haven for hundreds. It was hard work. I looked at the skeletal frame of the little lady as she disappeared around the corner. I had come in time to save her. Thank goodness. I did not think that she would have survived much longer in her physical state had I not been sent here. It was worth everything I had been through to know that my actions had helped so many and I wasn't even half done.

My tummy rumbled a little and felt sore so I decided to wander back to the clinic. The nurse who had been on duty earlier was still there.

'Are you feeling any better?' she asked me.

'A little, but my stomach is really sore.'

'Come in. I'll give you a quick once-over. Hurry though, before any of the other staff come.'

I followed her advice and slipped through the door. She shut the hatch behind me away from any prying eyes.

'What's going on? What was that about this morning?'

She put her fingers to her lips and pointed at the ceiling. I understood that we were being watched.

'I'll just give you a quick examination.'

'Ok. Is this room bugged?'

She nodded her head very slightly. 'I'm going to take your temperature and do your blood pressure.'

I sat still whilst she carried out her checks. She slipped a piece of paper into my hand and pointed at my top. I understood her meaning and hid the scrap in my cleavage. It had served me well as a good hiding place.

'You seem ok, but I need to just take some blood so I can send it off for some tests.'

'I had some taken the other day?' I questioned her as she looked for a vein in my inner elbow to stick a needle in.

'These are for different tests.'

Instead of blood filling up the syringe, I looked in horror as she pushed some clear liquid into my vein. I was about to pull away, but she gestured quickly that everything was ok. Somehow I believed her. I had become a very good judge of character. Came with the job description, I told myself, smiling at the irony.

'That's all for now. Just make sure you eat dry food only until tomorrow.'

I left her cleaning up the evidence and went into the toilet next door. I couldn't lock this one as it had a habit of locking you in. I had learnt this very early on in my stay here. I cleaned the carbon smutty marks off the windowsill and wiped the sink down first before daring to look at the note she had given me.

I understood now why she had injected me. It was an antidote to a drug that they had pushed into me last night as I slept. My suspicions had been confirmed, they were trying to finish me off before I could tell the world of the abuse that I had witnessed here every single day.

I joined my friends in the library.

'We are choosing some films to watch later in the purple lounge. Will you come too?' Shakira asked from where she sat cross legged next to a large box full of DVDs.

'That would be lovely. Yes, ok.'

'Pocahontas has been told she can go home tomorrow, so we thought we'd have a movie night with popcorn and everything,' Angel piped up happily. 'We're going to buy loads of sweets and chocolate from the hospital shop and have a proper girls' night in.'

'That's great news. I'm so happy for you. How are you getting home?' I asked my beautiful raven-haired friend.

'My boyfriend is coming for me. I wouldn't go in one of their hospital cars. You never know where you might end up.'

'What do you mean?' I asked, genuinely curious as to why she wouldn't get in a car that had been sent to take her home.

'I don't trust the bastards. I'm telling you, Kate, if they want to get rid of a body that's the way they do it. I've seen and heard a lot of bad things since I've been in here. I'm telling you, their transport is bad news.'

'Thanks for that. I'm going soon so I'll get my family to fetch me. I can't risk them doing anything. They've already been trying to get at me whilst I've been in here.'

'We know they have,' Angel replied.

'What do you mean?'

'Tell her, Angel,' Pocahontas said.

She lumbered over and sat her huge frame down next to me. 'I overheard two of the night staff talking. You know the ones who were on the other night. The blues. You know who I mean.'

'Yes, but surely they wouldn't say out loud if they were trying to bump any of us off?'

'They didn't know I was listening. They were stood outside our doors. I pretended to be asleep and snoring.'

'What did you hear?'

'I can't be sure of the exact conversation, but I heard one of them open your door. I'm sure they came in and injected you. It was the day after they took you into the isolation room.'

'Bloody hell, Angel, why didn't you tell me straight away?'

'I wasn't sure if I had just dreamt it or not. I'm so sorry.' Angel looked away shamefaced.

'It's not your fault. Don't worry. Forewarned is forearmed, they won't get a chance to do that again. Things are changing for the better.' I changed the subject. 'I'd like a Tom Cruise film if there are any,' I said picking up some of the DVDs and inspecting them.

'You're nuts about him aren't you?' Shakira laughed up at me.

'Him and Daniel Craig, too bloody right. Ooh, and Will Smith. Give me any film with them in and I'll be a happy lady.'

'Nuts.' The Oracle laughed and came out with another one of our catchphrases that had become the norm. 'Are you mental?'

'Yes, I am,' we all chorused before falling about laughing.

'Power up, ladies. We'll get these bastards. One by one, we will get out of here. I won't rest until we are all safe. I promise you.'

'Aww, come here, you,' Pocahontas joined in. 'Group hug everyone.'

'What am I going to do if anyone tries to harm any of us?' I asked.

Blank faces stared back at me.

'Rip off their heads and...'

'Shit down their necks,' they finished in unison.

We might all be under a section, we may well be all crazy and locked up, but we were united in hope for a better future. I knew that I would do my best to deliver us all safely back to where we belonged. I would never stop.

'I've found them!' Shakira shouted over the laughter.

James Bond in one hand and Tom in the other. 'Ta-dah!'

Alien Nations

Sunday 3rd April, 2016

Movie night was well underway. We had dragged quilts and pillows down to the 'Royal' lounge and set ourselves up for a girls' night in. It almost felt normal, like we were having a sleepover at a friends' where all the men folk had been banished from the house. There were a couple of nasty staff on tonight. One in particular seemed hell bent on spoiling our fun. She had been in a couple of times and switched the light on, telling us we weren't allowed to sit in the dark in case anyone decided to 'kick off'. We had ignored her and switched it back off after she had gone. After a couple of times doing this, she appeared to give up and left us to it.

Since the arrival of the thief, we had all made sure that our bedroom doors were locked when we weren't in occupancy. It gave us peace of mind that our belongings were safe. I wasn't worried that anything would be stolen because I had been stripped of everything when I came in anyway, but I did not like the thought of someone creeping around my room and looking through my things.

The rest of the ward was quiet. A kind of peace had settled over Chrysalis Ward. There were only eight of us now. Our four, the three new ones, and the little lady.

'Here, Kate, come and snuggle under the quilt with us,' Shakira called over.

There were five sofas in the room and we had stretched out on one each to start with. I looked over, and Shakira and Oracle were under a quilt on one. Angel had one to herself, as did I.

'Nah, I'm ok here, thanks. I like to spread out a bit and I can't be bothered to move.'

I liked having a sofa to myself. I could stretch out and enjoy the film. If I closed my eyes it was almost like being at home, curled up under a quilt watching TV, eating chocolate, enjoying a night in. I pretended that John was in the kitchen making the drinks. The thought made me shiver in anticipation. Not long now.

I watched the action on the screen, Tom doing what he did best. His eyes appeared to meet mine numerous times, and I had the feeling that what he was doing on there was real. I had the sudden thought that each and every film I had watched in here had been true. The actors who portrayed their characters so well were not really acting, they were living and breathing the role they had been given. They knew me. They knew where we were and each one was fighting for the good of the planet. Knowing this gave me every hope for the future of humanity. I could hardly wait to see what else developed over this night. Saturday night in The Hub was going to be a very interesting one. The players were coming down to land.

The first film was coming to an end. As the credits rolled, I made my excuses and followed my gut instincts. I had been told to go to the dining room once more. It was nearing midnight and I had work to do.

The bathrooms were all dirty. I checked each and every one on my route back to the northern most point of The Hub. I cleaned and wiped. Flushed toilets. Shut doors. I stopped to breathe in some oxygen at the Obs Room sign. I could feel the movement; we had taken off and were flying high above the earth. The ceiling lights were lined up, guiding the way for the others as they came in. A green tinged mist was present when I looked outside. I had been instructed to close all the curtains. We needed all the privacy we could get. I had to ensure that everything was as safe as it could be. Tonight was all about the culmination of the events that had brought us to this point. The players had been biding their time, taking a break and developing new strategies. The stakes were high. Tonight the big guns had been called in.

I checked the coffee machine. The creamy substance was seeping from underneath the tray at the front. My instinct kicked in. I flushed the polluted liquid away and purified it, rinsing it with hot water which I made holy by praying and doing each action three times. Black and white were flashing. The sledgehammer was flashing and the coffee cup on the display was landing. I checked the car park; a green mist, just a subtle colour change but enough to tell me that my Ares (Mars) had control. He was signalling green to me. Green, not for jealousy this time, but green for go. He had my back. The game was on.

I switched the radio on. Nothing but interference came through. I tried again, fiddled with the dial until I found the right station. I had been relieved of my DJ duties this time, a higher force had taken over, and I handed control over to the higher beings. They were arriving from every continent on the planet and from planets far away in time and space. The fabric of our reality thinning and allowing the subtle shifts necessary for access to The Hub. As I watched the crafts landing, the coffee cups on the machine changed to triangles. Not just triangles but pyramids. The ancient ones, the higher beings who had come to our planet so many years ago, were returning. This was the most important game I had been privy to. The stakes were high.

I kept myself respectfully out of the way as they came in; the Egyptians, the Mayans, the Incas, the Greeks, the Norse, the Romanys, the Native Americans. All the continents of the world had sent their representatives; they joined the representatives from other dimensions and the room filled up until every player had taken their seat. The fate of our world relied on the outcome of this game. We had the upper hand. Our nations on earth and beyond were all united in a quest to save our universe and preserve life on our earth. They had no choice, losing was not an option. We had all worked too hard. The Earth was worth saving. If we lost the game tonight, we would have no choice but to each leave it to its fate; we would abandon it to the darkness. The souls we had saved would come with us. They had already moved on from their physical boundaries and we were prepared to leave if necessary.

As each nation's player took their place at the game table, we waited for the opposition to arrive. The Hub held its breath, hovering above the Earth. We all waited for the moment when the darkness would make its first move.

I felt my guides start to take control of my brain. I had two main players within me. The radio sent out *'Dancing in the Streets',* David and Mick being the perfect accompaniment to our wait. Aphrodite came to the fore to speak on behalf of the Greeks, then a new entity awakened inside my mind. I heard his voice loud and clear, he was speaking in the ancient tongue of Quechua. He introduced himself as Atahualpa, one of the last rulers of the Inca Empire. He had died in prison on 26th July in the 1500s. He had died at the hands of the Spanish and I had been born nearly 500 years later, on the exact day he lost his battle. I understood then why I had always felt so drawn to Peru; it was the land of my ancestors. The reasons for my love of this distant land became clear. I allowed him to take me back there with his memories. We did a whistle stop tour. I had been and spent time in the Incan capital of Cusco. I had visited Machu Picchu. I had felt so at one with Mother Earth when I touched the ancient stones, unable to understand why I felt such a close connection with a land that was so many thousands of miles away from my current earthly home. He showed me places I had never been; the Nazca Lines in the south of the country no longer held a mystery for me as he showed me the meaning of the drawings so meticulously sketched out in the desert.

A pentagon had been drawn on the table. I took my place at the top point. To my left the Egyptian woman king, Hatshepsut; to my right one of the Jaguar Gods of the Maya. We formed a triangle in the shape of our buildings that had been called wonders by the humans. Only beings who had progressed to level five and above were allowed this much information; the origins of the human race laid out on the table in front of us.

I held my hands above my head, reaching up for the stars. The ceiling disappeared and the constellations glittered around us, still with the faint green tinge that reassured me we had our protection in place.

The dining room had been transformed into an arena, spinning like a top hovering in the glittering night sky. My spirits detached themselves from my body and took their rightful places. I was left in the centre of the pentagon. Each nation who had won their previous round had taken their place at each point of the pentagon. The rest of the nations joined hands and formed a complete circumference around the edge, their fingertips touching and coming together. I reached for the radio and the airwaves lit up.

The power of each nation as it united with its neighbour in this world and the hidden dimensions was indestructible. I could see the colours of the music as it washed over us and formed a protective dome above the arena. The representatives spoke in their native tongues. As their words entered the atmosphere, they were instantly transformed into a common language understood by all. We were winning. I had raised the stakes. I facilitated the game by watching in real time. The bad spirits that had possessed the members of staff in The Hub showed themselves under my scrutiny. I pointed each one out as they materialised and each nation took a shot at eliminating them. One by one, the badness present in each individual was identified and sent on its way. Each nation had its own way of dealing with evil and I left them to dispose of the bad spirits in their own way. We were starting to enjoy ourselves and as we approached three hours play, we called half time.

The atmosphere was jovial. It was like the ultimate dinner party. Spirits of human beings who had been long gone came to watch the event, taking a seat at the edge of the arena. The Greeks, known for their love of drama, had transformed the dining room into a representation of an ancient amphitheatre. Movers and shakers from the ancient days rubbed shoulders with the spirits of actors and well-known personalities from contemporary times. I was pleased to see some of the ones I had shepherded over to their correct plane enjoying the action.

Half time over, the atmosphere became more serious. Time for the last push. We were in the lead, but we all knew how sneaky and evil the darkness could be. They were experts at trickery and deceit. Three hours until the dawn. I had asked that I and my Greek (Roman) family could bring in the daylight again if we were triumphant. The general consensus was one of agreement. Glasses topped up and plates refilled, Dionysus (Bacchus) had taken over the festivities. The three graces, Aglaia, Thalia and Euphrosyne, had taken their rightful place at the side of Aphrodite (Venus). We loved nothing better than a challenge. I looked around at the scene as it unfolded. We were nearly there.

'Ladies, gentlemen, honoured players from around the universe, please take your seats. The interval is over. Time for the last push.' I turned up the music and let them take their places.

We were expecting some resistance and we were right to be on guard. The threat came in the form of the blues. The blues had once been trustworthy but they had in recent times become greedy. Their allegiance with the darkness was not entirely unexpected. The blues launched their attack. They had poisoned the half time provisions, sending burrowing parasites to contaminate the food. Not all of the players had eaten at half time. I had avoided anything wet and just eaten some dry bread. I had to enlist some help to remove the bugs that were burrowing into the internal organs of their hosts.

I left my post at the centre and made my way around to the clinic. The ship was spinning now and I had to put my trust in the airwaves. I called on each and every spirit that I had encountered to pull together and hold steady whilst I found help.

I recited incantations and raised the stakes whilst running against the forces that were trying to hold me back. I recited the Lord's Prayer over and over and found myself outside the clinic door. It had been such a fight to get there. It was locked. The nurse who had helped me earlier was nowhere to be seen.

'Hey, Miss DJ, what are you up to?'

I turned to see Angel slowly making her way towards me.

'I need to get into the clinic. No time to explain. Can you help me?'

Angel grinned. 'I'll give it a go. Move out of the way.'

She put her back against the door and pushed, getting her bodyweight behind her. A few pushes and I could see the hatch beginning to give way.

'If you can get the hatch open, I'll climb through.'

'Ok, nearly done it.' She gave one last push and the thinner wood of the hatch gave way under the force of Angel's weight.

'Thanks, wait here for me, I need to see if I can find something to help.'

'What's going on?'

'Poisoning, that's what.'

I looked around the clinic, opening cupboards and looking through files. I was hoping that something would jump out at me and give me a clue as to how I could help.

'What do you need?' Angel stuck her head through the hatch. 'I pretty much know where everything is in here.'

'Some type of antidote for poison or something to get rid of parasites.'

'Look in that cupboard in the corner. There should be some vials in there. I've noticed them before when they've taken my blood. Sometimes they've used that on me and I've been sick. They said I had to have an empty stomach before they could take my blood, not sure why.'

'That might do it. I'll grab some tweezers, too. Something is telling me they might come in handy.'

I crawled back through the hatch and ran back to the dining room. Angel followed. The scene that greeted us was one of complete chaos. Half of the players were still in their original positions, pinned to their chairs by an unseen force. The others were slumped over; a foul smell made me gag.

'Oh my God.' Angel backed off into the doorway.

'It's ok, they're still alive. You hold the bag, I need to get them to be sick.'

The room was full of flies. I hated the horrible dirty little bastards. 'Angel, get some paper, roll it up and start killing these little fuckers.'

I went to the body that was nearest to me, it was Hatshepsut. Her mouth was wide open, and as I looked, I saw something that looked like a claw sticking out from between her teeth.

I grabbed one of the vials and poured it in. She started retching. I stood in front of her and gently put the tweezers into her mouth. The thing was the size of a cockroach, similar to look at but bright red in colour. I grabbed it and squeezed the tweezers until I felt it pop in between the metal grips. It gave one last wriggle and I dropped it on the floor and stamped on it.

Once I had seen what needed to be done, I worked my way around the table until each player was clear of the parasites that had been sent by the demons. Angel had managed to swat most of the flies until only one or two remained. The players who were motionless in their seats had been put into a trance, but they came to as we finished up dealing with the ones who had eaten the vermin. I went to the drinks machine and poured hot water into half a dozen large jugs, rinsing them out and praying. I filled them with fresh cold water.

'We have removed all bugs. Please all cleanse yourselves with the holy water. Once you have washed your hands and faces, please signal when you are ready. We have only one hour left in which to close the proceedings.'

The players did as I had asked. The blues backed away, having been defeated for the moment. The darkness slunk back into the shadows and I thanked the Lord that the new day was nearly with us once more.

The Last Dance

Sunday 3rd April, 2016

The new day dawned. The Hub had been delivered back down to earth. The visitors from the night before had gradually departed once the light had begun to seep in through the green that had afforded us its protection, each nation satisfied that we had, between us, done enough to ward off the evil for the time being.

This year was a special one. It had been foretold that gods would come forth and make their presence on Earth felt. Luckily for the inhabitants of this world, we had all been prepared to fight for what we believed in. The aliens had gone back to their own realities, leaving us behind. The difference being now that we all had an understanding. We all knew our roles and the job we had been given. The world would not be allowed to slip down any further, its future turned around by the combining of resources. None of us were prepared to allow the evil to get that far again. We had sent out a message to the darkness; we would not be defeated.

Today belonged to us. It was a day of celebration and thanks. We were due to have a rest. Sunday would be honoured as a holy day, at least just for today. Angel and I had seen in the dawn; we were the only ones left in the dining room. The arena had been dissolved, and the dining room restored to its former self. The game had drawn to an end. We sat nursing a cup of coffee from the machine, and all the signs were as they should be. Black and white coffee, nothing flashing and no spillage. Things were coming right at last.

'I still don't really understand what just happened, Kate?' Angel quizzed me

'You don't need to have all the information. Just know that we have, for the moment, been given control. Everything will be ok. I promise.'

'I don't know if I will ever get out of here, Kate. It scares me sometimes if I think about it too deeply. I have nobody on the outside. It's just me who cares if I live or die.'

'Don't say that. You have me now. I can help you, Angel. You've been such a good friend to me. I know we will stay friends for always.'

'You care about everyone, don't you?' she asked looking at me intently.

'Of course I do. I care about things being right. The crap that goes on here day in day out is not right. I'm going to make sure this place is subjected to a massive investigation when I get out.'

'When do you think you will be going?'

'Tomorrow. It has to be tomorrow. I can't stay any longer than that. They've all said there is nothing wrong with me now so they can't keep me any longer.'

'I hope so, for your sake. I'm going to bed, Kate. It's been a lot for me to take in and I'm knackered.'

'I'm going to get some sleep too before they come and wake us for meds.' I got up and took our cups over to the worktop, leaving them in the bowl next to the coffee machine.

I did a last check around the room to make sure I had put everything back as it should be. I wiped the date of the whiteboards and rubbed away the names of the staff that were coming on duty. I couldn't let my guard down. We were very nearly there.

I slept soundly for the next couple of hours until the call for meds. I never really remembered dreams. I was convinced that the medication I now took completely wiped my memory so that I would be blissfully unaware of the fighting that I had to do whilst in the dream world. Sometimes, when I awoke, my arms would ache as if I had been doing a lot of exercise. I always put my black shawl under my covers when I went to bed. It concealed my notebook and other items that I did not want getting into the wrong hands. Occasionally I felt that I had been out flying all night, using my shawl as a tool for transforming. I flew with my demigods, the crows; sometimes there would be bits of twigs on the floor at the end of the bed, sometimes my feet would be black as coal, as if I had walked in the underworld barefoot as I slept. Whatever I got up to during the middle of the night I was sure that it was for a reason, and the exact actions were kept from me for a reason. No knowledge meant that no amount of torture would be able to glean any information from me.

This morning, I ached but I felt so good. My last full day in this awful place and I had things to attend to before I left. I took my meds and smiled at the staff. They all knew that I was to be released, soon to be out of their hair. I kept a close watch on them. I had not seen my abusers on the ward since the day of the statement. I had a feeling that they were being kept away from me, but that once I had been released they would resume their duties.

The day was as calm as I could ever remember. I even managed a phone call to John, catching one of the staff at an opportune moment; they were being unusually cooperative. He was so relieved to speak to me. I had assured him I would be coming home the next day. I had also told him in no uncertain terms that I would not be coming home in hospital transport. He didn't understand why I was so adamant that I got a taxi. He worried about the cost. I lost my temper and immediately regretted it.

'I can't trust them to bring me home. You have to understand how bad it's been in here.'

'But it will cost a fortune,' he complained.

'Depends if you want me back or not. Ok then, I'll ring Adam. He will come and fetch me. I'm telling you now, I am not getting into one of their ambulances. I will never see home again. You have to believe me.' I was starting to panic at the prospect.

'Ok. If you say so, but I really think you're being unreasonable, Kate. I'm sure they will bring you home safely.'

'No. I don't care about the cost. I'll pay it if that's all you're worried about. I won't let them take me away again, John. I mean it.'

The phone call had not quite gone as planned. I felt bad that I had lost my temper, but on the other hand I was furious that he didn't believe me. Would I have acted the same way as him if the tables were turned? I decided that I probably would have been exactly the same as him and my temper abated. I would make it up to him when I got home.

I went to the library and sat in my usual chair next to the bookcase. The books were all over the place again so I put them back as they should be. Everything had its place and the more in place and in order things were, the more it kept the evil at bay. I decided to have a final check around the whole ward. I cleaned the bathrooms, shut all the doors that had been left open, straightened the curtains. It was Sunday, a day of rest, but I pottered about taking my time to check that all was in order.

The call for fag break rang through the corridors and I joined the queue to escape to the outside for a little while. It felt good knowing that very soon I would be free and walk out of that gate to start the journey back to reclaim my life.

The girls sat around in a huddle, laughing and joking. I jumped up onto a bench and balanced my way along it, practicing some yoga moves. From my vantage point, I could see into the male exercise yard next door. It was empty and I felt sad that I probably wouldn't see my friend with the big smile again before I left. I looked around and took in the view: the smoking shelter in the corner, the artificial grass, the locks on the gate and the door. I stared up at the barred windows. This place was more prison than hospital. I wondered how in this day and age the staff were allowed to get away with so much abuse and mistakes when it came to medication and correct procedures. I had no clue, but I did know that once I was out I would rain hell down on them. I needed to get some strength back, but they would rue the day that they started on me. The fingerprint bruises that had been present on my thighs and breasts were no longer visible and I wondered what had happened to the photographic evidence. I suspected it had ended up the same place as the soiled linen, destroyed without a trace. I wished that I had had my mobile phone with me then I could have taken my own photographs. On the other hand, I was glad that I didn't have a phone because they would have stolen it anyway and then been able to access all my personal information.

I stared at the sky, watching the planes go past. I waved and blew kisses, my Ares flying overhead, checking on me. My mind was racing, mulling over all the events that had taken place since I had been brought here. I had such mixed emotions. I had been brought here in good faith; my family had put their trust in the authorities. They had no idea that they were sending me straight to hell. I had come for rest and to have all my problems melt away only to be delivered into the hands of devils in disguise. I had to forgive them before I went home because I could not blame them for what had happened to me. I had refused all calls from them. I hoped they would understand that I had only being trying to protect them. If they knew I had been abused they would be mortified. I had to deal with this shit on my own for the time being.

Fag break over, I climbed back up the stairs from the ground floor back to Chrysalis. I felt, as always, like I had the weight of the world on my shoulders getting back up the short flights of stairs. My legs felt like jelly as I reached the top. It was unnatural. I went straight to my room, not wanting to talk to any of my friends. All I needed was my bible. I sat and read until I was called for the evening meal. My faith was helping me to lay a lot of ghosts to rest. I knew now that it had been my destiny to be sent to this place. I had come here for a reason. My life had been in danger many times since I arrived, but I had overcome the evil and survived despite their best efforts to kill me. Tomorrow I would be free. I knew this to be the case. It had already happened. I was living in the past. The future had already been written. My story would be told around the world. It had happened in the next dimension, on a higher level. I would return home. I put my faith fully in my heavenly family to deliver me safely home to my earthly one.

Sweet Chariot

Monday 4th April, 2016

The call for medication came as it did every day, echoing around the corridors, bringing us forth, zombie-like, to queue up for the oral chemicals they administered to keep us under their control. Today was special. Today, I was going home. I couldn't wait to take my med and then rush to the shower. I sang and took my time as I used the last of my lovely shower gel, letting the soapy water wash away the dirt I felt clinging to my skin. I could have stayed there for an hour, luxuriating in the knowledge that I would soon be home free with my family.

Even the threadbare scratchy towels they provided here couldn't dampen my spirits today. I almost whistled as I made my way to breakfast.

'Morning, everyone,' I greeted my friends with a smile.

'Nice to see you so happy, Miss DJ.' The nice guy from the kitchen was on duty this morning.

'They've said I can go home,' I replied, greeting him with a massive grin on my face. 'Can I have muesli, a banana and some toast please?'

'Sure, no problem. I hope that you make it out of here today then. I wish you well.'

'Thanks, and thank you for the nice food you always serve. I don't know why the other staff can't do it like you?'

'Ah that's kind of you. I'll miss you, but I'm glad you're going.' He smiled back at me.

Breakfast was over in a flash. I ate quickly so that I could be first in the queue outside the office. I knocked loudly on the door.

'What is it?' one of the bad staff answered me abruptly.

'Just wondering if my support is in place for when I leave. I can go home when that's been done. Has anyone managed to speak to them?' I asked hopefully. 'I want to go home today.'

'I doubt it. Come back later,' he replied.

'No, I don't think I will. I'll stay here until someone has made the phone call.'

'You'll have a long wait; we are very busy.'

'You don't understand, I need to go home today. Please can you ring my local team? I shouldn't be here. The doctor says I'm fine to go home,' I pleaded with him trying to address his good side.

He shut the door in my face, leaving me standing. I had an awful sinking feeling that made me feel ill. In that moment, I could feel my release slipping away. I felt nauseous and it took me all my time to take some deep breaths to stop me hyperventilating. What the hell was I going to do? I was going to die in this place.

Panic seized me and I ran away from the office. I ran as fast as I could, tears blurring my vision. I did not know where I was going. Every door I passed was shut. I reached the isolation room; it was empty. Something drew me in. The cell door swung open and I was alone with the demon that had pursued me for the best part of a year. It had frightened the horses at the beach, it had followed me at New Year and I had sent it to another galaxy. Somehow it had come back to frighten us at the riding school and it had followed me here to The Hub.

'Leave me alone,' I screamed at it.

It did not reply. It stood exactly where it was, stock still. The moment lasted forever. The silence was heavy for a while until an ungodly sound filled the room, echoed off the walls of the cell. It laughed, a high-pitched, ear-splitting laugh. Mocking me.

'You thought you could cheat death. You thought you could cheat me. Don't you know that I will never give up? Your soul belongs to me. You will never see your earthly home again. Aphrodite, leave this human now. Go before I take you down with her.'

I took a deep breath, gagging on the stench of rotten flesh.

'What have I done that you want me dead?' I asked the demon in front of me.

'I told you that you would be dead by Christmas. I don't like to be kept waiting. Why should I tell you the reason?'

'I know why. You don't have to tell me. I have psychic powers; I was chosen to help shepherd souls. I am a soldier for the light. I control the airwaves.'

'Miss DJ. Don't make me laugh. You're nothing. I have come back every time you sent me away.'

'And I'll keep doing it. I'm not scared of you, not any more. I have the support of the light. Higher beings than you are in control. You have lost your grip. The real world is aligned with that of the dream world. You have failed in your mission to destroy our planet.'

'I will never give in.'

'And neither will we,' I screamed back at the figure and, taking a step forward, grabbed hold of the cell door. 'You don't get it do you. I'm the DJ. I control everything. Now go away and leave us alone.' I slammed the door shut and locked it.

My head was full of voices, each clamouring to be heard. 'I need help,' I asked the empty room. 'Sing with me.'

At once, a thousand voices filled my mind, and my body and soul were engulfed in the power. I almost lost my grip on the present.

'Enough. You have to get out of my head. It's too much. Show yourselves. All you souls who I have helped pass on, come now and we will get rid of this evil and send it back to the pit.'

The room filled with golden light. Kaleidoscope colours dancing and making patterns in the air in front of me and around me. I was enveloped as the painting on the wall of my room transformed the dismal isolation room into paradise. The most beautiful voices joined together and we sang.

The harmonies rose until the room throbbed with music. I watched the demon on the TV screen. It clawed at the walls. It covered its ears in a quest to blot out the heavenly singers. Slowly but surely, it started to fade.

'*Swing low, Sweet chariot.*' We chorused together. The music took over my soul. The golden ones beamed at me as we watched the evil fade away. I had never felt such a sense of peace in my whole life.

I waited for everyone to pass back to their own levels before I managed to leave the room, sad to be turning my back on the glorious vista. I made my way back to the office. I knocked again only to be told the same tale. I would not take no for an answer. Equally they would not make the call I needed.

I had to take drastic measures once again and snuck into the computer room to make the call to my advocate. It was a guy who answered my distress call this time. He promised to help, and true to his word he arrived at the ward ten minutes later. The staff reluctantly showed him into the Quiet Room and I filled him in on my predicament.

'This isn't right. I'll sort it for you.'

Ten minutes later, he was back. 'The transport will be here in an hour. I suggest you go and pack.'

'Really?' I couldn't believe he had managed it.

'I pointed out that they were keeping you here against what had been discussed last week. They had no choice but to organise your leaving. It should have been sorted out the day you saw the doctor. I just made an observation that I have the weight of the government behind my fist and I was prepared to use it. Soon got the ball rolling.'

'How can I ever thank you? Are you sure the transport is safe?'

'It's a different company, nothing to do with the hospital, so yes, I promise you are safe. And, my thanks is seeing you go on your way. I don't need any more than that, Kate.'

I burst into tears, the relief I felt was so overwhelming. My nightmare was coming to an end. I asked him to get them to ring John whilst he was on a roll. If looks could have killed, I was definitely in bad books now. I no longer cared. I was going home!

'We'll miss you,' my friends chorused when I told them the good news.

'You need to speak to the advocate. I promise he will help you. He's helped me so I'm sure he will be able to do something for you guys too.'

They didn't seem convinced. We swapped numbers and promised faithfully that we would keep in touch. They all lived fairly local to the area, and it was only me that had travelled hundreds of miles away from home.

I picked up my case. It hadn't taken me long to pack. The nice nurse that had given me the heads up about the dodgy medicine had said that I could keep my bible. I had to ask, somehow it didn't feel right just taking it.

The transport arrived an hour later. A driver and a security man, they wore black polo shirts with a company logo that told me they were nothing to do with the hospital. I knew they were on my side as soon as I saw them.

I said my goodbyes quickly, ignoring the staff and hugging my friends. The three of them left would look after each other. The little lady waved at me from her room when I passed. I knew that she would be ok, she had been improving in leaps and bounds since the last soul had left her. The other three patients we had labelled as bad had started to calm down a little and had begun making conversation with our group. I had the feeling that the evil that had threatened to devour their souls had gone. I said a prayer for them as I left. It was not my problem now.

As the car pulled away, I could hear my friends calling from the upstairs windows. I waved and blew kisses as they called out their love for me. I would miss them, our little band of brothers, but it was time for me to reclaim my life.

I felt the elements brighten. The nearer to home I got, the brighter the skies. Just an hour away and the cloud formations were the most spectacular I had seen for a long time. The golden rays of the sun shone down on us as we sped away leaving The Hub behind. I glanced at the trees, hoping to see my crows. I was not disappointed and they flew high, circling their nests, cawing loudly as we passed underneath.

'See you soon, guys,' I whispered and blew them a kiss.

The security guy was chatty; he had tattoos covering his arms and we spoke about their meanings. As we chatted, I realised that I knew him. He was my Ares/ Mars. His eyes scrutinised mine and the longer he stared at me, the more I understood. He had come to carry me home safely. To make sure that I was delivered back into the arms of my heavenly husband, Hephaestus. I smiled up at him. The sexual attraction was almost overwhelming. I had to look away before I went too deep. I could feel the power of Aphrodite surge through me and it took me all my strength to pull my gaze away from his. The driver caught my eye in the rear view mirror and winked. I looked out of the side window and took in every detail of the countryside we travelled through. I wanted to immerse my being into this journey. I wanted it to last forever, sat at the side of my Mars. Venus and Mars united. Our arms touched slightly and I managed to keep it there, soaking him up through my skin. The radio played our songs all the way home; songs for me and my loves. I closed my eyes, savouring every sweet second of the journey home. We passed a Romany camp and I saluted them. I knew they had all been doing their part to bring me home. At last we drew into the driveway of my earthly home. I was overwhelmed with emotion.

'Here we are then, Kate. Home sweet home.' He spoke softly and with a tinge of sorrow in his voice.

'Thank you so very much.'

Words were left unspoken, hanging in the air as he passed me my case and got back into the car. I stood and watched as they pulled away, leaving me on the driveway. I wanted to run after them and ask them to take me back. Back to our heavenly home. Aphrodite wanted to leave me. I felt sure that it would not be long before she left, but first she needed to be reunited with her husband, Hephaestus. Then I suspected a trip to the stables to see her Adonis would be on the cards. The overwhelming sexual yearning she had felt for Ares told me that she would soon be gone.

I picked up my case, blew them a kiss, and headed back to pick up the pieces of the life that I had fought so hard to come back to. The house that had been my home for as long as I could remember seemed strange and familiar at the same time. Weeks of incarceration had left an unnatural taste in my mouth. My family waited inside. I breathed in the fresh air and saluted the sky. Somewhere in the distance I heard my crows answer. I opened the back door and stepped over the threshold.

'Hi honey, I'm home.'

Our House in Order

Psalm 107, verse 41-42
'But he lifted the needy out of their affliction
and increased their families like flocks.
The upright see and rejoice,
but all the wicked shut their mouths.'

Six months later…

The radio is blaring out and I'm singing along to my boys. My heart is full of love and the future is looking better for the first time in many months. September is being kind to us, an Indian summer I think they call it.

Our house, although on a busy road, backs on to crop fields, and further behind stands a dairy farm that provides its own sounds and smells, reminding me of years gone by, transporting me back to my childhood as I stand outside the back door, steaming cup of coffee in hand, and breathing in the sweet air. John is putting his boots on ready for our daily trip to the stables. We go together now. I needed help when I first returned home and was grateful of John accompanying me before work in the mornings. We have fallen into a new routine, whilst trying to put the past behind us. We are closer than ever.

My main men, along with my beloved horse, are doing well. We have all reached an understanding, and we are rubbing along just fine. I am back to riding two or three times a week, and gradually our normal life is returning. Slowly, step by precious step, we are repairing the damage and rebuilding the foundations of our lives.

My eyes drink in the familiar surroundings, and although I have been at home for six months now, I know that I will never ever take it for granted. I read my bible daily. My family and friends are somewhat bemused by the fact that I have become a 'God-botherer', but I don't throw it down their necks and they don't question my reasons too deeply. Sometimes the truth is too hard to bear.

They all felt so helpless whilst I was locked away in that place. The staff fobbed them off every time they rang, and along with the fact that I often refused their calls, it seemed like they had abandoned me. They hadn't. We were all victims of a terrible system which let us all down. I have forgiven them for sending me there; none of us could possibly have known what lay in store for me. Despite all the shit we had gone through, we were still here.

The radio is playing a Bob Marley song *'Three Little Birds'*. I smile to myself. I won't Bob, I won't worry about a thing. Whether or not everything will be all right nobody knows, but it is a hell of a lot better now than it was just a few short months ago. Time to stop my daydreaming and to get on with my real life. I feel strong arms wrap themselves around my waist and pull me in tightly.

'Are you ready to go?' John squeezes me in closer and kisses my neck.

My heart swells with love for my husband, for my family, my friends, my beloved Ebony.

'Yeah, get the car started, I'll just take this in,' I say, holding my empty mug up. 'I'll be there in a minute.'

I deposit the mug in the sink, run some water, turn to leave it and turn back. I can't leave it dirty. My mind still has some traces of the fanatical cleaning I displayed whilst I was away. My home has always been clean so I feel happy here, but the part of my brain that is still healing won't let me leave a dirty mug, a fleck of dust, hair, and there are still routines that I have to do. It's going to be a long road to recovery, I know that, and I take the meds they prescribed. The voices I heard no longer shout at me, and not every colour, or every song is a sign from above.

My bag is on the table, its presence will not be ignored. The letter is stuffed inside, and sits lurking at the bottom, hidden from view. I have taken advice from the special investigation officer whom I saw in The Hub, and gave my original statement when the abuse first happened. He confirmed my suspicions that I was not alone; he, apparently, is the busiest member of his department and visits The Hub at least three times a week to investigate similar allegations. Patients furtively slip him notes containing heartbreaking stories of similar poor treatment.

He investigates, and nine times out of ten, no evidence can be found that anything untoward has taken place. They have been getting away with this type of thing for a long, long time. His suggestion, as no suspect can be identified – to write to my MP. They are too clever to be caught out. The normal channels notify establishments that they will be carrying out an inspection, so obviously on the day of the inspection, everything is shipshape and the troublesome patients are kept out of the way. It's catch-22; complain and you're spiralling or just plain crazy. Who'd believe a patient when qualified members of staff deny that anything untoward has occurred?

I switch the radio off and pick my bag up. I will post the letter today. Today, I will stand up for myself, for my friends, the ones I left behind in that place and the ones who have fought to be freed as I did. Free to build our lives back up again. I am lucky. I have a beautiful home, friends, family, and a massive support network that would not let me down again.

My story is contained within the envelope I have fished out from its hiding place. Time to step out of the shadows and tell the truths that have been hidden away as we were, out of sight, to bring mental health into full view. I'm not scared any more. Who am I? Kate Jones, wife, mum, daughter, sister, friend, survivor, your dream come true or your worst nightmare…

ACADEMIA – THE ESSAY – 2011

*In not more than **3,000 words** write an essay on a mythological figure of your choice.*

Your essay should:

◆ *Trace the development of the mythological figure in antiquity and (if you wish) beyond*

◆ *Include discussion of a **minimum of three** and a **maximum of eight** different sources; at least **one** choice of source **must be from antiquity***

◆ *Include critical discussion, contrasting examples and a coherent argument*

For this project, I have chosen the mythological figure of the goddess Aphrodite. In the following essay, I will be tracing the development, through antiquity and beyond, of this powerful and much worshipped deity. I have researched my work using a wide variety of sources which include both ancient text and more modern literary and visual representations. Whilst researching this formidable goddess, I have found the most difficult task presented to me to be selecting appropriate material on which to focus. Aphrodite has been the subject of many works which cover a broad spectrum and she is present in many guises in different formats throughout the arts and many genres including visual, literal and historical works, to name but a few.

In this essay, I will be focusing on the way Aphrodite developed from the original pre-historical goddesses of fertility through to her presence in the world of ancient Rome, her transformation with her new title of Venus and her descent and inclusion from the foundation myths of Rome in the lineage and genealogy of Julius Caesar himself. I will also be comparing the depiction in the famous painting *'The Birth of Venus'* by the Renaissance artist Sandro Botticelli to descriptions of Aphrodite and her attributes by earlier scholars.

To begin then, where did Aphrodite come from? How was her appearance first described? To trace her ancestry back through time, it is necessary to look back many thousands of years to early civilisations and their worship of fertility goddesses of pre-history. There have always been references to the worship of goddesses of fertility and it seems that early man gave votive and offerings to deities that protected and provided the base needs of survival. Fertility of body and sustenance is a fundamental need for the survival of any civilisation, so it is hardly surprising that any social community looked to divine intervention for help to ensure the success of both procreation in human, animal and crop production. Inanna was an early goddess of the Sumerians who was the goddess of above all the bed and fertility , responsible for the continuity of life. From her ancestor, Aphrodite inherited many of her attributes, including doves and temple prostitutes. (Grigson, *The Goddess of Love,* pp 19-39) It seems then that some items were carried through time to be either present as originally worshipped or, by making a transformation such as Inanna's husband Dumuzi, who shares similarities with Aphrodite's love Adonis, these poor unfortunates both suffering the fate of being gored to death by the tusks of a boar. From Inanna we move to Ishtar of the

Babylonians and the Assyrians. Ishtar is not only the goddess of the bed and of love but of violence and war, a similarity there with Aphrodite who has been cited as leading Paris to Helen of Troy and in effect causing the Trojan War.

One theme which has carried on is the worship and association of Aphrodite with prostitutes. Ishtar had sacred prostitutes in temples dedicated to her who were served by castrated priests. So from an unnamed goddesses of pre-history to Inanna of the Sumerians, Ishtar of the Babylonians, we then come to Astarte of the Phoenicians and from here we are getting closer to the birth of our heroine. In his book, Grigson, (1976) describes the trading routes and patterns of the Phoenicians and the Greeks and how a particular rich purple dye was sourced from molluscs from Kythira. Purple became a truly regal colour throughout antiquity and was a colour that was present in the senate of ancient Rome known as Imperial purple. From these beginnings, idea's, objects, and even colours passed from one civilisation to the next, ideas and identities changing and transforming along the way. As Ishtar began to fade in to the background, we then see Astarte, the Philistines called her Atargatis, transformed to Ashtoreth in Hebrew and then Aphthorethe which culminated in the name Aphrodite. We now have a succession of fertility goddesses traceable back thousands of years.

From here, her persona and birth become a little more complicated and there are a number of versions of her actual birth. The most popular version I have come across is that as cited by the ancient poet Hesiod, who wrote in the late eighth century BCE. His work *'Theogony'* is a basic genealogy of the gods of the Greek world and how the world began. In lines 161 – 225 of this poem, Hesiod describes the violent birth of Aphrodite; how Gaia (Earth) had conflict with her husband Ouranos (Heaven), made a sickle and gave it to her son Kronos, who then cut off his father's genitals. He tossed the genitals into the sea near the island of Cyprus, and from the blood of the genitals and the foam of the, sea the 'aphros' in Greek, grew a girl, Aphrodite, who first passed near the island of Cytherea then came ashore on the island of Cyprus at Paphos. (Hesiod, in West (trans) *Theogony*, pp 8-9, lines 161- 225) It could be argued that Aphrodite then, is the original root of sex and violence, or would it be fair to say, that she is the goddess of strong emotion, whether it is love, lust or violent tendencies? She is a passionate, powerful figure who, from her very beginnings, is surrounded by tempestuous and stormy waters as Hesiod describes her father's genitals being tossed into a 'surging sea'. An alternative beginning has her as the daughter of Zeus and the goddess Dione as suggested later by Homer, another ancient Greek poet responsible for epic poems such as *The Iliad* and *The Odyssey*. However, the Greeks seem to have stuck with Hesiod's more descriptive version of events for their lady of love.

From these descriptions and beginnings, I would like to now move on to objects and attributes that surround Aphrodite. Looking at different sources, there are certain things that have become significant and are mentioned in texts and shown in visual sources. Possibly one of the most well-known works of art showing Aphrodite is *'The Birth of Venus'* by the Italian Renaissance painter Sandro Botticelli. This work now hangs in the Uffizi Gallery in Florence and was commissioned by the wealthy Medici family of Florence in 1485. It is an impressive work of art which has drawn from the works of Homer and later works of art, the beauty and mythology of the goddess, unusual for this era because of the general penchant for painting religious works of art due to the popularity of the Catholic Church. A fundamental change obviously is the change of name from Aphrodite to Venus, this transformation occurring hundreds of years before the

Renaissance and coming from ancient Rome, who had their equivalent gods and goddesses that can be compared to those of the ancient Greeks. So, Botticelli was using the Roman goddess of love as the subject of his work.

This painting has Aphrodite blown to shore by Zephyrus, God of the winds and Aura of the gentle breeze, where she stands on the scallop shell and is received by The Goddess of the Seasons, The Horae. So, comparing this to the birth of Aphrodite as described by Hesiod, we have major differences here being the scallop shell and the presence of other deities who do not appear in *'Theogony'* at this point. Therefore, it is safe to assume that Botticelli did not take his influence from Hesiod, but from later descriptions of Aphrodite and much later works than Hesiod, embellishing the myth of birth from the sea with being carried on a sea-shell, the shell taking on more significance as a type of womb, giving birth to Aphrodite. Also, he may have been influenced or indeed inspired to paint this iconic figure of love by his own personal circumstances. The object of his affection as a model for Aphrodite was a beautiful woman by the name of Simonetta Cattaneo de Vespucci from the Medici court of Renaissance Florence, who it appears he not only used to depict Aphrodite but also as the face of Aura, so good he painted her twice in one work of art. This work of art is an iconic painting from a well-known artist of that era, and must have been the centre of some controversy due to the choice of subject matter. What is clear about the painting is that the main focus is on a beautiful goddess, an object of beauty and desire, who in turn influences love and passion in man (http://www.italian-renaissance-art.com/Birth-of-Venus.html, accessed 23.05.11)

Looking at the scallop shell that is central to the scene of the painting, in-depth analysis and significance can be placed on this object. During my research, I have found that the Greek word *'kteis'* for scallop, also means the genitals of a woman. This again links the shell with the womb, Aphrodite being born from the womb of a sea-shell. Also a species of scallop native to waters around the Mediterranean and Aegean contain a row of glittering white tentacles. These have been used in cult worship of a former Phoenician love goddess known as Margarito, or Lady of the Pearls, Grigson pp 38-39 (1976). Again linking her with genitals is the epithet given to her by Hesiod, Philomedes or Lover of Genitals. There is no getting away from sex with this goddess, it is all about the passion. From the scallop depicted, let us now look at the roses, which are being blown into land and surround Zephyrus and Aura. Romance, moonlight love and roses, it doesn't get much more romantic than that. These iconic floral symbols of love can be traced back to our lady and the Greeks. The scent of roses, the scent of love, and even the name of the rose depicted by Botticelli are very similar to a rose named the Nymph's Thigh or in a more prudish English form, Maiden's Blush, Grigson, p.194 (1976). The Greeks had it that a new shrub emerged on land at the same time as Aphrodite was born in the sea. The gods then dripped their nectar onto it and each drop became a rose. An alternative story goes back to the killing of Adonis by the boar as previously mentioned, and that each drop of his blood spilt on the ground transformed into a rose.

So, to move on from a brief analysis of *'The Birth of Venus'*, I am now going to move our goddess into the time of the poet Ovid and ancient Rome, under her Roman name Venus. Born in 43 BCE, Ovid grew up in a time of civil change, tranquillity after a period of much unrest. He had a prolific career as a writer of elegiac love poems, and of course Venus featured as a major player in these works which explored themes of love and Ovid gained fame with *'Amores'* which was known across the Empire, Raeburn (2004). Moving on from these elegiac love poems, he went on to create his most ambitious work, an epic poem called *'Metamorphoses',* written in the time of the Emperor Augustus, the adopted son of Julius Caesar, another link here into which I will expand a little later. This poem deals with the creation of the world and stories of transformation and has been drawn on ever since for its rich source of material concerning mythological figures and stories.

We find towards the end of Book 10, the last three stories are all related to or by Venus. In Orpheus' song, Ovid begins with the birth of Adonis from a tree and how Venus fell in love with him. In lines 518-559, we see the love story unfolding. Ovid beautifully describes how a goddess fell in love. From the first scratch of Cupid's arrow on her breast, Venus becomes entranced with the man's beauty. Ovid's use of imagery conjures up powerful emotions, set against the backdrop of Augustan Rome. This portrayal of love of a young man may have caused some concern in what was a quite austere society. Augustus was a ruler who was a firm believer in saving his citizens from moral decline. He was the 'princeps' or father of Rome, so it is well documented that although Ovid was once a favourite, his stories of incest, adultery, rape, inappropriate sexual encounters and the like ultimately contributed to his exile from Rome.

Venus, completely fallen in love with Adonis and by line 555, she is laid on the ground, reclining on him, line 557 'pressing her burning cheek to the naked breast of her lover'. From this position she recounts a story. Ovid has written a scene of great intimacy here, and as a reader it is almost so lifelike as to feel that you are an intruder into a moment of great love, her story culminating with a warning to her lover to beware whilst hunting. From Venus recounting a tale, we then move to a descriptive passage narrated once again by Orpheus. This story tells of the death of Adonis, and more detail is given here and Venus is named as being the deity responsible for the transformation of blood into roses. In lines 721-722, Venus 'Leaping down to the earth, she tore her dress from her bosom, she tore her hair and violently, bitterly, beat on her breast'. This reflects a lamentation going back to the time of ancient Greece when the women would wail and tear their hair as a mark of sorrow over the death of a loved one.

In keeping with this theme of tragedy and death, I am now moving Venus on to her role in the life and death of Julius Caesar. What could be more fitting for a Roman Emperor that to claim that he was descended from a goddess? Indeed, Venus is named in one of the foundation myths of Rome to be at the head of the Julian family tree from her communion with a mortal man. Being the mother of Aeneas and grandmother of Ascanius, also known as Iulus, Hughes (Block 2, p108). Some of her symbolic attributes present in a statue of Augustus, her son Cupid at his feet and the presence of a dolphin associated with Venus providing the link. For a Roman Emperor to associate with deities would certainly have increased his power and standing amongst the contemporary society. In 'Metamorphoses', towards the end of the work in Book 15, Ovid recounts his story entitled, 'The Apotheosis of Julius Caesar' so in the case of this family tree, we have now come full circle, descended from a goddess and being deified after his death as a god himself. In lines 759 Venus is named as 'Aeneas' golden mother' who foresees the death of Caesar at the hand of traitors and begs the gods of Olympus to intervene 775-780. Lines 800-815, Venus attempts to hide Aeneas descendant in cloud to save him from his death. Ovid repeatedly mentions Venus at key stages throughout this final chapter of the poem. By doing this, it is ensured that the reader is reminded of the association between Julius Caesar and his divine beginnings and his divine end. Line 842, we see Venus given the epithet ' life-giving' followed by 'catching the soul of Caesar up as it passed from his body'. From this moment, Caesar is carried by

Venus upwards on his way to the heavens to join the lofty heights of the other gods and goddesses. Ovid very neatly wraps up his epic in praise of the Augustan empire and one can only wonder at what scandal must have been involved for him to be exiled away from his beloved Rome.

As mentioned earlier, Venus was a prominent figure in the writings of Ovid, primarily because she was the Goddess of love, the main preoccupation of this poet. With titles such as *'Amores'* (Loves), *'Ars Amatoria'* ('Art of Love'/'Handbook of Sex Technique'); *'Remedia Amoris'* ('Cures for Love'/How to Fall out of Love now I've taught You How to Fall In') it is clear to see how he had many use for Venus as the love goddess within his works. I chose to write of her inclusion in *'Metamorphoses'* so I could illustrate her role within Imperial society, even bringing with her the purple of the mollusc from her Greek counterpart Aphrodite, now called Imperial purple and used on the robes of senators.

To sum up, this powerful female deity has been the subject of many, many works. I have been questioning whilst working on this project why such importance was placed on her and why she is such a prominent figure from mythology. I have come to the conclusion that this subject was as close to the hearts of men and women in ancient times as it is today. What other reason for the continuation and success of mankind than human relationships and

procreation. Without this, our very existence would grind to a halt. Attitudes and sensibilities may have evolved and changed throughout the development of culture and society but when it is all stripped to the bone, fundamentally sex, love and Aphrodite dwell in each and every one of us. Looking around our contemporary society, this beautiful goddess still has a place. Kylie Minogue, an iconic pop diva, has named her latest album 'Aphrodite'. Even everyday items are named after her, including a 'Venus' razor, promoting smoothness of skin for women. This goddess of love remains an influential figure even in our modern society; we do not have to dig deep to find her (http://www.kylie.com). I have traced Aphrodite and her Roman counterpart, Venus, from their beginnings of the fertility goddesses through to Kylie Minogue of our popular culture. I had no idea when I started this project that this would be possible. However, I am happy to find that this has been the case.

(3,000 words)

Bibliography

Primary sources

Botticelli, S. (1485) *The Birth of Venus,* tempera on canvas, 172.5cm x 278.5 cm, Uffizi, Florence

Hesiod, *Theogony* in West (trans.) (1988) Oxford, Oxford University Press

Ovid, *Metamorphoses,* in Raeburn, D. (trans.) (2004) *Metamorphoses,* London, Penguin Books

Secondary Sources

Grigson, G. (1976) *The Goddess of Love, the birth, triumph, death and return of Aphrodite,* Wallop, Constable and Company Limited